I0819861

DRAGON SCHOOL
EPISODES 16 - 20

Sarah K. L. Wilson

For all who ponder that final leap – this one is for you.

This is a work of fiction. Similarities to real people, places, or events are entirely coincidental.

DRAGON SCHOOL: EPISODES 16-20

First edition. October 11, 2018.

ISBN: 978-0-9878502-3-2

Written by Sarah K. L. Wilson.

Dragon School: Dragon Piper

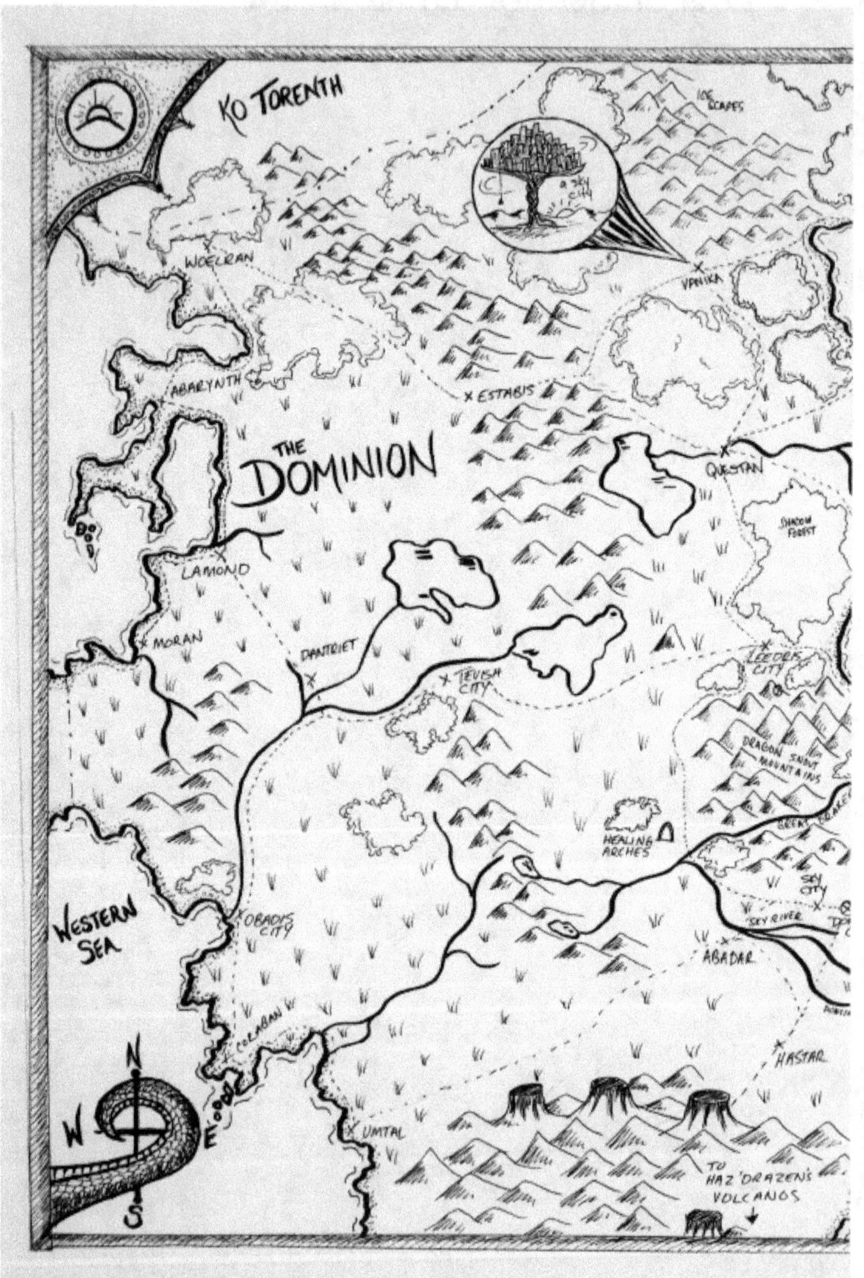
KO TORENTH
WOELRAN
ABARYNTH
ESTABIS
THE DOMINION
QUESTAN
SHADOW FOREST
LAMOND
MORAN
DANTRIET
TEVISH CITY
DRAGON SNOUT MOUNTAINS
HEALING ARCHES
WESTERN SEA
OBADYS CITY
SKY CITY
SKY RIVER
ABADAR
HASTAR
CORABAN
UMTAL
TO HAZ'DRAZEN'S VOLCANOS
N
W
E
S

BAOJANG
THE RUBY ISLES
Eastern Sea
HEALING ARCHES
CROFT
DRAGON SCHOOL
SALDRIN
TO THE LANDS OF THE ROCK EATERS
AVATLAR
FEET OF THE RIVER
BACKWATER MANOR
CASABAN
Eastern Sea
DRAGON HEAD ISLANDS
IEN
VA'LAREN
HEALING ARCHES
DRAGON
SCHOOL

Chapter One

Light painted my eyelids red and I let them flutter open, blinking at the brightness of the light. I felt hot – feverish, perhaps.

It's just me. You're lying propped up against me. That way I can keep an eye on you. You gave us a scare, spider.

Gave who a scare? I couldn't see anything from here. Just light and tree branches waving in beams of golden sunlight, their edges blurring in a golden haze.

"You *are* awake! I thought we'd lost you there for a moment." Ephretti's face swam into view and she smiled – actually smiled! – at me before turning to the side to cough into a handkerchief.

I tried to sit up, but she pushed my shoulder back down.

"None of that. You've been feverish for days. You need your rest." She looked awful – pale and drawn.

"I'm not dead yet," I said wryly, trying to sit again.

"Here, let me help you, at least." Ephretti reached out to help me shuffle up to a sitting position. With embarrassment, I realized I probably couldn't have done it without her. Why was she so keen to help me? This concerned, motherly Ephretti was a surprise.

Without her, you'd be dead. She has stayed by your side since you collapsed on the stones, refusing to let anyone else care for you except for a White who Lenora sent here from the Ruby Isles. She's done all the planning and ordering and dressing people down from right here.

What was he talking about?

Ephretti finished fussing with my positioning. "I'll get you some water."

"The water I brought from Baojang?" She gave me a curious look and shook her head.

"Renn took that with him. Don't ask me why it mattered so much to him. There's a natural spring here with all the water we could need."

I wasn't hooked again on the Silla. Good. I could just imagine Renn desperately negotiating for my water. Doubtless, Jalla had dosed him, too.

She moved to go get the water, letting me see what was in front of us for the first time. I was surprised to see that we were still at the Healing Arches, on the hill above the rolling forest glen. I felt like I was holding my breath as my eyes widened to take in the scene below.

The dragons were still here. Hundreds of them, scales gleaming in the sun, were moving stones, or clearing trees, or clustered in groups together. My eyes widened at the sight and also at all the people – almost a thousand, if my guess was correct. They filled the watchtowers and worked with the dragons repairing the stone structure, building bridges over the gash in the earth and constructing crude buildings.

What in the skies and stars was this?

It started when Lenora sent the White.

I needed a lot more information than that.

After you called the dragons and they defeated our enemies in dragon-like fashion.

In other words, with a lot of gratuitous flaming and the arrogant belief that no one else could get the job done.

You passed out from your wound. No surprise there. Fortunately, Ephretti was there. She freed the prisoners and they cleared this place of our enemies. Unfortunately, she only has battlefield healing skills, so when Renn arrived the next morning looking for you, she sent Lenora back with him instead, making them promise to stop at the Ruby Isles and send one of the White Dragon Riders back to us. How she thought they would convince him, I don't know, but they did.

Renn *was* quite the talker. It seemed I owed him a debt.

And after the Dragon Rider arrived, the people started to come, too. Apparently, the north is full of refugees. People who were just trying to survive and keep their families away from the war were hiding in every valley and forest and cave in this area. Fortunately, Ephretti sees everyone as a block in a wall – she just wants to know where to fit them in. She had no problem putting them to work building a stronghold here. Even the dragons, who she technically can't speak to-

Let me guess. You helped there.

There was a feeling of chagrin mixed with pride through our connection. *What makes you say that?*

You love arrogant women.

I also like people who know who they are. Who have a cause and a purpose.

I felt a sinking feeling as I glanced at Ephretti. What if Leng felt the same way about her when he saw her again?

Your jealousy is both misplaced and unbecoming.

Well, that was harsh.

Not really. Think, Amel. What happened to Bellrued and Tyalmae?

They'd been killed by the Magikas. But I'd seen Tyalmae reunited with Ephretti!

Just Tyalmae. Not all of those killed or injured in the arches were healed. Only a few. And Bellrued was not one of them.

Ephretti coughed again into her handkerchief before sitting down beside me and offering me a cup of water. I swallowed hard, my eyes misting as I accepted it.

"Thank you, Ephretti."

"It's my pleasure. Drink it, your body desperately needs the healing."

I obeyed, but my heart was sinking as I came to grips with the thought that I'd been nursed lovingly back to health by a rival who would likely die before the next moon.

Chapter Two

"How long has it been since that night?" I asked Ephretti.

She sipped her own water before answering. "Five days. Based on what Renn Woelran said to us, the armies of Baojang are only days from here by now. I sent Lenora with him to fulfill our bargain. She will work for Jalla, the Winged Prince, but she'll be faithful to the Dominion."

"You didn't go?"

"My time is ... limited." She coughed again, but her expression was firm. Ephretti wouldn't die quietly. "I'd like to spend it in a meaningful way."

I wasn't sure what to say to that. 'Sorry that you're dying' didn't seem like nearly enough. Should I even mention it?

"And you didn't think undermining Jalla was meaningful?"

"I decided that helping you was more meaningful."

It was hard not to keep my eyebrows from lifting. Ephretti didn't like me – or so I thought.

You don't know her as well as you think you do.

"I think that if we took your dragons west, we could retake Vanika. It would be a big win for the Dominion and good for all the people in the area. If we can take back their territory a bit at a time, we can start to rebuild. It's something worth giving everything for."

I glanced at her. She looked intense – like a woman dividing out the last few days of her life.

Which she is. I think her goal makes sense.

"If we bring fighting to a place currently at peace, aren't we the ones who will hurt innocent people?"

"Would you want to live under the rule of the Dusk Covenant? Freedom sometimes can only be bought with blood. Better to die for truth and freedom than live under the weight of lies and evil."

I wasn't convinced, but there were more things to consider. "Why Vanika when Cabradis is closer? I'd rather head south, to be honest. Maybe even to Dragon School. We need to get moving towards the conflict, not away from it."

"Vanika is-"

"Plotting for the future already?" A male voice spoke, and I twisted my head to see a man about the age of my father emerge from around Raolcan.

I hadn't noticed before, but someone had set up a pavilion over my dragon friend and me. There were more like it set up behind. I couldn't see them well and straining to look exhausted me.

The man was dressed in Dragon Rider leathers with a white scarf tied around his head, holding his braids back. White scarves with writing all over them were tied around his waist and at his left knee and a wide satchel hung from a strap across his body. He carried a wooden bowl that steamed even in the warm air.

"You need to eat," he said to me, smiling in a way that made his whole face fill with tiny lines. His eyes were warm and gentle.

"What's written on your scarves?" I asked weakly, noticing for the first time in a long time that he had writing on his leathers, too, just like Ephretti and every dragon rider I'd ever met.

He leaned in close and laughed. "No distracting me, eat this soup! Here, Ephretti, you can feed her."

"I-" Ephretti began to protest but he raised an eyebrow and she frowned reluctantly and offered me a spoonful. I ate obediently as the mysterious man sat down beside me.

"I'm Dax Cloudspinner, Dragon Rider of the White. You've been through a lot." Dax had a parental feeling about him. "No, no, Ephretti, gently. She's not a barn you're shoveling hay into, she's a human."

Ephretti rolled her eyes. "I know, Dax."

"Well, you didn't know when you almost drowned her last night, giving her water, or when you patched her up so badly that I barely saved her life from infection. I thought you said it was important that she doesn't die."

"I'd rather not die," I said, spluttering, as Ephretti took my open mouth as a sign to jam more soup in.

"You're not going to die, but you shouldn't go running off to Vanika with Ephretti, either."

"I don't have much time," Ephretti said with a grim look on her face.

"We don't know that either," Dax said.

Didn't we? I thought it was obvious. Her dragon was dead. She was coughing. The Ifrit was already out of the ground.

Whites. Typical.

There was a snort from over my shoulder.

"Despite grumpy dragons snorting at me," Dax gave Raolcan a pointed look. "We really don't know that, Ephretti. There have been very, very, few pairs of dragons that were bound to a human. I remember noting only one other pair in the records. There may have been more – the records get more inaccurate the further back you go – but there is nothing listed about the deaths of that group."

How did Ephretti even get two dragons?

They're twins. In Dragon culture, it means they have the right to do everything together. We wouldn't ask them to split, even if one was appointed to the humans.

So, they both adopted her?

That's a way to think about it.

I wondered what they'd thought about that when the pair had come to Dragon School.

They were surprised, but don't you think it sounds just like Ephretti to grab two dragons while she could? I think we should help her do this 'big thing' before she dies. We owe her.

Ephretti coughed, a little louder than last time as if to emphasize her condition. "I have all the signs, Dax. And I don't want to die coughing. I want to die doing something."

Dax made a suppressing motion with his hand. "We *don't know.* Maybe your connection with Tyallmae will counteract the effects of Bellrued's death. Maybe not. We need to wait and see."

"You can't do anything else for her?" I asked, fending off another spoonful of soup. I did feel better after the few mouthfuls I'd eaten.

"We have studied this carefully. If things are progressing as normal, I can only help ease Ephretti's pain. If this is different, then I will carefully record it for our records so that we know what to expect next time."

"Don't record this" Ephretti said horrified. "Promise me!"

"Calm down," Dax said.

"Promise!"

"Fine, fine," he soothed.

Ephretti looked upset as she stood, clutching the empty bowl. "I need to clean this."

When she was gone I turned to Dax. My head was still too weak to hold it up easily and I had to lean into Raolcan to stay upright.

"Are you really going to stop recording her condition?"

"Of course not." He already had a small book and stub of pencil pulled out of his satchel. "But she doesn't need to know that."

"And how long will it be until I can move again?"

"You should have recovered your strength by tomorrow if you eat your soup and rest. You need a lot of rest."

I watched him scribbling furiously in his book.

"You never told me what the writing is."

He looked up and smiled. "Oh. Well, the writing on the leathers is like all Dragon Rider writing – prophecies, portents, signs and well wishes inscribed on the leathers by those who blessed you on your raising day. The scarves are different. I'm always afraid of losing my books." He tapped the notebook he was writing in. "I keep the most important healing formulas on the scarves, too. You know, just in case."

He went back to writing and I let the seconds draw out into minutes as I gathered the courage to ask the final question.

"And my leg? Will it work again?"

"We'll see." His smile was not enough for me. I needed facts. "Just rest for now."

Resting was a terrible burden when all I wanted to do was to test my leg, but Dax kept his eagle eye on me and eventually I had no option but to drift back to sleep.

Chapter Three

The next few days were some of the worst of my life. I didn't like waiting. I hated all the fears that couldn't be dispelled because I had no way of knowing if they were true. Visions of my friends came fast and furious but combined with my nausea and aches they were too short to discern what anyone was doing beyond marching, sneaking or fighting. Being waited on by Ephretti was both embarrassing and infantilizing.

"Hold still while I comb it out," she said, jerking a comb roughly through my hair.

"I'm fine!" I protested, but Ephretti ignored me as usual.

"Dax says we can try your leg tomorrow and when it turns out to be healed, I don't want anything delaying us from the journey to Vanika. A surprise attack would be best, I think."

I still hadn't agreed to her plans, but she took my agreement for granted.

"You still haven't explained why it needs to be Vanika," I said.

"First things first, Ephretti," Dax said indulgently. It was his constant presence that kept me from trying out the leg. He slept only feet away from me, sitting up even in the night if I so much as stirred. He was like a prison warden, nurse, and mother all rolled into one, and Ephretti was his chosen apprentice.

See why I don't like Whites? They live for you. It's smothering and embarrassing.

"We've waited all we can, Dax. If she's crippled, then we'll need to deal with that. She's the only one who can play the Pipe."

I eased the Pipe out of the saddlebag Ephretti had placed beside me. I'd taken to examining it frequently. I didn't want to touch the positioning of the arm – I suspected it was set to dragons right now and I didn't want to forget where that was – but I did draw a sketch of the exact position in Talsan's book. Dax lent me a pencil for the job.

It would be better if I knew how to play it, that was for sure. I turned it over gently in my hands, placing my fingers on the holes along the shaft of the Pipe.

"Don't blow that Amel, it took us ages to bring the dragons you called out of their thrall last time," Ephretti chided.

"I wasn't planning on blowing it. I just wish I knew how to play a tune."

"Here." She snatched it from my hands and my heart did a flip for a second until I saw her bring it to her lips. The arm hadn't been bumped. At least it was still set correctly. "It won't work for anyone else, right?"

"I don't think so."

"Okay, watch. Ephretti raised it her lips, picking out a clumsy melody. I watched her carefully, trying to remember every note."

"Don't play it like that," Dax said without looking up. "It sounds awful."

"If you can do better, go ahead," Ephretti challenged. "We're going to need her to play it, so we can conquer Vanika and set the people there free. You haven't said yet whether you are coming with us, Dax."

"Who says that the people of Vanika want to be 'free?'" Dax looked up from his work. "Here, let me show you."

He took the Pipe in his hands and blew a light, lilting tune. It made me think of butterflies skipping over clover and light bursting through clouds.

"My mother taught me that," he said with a smile.

"Could you teach me?"

He laughed. "Only if you guarantee that you don't call up a cloud of mosquitos. Have you thought that there might be a neutral setting on the pipe?"

I hadn't thought of that. Perhaps, if I thought back to when it had been in the Kah'deem ...

"If you can find a way to make it neutral, I'll help you learn to play – after I finish my work here."

"And will you come with us to Vanika?" Ephretti had her fists on her hips. She was standing again – something that made me ache with jealousy, but when she tried to scowl she succumbed to a coughing fit.

Dax paused over his writing, hand quivering as it stayed poised over the paper as he spoke.

"I swore I'd never return there. I was stationed there before the fall of the city, you know. Or maybe you don't. In the Dragon Rider cotes. I enjoyed my work. Had a friend there named Riv Breadcutter who I worked with. The day the city fell he wasn't in the infirmary with me. When the fires began ... when the city finally fell ... there were so many who needed help. I spent days pulling survivors from the wreckage. Sometimes we were too late. People I knew. Children. Babies. I... I felt like something inside me was broken." He set the pencil aside as if it had grown too heavy. He wiped a hand over his forehead. "I found Riv one night in the makeshift infirmary we'd set up. He had a knife. He was undoing all the work I'd done that day, taking all the lives we'd saved. I asked him why. Why would he do such a thing?" his voice shook, and he fished a handkerchief out of his pocket. Even Ephretti was frozen, a look of deep grief on her face. "'I'm stuck,' he said. 'This isn't what I wanted.' He was holding this leather purse like it held his life. When ... when what had to be done was done I took the purse form his body. It had a spiral on it with a diagonal line through the spiral."

"What was inside?" Ephretti stood on the balls of her feet, as if she could lunge forward and seize the rest of the story right out of him.

"Dust."

Dust. Hmmm. Precious dust. Strange. And yet ... Ifrits were dust demons, weren't they?

"Dust? Are you kidding me? Did he have anything else on him?" Ephretti asked.

"Just a waterskin. Nothing significant. When we finished our work – helped all the people we could - I left for the Ruby Isles and I promised myself I'd never return. I just can't look at that place without remembering the things I saw. I thought everyone would leave, but ... well, people have rebuilt, or so they say. A shantytown of rubble and desperation."

"Which is why you won't go with us," Ephretti said, disappointed.

Dax's voice was quiet but clear when he replied. "Which is why I will."

Dust and water. Water and dust. I felt like I should know the answer to that riddle, like the solution was right in front of my eyes, but though I thought of it all night while Dax quietly showed me how he played the Pipe and as I combed over the Ibrenicus prophecies, nothing came to mind. There were mentions of water and dust in the prophecies I read but applying it to this felt like a stretch. Still, one section I had read rang in my mind when I finally fell asleep.

In dust and deception, I am made,
Bound by water and blood.
Who may retrain the dust storm or calm the call of water?
Who may feed the maw of the earth?
Is it not you, dark one?
Is it not your dusk descending upon us?

It was not a pleasant sentiment.

Chapter Four

I thought I'd found a neutral setting for the Pipe – or at least, nothing with wings had arrived, so it must be the neutral setting. I'd remembered it – suddenly – when I woke that morning. After blowing it carefully a few times, I'd settled into trying to copy Dax's tune. It was hard to be patient and hard to stay still. I wanted to fly south immediately, but I wasn't even sure that I could stay on Raolcan's back if both my legs were ruined.

I will never let you fall.

Or that he could fly properly with just one eye.

I can do more with one eye than anyone else can do with two.

Could he land when he couldn't see his spot accurately?

Seriously, this is getting insulting. Everything in life costs something. Sometimes it's time. Sometimes it's a physical wound. Sometimes it's a huge gaping emotional pit inside you that never fills again. Sometimes those things are taken from you against your will, but sometimes you trade a little bit of your life for something glorious – something so worth it that the pain, the scars, the permanent change are nothing in comparison. Like when I traded freedom for you.

I had no words good enough in return to that, so I went back to my efforts with the Pipe. My piping – or practice at piping – eventually made it impossible for Dax to sleep and I watched him furtively as he rose, straightened his things and strode off into the bushes. Now was my chance. I glanced around to make sure no one was watching before carefully easing my crutch over from where Ephretti had put it beside Raolcan. Was she as anxious for me to finally be mobile as I was?

I leaned myself against the crutch on one side and Raolcan on the other and pushed myself up onto all fours. My injury twinged painfully and felt –

strange – tight maybe? It was as if the injury was pulling at everything around it, grabbing at me so I wouldn't move and would sit here forever. But I gently pushed up, refusing to surrender, so I was kneeling and holding both Raolcan and the crutch. So far, so upright.

This was the moment of truth.

I shifted slowly, carefully, into place and then pushed upward on my injured leg, grimacing at the pain, but refusing to let it stop me. With an effort, I made it to my feet. I leaned there on my crutch, gasping and huffing. I was going to need two crutches. The leg was holding me, but it was already trembling with the effort.

I looked around and squeaked when I caught Dax looking at me with a blank expression.

"I told you to wait."

"I had to know." My voice was small, but I wouldn't apologize. I had the right to know how bad it was.

"Here." He handed me a makeshift crutch with a twinkle in his eye. "It's not a shining dragon-head crutch with a hidden weapon, but it's the best I could come up with on short notice."

"Thank you." His smile warmed me. He knew I'd try! I slipped the other crutch under my arm and carefully tried a few steps. I was mobile!

Painful? Yes.

Stiff and sore? Yes.

But I could move.

I could feel my eyes misting with relief, but I sniffed away tears. I didn't want Dax to catch me with tears in my eyes. He studied me carefully as I made a loop around the campsite.

"You're moving well," he said eventually. "The swelling is down, and the wound is closed, but you'll be sore for a week at least. You need to build your strength up again. And that means lots of rest."

"Can we leave today, then? It will take at least two days to get there." Ephretti emerged from behind the pavilion, braiding her hair as she walked. "I should start packing now if we're going to go."

"Wait." I pushed as much authority in my words as I could. It must have worked. Dax's eyebrows shot up and Ephretti frowned, but she stopped walking and looked at me.

"Cabradis is closer than Vanika to our west. Croft and Dragon School are closer to the south of here. Why are you so insistent that we go to Vanika?"

Ephretti looked affronted. "What difference does it make as long as we are helping the cause?"

"I'm needed in the south," I said it calmly, but tension coursed through me. I was certain she was holding something back.

"Vanika is where it all began."

"So, you want to retake Vanika for poetic reasons?"

She scoffed.

"Ephretti, if you don't give us a truthful answer, I won't be going with you." I kept my voice calm and quiet.

I could tell by her pursed lips and drawn eyebrows that she was angry, but seconds ticked out in awkward silence before she finally spoke.

"I just have a suspicion. When I lived in Vanika, there were rumors that under the city, on the ground – or maybe I should say *in* the ground, there was a passageway into the heart of the earth. I thought that perhaps if we retook Vanika, we could save weeks of travel for us and for the armies coming from Baojang. The rumor said that the passageway could take you instantly to a place near to Dominion City. If we managed it – well..."

It hit me like an arrow.

And you would know what that feels like.

"You don't want to miss the battle to the south. You want to get there before ... before you die."

Dax cleared his throat. "We still don't know for sure that she's dying."

Ephretti rolled her eyes but then she nodded. "I just thought it might be a way to get your dragons there that much sooner – maybe even these Baojang allies, too."

It's brilliant. The warrens. The perfect way to move an army into place quickly.

I shivered. I did not have fond memories of the warrens.

"Well?" Ephretti was rocking forward and back like she truly couldn't wait for my answer.

"It's a good plan," I said eventually. "And we'd be fools not to try."

We could get there in time to help Savette. Maybe.

"Interesting," was all Dax said, as he scribbled a note in his little book.

But as Dax and Ephretti made preparations to go and I sat on the ground sipping water and resting, little shivers of horror passed over me. My belly rolled too much to eat the fruit Ephretti brought me, even when Dax insisted that I needed it. I just kept seeing little bursts of memories in my mind's eye. The warrens were not a place to which I wanted to return.

Chapter Five

I *think you're getting the hang of it. It's sounding less like a dying rabbit all the time.*

Oh, ha ha. I adjusted myself carefully in my seat. Both of my legs hurt, and we hadn't even taken off yet. Ephretti had checked my safety straps four times – as if I couldn't do it myself – and now I was trying to ignore the fact that she was tying another rope around me. Mounting Raolcan had been worse. I could pull myself only about three-quarters of the way up with my arms and when Ephretti stuck a shoulder under me and pushed me up with both hands on my bottom I felt like I was about two years old. My face was still hot with the humiliation of it.

Next time I'll help you. I think I could get you most of the way up without help.

I was a Dragon Rider, not a sack of wheat. Or at least, I used to be one...

"Hold still, we don't want you falling off mid-flight. And you'd better stop playing with that pipe and get it ready to call the dragons to follow us. I've had a talk with the people here and set them up for while we're gone, but we can't leave these wild dragons here. They make everyone nervous and we will need them to retake Vanika."

I managed to suppress the irritation building up inside and simply say, "As you say, Ephretti."

She coughed, spitting black goo on the ground when she caught her breath and I felt my cheeks grow hot. I should be kinder to her. She was just trying her best. She just wanted her life to mean something while she still had a life to live. Besides, wouldn't it be nice to shave days or even weeks off of our trip south? And it would save that – wouldn't it?

Feeling better about using the warrens again?

The same terrified sickening sensation of being squeezed against Raolcan as we wriggled through a tunnel rushed over me and I shivered. No, I was not feeling better.

"Hold still! I need to get these ropes right or they'll chafe you!"

Was Raolcan ready for dealing with warrens again?

Ready for action!

Really?

Fear is the one great sin. It will make you do terrible things and winnow you away until you're nothing but a shadow.

Dax trotted up on the back of a sleek white dragon. Its skin gleamed in the light, just translucent enough to make me shiver at memories of Troglodytes but still opaque enough to be a White and not a Trog. This one had a frilly mane with long white tendrils floating in the breeze.

"What's your dragon's name, Dax?" I asked, noting that he was leading Tyalmae with him. Ephretti's dragon seemed healthy and strong. Hmmm. That was interesting, wasn't it? She was sick, but he seemed fine.

"Idlosias," Dax said, a smile on his face as he patted the White's neck. The dragon didn't seem to notice.

Typical White.

What did that even mean?

"Are you just about finished, Ephretti?" Dax asked.

"Just one more knot," Ephretti said, cinching it so that I grunted from the sudden jerk. "It would take a lot to knock you off of Raolcan now!"

The second she was done, Raolcan launched into the air.

See? No need for two eyes!

I gripped his saddle with both hands, trying to keep doubt from my thoughts. He needed my assurance that everything would be fine – just as I needed his. Ephretti and Dax leapt into the air behind us, Ephretti gesturing wildly. She made me feel anxious all the time. Could she not just rest for a moment?

I think she wants you to blow the pipe and call the dragons to follow us.

Oh. That made sense. I gently adjusted the arm on the Pipe, took a steadying breath and tried to play the simple song that Dax taught me as we circled up, up, up into the heavens. Below us, the Healing Arches and the new settlement became small – a tiny dot of life on a green landscape.

As I played, hundreds of tiny specks leapt into the air like a cloud of dust. I watched the multi-colored cloud as it coalesced and then began to follow us in a bubbling cloud of enthusiasm. The tune carried me into an almost trance like state so that – despite my terrible musical skills – all I could hear with the notes of the Pipe ringing in my ears.

STOP.

I froze, the pipe still on my lips. I swallowed and pulled it back to my lap. What had I done to draw the Troglodytes notice? The icy stab of their communication still rang through me.

To my right, an angry Ephretti signed rapidly. Something about 'are you trying to get us killed' if I understood correctly. I looked to the left and saw Dax shaking his head. We led a cloud of dragons, their eyes misted over as if they, too, were in a trance. What did that mean?

Raolcan? What did that mean?

He was silent and after a moment I realized why. Tyalmae and Idlosias looked just as vacant-eyed as they flew. My hands trembled slightly. What if I'd just kept playing?

This Pipe had too much power. It shouldn't be able to take free will away from dragons. I shivered. I must be very, very careful with this thing. It was far too dangerous – possibly even immoral. I placed a hand on Raolcan's neck as an apology. Sorry, old friend. This is no way to treat you.

What if the Trogs hadn't noticed and stopped me in time? How had they noticed, for that matter? They said that they watched me – was it through the eyes of the dragons or by some other means? It made me nervous to feel like I was being watched all the time – but also a little less alone. At least I couldn't completely mess things up if someone was watching and yelling in my mind when I made a mistake.

Fortunately, we were heading in the right direction before the trance set in. I was still nervous, though, and I didn't stop being nervous until an hour later when Raolcan shook himself lightly.

I gripped the saddle, grateful for Ephretti's extra caution with the ropes. My teeth chattered together as he jostled me and my injured leg flared with pain.

Now that was intense. Maybe just a note or two next time, hmmm? It's ... powerful. More powerful when it's an actual tune, it seems.

Was he okay?

Right as rain.

He seemed to be, but I didn't stop worrying about him as we flew for the rest of the day, or when we set up camp on the hills just past Cabradis. I could see the sky city from here, but with black holes in the distant structure, all did not appear to be well. Some sort of encampment had been set up at the base of the city and riders from there rode in our direction.

"We'll sleep for four hours and then set out again," Ephretti declared as we landed. "The horses won't get here before then. And this time be more careful. I don't want to ride a dragon who can't think for himself. You're their guide, not their master."

"It was a mistake," I replied, bristling a little. Ephretti was just so ... certain of herself all the time and certain that whatever I was doing just wasn't good enough. Oddly, it made me want to impress her, which was strange. Shouldn't I just want to strangle her?

I sort of do sometimes. She keeps on looking at my missing eye like I won't catch her doing it since I only have half my vision.

I gently caressed his neck as I gathered myself to dismount.

"Don't unsaddle him," Ephretti commanded. "We don't have time for that. We'll have to eat a cold supper and just sleep.

Oh, thanks for asking, Ephretti. Yes, I can sleep in a saddle since you asked so nicely.

"I'll help you down," she said.

"I can do it myself." If Raolcan helped me.

"You're going to reopen the wound if you aren't careful," Dax said from beside Idlosias. "Let her help you."

But I waved Ephretti away, slapping her hand when she tried to help me. She sighed and went to pull a cold dinner out of her bag, but her eyes stayed on me.

I finished untying the ropes and shuffled to the edge of Raolcan's back, carefully pulling my shot leg over the side of his back and gripping his neck tightly as I slid off to the ground. I slid faster than I'd expected and hit the ground too hard. A gasp escaped through my teeth and my head felt light. I'd have to be more careful next time.

Ephretti shook her head but no one said anything as I reached for my crutches and blanket.

The company that evening was as uninviting as the camp. Dax and Ephretti were silent as we ate our cold food, drank our cold water, and they set up cold tents. I lay against Raolcan, glad for something hot in a sea of cold, but I was still worried about him, and worried about the broken, occupied city not far from here, and worried – most of all – about conquering what was left of Vanika and entering the warrens again. I couldn't stop thinking of it as I drifted off and my dreams were all nightmares of fear and darkness.

Chapter Six

I was so tired by the time we reached Vanika that I wasn't thinking straight. Ephretti woke me just three hours after we fell asleep with mutters about misjudging how fast the horses were. I had to submit to her hoisting me up on Roalcan – there wasn't time to object – but it still took too long to get airborne. We were in the air just minutes before Baojang cavalry charged over the hillside, screaming battle cries and waving weapons.

As their weapons almost grazed our feet, I pulled out the Pipe and was more moderate this time, managing to call the dragons with two notes rather than putting them in a full trance. But the flight through the night was long and cold. We were nearing the mountains and as autumn approached the cold came with it. I needed a cloak. Fur-lined would be best.

It was mid-afternoon now, and we were in the foothills of the mountains near Vanika on the shores of a tiny mountain lake. Dismounting had been better this time with Raolcan helping me, his neck arched completely around so he could support me with his snout as I maneuvered down.

We were watching Vanika. It's one thing to talk about retaking a city and another thing to actually do it. Tension rolled over all of us with that realization. It was up to us to figure this out.

How must Savette feel in the middle of a siege against our own capital? Did she feel like worms were writhing in her belly, just like I did right now?

Our only hopes rested in the dragons. It was difficult to tell how they felt about this plan. They were following us – so that must be good, right? Every so often, a few flew away, but they always came back again.

They're eating. The mountain sheep are tasty, and some horses are lost in the mountains.

Seriously, he needed to stop it with the horse jokes.

The dragons are happy enough. They are interested in the idea of using the warrens. Many of them have never seen the pathways.

He told them about that?

They deserve to know.

And how did they feel about the possibility of attacking a human city?

We don't usually do that anymore. The Pipe is powerful, however.

I supposed we could assault the city front-on, but it didn't look as easy as it had sounded back at the Healing Arches.

The city below us was a ruin - a heap of broken buildings and tangled sky city structure like wreckage on a beach. Shanty houses and makeshift structures were scattered between the rubble. But despite the dilapidated state of the city, dark figures roamed the portion we could see and patrols ringed the city. There were men on horses and archers stationed on the makeshift walls. From here, it was hard to see clothing or read insignia, but if I had to guess I would have said it was a combination of Dusk Covenant, Baojang and possibly even some of those Rock Eaters we'd seen before.

I see Rock Eater costumes on the sentries. Your analysis seems to be right. They are fearless in battle. They'd fight in the middle of a storm and not even notice the hail and lightning.

If we just flew straight in there, we might encounter Magikas.

I've counted six so far.

Or catapults.

Also possible.

What we needed was an inside look.

"When do we attack?" Ephretti asked.

I yawned. But I didn't feel lazy. I felt tense and worried. We weren't the right people for this job. What if people who *weren't* Dusk Covenant got hurt in the attack? Maybe we should wait for Jalla and her armies.

Jalla will not have your concern for the innocent citizens in the city.

"Not tonight," Dax said, quietly coaxing Idlosias to light a small fire for his tea. The tiny fire was reflected across the waves of the lake. We watched him. "What? He's going to flame anyway, he might as well make tea. He can have some tea, too, if he wants. Idlosias? Tea?"

Idlosias snorted. No tea for him.

Dragons aren't big on muddy water. We don't mind a good beef broth, though.

"We need to know more before we attack, or we'll lose dragons for no reason," I said. "None of us are Reds. At the very least, we should have some sort of a plan we can follow. I'm worried that if we don't, we'll cause more damage than we should. Didn't you say there was a fortress around here?"

"Gerdath," Ephretti said. "The Dominar fled to it after the fall of Vanika. After he was driven from the fortress, it was abandoned. I was there for a time in the aftermath. It's nothing but ruins now. Any supplies it once had have been taken."

"So, we need to send someone to sneak in and find out the information we need," Dax said, noting something in his little book. "And it can't be a dragon. They won't blend in."

Har har.

I watched the city as he spoke, wishing I could see it better. Tiny figures traveled to and from the city despite the occupation – some allowed to enter, others turned away.

"I can sneak in as a merchant," Ephretti said with a cough.

"Because no one will notice you coughing up black tar," I said dryly as I watched the heap of rubble below us. How were people still living there? How were they eating and trading? How would we find this entrance to the warrens under the tumbledown buildings and wreckage?

"Well you can't go," Ephretti objected. "You still can barely walk. I've noticed that you won't step more than a few feet away from your dragon. Not even to-"

"Enough," Dax said gently. "She's healing well. We've made it this far. Let's think up a plan rather than fight, hmmm?"

"What we need," I said, still looking at the city despite my hot cheeks. I really would get better, I just needed time! "What we need, is a resident of that place to answer all our questions."

"Ha! Wouldn't that be nice!" Ephretti laughed.

"We should rest up for the afternoon and let the dragons hunt, and then in the evening we sneak down to a hidden spot along the road and grab someone coming out of the city."

"And how would we get them to talk?" Dax asked, gravely.

I shrugged. "If it's just a citizen and not a soldier, maybe she'll want to talk."

"And if it's a soldier?"

"We have a lot of dragons here and they can do more than light fires for tea," I said.

Some of us are very chatty.

Dax nodded but Ephretti was looking stubborn.

"And if they lie?" she asked. "If we find someone who betrays us?"

"Well, I hope you won't pick someone like that," I said mildly.

"Me?"

"It *is* you who is going to choose someone and grab them, isn't it Ephretti? I just assumed you'd want to..." I left the question hanging there, knowing she wouldn't be able to refuse.

"Yes, it will be me. You can't do it and Dax won't want to."

"Good," I said, lying down beside Dax's fire. "Then wake me up when it gets dark."

I felt the rush of air as Raolcan soared away to go and eat.

I won't be long. I'll have a half of an eye on you at all times.

It wasn't horses he was hunting, was it? That had to be a joke. I was too tired to worry more than that as I drifted off to sleep.

My mind filled with a vision of Hubric flying north, rain lashing at him. What was that city he was looking at? It seemed so familiar.

It wasn't until I woke up that I realized I'd been looking at Cabradis.

Chapter Seven

Rise and shine, spider.

I yawned. Dusk blanketed the forest and in the glimmer of the rising moon reflected over the lake, Ephretti was taking off her extra scarves and cinching her hair back.

"Wish me luck," she whispered before ghosting into the trees. Tyalmae would fly her close to the road so she wouldn't have to walk the whole way, but she'd have to sneak after that.

"Don't forget to choose your target well," Dax said. "Pick someone who won't be missed, preferably a common person, preferably someone who won't be inclined to report the incident."

"And how will I know all of that?" Ephretti sounded cranky.

"If you don't think you're able to do the job-"

"No, no, I'm fine. Stop delaying me."

She was gone before he could answer, leaping onto Tyalmae in a way I envied. Why couldn't I walk so easily? What in the skies and stars had planned to make me a cripple but still give me so many responsibilities?

I thought you were done with all the self-pity.

I coughed and adjusted my thoughts. He was right. We had a purpose and a goal and as long as our problems weren't keeping us from doing them we had no right to complain.

I'm not the one complaining.

Fine. *I* had no reason to complain.

"Want a cup of tea? I won't be able to sleep until she's done," Dax said.

"Should we be lighting fires out here? Won't people notice?"

"There are refugees everywhere," he said, gesturing to the horizon. I followed his hand, squinting as I realized I could see tiny glows across the landscape. "They can't investigate everything."

It still seemed like a needless risk.

If they send anyone to check it out, I'll eat them. Mmm. Tasty swords and chain mail and maybe even a horse or two...

"Tea sounds lovely," I said, but when Dax was done preparing it, we were both too tense to enjoy it. The minutes seemed to take too long.

It could take her all night to find the right person. Not many people travel at night. Especially not during a war. She'll need to find someone undesirable.

"Do you know anything about where a tunnel to the underground might be in Vanika?" I asked Dax, trying to make the most of my time waiting.

"I'd guess it would be under the base of the city. The bases are made of skysteel – woven, not solid. If I was going to hide something, that's where I'd put it. Anything else would be open to anyone to see."

"But how would someone even access that?"

He shrugged. "There were ways to get into the base of the cities. Hidden doors. I don't know if they are big enough for a dragon. It's more something a Magika engineer would know than a White Dragon Rider."

A Magika Engineer. Hmmm. "If Ephretti is right that it's a pathway to the south – a shortcut there – and if Magika Engineers built it, is it crazy to think our enemies might already be using it?"

"I'd say it would be crazy if they weren't – if these warrens really are accessible and really work the way you think they do."

I had a mental image of a stream of Ifrits disappearing down a dark tunnel into the warrens, flooding the channels underground with their spectral bodies. I shivered.

We both sat in silence after that, stewing on our own personal mix of fears. When Ephretti landed beside us with a rough skid, I was almost relieved to have a distraction.

Tyalmae hit the ground too hard, skidding through the trees until he hit one. It swayed precariously before a loud crack ripped through the air and the tree fell over. Tyalmae shook himself and Dax leapt to his feet, running across the scar on the earth to help.

I pulled myself painfully up on my crutches.

Don't worry, she's fine. She just got more than she bargained for. So did Tyalmae.

It was long moments before Ephretti and Dax emerged with a struggling figure. A green scarf was tied around his eyes and another around his mouth while his hands were trussed together, but that didn't stop him from bucking and lashing out in every direction. Dax leaned easily out of the way, but Ephretti took a knock to the gut and another to the ear.

"Would you stop already?" she asked, frustrated, as she shoved the captive to the ground beside me.

I sat back down. I couldn't help with the physical part anyway, and maybe seeing me sitting so calmly here would help him calm down when they took the blindfold away.

"I'm surprised you managed to get him on your own," Dax said. "This one has a lot of fight to him."

"I lured him to Tyalmae and we worked together. Dragon jaws are strong."

Tyalmae is still cursing because the boy punched him on the inside *of his mouth. It hurts.*

"Let's see what you found," Dax said.

He pulled off the blindfold and we were met with a burning glare that managed to take us all in. If Raolcan was a human, he'd look like this.

Ha! I think I like that.

He was about my age, I realized. Wiry, but muscular. Average height. Green eyes with a mischievous twinkle in them. A mouth shaped like a gash in a pie. He looked like more trouble than we'd bargained for.

I like him already. He has an entertaining mind.

As soon as Dax pulled the gag off the boy started talking. He opened his eyes so they were wide and innocent looking.

"I'm not in some kind of trouble, am I?"

Chapter Eight

"Listen to me-" Ephretti began, but he rode right over her.

He scowled, "I'm not sure I need to listen to kidnappers. If you think you'll get a good ransom price for me, you can think again. I make my own way in the world. There's no one paying my way." His expression changed slightly – just a flicker – as if he'd had a realization. "Not that no one will notice me gone. Sergeant Rickers in the Dusk Covenant Defense will notice. He runs patrols every day. In fact, I think I heard he was headed to the mountains tomorrow morning."

"We're not afraid of a single patrol," Ephretti said defiantly. "You're going to answer our questions!"

He looked up at the sky dramatically. "It's almost morning already..."

She rolled her eyes. "We'll start with a simple one. Are you Dusk Covenant?"

"You said you're not worried about patrols?" His eyes narrowed as he scanned the trees. "That means there's more than three of you. So why show me a sick woman, an old man, and a cripple? Where are the real Dragon Riders hiding?"

"We are real Dragon Riders!" Ephretti stormed, but Dax laid a hand on her arm. Dealing with irritating people was clearly not her strength.

"All we want is some information from a man who lives in the city. We can't get it on our own," Dax said reasonably. He sat down in front of the boy, the flickering fire illuminating both their faces.

"So, I'm really supposed to believe that all you want is to chat about where the best place for a drink is in Vanika?" the boy asked with a twist to his mouth. "You kidnapped me and trussed me up because you're just a really curious bunch and you just want to write down a few new facts for a book you're writing? I don't buy it."

"Let's start with your name," Dax said.

"Tor."

"Your real name."

"That's my real name. Or at least, that's what everyone calls me."

"Fine," Dax said. "Tor, can you tell us about the city? How well it is defended and by who?"

"Sergeant Rickers-"

Dax threw a hand up. "Let's start with something true. Are there Magikas in the city."

The boy tilted his head. "Before I go answering questions, let's talk about a price."

"The price is your freedom. Answer the questions well and we'll free you. Answer them poorly and you can get to know us a little better."

"I was thinking gold," Tor said.

Dax sighed. "We'll try this again. What-"

"Gold or nothing."

"You little rat!" Ephretti said, bursting back into the conversation like a maddened bull. She shook a finger under Tor's nose so he had to pull his head back to keep it from hitting him. He looked more entertained than threatened. "Don't you realize what we could do to you? These dragons aren't for show! They could light you on fire and watch you burn just for the fun of it."

I doubt that would be very fun. Make sure you never agree to an entertaining afternoon with Ephretti.

"Unless there's gold, I guess I'll live with the sunburn." He was examining his nails by the firelight, as if they were vastly more interesting than Ephretti, but I had a feeling that he noticed everything. The corner of his mouth had ticked slightly when Dax reached into a pocket for his pencil and only relaxed when Dax began to write. He was looking for weapons and opportunities.

This was clearly going nowhere. I'd known boys like Tor before. There was a man who ran a ferry in the neighboring town and sometimes his son would manage it while he was gone. He'd always ask for more than the agreed upon price and if anyone said no or that they'd tell his father, they'd find the ferry suddenly "jammed" for an hour halfway across the river. There was no point in trying to haggle with those people. You gave them what they wanted and moved on or you paid the price.

"This kind of gold?" I asked quietly, pulling one of Jalla's coins from my pocket.

His eyes narrowed as they met mine. "Who are you?"

"I'm the one paying you to talk."

He laughed. "That doesn't look like a Dominion coin."

"It's from Baojang."

His eyes glittered, and he smiled secretively. "I also have some water to sell if you need it. Direct from Baojang."

Ephretti looked puzzled but I laughed. "So, you've dealt with Baojang Princes before, have you?"

"Not really, though there was one visiting Vanika before the city fell. Rakturan, I think his name was. Supposed to marry someone special."

I smiled. "You've lived in Vanika a long time then."

"Maybe." He smiled confidently. "Any chance we can get these ropes off? They chafe."

"Maybe." I smiled back. I was pretty sure I knew what type of person Tor was. "You're the type of man who knows a little of everything. Like maybe how to get to things that no one else knows about."

"Things?" He tilted his head to the side, considering.

"There's a door leading underground. In the ruined base of the city."

Even by firelight, I could see the blood drain from his face, his features taking on a haunted look.

"I don't know anything about that."

"Or about dust demons using it as a passageway?" I asked.

He paled further.

"Or about who is really in charge in the ruined city and what the weaknesses in the defenses are?"

His features went hard. He didn't like the idea of us taking his city back, but that didn't mean he was Dusk Covenant. If he survived the fall of Vanika, he could be very scarred from that.

He is. He never wants to see that again.

"But I bet a clever man like you knows that an army is headed this way and they're going to take Vanika back by force. Maybe a clever man thinks he could survive this second conflict. But what about his friends. Do you have friends, Tor?"

He licked his lips. "A few. Are you saying you could protect them?"

His face was tight while he spoke. Now, he was bargaining for something *he* needed.

I smiled. "If you guide us correctly and tell us what we need to know, I'm sure it can be arranged."

He sagged with relief, nodding. "I think we have an agreement."

Nice work with the friends. How did you know he had people he cared about?

I wasn't sure. Maybe it was that twinkle in his eye, or maybe I just wanted as many civilians out of that city as possible before we attacked. Thinking about starting a battle had me nervous as a cat in a dog city.

Mmmm cats.

Now, *that* was going way too far!

Chapter Nine

It was hours before Tor was done talking. Surprisingly, he actually did know a lot about the inner workings of the city since it had been occupied.

"So," Dax said, summarizing. "There are still about a thousand citizens in Vanika trying to survive and pull a life back from the wreckage, and an occupying force of a few hundred. They're led by a contingent of about a dozen Magikas and about fifty Rock Eaters. They have a guard established, a central stone tower built from the wreckage to house them, and an established curfew. If we want to do the most damage to the occupying force and the least damage to the citizenry, a night attack is probably best, but they are scattered, so we can't just hit a few major targets and be done with that. On top of that, the enemy is housed along with civilians, so our dragons will have to be careful with their fire. They can't just set every building with enemy soldiers ablaze."

"Yes," Tor said, sipping the tea Dax had made for him. "Do you have anything to eat? I mean the tea is nice – I'm not complaining – but a man could use some real food, you know?"

Ephretti rolled her eyes – she still wasn't happy with Tor, but she fished some dried meat and berries out of a leather pouch for him. She kept her eyes on him, watching his hands no matter where she went in the camp. Perhaps she was still bitter that Dax and I had insisted on untying him.

"And you think you know where this entrance into the ground is."

"If it's where the ghost giants go, then yes." He was still nervous talking about Ifrits. He wouldn't meet our eyes when he did that.

"You don't like them," Dax said.

"We were curious about them at first." He chewed his meat, pausing and staring at the fire. "A group of us – boys like me, you know?"

Dax nodded. "People who live on the streets. Urchins."

Tor frowned. "I'm not an urchin. I'm twenty."

"You aren't twenty."

"Fine. I'm seventeen."

Dax snorted. "Are you thieves?"

Tor shrugged. "If you want to call us that. I've never stolen a person, though." He gave Ephretti a significant look and she scowled.

"There was a group of you," Dax prompted.

"Yeah, we were curious, so we tried to set a trap for one of them." How would he even do that? It's not like you could trap fire and dust. "We set up this big net we found from the ruined dragon cotes and tried to herd the demon to a dead end in the rubble and drop the net over it. It went ... bad." He cleared his throat. "Jimin and Relv ... well, I don't have many friends left and they were some of the last ones before ... before ..."

"Before you thought it was a good idea to trap a dust demon?" I offered. He was a fool.

But we're all fools from time to time.

"Yeah."

We sat in silence, letting the details he didn't share fill our minds. Watching your friends die like that – fleeing through the night listening to their screams echo in your ears -

"Okay," Dax said eventually when the silence became too much. "So, you can take us to the door and you can grab your friends and get them out of the city when we attack."

Tor nodded.

"Then we all need to get some sleep. Tomorrow night we'll be busy."

"And what will we do with *him*?" Ephretti asked, her eyes narrowed at Tor and her arms crossed over her chest.

"I have an extra blanket he can use," Dax said mildly.

"That's not what I meant," she muttered, but Dax was already fishing out the blanket from his saddlebags. Tor smirked at Ephretti while Dax's back was turned.

I took a sip of tea, trying to disguise my grin. It was fun to watch someone get Ephretti all wound up. At least, it was until a coughing fit left her gasping for air and spitting up black goo. What was it – a week maybe since her dragon died? That gave her only a week more. We needed to hurry.

I went to sleep resolving to help Ephretti get what she wanted before she died. I owed her that much.

Plus, it's what we want, too.

Even with the warrens involved?

Yes.

And who would work the central pillars to transport us?

I will.

In that case, I'd just have to trust him and stop worrying.

That's my spider.

Yeah. Right. As if sleep would come so early. But I must have been tired because I didn't even realize I'd fallen asleep until Raolcan nudged me with a toe.

You might want to wake up.

I sat up painfully, my leg still hurt all the time, but it was worse when I was going to sleep or first trying to move when I woke. Everything felt stiff and uncertain.

Forcing the pain from my mind, I scrambled for my crutches. It was still dark. I couldn't have slept for more than an hour at most. A haze on the horizon suggested dawn was not far off, but everything else was silent except for a few quiet grunts and a curse.

"Skies and stars! Just fly, would you! We're going to get caught! Do you need a magic word? What is it? Up! Fly! Giddyup! Go, dragon, go!"

I pulled myself up on my crutches and looked at Raolcan's dry expression. He looked like he was trying to suppress a laugh. Further up on his back, Tor sat without a saddle, slapping Raolcan with his hands and digging in his heels.

"That's a great way to get flamed," I said thickly, rubbing my eyes.

Tor froze, looking guilty. "What are you going to do about it?"

"Nothing," I said. "I generally don't interfere with his fun."

"Fun?"

Raolcan moved with smooth suddenness, his neck reaching around and his body moving so quickly that he knocked Tor loose and snatched him up with his mouth in a single fluid motion. Tor wriggled in his jaws until Raolcan neatly set him down in front of me, placing a heavy forefoot on Tor's back and shoulders to keep him pinned in a sitting position.

"He generally finds putting people in their place pretty fun."

I could really get to like this kid. I told you he was entertaining.

You shouldn't play with your food.

We don't eat humans. Not *anymore.*

"You're all crazy," Tor said, bent over by Raolcan's foot.

I sighed. "The thing about dragons that you should never forget, Tor, is that they are their own masters. It doesn't matter who rides them or what they choose to do, they belong to themselves. Kicking them and using 'magic' words isn't going to get you anywhere."

He grinned. "Then how do I get to ride one?"

"You should ask. Respectfully."

Tor twisted to look up at Raolcan. "How about we make a deal, dragon?"

"Can't this wait until morning?" I asked. "I'm really very tired."

Me, too.

"I can't exactly sleep like *this,*" Tor said, patting one of the toes wrapped around his shoulder.

I'm not letting go. He'll just get into trouble. Like a curious puppy.

"Then shift into a position you can sleep in," I said grumpily. I hobbled back to Raolcan's side and sank painfully back to the ground. It was too cold and hard on my aching legs. Fortunately, Raolcan was always warm as a cookstove. "Raolcan doesn't trust you on your own tonight."

"Are you suggesting that I should sleep under a dragon's foot?!"

"You're going to stay under that foot until after *we* get some sleep. Whether *you* sleep, is entirely up to you."

Nice. We need to work on your zingers, though. You always sound too nice when you're delivering them.

Chapter Ten

As I slept, I dreamt of Leng. Wherever he was now, he didn't seem to be helping refugees anymore. Had Savette assigned him to something new, or had he gone off on his own? It would be just like him to see an opportunity and take it.

He was dressed in rough city clothes – not his usual Dragon Rider leathers – and he slipped through a dark alley like he was hiding from something. He rounded a corner and I caught a glimpse of city buildings rising up all around him. The night was anything but peaceful, with children wailing in the night and harsh words coming from open doors. The glowing entrance to an inn peeked through a gap between the buildings and Leng shrank back into the shadows as a man was thrown roughly out the door to sprawl across the sky steel street. Sky steel! He was in a skycity somewhere. Leng pushed on, keeping to the shadows, and entered a poorly lit door.

"You're late," a voice said from the shadows.

"Two knaves and a dragon kept me at bay."

"What color is the dragon?" The way the question was asked seemed significant – like it meant something beyond just dragons.

"Gold," Leng answered and there was a sigh of relief from the other man, like the answer was a key to a lock.

"We've been expecting you. Come inside."

I woke to a yell and sat bolt upright, the dream of Leng still fogging my mind. At least he'd been safe, even if I couldn't puzzle out where he was or what he was doing.

Raolcan slept, snores coming up from his belly and smoke gusting through his nostrils with each rumbling snore. His foot was empty. Tor must have wriggled out of his grip while he slept. Around us, the other dragons slept, too, massive bodies heaving up and down with each breath. I scrambled up on my crutches, scanning the camp. Who yelled? Had Tor betrayed us somehow?

There was dew on the grass despite the bright light – so probably morning still. Ephretti and Dax's tents sparkled with dew droplets. They must still be in them or the dew would have shaken off when they were disturbed.

I scanned the horizon. No trail of people. No horses. No unfamiliar dragons that I could see. Our wild dragons roamed the hills and mountains, but in ones and twos not in clusters like an opposing force would be.

My breath was quick as my mind flittered from one possible scenario to another. What did I know? That Tor was missing and there had been a scream. It must be him screaming. He either fell off a cliff or was set upon by an enemy. Either way, I was in no condition to help. I'd need to wake Raolcan.

I was just moving to do that, when a pair of silhouettes entered the small hillside clearing, their backs to the sun so their faces were wreathed in shadow. I could tell that the skinny figure in front, with his arm pinned awkwardly behind him, was Tor. The golden halo of the sun lit him from behind. He limped forward but with the over-exaggerated movement of someone feigning more injury than was actually there. That was just like him. A trickster through and through.

It was the other figure that made me take a quavering step forward. There was something familiar about that confident stride. Was it ...?

The second the light finally hit his face, I rushed forward, clenching my jaw against the pain in my legs from my hurry. My crutches sped across the uneven ground as I almost launched myself into his hug.

"Hubric!"

"You're not dead! Skies and stars, Amel!" His tone was full of wonder, though one arm still pinned Tor in place. "I think I found something that might belong to you. He was sneaking out of here like a thief. He's lucky he didn't spook the wild dragons. I have no idea why so many of them are here, but the hills are crawling with them! I haven't seen a goat or horse alive in miles."

I really hoped he was joking about the horses.

"Hubric ... I ... I'm sorry. About Haskell." My mouth felt dry as I spoke. I was saying the wrong thing. There was something I was supposed to say, something to make things better, right? Some words of wisdom? But they were lost to me in the moment.

He ran a hand over his face, letting Tor's arm fall.

"Stay, boy," he growled, before turning to me. "You know?"

"I have a curse now – or a gift if you can believe the givers. I see little snatches of my friends lives."

"And you saw ...?"

"Yes."

Light glimmered off a single tear on his cheek but he sniffed and gave a jerky nod before saying. "This is not Baojang."

Why the sudden turn of conversation? "No, it's Vanika."

"You were sent to Baojang to bring reinforcements."

I laughed in relief. "They're on their way. We came here to find a faster way to bring them to Savette."

"A faster way? The fastest way is to march them straight to her or leave in ships."

"Or go through the warrens? Through a door under Vanika?"

His old face paled. "Never again."

"That's what I said, but Raolcan says that's silly. Either way, that's why we're here. Jalla's army is right behind us."

"Whose army?"

"Did I mention I'm a slave now?"

His big eyes and stunned expression were enough to almost make it worth it. Almost.

"Nonsense. You're my apprentice. I don't allow my apprentices to become slaves."

"You'll have to take that up with Jalla."

"Hrmph. I suppose I will, then." He had an affectionate humor in his eyes as he watched me.

"She's not very easy to talk to."

"Neither am I."

I laughed. Having Hubric back filled me with relief. It was like a part of myself had returned to me. His growls felt like home.

"Do you have a fire lit, Amel?"

I nodded.

"Good. You can brew caf and tell me all about it. And you, boy, are going to stay where I can see you. I know your type."

"I'm just a simple city boy," Tor said with an innocent smile. "Remember? I told you I was with these people and that I'd just needed a moment to myself. It's not my fault that you didn't believe me."

I rolled my eyes. Ephretti wasn't the only one who'd had enough of Tor.

"And why did you need a moment to yourself?" Hubric asked skeptically.

"I needed to ... meditate, I guess ... compose myself. You know, get ready for the battle in a few hours."

"Battle?" Hubric looked at me.

"Tonight we're going to take Vanika back."

He laughed, sobering when he realized I was serious.

"Well, you've gone and turned into a full Purple while you were gone, haven't you? Fully arrogant and certain you know what's best. We'll have to get you raised to Dragon Rider as soon as we can before your head is too swollen for a new scarf. Sit down and tell me all about it."

Chapter Eleven

By the time Ephretti joined us, yawning, Hubric was on his third mug of caf – he'd brought his own grinds – and was grinning hugely. She leapt when she saw him, like she'd seen a ghost.

"Hubric Duneshifter! You scared me half to death!"

"I see you've managed to mangle my apprentice," he barked. Her face went white until he said, "Not that she doesn't do most of this to herself."

But she had an ease about her after that, like she was safe again. Hubric had taken the group authority away from her as easily as reaching for another mug of caf.

Dax was also pleased. He asked Hubric about friends of his in Dominion City and White Dragon Riders who led their color, offering him food from his own packs. I was surprised by that. Whites and Purples didn't usually mix.

Times have been hard for Dax. He's – soft – now. Vulnerable after everything. The prejudice has evaporated and the old walls just aren't there.

Hubric also seemed indifferent to the color rivalry, gladly accepting the food and quizzing Dax on my health in a way that made me blush and shift uncomfortably. I resorted to reading my book of Ibrenicus Prophecies to drown out their conversation, but after just reading a short piece I felt stuck. My eyes scanned over it time and again, but I couldn't seem to get past that little paragraph, though it meant nothing to me:

Twice dead, she rises.
Her rising a sign of salvation.
Favor from the heavens.
Relief from the fires of hell

How could you be twice dead? The little verse haunted me as the afternoon wore on, but no matter how often I read and re-read it, no clarity came to me.

"You need to copy your own book soon," Hubric said when he caught me reading it yet again. "Talsan's is good, but having a copy in your own writing is important."

"When do I go back and round up my friends?" Tor asked, interrupting us. He'd spent the day leaning against a fallen log with an arm draped over his face and a flask of something in the other hand. I didn't want to know what was in it. Despite Raolcan's strange fondness for the boy, I found his irresponsibility grating.

He's doing his best. It's not easy for a stray to find his way in this world – particularly not during a war. His family was already poor and in trouble before the fall of the city and the last of them was lost to him that day. He lives how he can – scavenging and thieving. He doesn't know if he can trust us and he certainly doesn't feel part of this group. I think if he were given a chance he would be a different person.

I wasn't so sure. People usually were who they were.

"You'll need an escort," Hubric said. Someone who can help you find your friends and spirit them out of the city."

"Someone to babysit me and make sure I show you that tunnel entrance, you mean," Tor said with a wry twist to his grin.

Hubric laughed. "Well, you did say you wanted to ride a dragon and by that gleam in your eye, it might be all the incentive you need to get back here."

"Really?" Tor asked, warily. "You'll let me fly with you when I come back?"

"If you don't bring the guards with you, sure. But Kyrowat is temperamental, so you'd better treat him with respect or he'll flame the bottom of your breeches."

I snickered at the mental image of Kyrowat doing just that. Where was he?

Hiding. He's embarrassed and afraid to face me.

What did he have to be embarrassed about?

He wasn't fast enough to save Haskell. He's getting old.

I felt my heart sink at his words. None of us were fast enough in this war. None of us could prevent pain and evil and terror. All we could do was fight as hard as we could for the people we loved and be there to hold them and help them when we failed.

That's not just how war works. It's how all of life works. Accepting your limitations is important.

But so was rising above them. I gritted my teeth at yet another flare of pain from my wound. My old injury was giving me more trouble now that my good leg was injured, as if it was bearing more of the load.

Raolcan should go talk to Kyrowat face to face. Maybe if he saw that eye he'd stop hiding.

I hadn't thought of that.

Vulnerability helped hurt people come closer. It helped show them they weren't alone.

It's not vulnerability, it's a badge of honor.

Whatever it was, it might help.

Raolcan quietly snuck away through the tall trees and I watched as Tor and Ephretti loaded up on Tyalmae's back.

"No, he's not going to fly," I heard Ephretti saying. "He's going to sneak us down to the treeline so we can join the road and you can enter the city like a normal person. You'll have to come back and ride Kyrowat with Hubric if you want to fly."

"That dusty old corpse probably doesn't fly as fast as you," Tor said.

Hubric grunted from beside me.

"Don't let him hear you say that or he'll test your belly's fortitude. Have you ever barrel-rolled over a city? It's not fun the first time."

Their voices were already fading out.

"I hope this path through the warrens really works," Hubric said quietly. "Savette is in real trouble. Her forces are strong, but the Ifrits Starie has raised are numerous. Our people need help."

As if her name had triggered it, I saw through Savette's eyes for a moment. On a hill far away, a beacon of dark light descended on the hilltop. In its center a red-headed woman stood on the back of a golden dragon, darkness swirling around her and in the tangles of darkness, Ifrits clustered. They spread out around her like cattle on a hillside. I gasped and fell back into reality.

"Are they fighting every day?" I asked, tightly.

"Small skirmishes. Testing one another. The real live-or-die fight comes soon."

"We need to be there."

"Yes."

I shook out my leg and stood, hobbling to the area where Vanika could easily be seen through the trees. It looked daunting, but tonight we would do our best to take it back for the Dominion.

"Are you ready for this?" Hubric asked. He'd followed me, sipping his caf as he followed.

"I think so."

"Battles that you choose – sometimes they aren't what you expect."

I licked my lips, thinking hard. I didn't' know what else we could do to prepare that we hadn't already done.

"And you really can call up dragons with a pipe?" Hubric pressed.

I pulled it from my message pouch to show him. "Yes."

"Then I'd better make things formal. I've been ... thinking a lot lately. I don't want to leave anything undone."

I turned to him with wide eyes. "Please don't talk like you're dying! I just got you back!"

His gaze was misty as it drifted over the yellowing leaves of the trees. There was a tingle in the air of seasons changing. And that feeling of change made me nervous.

"War is uncertain. Amel. So is life. Sometimes, it's full and blossoming. Sometimes, it's a bare struggle. We never know what new, surprising gift is about to be given and what unexpected shattering is about to befall us. Nothing is ever certain. So, we strive, clinging to what we hold dear and being true to our word – because in the end truth is all we have."

"Yes," I agreed, my heart heavy.

"I have a gift for you. By my honor and the truth – which is all I have – I declare you complete in your training – a full Dragon Rider in all but name and you have my blessing to pursue that name with the Purple Council."

"Thank you," I said, my eyes misty. Having him declare me ready ... the honor was so real it felt like I could touch it. But I was thankful for more than that. I was thankful for the strange but powerful way that he had trained me. Not with words – though there had been words – but with his example and his way of being a Dragon Rider. I couldn't even think of doing it any other way.

Chapter Twelve

It was tense moments as dusk fell and we waited for Tor and Ephretti. I sat on Raolcan, glad to have time to adjust my straps after he helped me mount him. I was going to have to get used to this new way of doing such a simple thing.

"Remember the plan," Hubric said again. Kyrowat was grumpy under him, letting off puffs of smoke in irritable impatience.

He's doing better. He told me losing an eye would be good for me. That maybe I'd be less cynical if I only saw half as much.

"Amel flies up high," Hubric continued, not distracted like I was by Raolcan's interjection. "And uses the Pipe to call and direct the dragons." Although actually, it would be Raolcan directing them. But that was a secret for Purples only. "She'll lead the center charge while we stagger out to lead the edge of the attack in a long line. One pass where we hit the walls and towers, and then we circle back and try again. There will be Magikas. There will be archers. This is a city with a serious line of defense, not a ramshackle encampment or a few scattered Ifrits." Ha! Like fighting Ifrits was ever easy! "We give it our best shot and hit the hardest we can right from the beginning. We don't want any casualties in the citizenry. We're only attacking the defenses and the Dusk Covenant."

My stomach was bunched in knots. This wasn't what I'd trained for. None of us was Red. This just wasn't what we did.

Dragons have fought men before. They make easy targets.

That wasn't very comforting. What about the people like Tor who were just caught up in it? What if someone innocent died because of my plan to do this?

A lot more will die if you don't.

There were Magikas down there,

The Magikas are more of a challenge since they throw fire back, but it's all the more satisfying to singe one.

And the Ifrits? Did he have something glib to say about them?

Well, they're a little insubstantial, aren't they?

Oh, ha ha. There was a crashing sound of someone walking through the low bushes and then Tyalmae poked his green head out through the trees. Like most Greens, he had a very triangular head with very little mane, almost like a horse. Ephretti looked like her patience was exhausted and she practically threw Tor at Hubric.

"Take him."

Hubric chuckled and turned to Tor. "Climb up into the stirrups. That's it. Now, these straps are cinched tightly around your hips and those around your shoulders. These ones are for thighs. Don't look at me like that, I'm not strapping them for you. You do your own work around here, boy." Then in a quieter voice. "Are you friends safe then?"

"Yes," Tor said. "Let's go, old man."

"You don't want me to double check your straps?"

"I'm younger than you. I don't need my food fed to me on a spoon. I can take care of myself!"

"Uh huh."

I didn't catch anything else Hubric said, but I saw the wicked gleam in Kyrowat's eye and saw Raolcan shaking with laughter as they launched into the sky. Kyrowat barrel-rolled almost before he had enough height for the maneuver, brushing the tops of the trees with his wing tips and loosening Tor from his saddle. He was dangling by one strap and yelling when we streaked past. I wasn't worried. Hubric wouldn't actually kill him while he knocked sense into him ... would he?

Doubtful. He finds the boy as entertaining as I do. Wants to make a Dragon Rider out of him, which would be a good idea. He has the guts for it. And he could use a dragon to keep him in the right place.

And where was the 'right place'?

In the sky of course!

And with that, I was loosened out of my nerves and we were streaking away from the mountain lake and toward the city as I fumbled in my bag and pulled out the Pipe. Hubric – always cleverer than I was – had offered me a gift while we waited – a narrow leather strap to loop it around my belt.

If you lose your seat or get knocked around, you don't want to lose a thing like that.

I blew the first note with shaking fingers, watching as the dragons on the hills leapt into the air. Was it right to call them this way?

Just stick to a few notes. That calls us like a horn to battle, but we can still resist. It's when you play a song that it's irresistible.

Their silhouettes surrounded us. I could feel the wind from their wings as they joined us in the sky. At first, there were only a few, flapping beside us, soaring through the cool evening air. Then there were a dozen, thirty, a hundred. By the time we approached the city walls, they had all joined us. It was strange to think so many had been hiding in the hills waiting, as we chose our time to carry out this plan. What made them so patient?

Good leadership. I've always been an excellent leader.

Was there anything he wasn't a master of?

I'm not very good at table manners, if you must know. But I think we should revise the rules for those, anyway. Points should be awarded for clear enjoyment of food and overall enthusiasm.

And how would he award points in the coming battle?

Everyone who survives gets a point. Make sure you get a point, Amel. That's an order.

He was silent after that, clearly focused on directing the dragons. More than one fight broke out between them and a single clash of his mighty jaws or half-snarl towards them was enough to stop the fight immediately.

My grip on the saddle was moist, but I kept the Pipe in one nervous hand, just in case. On our final approach toward the city, I kept my back straight and my gaze level. The walls – made of timber, chunks of rock and crumpled sky steel – were formidable despite our dragons. There were so many places for the tiny figures below to hide.

Magikas and archers scrambled for places on the makeshift walls and towers, letting off arrows a little too soon, so they fell before they reached us.

They followed up immediately with a raft of fireballs, as if to announce their intentions. They knew they were under attack and they were ready to fight.

Raolcan's emotions through our connection were almost giddy as he swooped toward the choppy wall, his dragon cohort at his back. He flamed dramatically, setting the part of the wall aflame in our first pass. Behind him, dragon after dragon set their flames loose on the towers and walls.

I hadn't seen rain since I'd returned to the Dominion – even longer than that perhaps, and the timbers were dry. They went up like a fire made of aged split wood. This close to the first frost, there were usually rains and mud. I hadn't really thought about that until now. I hadn't factored in wall-burnability to the plan. But with them so easily set aflame, it was almost too easy!

I was already beginning to celebrate when I heard a cry from Hubric. I spun in my saddle to follow his pointing finger.

Flames leapt from the burning walls, licking up the towers as men leapt from their heights to the ground below. I gasped as the first one dashed on the rocks. Even from a low tower, the height was too high to survive.

My grip tightened on Raolcan's saddle, and I watched, helplessly, as the flames kicked up in the wind like waves crashing into the shore. They swirled into the make-shift shanty-like structures behind them, consuming a dozen in a single breath and rushing further.

Wait! No! It wasn't supposed to go this way!

My breath was growing faster as my gaze flickered from one scene of horror to the next. The dragons hadn't stopped – they were still flaming towers and walls further into the city. I fumbled for the pipe, my fingers too thick to grab it the first time. I brought it to my lips the second time but paused, uncertain about what to do. I knew how to gather them up, but how did I make them stop?

They had to stop!

There was a tall building – two storys high – the base of it on fire. Like a vision from the Troglodytes, it flashed into my vision and then out again just long enough to see a mother passing her children to the building beside it. I gasped as Kyrowat skidded to a landing within the inferno, Hubric and Tor rushing into the building the children were being passed to. It was already smoldering. They'd been passed from one danger to another.

I never expected this. This wasn't the plan!

I spun to the side to see Ephretti, frustration on her face, signaling sharply to me to stop this.

Dax was nowhere to be seen. He must be in the flames like Hubric. It would just make sense that his soft heart would leap to help.

I put the pipe to my lips and blew the first note I could think of, but nothing happened. I blew and blew as gnats filled the sky.

Panicked, my fingers fumbled with the lever. I must have accidentally bumped it. It wasn't set to dragons anymore.

Raolcan! Help!

Trying... too much for me...

They must not be listening to him. They needed help. I adjusted the wing with trembling hands and blew again, seeing the dragons on the edges of the city swirl toward me. That must be right. For good measure, I kept blowing, and blowing and-

Stop! Stop!

I stopped.

It's too much! They aren't thinking now!

A cluster of Magikas on the far end of the city fired in unison, their fireballs surrounding a white dragon whose expression was in a daze. He crumpled, falling from the sky like burning ash over a campfire. He fell to the ground, breaking the buildings beneath him and setting them on fire as the magenta, sticky Magika fire spread from him to the area around his fall.

I'd gone too far in the other direction!

Dragons were falling as quick as I could spot them. Dozens of them. Each fall lit a new blaze.

Help! I screamed to Raolcan. Help!

Trying.

Help!

THINK.

The message of the Troglodytes pounded in my brain like a nail into wood. I shuddered. Think about what? But the message wasn't for me. Around us, I saw dragons shaking themselves out of their stupor and turning on their adversaries.

But that was wrong. Right now, Magikas were not our problem, and nor were archers, or even Ifrits. The fire was stealing innocent lives. The fire that *I*

set, that *I* ordered. I hadn't known – hadn't realized – what I was doing, but every choking, screaming, dying soul below us was my fault.

Shuddering with horror. I laid my hands on Raolcan's scales, forcing my thoughts from incoherent panic to a plan. We needed water. The lake!

I didn't even need to clearly think of what I was planning before the entire mass of dragons was wheeling from the city and back toward the mountain. We dove toward the lake at full speed, the cool night air washing over us, so peaceful and different from the fires in the city below. Raolcan opened his mouth as wide as it would go. On either side of me, I saw dragons doing the same, taking huge, gulping mouthfuls of water and spinning in the air to turn back on the city.

Would a hundred mouthfuls help? Two hundred? Three hundred? Would that even dent the infernos raging beneath us?

Between the pounding of my terrified heart and the desperate speed of my beloved dragon, I felt completely turned around as we shot toward the city. Something was on the horizon where the road led to Vanika – a dark moving mass. I prayed it wasn't Ifrits, but there was no time to plan for them or even worry.

We swept over the creeping line of fire, each dragon spitting water down on the licking flames and arcing back into the air to fill their mouths again. Steam rose up into the air and in the hellish orange light the city flickered and melted light into dark and shadow into brilliance.

I had a horrible feeling that the city was me. It was shadow that thought it was light. It was smoke that thought it was clarity. I was trying hard not to imagine the fates of those already lost, trying desperately not to think of how few would be saved by the Dragon Riders in the city. If I stopped for a moment and thought of those children with Hubic racing toward them...

I was in a steady rhythm of dive, scoop, ascend, swoop, spit, ascend. Over and over and over until my mind grew numb with it.

Chapter Thirteen

We can leave them to this pattern now.

It felt like we'd been doing it for hours.

At most, it's been twenty minutes.

We flew toward the city again, my mind spinning with a brew of guilt mixed with terrible despair.

Your despair helps no one. Shake out of it!

It was all my fault. My plan. My execution.

Your responsibility now to save who you can.

I couldn't shake off the horror of what I'd done so easily.

You have to.

We landed in a swirl of flame. I was high enough on his back to be shielded from the worst of it, but here on the ground of the ruined city things were so much worse than in the air. People ran, screaming, from the fire, children, and belongings in their arms. Magikas on horses sped through the streets, not caring who they trampled in a flurry of flame and choking smoke. Soldiers barrelled through in knots of five or more, ignoring cries for help.

Tor ran out of a building nearby, a pair of grimy children in his arms. He rushed to me and shoved them at me.

"Hubric is setting them down outside the city. Dax has a fire. Look for it."

He was gone, rushing back to the building before I had time to question him. I barely managed to grip the too-silent little ones before Raolcan leapt into the air. He sped over the city toward a mark only he could see. The tiny bundles in my arms were so fragile, so small. I clung to them, tears flowing down my face. I'd destroyed their world.

So that's *what that fire is!*

Where were their parents? Who would look after them when all this was done?

Keep your mind on what you can do. Big chasms can only be crossed one step at a time. Take the step right in front of you first. The next one after that and the next after that. Eventually, you'll find you've crossed the chasm without realizing it.

The children were coughing by the time we set down at the campfire, their huge eyes glassy with tears. I gathered them in a hug, cooing gentle words until Ephretti came running out to take them from my arms. Behind her, Dax worked over a burnt man, speaking quietly. Someone had found the time to throw up a canvas over him like a makeshift tent. I squinted at it.

"Once a White, always a White," Ephretti said as she took the children. She waited until I met her eyes. "Your plan is a terrible failure."

Like I needed to be reminded. My arms felt empty with the children gone. Just like my mind was empty of everything but fear and shame.

I watched her bring them to a group of people huddled under another canvas and settle them in with a few other children under a single blanket – Ephretti's own blanket, I realized.

We leapt again into the air. My heart was breaking, my eyes stinging. I barely noticed when we flew over a group of archers fleeing the city on horseback. Their arrows swooshed around me, deflecting off of Raolcan's belly armor. But I felt heavy and dead inside. So what if one of them hit me? I'd been hit before. I could be hit again. All this was my fault.

Beating yourself up and being the sorriest of sorries isn't going to fix this, Amel. It might make you feel better to punish yourself, but it won't help right now. Focus! Shake yourself out of this! You're no help to anyone when you're focused on yourself!

I focused.

The dragons were still circling, battling the expanding line of flames. They were keeping it from engulfing the entire city, but the flames continued to march slowly forward. At least half the city was aflame now and the dragons were forced to weave in and out of the billowing black towers of smoke. Despite the darkness around us, the countryside looked orange in the light of the fires.

That dark mass down the road continued to creep toward us, and if it were Ifrits, we were dead already. Between the fires and the clumps of Magikas and warriors still fighting, we didn't have enough people and dragons. I glanced at the newly built tower in the center of the city – still untouched, it bristled with archers and Magikas ready to fight. But, along the walls and further out, every able-bodied person who could flee, was fleeing. Tiny figures and their long shadows ran from the city in every direction like ants from a kicked anthill.

I gritted my teeth as we descended again into the blazing hell below, dodging dragons with water-filled mouths and whizzing magenta fireballs from the Magikas still too loyal to turn coat and flee. We met Kyrowat flying up as we swooped down. He was heavy in the air with eight people clinging to him like barnacles. Shockingly, Tor was holding four people, one of his straps on each of them, calling out sharp instructions.

"Hold on to your strap! Eyes on the dragon, not the sky or the ground! It's not far, just be brave! I've got you!"

Hubric's teeth were gritted, ash and soot streaked across his face and through his wild white braids. He held the people around him expertly, not even pretending to steer his old dragon. Kyrowat flew like rescuing panicked people was his daily profession. He was as competent and steady as Raolcan, but as I looked into the burning city I knew it wouldn't be enough.

The wind was picking up and as it did, the flames burst forward like a dam opening. A gust of hot air shoved us back, spinning Raolcan off course. I hung on tight, watching as the central tower spun closer and closer.

Chapter Fourteen

We smacked against the tower, tumbling away as arrows and fireballs arched through the air around us. The gust of fire pushed the line of the blaze forward, gobbling up a new line of tumble-down shanties. I gasped, clinging to Raolcan's neck as he righted himself. Heat flashed against my skin and I hissed at the pain and intensity.

The fires were almost to the tower, but the Magikas seemed more intent than ever on fighting us instead of the flames. I felt tight and edgy as I watched them. If the fires made me feel like my skin was curling in on itself, what must it feel like in that tower?

Fools.

I tried to focus instead of being distracted by them. Raolcan was fighting them flame for flame, fire for fire. A magenta ball of fire came so close that my face felt suddenly hot, the smell of burning hair filled the air.

Oops. It's okay. You'll look fine without eyebrows.

Somewhere in that panicked darkness, innocents were fleeing the conflict. How would I get them all out? There weren't enough Dragon Riders and the wild dragons wouldn't allow people on their backs. There had to be some way...

What if the dragons cleared a path for them out of the city and toward Dax's encampment?

It might work. A lot of the problems down there come from confusion. They don't know how the fires are moving, but we *can see them from the air.*

He spun, and I heard arrows clatter behind us. Why were we so close to the tower?

I'm keeping them occupied while the others work. The fools don't know they've been beaten.

So, if the dragons cleared a safe lane out of the city and kept it clear and wet, that would be a start. Then, if we could just get people to touch down and tell the people which way to go...

Kyrowat thinks it will work. I'm changing the orders for the dragons.

I felt tense as we circled the tower again drawing the fire of the Magikas to us. Fireballs landed uselessly behind us in the flaming parts of the city instead of arching towards the areas untouched by flames. Raolcan was keeping their fire away from the tinder-pile city one swoop at a time.

Little steps. One after another.

A pair of black dragons landed in the smoky city, and as if by magic, began to clear a path, pulling rubble out from a road and widening it. Behind them, the dragons bearing water began to drop their mouthfuls on the cleared path. Kyrowat dropped down nearby and moments later tiny figures pushed their way through the rubble to the path, rushing down it almost as quickly as the Blacks could clear the path.

Tyalmae flew past, Ephretti signing like she thought I could even keep up with what she was saying.

Hubric told her to fly to the other side of the line and start herding people to the clear path.

We just had to hold on. We just had to get as many people clear as we could.

Something changed.

My brow wrinkled as I tried to think of what it was.

They've stopped firing at us. They're leaving the tower.

A gust of steam puffed up from the base of the tower and my eyes widened as I realized the Magikas could throw orbs of water as easily as they'd thrown balls of fire. Where had that been during the fire? Why hadn't they helped the people?

Selfish. They care only for themselves. Wrap your scarf around your mouth and come on.

We dove down past the flames to the thick fog of smoke. I poured water from my waterskin over the scarf covering my mouth. Raolcan set down in a crossroads between heaps of stone rubble from when this had been a skycity and makeshift vendor booths made of wood planking and salvaged rock. People huddled in the rock openings.

"Hurry!" I called to them through the scarf. "There's a clear way out of the city that way!"

"It's safer to stay here," someone shouted from an alcove. "We're under attack and we need to be where the Magikas can defend us."

"The whole city is on fire. You need-"

A dark figure leapt off the top of a heap of rubble, crashing into me. Raolcan reared up, but my attacker grabbed my shoulders.

"Die, Lightbringer!"

I tried to dodge his grasping hands, but I was tied in the saddle and he was too quick for me. Raolcan writhed beneath me, but there was nothing he could do to the man attacking me that wouldn't hurt me, too. The man's rugged face was inches from mine when his hands grabbed my neck. He held on tight as I wriggled, trying to escape his grasp. His grip was too tight! Every movement only made it worse.

"The Dusk Covenant will never surrender. We are fuelled by the dust of the earth, the blood of the fallen, and the power of the One. The brothers of Ko'Torenth have prophesied our victory."

Ko'Torenth? The thought fell from my mind before I even had it fully in place.

I couldn't breathe.

I couldn't think.

It hurt so much.

My neck felt weak and fragile as his fingers dug deep into flesh and muscle, cutting off my breath, pinning me in place, forcing me to plunge toward death... darkness flashed across my vision.

I saw Savette for a moment, battling in a rain-slicked field, her troops forced forward through the storm and knee-deep mud to fight against raging foes. She reached out both her hands, shouting as her light hit the darkness of Starie Atrelan. Starie's eyes were wild, the mark on her arm emanating black light as her dark, cloying mists wrapped around the dragons fighting for Savette, pulling them down from the sky and into the muck. Savette's light severed the bands of darkness at the last moment and the scene went dark.

But now, everything was dark.

Dark. Painful. Desperate.

“This isn’t over, Lightbringer. The One will avenge us.” I could barely hear him through the hissing in my ears.

So, this was death. Being shaken and squeezed to pulp in the hands of a madman spouting vitriol.

Not yet. Not yet, spider. Hold on.

But life was slipping from me and as my hands went limp and then my body, I was glad my last thoughts would be of Raolcan.

Chapter Fifteen

A flash of pain seared through my throat as the air finally escaped. I gasped, sucking in air and choking violently on the smoke that came in with it.

"Take off! We need to get her to fresh air. Now!"

My vision crackled with black and white spots, swirling so badly that I shut my eyes against the nauseating whir. I felt Raolcan lift into the air, felt a cool breeze on my face. Through my aching throat, the air felt fresher. I sucked in painful breath after painful breath. Strong hands held me.

"There you go. Breathe. You're okay."

"Tor?" I cracked an eyelid to try to get a look at him.

See? I told you he wasn't a bad guy. Hubric and Kyrowat landed nearby to help with the city and when he saw you he leapt into the fight.

"Don't tell anyone, but I have a soft spot for cranky girls who ride dragons."

"Cranky-?" my voice cut off into a fit of coughing. It felt like my throat was being shredded.

"Yeah, you probably shouldn't talk. Even blowing that whistle is going to hurt for a while. I think I'd better ride with you for now – unless you want to go to the infirmary."

I shook my head, not trusting my voice. Each breath was like a gift, clean, pure and full of gratitude. I leaned into that feeling, focused on one breath after another. I'd have to let Raolcan take charge while I recovered.

I'm glad you're okay, spider. You had me worried.

Affection poured through our bond, but we were already descending.

"I wonder who those guys are," Tor muttered, watching the black mass as it approached the city, but a moment later we'd landed and as I slumped forward in the saddle, he leapt off and started shouting to the people surrounding us.

The mass of people on the road grows closer as the hours pass.

How long had we battled this fire?

It's past midnight. A strange time for an army to march.

Army?

"Come on, dragon!" Tor yelled, vaulting back onto Raolcan. "Let's fly!"

Raolcan hissed.

"Get over yourself," Tor muttered as Raolcan launched suddenly, knocking Tor backward so he had to cling to my saddle.

Maybe I don't like him after all. How are your lungs?

They felt like they were on fire and I was barely keeping my seat – but I was alive. Sweat ran down my forehead, stinging my eyes and making trails through the soot. I glanced at Tor and found he looked the same way.

We were all marked by this night.

Raolcan gained height and as he did, I saw a burst of magenta light a little way northeast of the city. I was too tired to even think of what question I should be asking.

You want to know why the Magikas are flinging fireballs outside the city. Our dragons are not there. They're busy fighting the fires and rescuing people.

Yes.

It's hard to tell, but I think they just washed up on the shore of that massive army.

Those were morning problems. Right now, we still had night problems.

Isn't that the truth!

I looked down over the city, my head aching and my mind reeling. The line of the fire had crept over three-quarters of the city, but it seemed to be holding there. Our weariness was proof that it could be fought. Proof we could still snatch souls from the gaping maw of the fire.

If we don't stop it completely, then we'll need a miracle. The fire will spread beyond the city to the forest surrounding it and if that happens, all the people we've saved will die anyway.

What a cheerful outlook. I felt too tired to even know what to do. The Pipe wouldn't help now. We had no miracles to stop fires. It suddenly occurred to me that we hadn't seen any Ifrits yet. Where were they hiding?

I don't want to know. Don't wish them on us now.

We needed a miracle.

The wind picked up, and fire kicked up with it, surging across the city so suddenly that my breath caught in my throat. Out of a spurt of flame, Kyrowat shot into the air, loaded with people clinging to him. Tyalmae was right behind him with Ephretti.

Ephretti was signing – of course.

She thinks they've cleared all the people they can. Anyone left will be taken by the fire.

But that wasn't acceptable. It was my responsibility to stop this. There had to be something, anything to stop this fire! I turned my head upward, looking at the swirling clouds above. The light came from the heavens and bathed the earth. It streamed from between clouds and filled up dark places. It crept across the ground and revealed hidden things.

You sound delusional.

But I wasn't. Wherever that light came from, somehow, Savette could tap it, and bring that strength to bear. It had even come through me once. But this time, I didn't have a prophecy on the tip of my tongue and I didn't have light to read the book by – except for by the light of the raging fires.

"We need to do something. We can't just circle here," Tor said from behind me. "Wait! Ephretti must have seen something!"

I followed his line of vision to see her diving down into the flames. What was she doing? That was too close! She wasn't just on the edge, like we'd been. She was deep in the heart of the burning shanty-city, flames licking around her and Tyalmae. She disappeared from sight and I gasped. She was going to die down there.

Chapter Sixteen

"Come on, dragon! Go after her!" Tor said, kicking his heels into Raolcan.

Raolcan circled the area around where she disappeared, the heat – even from so high up – searing the soles of our feet and legs as he tried to find her in the flames.

Please light, please. We just needed a miracle. Something to break the raging fires. Something to help!

"Well? What are you waiting for? Get in there!" Tor's feet were flapping like he thought he could do the flying as he tried to spur Raolcan into the flames. Fool. Raolcan knew what he was doing. "I know what it's like to live down there, okay? I know what it's like to forage for food and never feel safe. Whoever she's saving *needs* that help." He sounded desperate. "Come on, dragon, please!"

"She can't have survived that," I said through my raw throat. It was like Ephretti was dead all over again – first when her dragon was slain, and now again in the flames. Wait. What was that prophecy I'd read yesterday afternoon? The one that stuck in my head, so I couldn't move on.

Twice dead, she rises.

I didn't see her rising.

I can't hear her mind, Raolcan said. His mental voice sounded sad and mine was, too.

What was the rest of that prophecy? It was only the first line that kept ringing in my mind. *Twice dead, she rises. Twice dead, she rises.*

I said it aloud.

"What does that mean?" Tor asked.

"It's one of the Ibrenicus prophecies." I couldn't stop the tears that filled my eyes. Ephretti hadn't deserved one death, never mind two. She was just so keen on doing what was good and right. She just cared so much. Enough to fly into the flames for what seemed to be no reason. We needed to go down there and look.

It's too hot. You and Tor will die if I go in there.

"The what?" Tor asked.

"Prophecies for our time and the times to come. I read them to help guide me." My eyes were fixed on where we last saw her.

"I generally find common sense is best," he said with a sniff, but his shaking voice told me he was trying to disguise emotion just as I was.

"Look! What's that?" I pointed. There was a puff of steam from the center of the flames. We stared at it, frozen in place, unable to look away.

"There's a pool there," Tor said. In the middle of the square. It used to be a fancy fountain in the old times, but now it just holds dirty water."

"So, it's just water evaporating in the flames?" I didn't want to get my hopes up. It was just steam.

The wind grabbed the steam, brushing it away like a curtain. I drew in a breath and held it, watching the shreds of mist tear away, staring at crimson glow. Was that? It couldn't be...

Lancing up through the flames shot a green dragon, streaked with soot and the rainbow burnish of flame on scale. On his back, his rider huddled over a small bundle of rags, both of them blackened and seared.

Twice dead, she rises.

The rest of the prophecy came back to me as I watched her soar into the air, Tyalmae's wings extending outward in victory. It barely seemed real.

Twice dead, she rises.

Her rising a sign of salvation.

Favor from the heavens.

Relief from the fires of hell.

The first drop of rain hit my nose, like a splashing tear.

And then a second.

And then whatever great dragon surrounded the earth and held it in place opened his mouth and water flooded over us.

Her rising. The sign of salvation.

Or, it's just raining.

This was the miracle we needed!

It won't save the city. It's too late for that.

But it would save the countryside and the people we'd helped escape and maybe even the ones still fleeing the burning hell below.

I still couldn't believe it was real. I was afraid to breathe.

"Amel?" Tor asked. "That's your name, right?"

I ignored Tor. Ephretti must have landed in that pool of water and scooped up some poor soul huddling there to escape the flames. She wouldn't have even realized that she was the sign...

"Look, it's not like I expected you to have the good sense to come out of the rain, but I did think you might want to look at this." His voice had taken on an urgent tone.

I opened my eyes. Across the burning city, a golden dragon flew toward us and the fierce woman on his back was staring directly at me.

Jalla.

Chapter Seventeen

Oh great. My master was back. We'd better head toward the infirmary. Any meeting with Jalla was going to be hot enough without adding a flaming city in the mix.

She's not going to like that. She'll think you're making her follow you.

She could think whatever she wanted. Where was she a few hours ago when we could have used her army?

Marching across the landscape, I'd guess.

Why was Raolcan always so easy on Jalla? She didn't deserve it!

No one deserves mercy or kindness. But it's a gift that the merciful give, regardless.

My cheeks felt hot.

That wasn't a rebuke. It was just a reminder.

"Who's the woman on the golden dragon?" Tor asked.

"Jalla the Winged Prince of Baojang."

"Pretty, isn't she?"

I scowled. Pretty? Of all the adjectives I thought fit Jalla, that was not one of them.

"If you're attracted to snakes."

"I might be. I've never met a snake before who was also a beautiful woman."

We landed on the hillside not far from the makeshift infirmary. As if our landing was a catalyst, Kyrowat leapt into the air and landed roughly beside us.

"That dragon came from the approaching army," Hubric said as Kyrowat shifted under him. "I figured you could use some backup." He nodded to Tor. "Good work back there."

Tor dismounted but I stayed on Raolcan's back. I preferred it here – especially now that walking was even more difficult.

I'm happy to be your legs, Hopebringer.

I felt a pang of guilt. I hadn't brought much hope here.

It wasn't hope that you brought when you sent dragons to spit on a fire? Not hope when you helped make a way for fleeing innocents? I'm not sure what you think hope is.

I just thought I wouldn't make mistakes like this. I didn't think I'd ever be the one to destroy something or to hurt people. I was starting to think now that I didn't know who I was. Maybe I just knew what I'd done – and it wasn't all good.

I know who you are. You're Amel Leafbrought, Raolcan's human. Your aching heart of compassion is what defines you. Your desperate attempts to save the innocent in both small ways and huge designs, are what makes you Amel. I won't let you forget that. You are what you've done – sure. But you're more than that, too.

Tears pricked my eyes and I let my hands spread out across Raolcan's back, basking in the love of someone who still accepted me when I had nothing to offer but failure, brokenness, and exhaustion. What would I do without this dragon?

What would I do without this human?

Conquer the world?

Lose my heart.

Ahummal landed in front of us, spoiling the moment.

He smells like feet. How can he travel so far and still smell like feet?

Chapter Eighteen

Jalla didn't wait for his feet to skid to a stop before she leapt off Ahummal's back and strode toward me, her long curly hair whipping in wet ropes behind her and the rain lashing at her from every direction. Her loose desert clothing was soaked, but she seemed completely unaffected by the storm.

"Ruined!" she yelled over the pounding rain. "I get here, and you've burnt the place to the ground! Well? What do you have to say for yourself, slave?"

"I-"

"Don't even begin with me! I sent you to find me more dragons and I find you attacking cities and burning them to the ever-loving ground!"

"So," Hubric said laconically. "This is Jalla the Winged Prince. She's smaller than I expected."

Raolcan snorted a laugh, but Jalla's eyes narrowed as she turned to Hubric. "Silence, old man."

"I can't be silent if you insist on speaking to my apprentice that way, Winged Prince."

"Your apprentice? She's my slave!"

I coughed, suddenly realizing that no matter what labels people put on me there was only one that mattered. "Actually, I'm Raolcan's human and everything else just seems a little inconsequential at the moment."

"And *where*," Jalla asked. "Is my Pipe?"

I ignored her, turning to Hubric. "The survivors?"

Hubric smiled. "Dax has the infirmary under control, but the rain will be a problem for the survivors. They lost everything in those fires. And even with the rain it will be days before they stop smoldering."

"And days before we can access the door to the warrens – if it's still intact," I agreed.

Tor coughed. "Well, since it is at the base of the stone tower and since the tower is still standing, I think it will be fine." He stepped back as all eyes turned to him and threw his hands up defensively. "Not that I know anything about that."

"Explain," Jalla demanded.

I sat up straight in my saddle, steeling myself to stand up to Jalla. "There are underground pathways from here that can lead your armies south to the cities below in mere days instead of weeks. There is a door leading to them beneath this fallen city. We took the city in battle – and fire, it seems – and now we have survivors to care for and a path to find to the main battle south of here."

"Good work," she said, as if none of her former criticisms had ever been voiced. "We'll have our men fight the fires in the morning and drive a path to this door. A small occupational force can be left to deal with the survivors of this city."

"No need," Ephretti called as Tyalmae landed behind us. Raolcan spun so I could see her. I barely supressed a gasp. Ephretti's face and clothing were smeared with rain and soot, but behind the soot was a glow to her face that overshadowed exhaustion and pain. Was that the same glow that Rakturan and Savette had?

Twice dead, she rises.

"Dax Cloudspinner, Dragon Rider of the White and Ephretti Oakboon, Dragon Rider of the Green have claimed the fallen city of Vanika as our charge and responsibility and by the formal vows of the Dominion we assume the responsibility of the Dominion for them and will exercise the authority of the Dominar on his behalf and in his absence and of any relevant Castelan to shelter and aid, protect and guide them as expressed in the founding letters of the Dominion."

They could do that?

It's an old provision, but still valid ... in the Dominion. The question is, will Jalla accept that? She's the one with the army here.

Jalla frowned, tilted her head to one side as she thought but eventually she nodded. "I have better things to do than try to keep up a char heap. Be about it."

Ephretti was gone before anyone else could speak a word. She hadn't asked about Lenora. She hadn't acknowledged us at all. She moved with an other-worldy certainty and authority. What happened to Ephretti in that fire?

Purification. She's still Ephretti – but she's something more now.

She was reborn.

Twice dead, she rises.

Her rising a sign of salvation.

Favor from the heavens.

Relief from the fires of hell.

I could only hope that the prophecy wasn't just literal. Could Ephretti's rising be a sign of something more? A sign of a greater turn in this battle?

"I have business to attend to," Jalla said, still ignoring the rain as it washed over her face. "I'll send Renn to you in the morning and we'll find this path. And you'll return what you stole from me."

I ignored the dig. I hadn't stolen anything. There was a cough from behind Jalla and I looked to Ahummal and saw Renn sitting on his back, hunched against the rain and wind.

Jalla crossed her arms over her chest. "You didn't tell me he was a Castelan, Amel. That's practically a war leader in your Dominion. As soon as he told me, I realized what an opportunity that was. After all, if I'm going to rule this land, I'll need a proper partner. I ordered him to wed me two days ago."

My mouth dropped open. Jalla had married Renn?

She smirked. "Don't look so horrified. We won't step through the arches until after the war is over."

That's how Baojang war leaders wed. They step through sacred arches together.

"I don't plan to be a widow before I'm a wife. But really, Amel, you should have said something. I'm only forgiving you for that slip up because I've conquered this city and brought glory to Baojang. At least you can be relied upon for victories, even if you aren't the brightest among my slaves." She sighed dramatically. "Sleep. We need you to be sharper tomorrow when you take me to the heart of the earth. You won't just be able to burn a city down to save your reputation if you mess *that* up."

She turned on her heel and strode off.

"A lovely woman. Charming personality," Hubric said dryly.

"I still think she's pretty." Tor's voice surprised me. He was still here?

I watched silently as the pouring rains reduced the city's fire to a crimson smolder. At least the firestorm had lessened. But tomorrow we would march down into the ashes below and open a door into the belly of the earth. I bit my lip as I thought about all the ways that could go wrong.

"Down into the depths for a second time, into the passage of death," Hubric said, as if reading my mind. "We'll rise again – a second time – when it spits us out on the other side. It makes me think of a prophecy:

Twice dead, she rises.
Her rising a sign of salvation.
Favor from the heavens.
Relief from the fires of hell."

I laughed.

"What's so funny?"

"I thought that prophecy was about Ephretti."

He smiled, shaking the rain out of his hair, only to have it soaked again a moment later.

"I suspect it will be about both."

Dragon School: Dust of Death

Chapter One

"I don't think I'm dying after all," Ephretti said quietly as we stood, side by side watching the smouldering city below us. The rain had not stopped. It still lashed around us in a torrential downpour, as if the heavens themselves were furious that the fires of Vanika had ever been lit.

My fault. Still my fault.

It was hard to even tell it was morning, the sky was so dark. Behind us, Hubric cursed steadily as his little fire caught and then went out again.

"I can do it myself," he growled to Kyrowat, but I knew he just wanted the dragon to rest. Kyrowat had smoked and moaned all night. Dragons had protection from the fires, but not from exhaustion and carrying so many people in energetic sprints had been too much for the old dragon.

He'll be fine. He's a huge whiner.

But Hubric didn't usually fuss over him and he was fussing this morning. I huddled a little closer to Raolcan. The Autumn rain was cold and my leathers were poor protection against the storm. I had no reason to complain, though. The refugees from the fire had left with only the clothing on their backs. Our tents and blankets had only gone far enough to protect the most vulnerable.

"I'm glad you aren't dying, Ephretti." I meant it. The world would be a poorer place without her stubborn determination. And this place needed her passion and her willingness to risk everything to help the people here.

"Tell the Winged Prince to leave me Lenora. I need help here. Dax and I have our hands full."

I stole a glance at her – soaked as she was, she was still glowing faintly. Whatever had happened in the depths of the inferno had changed her.

"The fires are almost out," I said.

"They'll burn under the ashes for days or weeks," Ephretti said, shaking her head. "You must continue through the heart of the earth, just as we planned. But Dax and I have other work. There are people here who desperately need us and a city to rebuild."

She looked certain and hopeful. I felt my bottom lip begin to quiver.

"I'm so sorry about what happened. I didn't realize when we attacked that this was even possible."

She sighed. "I'm sorry, too. We were all at fault, Amel. It was not you who brought us here – not really. That was me. It wasn't you who made the plan of attack. That was Hubric. It wasn't even you who lit the fires. That was the dragons."

"I ordered them. I blew the Pipe."

"Yes. And when you leave this place to fight other battles, don't forget this. Don't forget what one terrible error can do. Don't forget how many people have suffered – have died – because of us." She ran her hands through her dark hair, combing it back out of her face. Little rivulets of water ran down her cheeks like the heavens were washing away her guilt ... and mine.

"I won't." My voice was small and trembling. I barely heard it above the pounding of the rain.

"But Dax and I will work now to restore this place and these people. Don't forget us here when the war is over, Amel. You owe these people a debt."

I nodded. "I won't forget, Ephretti."

"And don't forget that I'm proud of you." She felt embarrassed by the admission. I knew that because she immediately frowned. "Can you mount that dragon of yours without constant assistance?"

"Yes," I mumbled.

"Hmmm? Speak up!"

I felt my face heat – the only warm part of me right now. "Yes."

"Then we both have work to be done. The dark night is not over yet. Dawn has not yet come."

"Dawn has not yet come," Hubric intoned from behind me. It must be a Lightbringer thing. "Are you going to jaw all day, Ephretti, or go get some real work done?"

Ephretti ignored Hubric, surprising me with a hug. "Goodbye, Amel. I won't be able to say it later. There's too much to do. Stay alive. Watch out for that leg. Try not to do anything stupid."

"I'll try." I surprised myself by getting teary as she left us. Through the downpour, she disappeared in moments. I was going to miss all her orders and the way she had of organizing everything.

I jumped when Raolcan lit Hubric's fire with a burst of orange flame. Hubric muttered thanks and set his caf pot roughly on the ring of stones he'd made.

"She's a good woman, Ephretti. She and Dax will do what's needed here," Hubric said after long minutes had passed. I turned to look at the fire he was still nursing in the rain. He never would have managed to light it without Raolcan. "Come and drink some caf and warm up. We have things to talk about."

I sat beside him on a sodden log and accepted the caf. At least it could warm my wrinkled fingers.

That's why I lit it. You two fools would have dissolved before asking for help.

"We have to go back down into those warrens," Hubric said. "And we have to bring an army with us, Amel."

"Raolcan thinks he can work those portals – if they're undamaged. Remember how some were burned out last time?"

"That's not the thing I'm most worried about."

We sat in silence for a few moments before I said the word ringing in both our heads. "Ifrits."

"They've been going down into those tunnels, but none came up to fight in the city last night."

I followed his thought. "Which means that they have either gone to their destination-"

"-or they are still under there, waiting for us," Hubric finished.

I drank my caf and thought about hundreds of Ifrits under the ground with glowing mouths and eyes. I swallowed down the bile that rose at the thought of them. But what else could we do? I'd burned down a city for the chance to use the warrens. I didn't have the right to back out now.

No, you don't. The course is set.

"The man who tried to kill me – the one in the city – he said our destruction was prophesied by Ko'Torenth."

"False prophecies," Hubric said waving a hand.

"And there were Rock Eaters here when we attacked, although I didn't see any after in the chaos."

"They may have fled." But now he had a thoughtful look on his face.

"And before we recruited Rakturan and Jalla to our side, Baojang led the war against the Dominion."

"Don't think they are fully your allies now – not really. In the end, they want what we have." Hubric was a sharp man. One conversation with Jalla and he'd seen that.

"So, what makes three other nations attack us at once? Why band together to destroy us?"

"Maybe they just saw an opportunity. The Dusk Covenant had struck and our Dominar was in jeopardy. Maybe it was just good timing." He sipped his caf, watching me, like he was expecting something.

"Or maybe they pushed the Dusk Covenant. They've lain dormant in our land for generations. Why strike now? What if these nations pushed them, secretly, in the quiet of peaceful times."

"It's possible. But why would they do that?" He wasn't doubting me, but he was pushing me.

"What do we have that they want?"

We sat there in the rain, thinking about it in shared silence. That was the question, wasn't it? What did they want? The Dominion, maybe. We had wealth and resources. Perhaps it was our sky cities that tempted them. After all, they seemed to have turned all the Magikas against us – but why not just steal the Magikas away if that was what they wanted?

I felt like I should know this answer, like it was obvious somehow, but I just wasn't seeing it. I pursed my lips and thought about it, but whatever insight I might have found was interrupted.

Chapter Two

Lenora's face had a panicked look when she landed. Lypukrm skidded to a wet, mud-flinging stop in front of us and she didn't even dismount before calling through the rain.

"The Winged Prince wants you, Amel!"

She looked so entirely different from the haughty noblewoman I'd met only a handful of months ago that it still surprised me. We'd been through a lot in the road-worn Dragon School we'd ended up in. No matter how difficult they crafted the courses in the original school, they couldn't have worked us this hard.

"Lenora," I said. "Would you like caf?"

Her eyes went big. "Aren't you coming to see Jalla? She wants you right away."

"When I'm ready. Have a drink with us."

She shook her head. "When I get back-"

"You aren't going back," Hubric said with a grunt. There was a twinkle in his eye and we shared a smile. We were still on the same page.

"Ephretti says she needs you back now," I said. Lenora's eyes became sad. She glanced toward the camp Ephretti and Dax had set up for the refugees as if everything in her were drawing her that way. "You have your things with you in your saddlebags, don't you?"

"But, Jalla-"

"Will still have an army and a future husband to wait on her with or without you." Hubric was making interruptions a habit.

"What did Jalla do with the Rock Eaters that fled the city?" I asked.

Lenora looked surprised. "She killed them to a man. Even those who surrendered."

"And the Magikas?"

"She told us not to go after them. They fled toward Cabradis."

"And the other soldiers? Archers? Men on horse."

"Some are prisoners. Some are dead."

Interesting. So, she didn't want to fight the Magikas, for whatever reason, and she didn't want any of the Rock Eaters to live. What if my theory was right and there was some kind of conspiracy between our neighbors? What if Jalla knew more about it than I ever imagined?

"I didn't get a chance to tell you after the Healing Arches," I began, but I had to stop and clear my throat. "How glad I am that you survived." A bit of the old Lenora came back with those words. She sat up a little straighter and held her head a little higher. "Do you want to go back to Ephretti?"

"Yes," she said fiercely.

"Then I'll miss you." We were both smiling, now. "And you'd better be about it. I can see Renn on his way. Jalla was too impatient to wait for you to return with me."

Lenora glanced over her shoulder, the edgy look back in her eyes for a moment, before calling out, "Thank you!" and leaning low over Lypukrm. His muscles bunched and then he leapt into the air, power and grace uniting in a single motion.

We're beautiful when we fly. We were made for it. People are always the most beautiful when they're doing what they were designed for.

And the most miserable when they weren't. And Renn seemed surprisingly miserable for someone about to seal the biggest negotiation he could manage in a lifetime. He was almost green in the face when he landed at our camp.

We should just call this tiny fire "the Dragon Cotes" and be done with it, there's so much traffic here.

"Where did Lenora go?" he asked. His good looks were marred by dark circles under his eyes. Sleeplessness didn't suit him.

"She's off to bring equality to all people," I teased.

He didn't even notice. "As long as she gets back to Jalla soon. The Winged Prince does not like delays. She wants to know where you are and why it's taking so long. Dawn is more than an hour past."

"If she's the Winged *Prince*, what will you be called when you marry?"

I almost laughed at his pale face and wide eyes – but I felt too sorry for him. He was bound to a force of nature. It was kind of like strapping yourself to the back of an Ifrit and holding on for the ride. What would that do to a person?

"I'll be whatever she decides. What are we waiting for?"

"We're waiting for the talent," I said calmly, sipping my caf.

Hubric chuckled into his coffee. For someone who seemed to derive all his pleasure from watching people, he was having the time of his life here. I wouldn't have known he was on edge if I didn't know him so well, but he was twisting and turning one of his scarves when he thought no one was looking. He was as worried about the warrens as I was.

"I'm here," Tor said, stepping out from behind us. "Have you modified that saddle to fit me, too, old man?"

"Hardly," Hubric's tone was gruff, which I'd come to know disguised true affection for someone. "I can hardly carry a sack of potatoes behind me all the way south. You'll show us the entrance and then you'll go help Dax and Ephretti until after this war is over."

"And then?" Tor froze as he waited for the answer. Interesting. This meant something to him.

Last night he had a taste of the life he really wants – dragon riding. Hubric was right. He's a natural. A perfect fit for a dragon, but boy would it be a job taking him on. I wouldn't want it.

Maybe his dragon wouldn't pick. Maybe he would.

I doubt it. He feels sort of Purple to me. Sort of.

Even more interesting.

Hubric had let the answer hang in the air for so long that Renn cursed. "Just answer him, will you? Jalla is waiting and if I'm late..."

I didn't even want to know what Jalla would do to him. Well, maybe I did. After all, I wouldn't be stuck with her if it hadn't been for him.

And you wouldn't have the Pipe.

And I wouldn't have burned a city down.

Or saved us all at the Healing Arches.

Hubric's roar of an answer surprised me so much that I almost dropped my mug.

"And then we'll throw you off a cliff and see if you can fly! What did you think we'd do, boy?"

"Promise?" Tor's eyes were alight. He was crazy. That was the only word for that – crazy.

Or maybe dragon-y.

Chapter Three

The army or Baojang was surprisingly well organized considering how disorganized everything else about them seemed. Their traditions and laws were still opaque to me and their various leaders seemed to come and go in such a haphazard manner that it surprised me to see their tents laid out in careful rows with group fires spaced equidistantly along the lines. A large pavilion at the center of the camp was dominated by Jalla and her war leaders. It was positioned at the top of a hill, which made it easy to see from even outside the camp – and it also made it possible for her to see everything that happened in her camp.

We landed outside the camp on the city side of it.

"I'll wait here with the boy," Hubric said, nodding at Tor. He watched Renn suspiciously.

You aren't the only one who doesn't trust that foot eater. Oh, great, he's leaving that moldy old rug of a dragon with us.

Why did Raolcan hate Ahummal so much? He hadn't seemed that bad of a dragon.

You aren't the only one who feels betrayed by events in Baojang.

Interesting.

My progress was slow as I worked with both crutches and my slowly healing leg. It could move and bend and bear my weight, but I was tired from the night before and both legs were stiff from being pushed too far during last night's flights.

"Can you hurry?" Renn asked impatiently. "You've already taken too long!"

Rakturan stepped out from the shadow of one of the tents. "Why don't you go soothe your lady love, Renn, and I'll escort Amel."

Renn's expression looked like it didn't know if it should be offended or grateful. After a moment he just turned on his heel and rushed away.

"You think you have a faster way to get this army to Savette?" Rakturan said without preamble.

"We hope so. Have you decided if you are for us or against us, Dark Prince?" If he didn't have time for niceties, neither did I.

His eyes glowed behind his blindfold as he said, "I told you before, and I grow tired of telling you – I am for Savette. I will give my life's blood for her."

"And your people?" I was slowing as the ache in my leg increased, bringing tears to my eyes. I should have ridden Raolcan in here instead of worrying about crushing the tents along the way.

The soldiers along the way stared at us and I didn't know if it was Rakturan's glowing eyes or the foreign Dragon Rider who had their curiosity piqued.

"I brought them here, didn't I? To fight and die in a war not their own? What more do you want, Amel?"

"I want what you wanted when you asked me to stay in Baojang with you."

He sighed, but he wouldn't meet my eye and I knew he felt the shame of knowing it was his request that enslaved me to Jalla – or so he thought. I still was certain I could wiggle out of it somehow. After all, if she could declare me a slave just like that, I could declare myself not a slave just like that, too – just not when her army was nearby. Or any of her relatives. Or anyone else who might kill me for thinking that.

"Listen," he put a hand on my arm and I stopped. It didn't take much to make me want to take a break. I felt lightheaded. I needed sleep and rest. I wasn't going to get either. "Have you stopped to consider why Baojang chose to attack the Dominion?"

"As a matter of fact-"

"Because that reason hasn't gone away, and since you arrived in Baojang, your presence has only fuelled our war leaders desire to see the Dominion under the feet of Baojang."

It had?

"But Jalla has big plans."

Big plans, hmmm? What did that mean? "Is that why she ordered the Rock Eaters killed?"

Rakturan looked around furtively before saying, "Jalla doesn't like to share." He paused, but we were almost to the pavilion now and he had to be quick. "If I can save your Dominion, I will – for Savette. But there's no guarantee that I can, and better a vassal of Baojang than a slave of the Rock Eaters or a puppet of Ko'Torenth. At least we have honor."

What did that mean?

You still have a lot to learn about our neighbors. He's right about one thing – the other options are definitely worse than Baojang.

Worse? Worse than slavery and bickering war leaders and those awful Sentries? Worse than deserts and heat and holes in the ground with people hung over the side in baskets?

Yep. Worse than that.

My stomach flipped at the thought.

"And now I want a similar promise from you, Amel." Rakturan's eyes flared, like his emotions were triggering greater light.

"What promise?"

"I want you to treat my people like they are your own. You're about to lead them down an unsafe path under the ground. I want to know you are looking out for them, that in your eyes they aren't just a tool to help Savette."

"I thought you *wanted* to help Savette."

"I thought *you* wanted to save lives." He was quicker than I was.

"Okay, I promise. We're still driving for the same goal, aren't we Rakturan? Can you promise me that?" I thought that perhaps Rakturan was a good man, an honorable man, but why did he always leave me guessing? Why couldn't he just be who he was instead of always showing this opaque exterior?

"I will die trying to rid this world of Ifrits and give my wife what she needs. Is that what you need to hear?"

"Yes," I said.

"Then the covenant is made between us. Together, we will destroy the Ifrits and help Savette. So let it be soaked in our spirit. So let it be accomplished." He offered me a waterskin. "In Baojang we seal an oath with a sip of water."

"I bet you do," I muttered, but I wouldn't be sipping Silla-laced water ever again. Instead, I grabbed his hand. "In the Dominion, we seal it with a handclasp. Since we're in the Dominion, let's do it that way."

He hesitated before nodding.

"As you say."

There. I might not understand the Dark Prince, but this was probably the clearest words I'd ever get from him. I needed to just be grateful for what I had.

I think that in the end, you will have been glad to know Rakturan.

Was Raolcan a prophet now?

No, but I'm good at judging people.

I almost believed him ... but then I remembered that he liked Jalla.

Chapter Four

"You're late," Jalla said as soon as I was in earshot. "Come and tell my war leaders what they can expect from this underground shortcut."

"I don't know, exactly," I said. There were sounds of disbelief around me.

Jalla raised an eyebrow, peering down her nose at me like I was an insect crawling on her clothing. "That's unlikely."

I sighed, but the war leaders were all watching me like a ring of rodents and I *had* promised Rakturan to take care of them.

"The warrens extend underground," I said, letting my gaze sweep the gathering. I kept my head held high, refusing to look down and lower my gaze like the servants pouring wine and water throughout the pavilion. "They were built by the Elders of the dragons."

Don't get too specific. This is not their business.

"If you are knowledgeable about how to use the hub points, you can shorten travel time between points by use of the power of the ancients."

There was a murmuring and one war leader spoke up. "Like how you used the Kah'deem in the service of the Winged Prince to establish her power over Baojang?"

Jalla smiled indulgently and it took all my fortitude not to roll my eyes.

"It's similar, yes." I couldn't keep the tightness out of my voice despite all my effort. They all saw my victories as Jalla's!

"Then why are these warrens not used all the time?" the same war leader asked. He was young for the role, not much older than Jalla and his armor was finely tooled speaking of status. I didn't like how soft his hands and face looked – as if he had never seen hardship.

"They are very dangerous, and their entrances are a secret to all but a few."

"Dangerous?"

"The warrens are dark." How did I convey just how bowel-churning my last passage through them had been? "And narrow. There are vast chasms bridged only by small rock bridges. Any fall would plunge you to the depths."

"So, it is like climbing in the mountains at night. Soldiers can do this with good leadership," the man said with a shrug. He motioned to one of the servants to refill his cup. "Your slave is overly timorous, Jalla. No true war leader shies away from danger or trembles at the hardship of losing a few men. I hope she has not learned this from you."

Jalla's face flared red and her eyes took on a fiery spark. "I fear no caves of stone, Habrida. Nor does anyone who serves me. She must be concerned only for your lily-white hands."

I hid a smile as Jalla's insult hit home and the man flinched.

"Mostly, I am concerned about the Ifrits reported to have entered the tunnels," I said. "In my last journey through the warrens, I was relentlessly pursued by them. They filled any space we found with violence and terror."

"A rumor," Habrida said, waving a hand. "The Ifrits were an evil brought to us by the Crescent Prince. They are no longer a problem. The Rock Eaters only spread such rumors to keep us from our prize."

I gritted my teeth but Jalla smiled at Habrida. "The Serpent Prince's words tell me that he has chosen to enter the warrens first. He and his soldiers will hold the honor of Baojang at the front of the line."

Habrida arched a single brow like he found all of this amusing. "We would never take that honor from your most excellent person, Winged Prince. Can I assume that you and your guides will ride before us – the glory and majesty of Baojang? We would never ask for more than the second honor."

Jalla's smile fell. Whatever scheme she'd been planning had hit a bump in the road. "As you say, Serpent Prince."

I didn't know why anyone would want to have someone named the "Serpent Prince" at their back.

What about the Dragon Prince?

That was the name of the only one I ever wanted to have watch out for me.

"The Serpent Prince will designate the placements of the other war divisions," Jalla announced. "Strike camp. When the men are ready to march, my slave will lead the way."

She swept away from the table like a queen in a castle. Which, I supposed, she was. She was the closest thing Baojang had to queens.

I was worried by Habrida's words, though. What did he mean by their "prize?"

There are deep waters running here. Motivations are tangled and diverse, but there is one thread running through every heart – greed. They are all slick with greed and want.

I swallowed. Of all things to bring with you into the warrens, greed might be the most dangerous. It had bent Iskaris into a traitor in these very dark corridors. What would it do to these war leaders and their men?

"Amel? A word?" Jalla said, grabbing me by the arm and pulling me from the tent.

"My injuries-"

"Are not preventing you from causing me problems."

"What is it this time?" I asked.

She leaned in, so her lips were inches from mine. "You have only two jobs in the warrens. The first is to lead us through without trouble." If only she knew how hard that was! "And the second is to see that the Serpent Prince does not survive the journey."

Chapter Five

The dragons cleared the way to the central tower under Raolcan's direction while the Baojang camp packed up. As much as I hated entering the warrens again, I was glad to take the army away from Vanika. I didn't like the way the Baojang war leaders were watching the city or the glances they sent toward the camp Ephretti and Dax had set up on the mountainside. The sooner we took them away from here, the better.

We're almost through to the tower, but the path is still ember-strewn and hot. For anyone less than a dragon, it will be impossible to cross.

But it would cool. And if it didn't, we would dump water on it to cool it faster. I sat on a large portion of wreckage from Vanika's original destruction, just outside the new city walls and massaged my healing leg. The wound was closed now, leaving only a red scar, but the muscles were still tender, and I just didn't have the confidence in it that I used to.

It just needs time. Be patient with it.

I was trying to keep my mind busy so I wouldn't fall asleep. The sounds of the army assembling behind me combined with the moment of rest were lulling me into a sleepy state. I was reading the Ibrenicus Prophecies off an on between watching, but the page I was reading today made no sense to me.

Tide of the north rushing, rushing,
Longing for sea to meet sky and conquer,
Longing to take to wing,
But by blood they grasp,
And the innocent fall with the guilty.
But one shall rise,
To stand in the place of the other,

to bear the debt of nations,
to give up the breath of life to dispel the dust of death.

I watched as Raolcan and Kyrowat slowly cleared a path with the wild dragons helping them. I hadn't taken out the pipe yet. I didn't want to remind Jalla about it. She was distracted right now, but eventually, she would ask me for it and I didn't want to give it to her – not now that I knew what it did. It was too powerful. No human should own such a thing.

I couldn't agree more. I don't like being piped into a trance.

After this war, it would need to be destroyed.

After?

Well, we still needed it right now.

You should think about whether that is really true. Real strength will give up an advantage for the good of others.

I let the moments tick by, thinking. I supposed that I could destroy the pipe. Smash it? Something told me it was unlikely to break easily. Despite the general delicate look, it had sat in that Kah'deem for generations, and it hadn't broken or even cracked in all my rough adventures. Set it on fire? It was metal. The worst that was likely to happen was soot covering it. Should I throw it into an ocean or hide it in the forest or drop it off a cliff? The thing was – in any scenario like that it would be found eventually, wouldn't it? It would be found and manipulated and used against the dragons and I just didn't think that was right.

I watched in the distance as Baojang loaded their horses and Sentries. The Sentries buzzed in their unnaturally straight line as their riders mounted. I could probably force them all to do my bidding, too, if I found the right setting. And that was just plain wrong. I needed time to think about it.

"Are they almost done?" Tor and Hubric were waiting with me – Tor less patiently than my mentor.

Surprisingly, the base of the tower is mostly intact. It was built on a part of the original base of the skycity – of course, most of the ruins are, but this part is bent and twisted, but mostly still intact. Hmmm. Look at this, Kyrowat! The door still opens and... Amel?

Yes! I was still listening.

It's a door into a carefully dressed stone cavern. There are ancient carvings of troglodytes ringing the entrance. This is it. And it was shockingly easy to find. I don't like that at all.

It would have been harder when it was tucked into the base of the city.

If we go down there, there will be nothing to prevent anyone from following us. People shouldn't be able to just wander inside. We'll need to block it up behind us.

"They found the entrance," I said, grimly. I didn't like the idea of being blocked up inside the underground caves. Only a fool would stop up their only chance of escape.

"Once we go down, you'll need to get Ephretti to block up the entrance after us," Hubric told Tor. "Let nothing back up after it has gone down. Who knows what ancient evils lie in the dark?"

Tor frowned. "You'll be down there."

Hubric snorted. "I appreciate the confidence, boy, but even I have limitations."

"Will they all fit down there?" Tor asked, watching the hundreds of Baojang soldiers form up.

I wondered the same thing. The warrens were huge – but were they big enough to move hundreds of people, animals, and Sentries, never mind the wild dragons?

They were built for dragons.

And yet that made me more nervous than I could justify. Somehow the idea of bringing all those dragons and people down into the warrens filled me with dread.

"Lazing around, slave?" Jalla asked as she approached us. Renn hovered at her elbow, his expression a mix of smugness and anticipation.

Hubric cleared his throat and gave her a pointed look.

"We're waiting for the path to be clear," I said stiffly. When Baojang was through the warrens and helping Savette I would find a way to make her eat that word.

"It looks clear enough to me. I'm here for the Pipe. I'll call the dragons to follow us into the warrens." My face must have betrayed me, but she smirked. "You can't keep secrets from me, Amel. Did you think I didn't know? That Lenora didn't tell me what happened at the arches? For that matter, why do you think I came to Vanika and not Cabradis, which was closer. I know more than you think I do."

My brow crinkled as a wave of cold washed over me. How did she know about Vanika? How had they arrived here? She was insinuating that she had some way to track me – to watch me – when she wasn't there. That couldn't be true ... could it?

We'll have to find out.

Behind Jalla, Rakturan and Enkenay landed on the scorched earth.

"Your War Princes are ready to move, War Leader," Rakturan called.

My eyes narrowed. We'd made promises to each other about keeping his people and mine safe and helping Savette, but we'd never said anything about information. And I knew the Troglodytes had chosen him as much as they'd chosen me. Perhaps he had watched me in visions and told the Winged Prince.

It's a good theory.

I would have to be careful what I told Rakturan.

Chapter Six

My first step back into the warrens was the most terrifying. My will told me to press forward but my mind and heart were a gibbering terrified mess in the background wailing as my crutches led the way into the darkness. Jalla had insisted we wait to mount the dragons until we were inside.

"Otherwise the soldiers won't believe it is safe to walk into the tunnel," was her excuse. As if the warrens were ever 'safe' for anyone.

I leaned a shoulder against Raolcan as I walked. I would have liked to place a hand on him, but I was still using both crutches even though I thought I might be able to get away with just one again. Dax's was carved wood and nice, but it didn't move as easily or fit nearly as well as the one Hubric had given me and I was growing weary of having both hands full.

As soon as I leaned against him, a vision washed through me. Leng was shifting in a dark space that smelled of dust. He moved and I could feel wool against his skin. Was he behind a tapestry? Voices filtered in from behind the curtain.

"... only a month and Ko'Torenth will be ready to send troops to support us. Are you really telling me this rebellion can't be held back for a few more weeks?"

That voice! I would recognize it anywhere. Iskaris!"

My mouth went dry as Leng shifted his weight. What was he doing in such a dangerous place? He shouldn't be there! He must be at the very heart of Dominion City!

"Did you hear something?"

Iskaris' question set my heart pounding, but before I could see what happened next, I was back in the real world, stepping into the cool darkness of the cave.

"There, see? She walked through a stone door without dying." Hubric's tone was dry as he spoke to Jalla. "Can the rest of us get a move on? I've already lit my lantern and I don't want to lose the light. Do you know how hard it was to find fuel oil in this city after a fire? And now that you've put the dragons at the very back it will be hard for them to light anything for us along the way. Only those disgusting Sentries are behind them."

I hated his reminder of the dark, but he was right. We were lined up in the rubble of the tower – me in the warren, Hubric, Rakturan, Jalla, Renn and their dragons next, and the Baojang army after them. The Serpent Prince had relegated the dragons to the tail end of the procession and the Sentries were to follow them at the very end. I thought he was treating them like herd dogs and the dragons like sheep – which showed a lot of ignorance about each species.

We could shred those lampreys like torn noodles if we needed to.

Ugh.

"First, hand me the Pipe, Amel." At my reluctance, Jalla raised an eyebrow looking at the army at her back.

I gave her the Pipe, but the moment it left my hands I was rocked by a second vision. Savette studied a paper in her hand.

"And there was nothing else?" she asked the man in front of her. "Only a satchel of dust and this note?"

"I swear it."

"Hmmm." She opened the note as she spoke. "A strange thing for an assassin to sneak into the heart of our camp with nothing more than a knife, a bag of dust and a note."

"What does it say?" a voice asked from beside her. I turned to see a woman dressed in fine wools – a Castelan. Was she one of Savette's allies?

Savette glanced down and I read the words on the paper.

"We will take the strength of the Dominion from under your seat. Your lives are forfeit for hoarding it throughout this age. The wealth shall be redistributed. The privilege removed. The strength given to the weak. Take warning."

There was the sign of a tower under the writing.

What did it mean? It sounded like something Renn might say but carried by an assassin ... that was different. What sort of an assassin brought a bag of dust with them.

"The man was from Ko'Torenth," the messenger told Savette. "We found coins and dried fire vines in his clothing."

"But why would they send this vague message?" The Castelan asked. Her wrinkled face twisted in thought as she spoke.

That bag of dust was just like the one Dax had found on his dead friend – a strange thing to bring with you to kill. Was it a symbol? Some sort of token or talisman?

I returned to the real world just as Jalla threw the Pipe at me. "This thing is junk!"

It bounced off Raolcan's flank and Tor caught it, offering it respectfully to me.

"Thank you," I said. Turning back to Jalla as Hubric began to whisper to Tor about remembering his part of the bargain and returning to Ephretti until Hubric came back for him. I held the Pipe up and caught Jalla's eye. "Do you want the dragons to follow us into the warrens and fight with us on the other side?"

It was lucky for her that so few people could see me from here - only her and my friends and a handful of Baojang princes. If I had been on a hill where everyone could listen, this would have been the perfect speech.

"The dragons are not our slaves, Jalla. They are free to come as they wish and go as they must. But let's see if they would like to come with us."

I adjusted the arm and blew a three-note tune. I couldn't even see from here if it worked.

They come, Raolcan said to me. *I have instructed them to follow at the back of the line in the place they were assigned – between the army and the Sentries.*

How did they feel about the Sentries?

No one knows if they taste good or not. It's hard to live with an unanswered question like that looming over us...

Jalla's face was so cold that I didn't know whether it was rage or jealousy making it look like death had come early to her.

Both. Be careful, Amel. Petty people can do very cruel things.

But I had already turned around and begun to mount Raolcan. What did I care if the Winged Prince hated me? She had already taken me as a "slave" and taken all my victories for her own. What more could her anger take?

The warrens, now. They were a different matter. They had almost taken my life last time. I would not let them finish the job this time.

Chapter Seven

At least I didn't need to walk on crutches the whole way through the warrens. I kept reminding myself of that as the cool damp of the first tunnel penetrated through to my bones and filled me with remembered dread. Raolcan and I led the group at the very front, a lantern from Hubric attached to the saddle on a long pole he'd hewn from a sapling before we left. He followed me, a similar pole holding his own lantern. Jalla rode behind him with Renn and I could hear her chastising him - a background noise as we wound through the tunnel, moving ever downward into the belly of the earth.

"If we incorporate the citizens of the Dominion into your rule they will finally be equal – subject to the same rules and strictures instead of the tyranny of merit."

"What, exactly, do you mean by that, Castelan?"

"Well, citizens of the Dominion have to work and fight all their lives for respect and position, but in Baojang it is granted by a higher authority, equally to all."

"You think you are my equal?"

"Well, we *are* getting married..."

"You will never be my equal, Castelan. You should feel great honor that I have chosen you for a consort. And you should be thinking about how your lands and blood can purchase for us greater dominance and influence."

"Ummm..."

"And if you can't think of that, then perhaps I can find someone more useful."

I tuned them out, focusing on the way ahead. I could almost smell the stink of Ifrits ahead.

It's all in your mind. Ifrits smell of nothing but dust.

Dust. Bags of dust.

Wait. How, exactly, did Magikas bring up Ifrits from the ground? When I had been shot and lying on the ground to bleed to death the Magika had screamed at Lenora.

He said that without the aid to his magic brought by the Healing Arches he would need blood instead.

Bags of dust and knives ... could it really be so simple? Could these assassins – like the one found by Savette – be there to unleash an Ifrit? Did they just need the blood to finish the effort?

It couldn't be just any kind of dust, could it? Or why bring it with them?

Well, there wouldn't be much dust in a city – or at least not all in one place.

So, they kill an innocent person and use their lifeblood in some sort of dark magic to raise up an Ifrit? How chilling.

How utterly unstoppable. A man could bring a bag of dust anywhere. He could open it up and kill someone anywhere. I looked behind me nervously. There were hundreds of people behind me with bags.

Soldiers. With their equipment on their backs. Not assassins.

But how did he know? Now that I knew, I couldn't help but suspect everyone.

Even me?

Okay, not everyone.

The air felt too thin with so many people jammed into the narrow tunnel. I hadn't wondered if we would run out of air. But I should have, shouldn't I? They had probably already blocked up the entrance...

Actually, even though we've been walking for two hours, there are still dragons entering the tunnel behind us. We're taking a massive horde with us through here.

And did he really think he could work the portal if we got to it? He hadn't been able to before.

No guarantees, but I wasn't completely idle at the Dawn Gate.

What?

Well, there were a lot of dragons there. I asked around. Some of them were curiously well-informed.

How did I not know this?

I can't possibly tell you everything.

I felt so stunned that I rode in mental silence for a few minutes before the chagrin of it hit me. Raolcan was *always* one step ahead of me.

A dragon has to try.

And what about the dust and the knives? Was he ahead on that, too?

No. We both thought of that at the same time. So, I guess there is only one last puzzle for you. What do the Rock Eaters, Baojang, and Ko'Torenth have in common?

They are neighbors of the Dominion.

And?

They are allied against us.

And?

They want something from us.

You are very close. Keep thinking.

Why didn't he just tell me if he'd already figured this one out?

Because I think you need to get there by yourself. There are implications to it that will make a huge difference to you.

Well, now I really wanted to know.

I think I see the first marker ahead.

A hub?

Yes. And I see the glow of the sigil. If we are lucky, it's undamaged.

Would that be lucky or unlucky? After all, if it was undamaged then the Ifrits may have been using it all this time to plunge deep into the heart of the Dominion.

But now we know they can come from anywhere with the right ingredients.

What were they? Products of magic or true living entities?

Enemies. That is all we need to know. We will rip and tear them to pieces.

We stepped out onto the bridge that led to the center hub. I could sense it immediately. Something was not right.

Chapter Eight

"What is that?" The murmur came from the ground beside us. How had the Serpent Prince snuck up here?

"You shouldn't be at the front," I whispered.

"What is that monstrous thing?"

Above the carved dragon figure in the center of the hub, an Ifrit floated, detached from the ground. It was as if it slept, its usual gashes of fire and brimstone that served as eyes and mouth were shut. Was it alone? I glanced furtively from side to side, my breath coming quicker.

Even if we wanted to turn around there are hundreds behind us. We cannot run.

I settled for venting at the Serpent Prince. "Weren't you at the Kah'deem?"

"I was not. I did not see Jalla's victory."

Hubric pressed forward so that Kyrowat's head was almost touching me as he pushed into Raolcan's back.

His voice was hushed. "Whatever it's doing, we'll have to fight it. If you sweep wide to the right, I'll take the left and we can try to pinch it between us."

Solid enough plan.

I didn't like that it was sleeping. Somehow, an Ifrit in motion felt better than one lying in wait. What did it know that we didn't?

"Take me with you!" the Serpent Prince said, his eyes alight.

I ignored him, hunching low in the saddle as I prepared for Raolcan's leap. As he leapt, I felt myself slipping to the left. I gripped the saddle hard, hoping my straps would hold. My bad leg was caught on something! Fear rose as I tugged at it. But no – we hadn't stopped, we were still rising!

And then I felt the pressure moving higher and I looked down to see the Serpent Prince holding my leg as we flew through the black of night.

"You're insane!"

Grab him and get him up quickly! He's thrown us off balance.

"What does it matter?" he asked. "It's the useless one, isn't it?"

"It's still useful to me!"

I reached down, trying to push back nerves as I pulled him up. I wished I could just push him off and let him fall. His comment disgusted me.

This felt too much like last time. It was almost as if I could still hear the pounding of hundreds of Ifrits on the door, feel them rushing behind us, see again Iskaris stealing the mask and pulling the Dominar out of the circle of safety and now another enemy sought to take what wasn't his.

"Jalla isn't the only one who should have a dragon rider to serve her," he said with a grunt, pulling himself up into the saddle behind me. "And I think she owes me your service. After all, most of the soldiers here are mine. How do you steer this beast?"

"I'm not available for the taking," I said tightly.

He whispered his response in my ear, and the act was too close – too intimate. It made me shiver with revulsion. Perhaps this was why they called him 'Serpent Prince.'

"I know who wins Jalla's battles. I think you could win some for me. I'll even offer you something she can't. I'll marry you – with all the status that brings – and just like Renn manages her dragon, you can manage mine. Obviously, with that leg, you won't be bearing my children, but the arrangements I make for that will not impinge upon your standing. Now *that* is a better offer than you'll receive from anyone."

"No," I said, my voice a ghost as the horror of his proposal washed over me. Would Jalla really give me to him? With this army, how could I stop them? I swallowed as I watched the Ifrit growing closer, worry knotting deep in my belly. I could see my life playing out just as he said – forced to fly him here and there as he whispered directions I couldn't stop in my ear. I felt sick.

"Then how about this, instead?" His tone remained low – pitched only for my ears as we soared toward the sleeping monster. "How about if you kill

Jalla for me down here in these caverns? It's so dark that no one will know. You'll be free of her, and I promise that once you return us to the surface you'll be free of me."

"I won't be killing anyone," I said tightly. I didn't like how close he was sitting or how he chuckled in my ear.

"I can guarantee you one thing. You will give me Jalla or she will give me you. There is no third option."

Or you could kill him like Jalla asked you to.

But I didn't think I could do that. I remembered when I wanted to kill Iskaris. What had Hubric said? He'd said that the consequences went a lot further than I thought. And what about when I thought I could conquer a city? Just thinking of it now brought thoughts that stabbed through my brain like jagged glass shards. The mind-numbing shame of what I had done hurt too much to dwell on. Thinking about it again was like picking up red-hot metal with your bare hands. My mind shied away from even allowing it.

My fault. Still my fault.

No, I wouldn't be killing anyone.

We circled the Ifrit, my fear of the dust creature lessened by my horror of the human creature on my back. One loop and no reaction. Hubric shook his head with a frown.

Strange. What was it doing here, still as a statue?

Raolcan slowly circled lower around the glowing dragon statue at the center of the hub. The huge glyph at its feet glowed a bright purple over the dusty stone floor and the runes along its base flickered with light. I tensed, anticipating his landing, but had to grab for support when he spun suddenly, neck arching around and wings shooting upward so quickly that the Serpent Prince fell from his seat. Raolcan snatched him in his jaws, shook him twice and spat him into the circle.

No one talks to my human like that.

I didn't know if I should laugh or choke on my laughter. There would be a price to pay for that. And I wasn't even a little bit sorry.

Chapter Nine

"So, why is there an Ifrit hanging over us looking like he might dive down and shred us to pieces at any moment?" Jalla asked as Ahummal landed beside us.

I hadn't been able to tear my eyes away from the motionless statue since we landed. It gave me the creeps. I had the horrible suspicion that if I turned my back for even a second it would come to life and gobble me up.

"If we had answers, Winged Prince, we'd be sure to offer them," Habrida, the Serpent Prince, said with a smirk. Even a good shaking by a dragon couldn't wipe the confidence out of him – though I noticed he wouldn't look at Raolcan or me.

Good. If he so much as looks my way, I'll shake him again.

But you couldn't treat people like that. Especially not powerful leaders of armies.

I'm pretty sure that I just did...

"I'd like an answer, Amel," Jalla said. I glanced at her for a moment. "If you don't know what the Ifrit is doing there, or why it is motionless, then can I suggest you at least find a way to carry out my orders?"

She shot a significant look at Habrida. It was true. When he grabbed my leg it had been the opportunity to kick him into the darkness and let him fall to his death. But if she didn't realize I wasn't the kind of woman who would do that, then she didn't know me at all.

I settled on something safer to say aloud. "We're figuring out how to transport your army, Winged Prince."

Raolcan was focused on the center statue, studying it carefully, just as I'd said.

It's intact and working. Well, mostly working. It looks like it can only take us two places – the other runes are damaged.

And where were those places?

Somewhere near Dominion City and somewhere close to Leedris City. I can't tell specifically.

Perhaps the Leedris City entrance let to the caves we'd sheltered in before we entered the warrens the first time.

Possibly, but I don't think so.

"What's taking so long?" Jalla asked.

"It's not like gutting fish," Hubric said lazily. He must have landed behind us. "If you're lucky enough to find someone able to tune the hub, it still takes time."

Hmm... it's tuned right now for Leedris City. And the runes are ... stiff would be a way to put it, although it feels more complex than that. I'm a little worried that if I try to change it I might break it.

"The Hub is tuned to Leedris City," I said.

Jalla motioned to Renn who pulled a map from his saddlebags to show her in the lantern light.

"Remember when I told you it would be better to go to Leedris first?" he said, excitedly. "Better to establish a stronghold there, so we don't have enemies on every side. And it will be harder for the Dominion to ask for it back if we take it and occupy it before a decisive conflict to the south."

He was sharing strategies to defeat his own country with her? My eyes went large and I felt hot at his words. This was outrageous! It was hard to think clearly when all I wanted to do was shout at him.

"Leedris will be just right," Jalla said, as if it were as easy as ordering more wine from her servants.

But I didn't want to go to Leedris. That was days away from where we could help Savette! If we went to all this trouble I wanted to go to Dominion City.

I'm really not sure that tampering with the hub is a good idea right now. If it's working, why risk it? You've seen how easy it is for them to stop working entirely.

How many times would this one work?

There's no way to know.

And how many times would it take to get all these people through?

Many.

Like how many?

Many. Many. Many.

Well, that was helpful.

Don't blame me! It's not me who brought an army down here.

I clenched my jaw. No. It was me who brought the army down here. Me, who was relying on him to use this hub over and over. Me, who knew that if we went to Leedris City there would be another battle like the one I started at Vanika, another chance to be responsible for the deaths of hundreds of innocents. I could still smell the smoke on me from when Vanika burned.

If I agreed to let Raolcan open that portal for Jalla's people, then I was agreeing to do that all over again. I might as well start bathing in the blood.

Don't be over-dramatic.

Well, what would he call it then? To my shame, there were people gone from this earth who should still be here – because of me. And to my shame, I would do it again.

"What's taking so long?" Jalla asked. Her arms were crossed and her foot tapped on the stone. "The army is almost across the bridges."

I looked where she was pointing, eager for the distraction. The line of lanterns moved slowly towards us, hundreds of feet crossing the narrow stone bridge to the center hub. The snorts of horses and distant babble of low voices met us. One of the lights fell over the side, slowly plunging into the darkness and falling, falling, falling, until I lost sight of it.

In reaction, the crowd pushed the other direction. I thought I heard someone yell and then a second lantern dropped. If they weren't careful, they would lose all their lights.

The lights are attached to men.

A wave of nausea washed over me and I closed my eyes, clamping my jaw shut as I spread my palms across Raolcan's scales looking for support. Horror rocked me and burrowed into my mind tentacle-like. How long would they fall before they died? How many minutes of knowing it was too late. What if that had been someone I knew? Lenora? Or Ephretti.

Stop. You're spiralling out of control.

But they were here because I led them here.

Enough. It's time to decide. Shall I open the portal?

"Did you see that?" I asked with a shaky voice.

"The way is narrow. And this rock island is small," Jalla said, her voice hard and unyielding. "If you don't like lives wasted, then pick up the pace. Once they crowd onto this hub we need to start moving them or many more will fall."

Do I open it?

No.

Really? Do you know what it would take to back all of this up?

I mean ...

The fight in Vanika was for this. The lives lost were for this. You can't back out now. You have to finish what you started.

I didn't want to do it. I swallowed, and my throat ached so much it was hard to even swallow my own saliva. I cleared my throat roughly, biting back an anxious whimper.

Yes, okay, yes.

There was no turning back now.

Chapter Ten

Once this starts, I won't be able to stop while people are going through the portal.

I thought they just stood in the circle and you activated it and it transported them.

That's one way to do it. The dragon I spoke to at the Dawn's Gate says it's possible to trigger the gate to stay open as long as I hold the flow of magic in place.

And how are you supposed to do that? It didn't sound like a real thing.

With a mental trick.

It sounded too easy. He'd just 'happened' on a dragon who knew the legends of these portals when he, a dragon prince, hadn't known them. And then it just 'happened' to be a mental trick that made it work perfectly for our situation?

My, are you cynical these days. Where did sweet little Amel go?

She burned up in the fire.

There was a pause, like he was processing what I'd thought before a burst of chagrin came through our link.

I asked my brother. He was always more studious than I was.

He'd talked to his brother about this?! He hadn't mentioned it.

Just because you're getting cynical it doesn't mean that I need to get all gooey to balance you out. You were busy planning your bright future with Leng while we were at the Dawn's Gate. I wasn't just sitting there idly.

So, he had to focus, and he had to stay focused while the portal was open.

And practically motionless. Do you want to stay on my back or get down before I start?

He shuffled slightly, positioning himself so he could access the glowing runes while looking down the bridge before us. The torches were growing closer. I kept my eyes unfocused when I glanced up, trying to judge distance without noting specifics. I didn't want to know if someone else fell in their hurry to arrive at the bridge.

Pretending it isn't happening doesn't make it stop.

But feeling the pain of it didn't make it stop either. Who were these crazy people who would push forward to battle so intently that they lost their footing and then not even show compassion for those who fell?

These people are your enemies who are temporarily your allies. Note how they think differently than you do. Note how their values and ways of expressing themselves are different. You may need to understand that someday. But don't ever forget that they are human just like you. No matter how different, no matter how foreign - they are human.

I let my eyes focus. I'd stay up here on Raolcan's back – solidarity with my dragon. Whatever befell him would befall me. The first marching feet reached the hub at the same moment that Raolcan's mind began to feel distant from me. The glowing circle grew brighter.

"Finally!" Jalla said from the sidelines. "Are we ready?"

I cleared my throat, nervous suddenly. What if it went wrong?

"We're ready."

"Test it out, Dragon Rider," Jalla said to Hubric, but he just raised an eyebrow.

"I'm on Ifrit watch, Baojang," he said, calling her by the nation she led like she was a real monarch. I supposed she was, whether it felt that way to me or not.

Kyrowat shifted to stand shoulder to shoulder with Raolcan and I smiled gratefully at Hubric. At least if we were pinned here we could have him at our back.

"Fine." Jalla looked around herself with a frown, clearly trying to think quickly.

With Hubric and me stuck at the hub that only left Ahummal for her to ride, but if she was the first to go through the portal she'd have to leave her army behind her – uncertain about whether they could follow her. She glanced at the Serpent Prince, her mouth forming a worried moue. He smirked, clearly realizing, as I did, that if she sent him through first he would be in command of the forces on that side until she joined him.

She cleared her throat. "The Serpent Prince will have the honor of leading us through the portal."

I felt a vibration.

I looked up, slowly.

Bright, fiery eyes were looking down at me.

Chapter Eleven

I've already started. I can't stop.

The Ifrit stirred.

"Hubric!" I whispered. Just a whisper in a cavern full of people talking at full volume. But the Ifrit shifted slightly – like I suddenly had his full attention.

Everything seemed to happen very slowly – too slowly.

The Serpent Prince yelled a command in his language, pushing past Jalla and rushing into the circle. As soon as he reached the midway point he startled, freezing in place for a moment – his eyes wild – before he disappeared. He didn't fade slowly or seem to walk through a door or anything else, he was just gone.

I didn't have time to gasp before Jalla drew her sword, raised it in the air and yelled, pointing at the glowing glyph on the floor. The army rushed forward from the bridge onto the central hub, charging for the glyph at full speed. The man leading the charge didn't even pause as he hit the same point as Habrida had and vanished midstride, just like his leader. I barely saw the faces of the men and women who followed him before they vanished into the portal, too.

And then everything was moving too quickly. I held my breath as I watched, unwilling to be distracted by the need to breathe.

The army continued its headlong charge into the portal. Kyrowat launched into the air beside me while Jalla screamed at Renn to follow him. Renn argued back, his face flushed in his intensity. It would take a lot to force Renn to fly into the face of danger.

He finally launched into the air, cursing so loudly that I could hear him over the pandemonium of the jostling army. I couldn't understand the shouted orders or loud calls, but I caught their meaning well enough. The army was both charging into the unknown, and fleeing this dank underground hell, in the same action. Occasionally, one of them would stumble or be pushed to the side, careening into Raolcan and bouncing off his side as he focused on his task. I held my seat and my nerve carefully, refusing to let fear rise up inside me even as I was jostled and pressed.

The Ifrit shot into the air so suddenly that my heart pounded in my ears. I kept my lips pressed firmly together, my hands on Raolcan's neck. If a dragon could keep him at bay until the other dragons could get down the passage and burst into the hub cavern, then Kyrowat would have to be that dragon. If a dragon was not enough, there was nothing that I could do.

The Ifrit spun, sailing through the air like a spark-filled cloud of death. He elongated and then snapped back to his usual size, flying low over the bridge of soldiers so that his belly brushed against their lantern poles. More than one lantern fell from terrified hands and the charge I had thought was at full speed, suddenly sped up to an even faster pace.

A soldier fell into Jalla, making her stumble backward. She shoved him back with a roar and an order in her language before rounding on me.

"I'm coming up. Make space."

I opened my mouth to protest, but she was already scrambling up Raolcan's motionless side and settling into the saddle.

"We wouldn't have this problem if our soldiers were riding those dragons. Instead, we have fleeing soldiers trying to get through this portal and the dragons that could help are behind them, clogging up the rear."

I could barely hear her over the shouting. The Ifrit charged down again, this time knocking soldiers off the bridge and grabbing them by the fistful to fling into the dark. My breath caught in my throat. This is what I first feared when we returned to this terrible place. And there was no way to go more quickly. No way to save those who had fallen. No way to prevent more from falling, too.

"Your soldiers," I gasped.

"They are men and women of Baojang, not withered flowers like the people of the Dominion. We accept risk for the prospect of glory. We are made of courage and honed by risk." She sounded proud.

Kyrowat swooped toward the Ifrit – flaming as he passed – Ahummal hot on his heels. My eyes widened as I watched Renn lean low over his mount as they unleashed their own flame. Who would have thought he had it in him?

"Look at my future husband," Jalla continued. "He fights bravely – like one of us. But he shouldn't be alone. Our people should be mounted on dragons by the hundred instead of leading them as a vanguard. It has always been our destiny to fill the skies."

"Well, you do have the Sentries. But let's just get as many of your soldiers as we can through the portal," I said tightly.

Jalla nodded. "And then we will conquer the Dominion and every man and woman who survived here today will be a war leader with their own fertile lands to rule."

I clenched my jaw, not sure what to do with the mixed emotions I felt now that she was mentally dividing up my home. Every person who fell on that bridge was a human person, dying a horrible death they didn't deserve. And every one that survived was a potential Jalla – a careless slave master who would take everything from my people. I did not like either prospect.

Raolcan shifted slightly under me. Was the strain becoming too much for him? How long could he hold on?

I glanced up to where Kyrowat and Ahummal were distracting the Ifrit, one tempting it in one direction and the other swooping in to distract it somewhere else just before it caught the first dragon.

How long could they keep that up? They only needed to remain steady until the dragons arrived. I reached for the Pipe. Holding it tight in my hand and ready to start piping when the first dragon emerged.

"You'll have to give that back eventually," Jalla said and there was a strange tone in her voice when she said it.

"It doesn't work for you." My voice was tight with stress as I followed the battle, feeling helpless as I sat in one place while others fought and dodged and ran.

"For now. It seems bound up with you. With your life."

Was she suggesting she would kill me if that's what it took to get the Pipe? I glanced over at her, surprised to see the calculating look in her eye. Why was I surprised? Jalla had been this way from the moment I met her. The thing is – her bark was always worse than her bite. When she made me her slave that mostly involved playing cards and passing the time with her. It also involved loyalty demands and chores – but I thought that maybe from her perspective she'd gone easy on me. What would it mean to go easy on me when it came to acquiring this artifact back?

Her eyes were hungry as she watched it.

"I'm not going to die anytime soon," I said, but my eyes were moving tensely from the Ifrit to the fleeing soldiers. He ignored Kyrowat trying to draw his attention and made a second sweep across the rock bridge. My whole face tensed as my eyes fought to close, but I couldn't close them – I had to watch. It was wrong to pretend that people weren't dying. Behind me, Jalla stiffened. So, she did care. No matter what she said, she cared that her people were dying.

How much longer would it be until the first dragon emerged?

The army wasn't coming through the tunnels anymore. There! At the very rear! Rakturan and Enkenay brought up the rear for Baojang, launching immediately into the air as soon as they entered the larger cavern. Enkenay rushed toward the Ifrit with a roar as the last of the Baojang soldiers' feet pounded toward the glyph.

But where were the dragons? I expected them to emerge by now.

The platform suddenly felt darker, as if a shadow had passed over it. Raolcan swayed underneath me and then slumped suddenly against the statue.

The glyph was dark. The portal was closed.

Chapter Twelve

"Get it back!" Jalla shouted. She kicked her heels into Raolcan. "Back, I said."

I spun around, my teeth clenched in anger. She kicked Raolcan! Kicked him when he was clearly hurting! With all my strength, I shoved her off his back, not concerned when her eyes went large and she toppled down to the stone. She shot me a look of death before scrambling in the dust on the stone floor and leaping back to her feet and drawing her sword.

"Baojang! To me! We'll form defensive lines!" Jalla called. She yelled a second time in her own language, clearly repeating her orders.

There was no other choice for Baojang, but I had other things on my mind. I blew my Pipe, calling to the dragons in the caverns. If they could only hurry, there were more than enough of them to deal with one Ifrit. Even the addition of Enkenay was helping Kyrowat and Ahummal in their desperate battle to keep the Ifrit occupied.

I'd thought that too soon. The Ifrit reached out and batted Ahummal. He fell backward, tumbling and crashing before landing limply on the platform. The Baojang soldiers around where he fell, scrambled to clear the area for him before he landed, half tripping over each other in their haste.

That hurt.

Raolcan! He was back with us from wherever he'd been!

No time. Concentrate on calling the wild dragons while I direct them.

I blew my Pipe in the three-note melody that had worked so well last time as Raolcan found his feet, sliding them in the dust a little as he shook himself. Was he really okay?

I'll live. I just need to get my bearings. It's a lot of work to do so many things at once.

Where were the dragons? Could they not hear my Pipe? I raised it to my lips.

Not again! Not yet. It's too strong for those of us nearby. They're held up at a narrow point. It has slowed them.

I held the Pipe tightly, trying not to pay attention as the moments ticked by and Jalla finished chivvying the Baojang soldiers into line. I tried not to worry as she pulled a limp Renn out from under Ahummal. He didn't seem to be bloody or battered, but he was pale as a ghost.

I focused on breathing evenly as Kyrowat flew low overhead, favoring his left side. Hubric rode slumped slightly over his neck. Were they struck by the Ifrit while I was distracted?

Yes.

Kyrowat landed awkwardly behind me, shaking slightly as if from shock. Only Rakturan and Enkenay still dominated the air, but the Ifrit had them on the run. They flew toward the island, barely ahead of his snatching hands. At the last second, it looked as if the creature would grab Rakturan from the saddle, but Enkenay rolled into a summersault, corkscrewing out of the flip in an unexpected direction and the Ifrit's fist came away empty.

He surged forward, and I clenched every muscle, willing my eyes to stay open as he charged towards us. All I saw was his inferno mouth as he opened it in a wide shriek. There was nowhere for me to run, nothing I could do, no way to fight. Which also meant that there was no point running and screaming in the face of this charge.

Hot air blasted over us and the high-pitched squeal of his shriek stabbed through my ears. My fists balled, but I refused to give in to the fear rolling through my belly and making my bowels feel like water inside me.

Jalla shouted and her line of defenders seemed to stand straighter as the Ifrit dove. Another shout and their weapons moved, stabbing, slashing into the Ifrit at the same moment that he plunged through their ranks, snatching them up by the handful and bowling over anyone in his path.

It was like a living tornado had spun through our soldiers. On every side bodies scattered like fallen tree limbs. Broken, torn and bleeding, they dropped to the dust below. I stared in shock at the tattered few who still remained. Jalla was among them, her face hard, her sword held high, preparing for another charge. Raolcan had his forehead pressed against the center statue.

Trying to fix it.

I blew the Pipe again. Where were the dragons? All my attention was concentrated on the opening at the far end of the stone bridge. Was that movement I saw? He'd be back at any moment. We needed help and we needed it now!

Yes, it was movement! There was a dragon head coming through from the warrens. I felt hope swell up inside me and drew in a breath of relief. I was just about to cheer when I heard Jalla make a sound like I'd never heard before. The surprise and horror of it drained every sliver of excitement from me.

I turned to look just in time to see a dozen figures rising up from the dust of the earth, spinning, like a dust devil kicking up. Black light poured from them and little slivers of fire seemed to peek out as they were built dust layer by dust layer from the ground up.

In every place where the blood of Jalla's soldiers had been spilled in the dust, an Ifrit was rising.

And suddenly I realized why one Ifrit had been left behind. He'd been there to trigger the ultimate trap.

Chapter Thirteen

Yells in Baojang filled the air and I felt helpless on Raolcan's back. He was frozen here again, his mind busy at the controls of the hub, but even if he wasn't busy, I would be useless in this conflict.

Ifrits filled the platform, as the tiny figures of humans tried to dodge and weave around them. Jalla slashed at one with her sword, flying through a series of intricate swordplay poses that would have impressed me and reduced an enemy to tiny shreds – if that enemy wasn't a demon made from dust.

I blew the Pipe, worry filling me as Kyrowat skidded in front of me, trying to protect Ahummal and Renn. The dragons were coming - I could already see them flying into the main hub area, one by one – but by the time they made it here we would be dead, and they would be trapped here with the Ifrits.

I'm trying...

Soldiers of Baojang flew through the air as the Ifrits tossed them out of their way. Screams and the scuffling of feet filling the air. Somehow Jalla was still on her feet, her eyes blazing as she slashed and danced around the Ifrits.

A fiery mouth crashed toward me. Kyrowat leapt in a single jump, darting between me and the Ifrit. The Ifrit swiped at him, sending him careening away into the dark. Hubric!

I screamed.

As if my scream had triggered it, the glyph sprang to life, flooding the platform with purple light for only a second before disappearing again. But with it went Jalla, Ahummal and Renn, a dozen injured soldiers, and half the Ifrits.

I gasped.

Almost had it there.

The last Ifrits turned on me, racing forward. I blew into the Pipe, but I knew this was the end. My final moments. At least I hadn't died a coward. At least I hadn't died alone.

The closest one was inches away, his scream shredding my hearing, his open mouth burning me with the intensity of the fire within. I braced for the violence, my eyes closing involuntarily. I took a breath.

There was a shriek and a scuffle and then I opened my eyes again.

A dragon passed inches from my face, scales flashing as he passed. I sucked in a breath at the nearness of him. It was easy to forget how massive a dragon was. Easy to forget until they almost knock you over.

Which dragon was this? Those scales were red!

As soon as he passed, I gasped as the scene in front of me unfolded. Dragons tore into Ifrits on every side, flaming and snapping and roaring. Showers of dust flew through the air as one Ifrit after another burst into dust. Hundreds of dragons of every color, size, and texture swirled through the air, dominating the battle.

I remembered Jalla's words, 'Our people should be mounted on dragons by the hundreds. It has always been our destiny.' This is what she wanted. And now I could see why. The sheer power and dominance of the dragons... wait! *This* was what the other nations wanted. They wanted our dragons. They wanted this power.

The words of the Ibrenicus Prophecies filled my mind:

Tide of the north rushing, rushing,
Longing for sea to meet sky and conquer,
Longing to take to wing,
But by blood they grasp,
And the innocent fall with the guilty.
But one shall rise,
To stand in the place of the other,
to bear the debt of nations,
to give up the breath of life to dispel the dust of death.

But the dragons weren't ours. They belonged to themselves. It didn't matter that the nations of the north wanted them. They weren't ours to give.

I knew you'd get there on your own eventually.

Purple light flared as the glyph sprang back to life, but now it wasn't illuminating Ifrits. There wasn't a single one left. The dragons on the platform glanced at us before diving toward the glyph.

I managed to lock it open this time. They can go through without me concentrating on it or staying in place.

I scanned the darkness looking for the one purple dragon I'd lost track of.

"Why are you staring into space?"

He was behind me. I spun in the saddle.

"Hubric!"

"We don't die so easily, do we, Kyro?" He was battered and dirty – and so was Kyrowat, but they were still whole. "Where's Jalla?"

"Through the portal."

"I don't trust her out of my sight."

"Hubric?" I asked. I needed someone else to know.

"Yes?"

"I know why the nations are fighting us. I know why they planned together to destroy the Dominion – to feed the rebellion of the Dusk Covenant and turn the hearts of the Magikas and attack us on every side."

"They want the dragons," Hubric said, smirking when my eyes went wide. "Tell me something we don't know. It's why the dragons give us some of their own – why we have our own side of the bargain to keep. We are part of their buffer against humanity – part of what keeps the world from a dragon - human war. The nations can't steal the dragons. But they could extinguish them from the earth. The pact between Haz and Haz'drazen was made to prevent that. The story gets twisted into something about how the Dominion Sky People were established to rule this land, but it was really a pact between two desperate groups to save each other. And that's still what it is. See these dragons flying free and strong? That's why Raolcan and Kyrowat and all the others live their lives as slaves and it's why you and I live our lives that way, too. Or haven't you noticed that is what we are? We live to serve the people and the prophecies and the dragons."

I stared at him, letting the words sink in.

We're proud to serve.

And so was I.

"Enough introspection. The battle has only just begun." Hubric grinned and Kyrowat ran to the glyph to join the stream of dragons darting one after another into the portal.

Ready?

I was still reeling with the knowledge of why we were fighting.

Reel later. We have work to do.

Chapter Fourteen

Raolcan was already leaping toward the bright glyph before I could answer and as soon as his feet hit the pattern, everything changed. We were still standing on a glyph on a pattern, but where we had left dragons darting into the portal, here they were rushing from the central hub and through a dark entrance on the other side of the bridge. I didn't know exactly what I'd expected, but I think it had been light and the outside world, not more portals. I didn't remember what had happened last time – I'd been unconscious – but I knew it wasn't like this.

We're below the base of Leedris City.

Raolcan flew after the stream of dragons, pausing for a moment beside Ahummal who was slumped beside the statue. Around the statue, bodies were piled. When Jalla and the Ifrits came through the portal, they must have surprised the Baojang soldiers here. Renn sat beside him, head in his hands.

"Renn?" I asked, "Are you hurt?"

"My head is ringing. I just need a rest."

I shouldn't leave him here, but I felt torn. I didn't trust the army of Baojang near a Dominion city.

"Where is Jalla?"

"She went on ahead. I just need a rest ..." his voice faded but my guilty feeling was interrupted by Hubric.

"We'll come back for him," he called to me as he and Kyrowat raced forward.

I sighed, not sure what to do, but Raolcan was already dashing after Kyrowat. Maybe when the Sentries followed they would pick up Renn and Ahummal.

Do you really want Jalla loose in Leedris? Who knows what she'll do next.

Who knew whether I could stop her if she tried to hack or slash her way through the city? We flew on, across the bridge and through the dark entrance. A pair of Baojang soldiers stood on either side of the opening with grim expressions, but they made no move to stop us.

"Jalla?" I asked, and they motioned into the door.

We flew through, directly on Kyrowat's heels. No Ifrits so far.

The dragons that went through before us dispatched them.

I blinked at the light as we exited the cavern. It was late afternoon here. Had we been in the warrens so long?

It was bright compared to the caves. I grabbed the light from Raolcan's saddle and extinguished it. No need to let anyone know where we were. And where was that, exactly?

We were in the base of a skycity, I realized. It was hollow and wide at the bottom, the woven human-thick threads of skysteel that supported the city surrounded us, woven into an impenetrable basket of strength – inaccessible by the outside world. Up above the structure supporting the sky city narrowed to a slender stem and through the center of the stem were a series of steel baskets on a thick cable. I watched as three dozen men and women in Baojang armor worked a huge pulley and crank system that was marching the baskets up the line – like a watermill of sorts, but for bringing people and supplies high up in the air to the sky city. Behind them, other soldiers waited for their turn.

Around the baskets, the dragons flew upward, outstripping the human warriors in their speed of ascent. The entire center of the skysteel structure was clogged with bodies moving upward like a spurting fountain to the city above. I shivered at the thought of what was to come.

Raolcan didn't even hesitate.

Hang on. Lie as flat on my neck as you can.

I crunched forward, leaning out across Raolcan's neck and clasping my arms around it. His launch was so powerful that I felt my belly tense as we shot through the air.

Don't look up.

I thought I felt something scrape across my back. I shut my eyes tight and pressed my cheek against his scales.

Just reminding everyone who leads this expedition.

Isn't that Jalla?

It's Raolcan, Prince of Dragons.

He was as arrogant as a Baojang war leader.

Oh, I'm far worse than that. Prepare yourself!

For what?

For battle. I know you don't like it.

Warm air burst across my face suddenly and I opened my eyes to chaos. We launched through a small room packed with soldiers helping others out of baskets and onto a platform to the side. This must be a sub-floor room of the city.

Someone – a dragon most certainly – had torn the entrance from the room into one above that was a lot larger. Teeth and claw marks bit into the crumpled scrap left at the edges.

I barely had time to take in the details of the tight room before we were pushing past other dragons and humans through what had been the floor. The humans were still using the stairs, but the dragons had burrowed upward like groundhogs in a farmer's field, tearing holes through one floor up to the next and through that floor again. We burst up through it with at least a dozen other dragons and into a courtyard. We were finally at city level.

Pandemonium reigned.

Dragons swirled above us – some the free dragons who had come with us, others the Blacks stationed here to guard the city. Fire lanced from one group to the other, but in the chaos, the exact battle was hard to follow. Around us, Baojang soldiers marched in steady streams to the surrounding walls and towers. Burn marks and limp bodies told me we were late to arrive.

Habrida, the Serpent Prince, had arrived much too far ahead of us.

Raolcan gained height over the courtyard, giving me a chance to survey what was taking place below.

I'd say he has conquered half the city, but the battle is far from won. Even the skies are in contest. Look.

On one side of the city lines of Magikas were assembled on every wall and tower, taking aim at the wild dragons around us. Why did it seem like every Magika had chosen our enemies over us?

That's an answer for another day.

That's where we needed to be – directing and coaching them to do the least harm while still gaining victory.

This force seems much stronger than I'd expect, even defending a city the size of Leedris. There are armies spread out across the plain. And look! There are Ifrits in the sky city and all around the city!

I saw what he meant – clusters of the dust demons fought in the cramped city streets and out over the plains around the city there were lines of dust clouds that I had come to recognize as Ifrits on the move.

I bit my lip nervously. I didn't want to think about the battle below, about the innocents hiding in their homes, about collapsing cities and digging people out of the rubble.

If we don't do it, things will be just as bad – worse. The Dominion ruled by Ifrits and the Dusk Covenant won't care about those children. The neighboring nations won't care when they enslave or kill every dragon they can find. You must choose this path because the other one is so much worse.

But I didn't want to choose any path if both were full of violence.

Amel, you can't control everything. You can't save everyone. If you try to opt out, all you do is strengthen the enemy. You must choose to do all the good that you *can and limit as much evil as you are able to do. Be courageous.*

I took a deep breath. Okay. Assess the situation. Figure out a plan that didn't end with a burning or toppled city...

But where was Jalla? She had been only a little ahead of us and she didn't have a dragon to ride with Ahummal injured.

No time to think of her.

But he was wrong. Because wherever Jalla was, that would be the main event. And if I wasn't there to rein her in, there was no telling what she would do.

We need to focus on the wild dragons. With the Pipe, you are their leader.

But I wasn't, really. Raolcan was. I tried to listen to him, scanning the sky for dragons to pick out where our dragons were and figure out what to tell them to do, but my eye was caught by a lone purple – riderless – but saddled. He flew toward us with a gait so familiar that I felt my forehead wrinkle as I watched.

Realization dawned on me and my eyes went large. Raolcan...?

Ahlskibi!

Chapter Fifteen

He flew toward us and I sensed a shift in Raolcan's flying, as he moved upward and into an observing arc, waiting for the other dragon. As we soared there, Hubric and Kyrowat joined us.

Ahlskibi is riderless.

Did he mean...?

Leng is not dead. Not yet. But he needs help within the Castel.

The dragons out here needed direction but now I wanted nothing more than to dive into the Castel and find Leng hiding behind a tapestry or doing whatever other thing was going to get him caught.

Blow your Pipe to get their attention and I will pass authority to Kyrowat to lead them while we storm the Castel. I didn't expect... but no, just blow the Pipe and I'll tell you on the way.

I signaled to Hubric, asking if he understood the plan and he signaled agreement and gave me a firm nod. That was as close to a blessing as he gave. I nodded back and blew my three-note tune on the Pipe. The swirling dragons below took on a more certain look before Kyrowat dove into their ranks to lead from the front.

My hands shook as I tucked the Pipe back into my belt. Where was Leng and what was happening in the Castel? Ahlskibi reached us, his expression agitated. He plunged past and then dove toward the Castel just off to the east side of the center of the city.

From above, it was easy to see that the Castel remained in the hands of the Dominion – or rather the Dusk Covenant who had seized our empire when Iskaris took power, but Baojang pressed against the edges of their defense. Likely, it would be the last part of the city to be conquered.

As we raced toward it I saw a swirl of Baojang soldiers rush around one side, attacking a slowly retreating group of soldiers in Dominion uniform. It bothered me to see them dressed as loyal soldiers, knowing their strings were pulled by the Dusk Covenant. The Serpent Prince was at their head, fighting with the same chilling precision with which he'd made his threat to me. I didn't think I should want people to die, but would it be so bad if he just got sick of the Dominion after this and went home?

Almost there. I can't land on the battlements.

That was an understatement. The battlements bristled with archers and Magikas. A pair of Ifrits were on the uppermost portion. Why were there battlements on a Castel in a sky city?

The Dominion has always feared dragon attack.

They were right to fear. But if we couldn't land there, where would we land? I ducked as a fireball was lobbed toward us.

See that balcony?

I did. It was very close to the fireball-lobber.

I'm going to fly at it full speed and hope we can squeeze through the wide window.

It was big. But was it big enough? And what if we got stuck halfway through?

There are no defenders there besides a single pair of guards. It's our best bet.

Why the urgency?

Ahlskibi says the Dominar is here.

Shonan? Was he in trouble?

The other Dominar.

Iskaris! A flare of heat rushed through me. Stopping Iskaris was worth the risk of diving through that balcony.

I'm glad you think so.

The window was getting closer. I hunched low over Raolcan's back as fireballs and arrows from the battlements above us crashed and smoked around us. I could hear the yells and screams below, smell the sulfur in the air, and see the window growing closer.

Twice dead, she rises.

Her rising a sign of salvation.

Favor from the heavens.

Relief from the fires of hell.

Raolcan quoted the ancient prophecy as we dodged and spun, always getting closer to the gaping window.

Let's show them a little favor from the heavens, shall we?

And then we were darting through the window head first and I was clutching his neck, pressing my cheek to it to make myself small so we could fit. We were here to stop Iskaris and if I had to die to do that, I would. I had seen the evil in his heart.

I gritted my teeth as it occurred to me that he might have captured Leng. Being at the mercy of Iskaris was one of the worst things I could imagine.

Chapter Sixteen

Raolcan's speed slowed and he wriggled through the tightest part of the window before tumbling forward. I waited until we'd stopped moving before I looked up, still gasping to fill my lungs after that tight compression.

We were in the audience hall. And we were not alone.

I'd never seen so many Magikas in my life. My breath caught in my throat as I saw them, row upon row, their rune-bedecked robes fluttering in the wind of our passage. I could almost feel every hair of my body rise at the sight of them.

The ceiling of the room soared upward – three Raolcan's high – and was bedecked with hanging chandeliers, the lanterns and candles hanging from them lit despite the daylight.

The walls of the chambers were hung with tapestry after tapestry that looked so foreign that I gasped. The symbol of the Dusk Covenant – a diagonal slash through a spiral – was everywhere and the scenes in the tapestries were of Ifrits, fire, and death. But a tapestry wasn't made in a day – much less a dozen of them. How long had artisans labored over such a grizzly craft? And who had employed them? Wasn't Leedris Savette's family? How could this have been done in their Castel without their knowledge?

And what would make you assume that they are good?

They were loyal to the Dominar – to Shonan.

Or so it was thought. Sometimes, friends deceive.

At the end of the room, on a raised dais, the Dominar sat on a steel chair, his mask gleaming in the light of a hundred lanterns. He stood abruptly, but it wasn't him who had my attention. I knew what treacherous scum he was.

I knew we needed to rip that mask off his face and return it to our rightful ruler.

It was the figure beside him, hands and feet lashed to an "X" of wooden beams who caught my attention. Someone had thrown a hood over that person's head. Strung across the wooden cross with a swath of cloth thrown over him like a curtain, his identity was impossible to discern.

Leng? I hoped not with all my heart but somehow my lungs just weren't working right anymore and my faulty heart was stuttering in my chest. My hands gripped and twisted at the saddle under me while Raolcan shifted back and forth. Could he read the prisoner's thoughts?

I'm not finding anything. He must be unconscious.

Behind us, Ahlskibi pushed through the narrow window, struggling to pull his bulk through. He was bigger than Raolcan and I heard him snarl as a stone knocked loose from the masonry and crashed to the ground.

"An audience," the Dominar said, stilling the whispers of the crowd. "I like audiences. And this one, while few, makes up for it in sheer size."

There was a tittering from some of the nobles at the front of the crowd. They must be starved for humor.

Or just plain starved. Iskaris is not a kind master.

Iskaris sounded as though he were smiling behind that mask, but I wasn't fooled. Iskaris didn't smile.

"You didn't like having an audience on that platform in the warrens," I said.

My voice sounded too high pitched. I could feel the tremble in my throat as I spoke. I had watched a city burn because I didn't have the foresight to prevent it. I'd watched an evil man become a ruler for the same reason. I wasn't willing to let him do whatever evil thing he was planning now. He needed to remember that he was nothing but a traitor. I needed to remind him.

"We've found a traitor among us," he said, as if he could hear the chant of 'traitor, traitor, traitor,' in my thoughts.

"We certainly have," I agreed. It was only when I heard the gasp that I realized what the Magikas were seeing – I, a fledgling Dragon Rider, was speaking like an equal to the Dominar. But he wasn't my Dominar and I didn't buy this idea that the mask was the man. The man only wore the mask, and this one wore it poorly. A mask like that could never be taken in treachery, it could only be received in self-sacrifice.

Ahlskibi moved to tuck in beside Roalcan where they could defend each other if attacked. The crowd shifted at his movement.

"And now we are deciding what to do with this traitor. And here I find a Dragon Rider, at the perfect time, has joined us. Your color is purple – the color of truth. Tell me, Dragon Rider and tell me true – what should be done to a traitor of the land, hmm?"

Was he asking what I should do to him? Or to whatever poor soul was under that sheet? I knew I should say something moderate – what if that was Leng? But it was hard not to answer him directly.

"Any traitor should see with his own eyes the destruction he has caused," I said. "He should have to make a recompense for his crimes to every person he has hurt. He should hear from them what he has done."

"An excellent verdict."

There was a murmur of approval around me, but I felt like someone had lined my seat with pins and needles. There was a catch here. I could feel it coming. This was no ordinary person under the cloth and Iskaris was only baiting me, knowing that we both knew that he was the ultimate traitor here.

He motioned to the guards and my whole heart was screaming within me, Please don't be Leng! Please don't be Leng!

They ripped the cloth off the figure and flung it to the ground.

It wasn't Leng fixed to that wooden X. It was Jalla.

Her head hung limply to the side until one of the guards slapped her awake.

Had someone nailed her hair to the beams? Her eyes flashed defiantly in the light, but the tiny trickle of sweat at her temple – or was it blood? – gave away how desperate her situation was. I tensed as I watched her, trying not to quake at the thought of how Iskaris would use my words against her.

How did she get here so quickly? That's dragon-hard.

But I'd known that where there was trouble, there would be Jalla. And I knew something else – we needed her alive. No matter how troublesome and entitled and all-out frustrating Jalla was – the Serpent Prince would be worse. My lips tightened as I tried to assess the situation. What could I do to free her?

"This woman has betrayed our land into the hands of the armies of Baojang," Iskaris said.

"Only a friend can betray," I said, my voice squeaking at the end of my sentence. I needed better control of myself when I was nervous.

"And Baojang was a friend and an ally. And now she is not. Now, she is tethered to these sticks, like a feast-day goat. And we shall do to her exactly as you suggested, Amel Leafbrought, Dragon Rider of the Purple. We will lower her down from this window on these very sticks so she can watch the results of her treachery and learn with her own eyes what she has done."

"You'll doom us all," I breathed. This was what he was doing? While his city was attacked? While his soldiers bled and died? He was playing games with Jalla instead of fighting for his life?

He paused, appearing to consider the question before the eyes behind the mask twinkled and his voice went velvet smooth.

"Or..."

"Or what?"

Every set of lungs in the room froze as we waited for his reply. Every person rose up on toes, head lifted high, eyes fixed on their master.

"I'm reminded of the words of the Ibrenicus Prophecies," the Dominar said, tapping a finger to his masked chin as if he could twist the prophecies against me. "'Healing comes from the one who pays a steep price.' Would you like to heal this land, Dragon Rider? And again it says, 'To stand in the place of the other, to bear the debt of nations, to give up the breath of life to dispel the dust of death.' There is death in the air tonight. There is one who will pay a price. Will it be this one? Or will it be you in her place?"

Chapter Seventeen

I stared at the wooden X. Iskaris was mad. Raving, insanely mad. But as I watched the Magikas and Castelans in the room watching him, their breath held and their eyes bright, waiting to see what he would do next, I realized that he wasn't the only one who was crazy.

It's infected them. There's this thing that happens to people when all their hopes are crumbling – it turns them like bad meat. They don't dare look at their crumbling hopes in case that makes it more real. They can't force themselves to fix the problem, because underneath it all they know that they have already lost and no amount of climbing will get them out of the hole they have dug for themselves. So, they lean into it. They let themselves be distracted and they throw themselves into insane causes that are so far from their initial goal that it's almost impossible to draw a line from one thing to the other.

And now they were waiting to torture and kill either Jalla or me on that wooden X.

Well, it won't be you.

But it couldn't be Jalla. If it was Jalla, then there was an army in Baojang led by the Serpent Prince, and while Jalla was irritating and arrogant, I had begun to realize that underneath it all she had a set of ethics that governed her. The Serpent Prince had shown me that he was pure danger.

Raolcan shifted under me.

I can fly out of here as easily as I flew in. We can just leave.

But what about Jalla?

We can save her. We'll get some allies to help.

I locked gazes with Jalla and her firm gaze told me that she agreed with Raolcan. And yet ...

No, 'and yet!'

Was that fear I felt in his mind?

It's all-out panic. Don't go crazy on me now, Amel!

Raolcan shifted, backing toward the window we'd flown in by. The Dominar made a small sign with his two first fingers and thumb of his only hand. Raolcan bucked under me.

I wasn't fast enough! They have me pinned in place. Ahlskibi, too. There was a wild note to his thoughts. *I shouldn't have let you think about it! I should have just flown away.*

No. I could see clearly now what was required of me. Iskaris, insane as he was, was right about the prophecy.

To stand in the place of the other, to bear the debt of nations, to give up the breath of life to dispel the dust of death.

But he was wrong about the outcome, wasn't he? The part before was about how badly the north wanted the dragons and how this was the one way to stop that from happening. Besides, what was the dust of death if not the Ifrit scourge? And someone needed to win today – to push back the Ifrits. Below us, our army was doing just that. The dragons were shredding them to pieces beneath us. But it wouldn't be enough if Baojang lost her leader. It wouldn't be enough if Jalla died here.

I could almost see Iskaris' arrogant expression behind that mask as I took my crutches out and slid down Raolcan's back.

Please don't do this.

The crowd around us breathed out softly, their expressions anticipatory and greedy. Blood was what they wanted, and blood they would receive.

This is madness. No one else knows we are here. Ahlskibi is stuck here, too.

Which meant that no one else could save Jalla. And no one else would know what I was doing as I deftly unfastened the pipe from my belt and offered it to Raolcan. If he took it in his mouth, they couldn't take it from him. It was utterly essential that no one else had the power to control dragons against their will. It struck me, suddenly, that it always should have been his. After all, he was the Prince of Dragons. He had suffered those trials with me. It belonged to him as much as it did to me.

Thank you for that acknowledgment.

Of course.

He took the Pipe delicately in his huge mouth.

Now get back in your saddle, you foot-eating fool!

But I couldn't do that. If the choice was Jalla or me, I knew who was essential to save the Dominion – to save the whole world from these Ifrits. And it wasn't a crippled Dragon Rider from a mud hut on the plains.

Please don't do this. If you care about saving the world, it's you who should be here to save it.

And I appreciated that, but it was Jalla who was needed.

We'll find another way. We always do.

Yes, we always found a way. And this was the way. I remembered what Ephretti said as we watched that smoldering city together. She'd said, 'Remember what one mistake can do.' I couldn't afford any more mistakes.

I hobbled forward to stand before the dais. I didn't look back. Now was not the time for tears and if I looked back at his big eyes so full of loyalty to me, I would crumble.

"I'll take her place," I said simply. Who knew? Maybe our army below would conquer this city before he was finished with me. There was still hope that someone – Rakturan perhaps – would arrive in time to save Jalla and keep this war from spiraling out of control.

You can't see smiles behind a mask, but I was sure Iskaris was smiling as much as the people on every side of him. Raolcan was right, they were all infected with his insanity.

And now you are, too.

Chapter Eighteen

The most surprising part of the whole situation was Jalla. She didn't say a word – which was strange for her. Was this the princess who never paused even for breath as she spewed out a steady stream of commands? Was this the woman who I'd seen fighting bravely between Ifrits and watching coldly as cities fell? She didn't seem like the same woman as she silently let them unbind her and shove her to the side. I thought she might be trying to tell me something with her eyes, but if she was, I didn't hear it.

She is surprised, and very little surprises Jalla. And she is afraid.

Didn't she expect her slaves to die for her?

Not by choice. That is why she is afraid.

"Make sure she doesn't leave the room," the Dominar ordered. Wise. After all, by the rising noise outside, the battle must have moved into the lower floors of the Castel. All I had to do was stay calm and try not to die before the army reached this level and freed Jalla and Raolcan.

One day, you will learn I am wiser than you and you will finally listen to me. This is madness!

That was good. He was still talking like I had a future. He needed that hope. I swallowed back the hitch in my throat as the Dominar's guards grabbed me roughly, shaking my second crutch away in their haste. They didn't bother to unstrap the other one and it bounced along the stone floor as they hauled me to the wooden beams and shoved me roughly against them.

I could feel the blood draining from my face as my body processed what was happening quicker than my mind could. Already my belly was churning, and a sour taste was in the back of my throat. Please don't throw up, Amel. It would be so undignified. A bubbling sound in my belly made me fear even worse consequences as they cinched leather straps tightly around my wrists and ankles and through a slit in the beams, tightening and tying them on the other side. I was firmly fixed in place.

Sweat stung my eyes and I blinked it away.

I unfocused my eyes so that no one would notice me watching Jalla, edge step by step, behind the watchers and slowly climb onto Roalcan. He wouldn't mind that. He'd always had a soft spot for her.

Not today. Not when you choose to take her place.

He sounded raw in my mind. Like he couldn't bear this, but he would bear up under it just fine. He was always a survivor.

Not without you. You know that.

If Savette could survive without her dragon, then Raolcan could survive without his rider. He would need to find Shonan and ask him to help – or perhaps his mother could help. Or even the Troglodytes. He carried their talisman now. They would have to listen.

You are gambling both our lives on this!

But if I hadn't then we could have lost Jalla. And Raolcan should know as well as I did that we couldn't win a battle in this room full of magic, and Iskaris would not have let us leave without one.

The guards – ten of them – gathered around the crossbeams and with one great heave, lifted the beams with me strapped to them up into the air. I gritted my teeth, holding tight to my mind to keep it from skittering away in fear.

I knew the trick of this. Concentrate on little details. Concentrate on the ceiling. Someone had taken a lot of care with the wooden beams, painting them white and carefully carving them in designs and swirls.

A little dust fell from the ceiling.

"Fasten the rope tightly," Iskaris called from behind me. I felt someone working to tie ropes through loops at the top of the beams. What had this thing been for before they made it into this instrument of terror?

I think it held lanterns from the ceiling above the audience chamber. It should not be holding you!

A strip of the ceiling seemed to rip free, torn upward. Was I imagining things? The window was close ... so close now that I could smell the battle beyond the window.

"Heave her over!" Iskaris called. "Let all the city see their traitor!"

The ceiling above me peeled away suddenly, as if someone had ripped it up with a massive hand full of claws. Wood beams shredded into splinters raining down on me. Was I the only one seeing this? Was the I the only one watching as light poured in through the rent ceiling and a massive white hand ripped beams and white plaster to widen the gash? The guards carrying me were steps from the window.

No wonder I was seeing things.

No wonder I was going crazy.

The murmurs of the crowd still carried the same tone. I watched the ceiling like a person in a dream, not sure what I was seeing as the dust of the floor above us fell down, stinging my eyes and scattering over the crowd and then, through the glittering beams of dust, a huge white head plunged through the ceiling and burped a stinking cloud of sulfur onto the crowd below.

Someone screamed.

This was real after all.

Chapter Nineteen

The guards dropped my beam and I crashed to the floor, my head feeling like it had been cracked in two as I landed. The crossbeams hit the floor so firmly that I felt the reverberations running through my whole body. I gritted my teeth against the pain, but there was no way to defend myself spread-eagled as I was across the beams.

A hundred other throats screamed all around me as Enkenay shoved himself through the ruined floor and landed heavily over me. All I could see was the ghost-like white of his semi-transparent scales as his belly settled over me, one leg between each beam. But I could hear the sound of running feet and screaming enemies, and then the rippling sound of fire through the air.

Smoke and ash washed back over me and blinded my eyes, but my heart still thudded on like a drummer who hadn't noticed that the song was over.

Rakturan – who must have been on Enkenay's back – bellowed something in Baojang and Jalla replied and then the sounds of battle extinguished everything else. I could smell sulfur and burning clothing. I could hear shouting and cursing and steel on steel. I tried not to think of what else I was smelling.

Amel? Are you okay?

I was okay. Sore, shaken, my heart felt like it didn't fit in my chest anymore. But I was okay. I shook slightly on the beams, twisting my head to try to see, but all I could see between Enkenay's thick legs were the hummocks of fallen Magikas across the stone floor. Was Raolcan hurt?

No, but Enkenay hasn't found the Magika who holds me fast. I'm stuck here until he does. Thank goodness for Jalla!

Jalla?

She is fighting for Ahlskibi and me.

Jalla?!

There was a crash from the other end of the room.

The army has arrived.

Whose army?

Who even knows anymore.

And Enkenay moved and I shut my eyes tight and gritted my teeth as his scales brushed my nose. I opened my eyes too soon as the tip of his tail smacked my face. Ouch.

I blinked in the glittering dust ray that shone over me now that he was gone. Dust shone like tiny rainbow gems drifting down to me.

In the torn remnants of the ceiling, a dark figure crouched, lit from behind. He was holding a rope. He descended, arms and legs flung out like a dragon's wings. I could hear the sound of the rope playing out across the edge of the gash. Behind him, the ceiling of the room above – a golden network of crossbeams – looked like the sort of place I imagined angels would live in. Perhaps the man was an angel.

He was slowing as he grew nearer – that ceiling really was high! – and I tried, helplessly, to repress my feeling of vulnerability. I couldn't move an inch, not to protect myself, or even cover my eyes as he fell from directly above me, his own face still wreathed in shadow.

His descent slowed abruptly and I just barely recognized his face before we were nose to nose, his breath gentle on my cheeks.

He kissed me – tender and treasuring, as if he were afraid I would crumble. I was far from crumbling. My heart soared, my breath quickened, my arms ached to hold him.

Leng scrambled to the side, moving into an easy crouch of readiness, quickly sliding the rope he'd glided down on from a network of larger ropes tangled around his waist and thighs. He drew a small knife, darting back as an enemy guard leapt from out of nowhere and lashed out at him.

Leng danced back and forth like a snake between the rocks, keeping the guard at bay and away from me before something hit the guard from behind and he slumped to the ground.

Leng didn't hesitate. He spun back to me, smiling like he was trying to make me brave with his smile and then darting to slice the leather cords that held my right wrist. I wiped dust from my eyes as he scrambled over me to cut the cord from my left wrist and help me sit up. I ached from head to foot but I couldn't take my eyes off of him as he worked to free my feet without harming me and help me gain control of my crutch.

He was alive! He was safe! Or at least, as safe as any of us ...

"It's my turn to save you again, heart of hope."

"What are you doing here?" I gasped. It was hard to tear my eyes from his familiar face but behind us, the sound of steel on steel continued and so did the shouting. I glanced to Raolcan still frozen where he stood. How would I help him?

"Helping Savette spy out the source of the Ifrits," he replied.

"Dust," we said both at once, but we were both looking at our dragons, worried about them.

He nodded. "And blood – or deep flows of magic. They seem to use both. But now that your army has scattered the Magikas, I won't be able to hatch my plan."

The battle had moved across the hall, the Boajang army fighting with the guards, but where had the Dominar gone? Where were the Magikas? Or Rakturan?

"Your plan?" I wanted to give him my full attention, but I was distracted as I slowly pulled myself to my feet. Leng hurried to help me up.

"I was going to burn down this tower with all of them assembled here."

"But you were above them! You would have burned, too!"

His gaze held a guilty look.

"No wonder Ahlskibi was worried!"

I looked toward Raolcan and Ahlskibi at the same time that Raolcan shook himself.

Finally! And now, if you're about done making puppy-eyes at each other, spider, I'd like to show some of those Magikas what helplessness feels like.

"I wasn't trying to die. I planned to get out through the escape hatch. There's one here in the audience chamber, just like there was in Vanika."

And that's where the Dominar and his Magikas went and where Rakturan followed.

The hatch opened suddenly and Jalla poked her head up through the trapdoor, noticing me first.

"Good. You're still alive. Rakturan needs reinforcements. Take your dragon and follow him, slave."

"I'm not your slave anymore, Jalla," I said firmly, feeling more strongly about that word than ever as I saw shock flash across Leng's face. "I gave my life for you – I didn't die, but the offer means something – and here in the Dominion that would make *you* my slave – so we're even now."

That wasn't true – that I knew of – but I was betting that Jalla didn't know that either and it sounded like just the kind of nonsense they would use in her land. I held my breath, waiting to see if she would believe me.

Jalla stared at me for a shocked second before jumping out of the hatch and slamming it behind her. She strode forward so forcefully that Leng moved to intercept her, but I put a hand on his arm. I could deal with Jalla.

I expected a blow or a raging outburst. I didn't expect a violent hug. Before I'd even shaken off the shock she drew a knife, slashed her palm and wiped it across my cheek. Yuck!

"We're blood sisters now," Jalla said urgently. "Marked by blood and honor. This is good, yes, even better than before," she nodded as if to herself before looking me in the eyes. "Send help as soon as you can."

She turned and ran back to the hatch so quickly that I was still wiping blood off my face and looking at it on my fingers and she was already gone.

I had a terrible feeling that being Jalla's blood sister might be even more dangerous than being her slave.

You're getting wiser.

Dragon School: Troubled War

Chapter One

"They fled like rats from a flaming city," Jalla said, looking out across the plains below Leedris where Ifrits, dragons, and soldiers left a long trail of dust. Broken brush and abandoned items were scattered across the sides of the road, evidence of their flight.

I shivered at her analogy. The thought of a flaming city still filled me with shame. Especially now that we stood in yet another ravaged city. I looked behind my shoulder at the smoke trails rising up through Leedris City. It hadn't burned like Vanika, but there had been a half a dozen small fires in the conquest. And other horrors that my mind shied away from.

Our army had worked through most of the night to clean out the last pockets of resistance from the city and now Habrida's war leaders had guards stationed on the walls and the turrets of the Castel. They were looking for any Castelans they could find among the people. I doubted they would find many. Any who had been here were either fleeing with the Dominar across the plains below or already dead. It was a grim day for the Dominion – and a grim day for Leedris. My heart felt heavy at the thought of having to tell Savette about her family's involvement. She had believed them to be loyal to the Dominion. Perhaps it was that connection with the underground plots and not their loyalty that had pressed them to offer her as a bride to Baojang. Perhaps, this had been going on for far longer than we suspected.

"And now we need to discuss the governance of the city," Hubric said to Jalla. It wasn't like him to talk about something like that – not like him to thrust himself into the spotlight, but by the gleam in his eye, I could tell he was as worried as I was about the citizenry here. These were our people. We needed to protect them as much as we needed to pursue Iskaris.

It had been hours before Rakturan and Jalla returned from chasing the Dominar the night before. Grimy and weary, they had been forced to admit that it would take more than a pair of war leaders to hunt down and destroy an army. Iskaris' escape had been too well executed to catch him before he reached his greater forces.

I would have been irritated at them, but I was too grateful to be angry. Without Rakturan, I would have died on a wooden 'X' hung over the city.

"I'll leave a War Leader here, Dragon Rider. He will maintain order." Jalla looked tired. I didn't think she'd slept the night before, making this the third night in a row for her without sleep.

"Not Habrida?"

"That wouldn't be a question if you had obeyed orders in the warrens. But no, not Habrida."

I'd finally fallen asleep halfway through the night when my own exhaustion would wait no longer. Raolcan, Ahlskibi, Leng and I had formed a ring in the attic above the audience room – away from the massive hole torn in the floor – and fallen asleep under the high beams of the ceiling there. Doubtless, there were other more comfortable rooms, but the attic was high up in the Castel, hard to access, and it was easy to hear any intruders enter. I'd fallen immediately into a deep sleep and hadn't woken until Jalla stormed into the room and demanded we talk about the present situation.

We were standing now in the rubble-strewn attic, looking out from the wide windows over the city and the surrounding plains. The attic was large enough for dragons to stand easily and as we spoke, Raolcan yawned dramatically, stretching like a cat.

"You could use the current systems and structures to run the city until you return," Hubric suggested in a way that was incredibly diffident for him. "Not to rule, obviously, but to keep everything working – food coming in and waste going out, business and commerce, the care of the people and prevention of disease."

Jalla's gaze was eagle-like as she turned from the window to consider him through narrowed eyes. "You could arrange for that?"

"I have contacts here with the Lightbringers-"

"The religious sect," Jalla said.

"If you want to call it that. They are seeded throughout the city infrastructure and could help to maintain order and commerce under whoever you leave to govern."

Jalla considered for a long moment. "I will leave Avdam, the Sand Prince, to guard our hold here. Go and arrange to have the city work under his rule. Work quickly. We march again tomorrow."

Hubric nodded briskly, hopefulness in his eyes. I breathed a sigh of relief. He would arrange to protect the people here. We would do what we could to make there suffering more endurable. At least that was done.

"And now we make plans," Jalla said as Leng joined us. He adjusted his scarves as if he wasn't really paying attention, but I knew he was.

"An army on the run is vulnerable," he said, looking through the window.

"Exactly," Jalla said with a smile. "I have half a mind to chase them now, but that would be irresponsible. I have armies to lead, and Amel failed to kill the Serpent Prince, so I have that headache to deal with."

My eyes widened, and I saw Leng's start to widen before he fought them under control. She thought of killing a man as a mere headache! Jalla's ruthlessness would never stop surprising me.

"You need scouts to keep an eye on where they are going," Leng said. He must have some sort of plan. "Amel and I could scout for you."

Ah, that was the plan. I couldn't fault him for it. I wanted to be away from all of this, too, but life was rarely so simple.

Jalla tapped her chin with a finger. "Yes. But more than that. We need to lay a trap ahead of them and hold them in place so my army can catch up and destroy them."

I cleared my throat. "Shouldn't we wait and attack them from the rear when they hit Savette's army to the south? Then they will have enemies on every side."

Jalla shook her head. "We don't know how well or poorly your friend is faring. Perhaps her army is already destroyed. Better to take this army on the run before he can find his own allies or a place to make a stand. You and this bald one can go and scout for me. Take the Pipe and the dragons. When you find a likely place for a trap, set it up and send back a message to let me know where you are. If you can hold the Dominar's army in a likely place until we arrive, we can pinch him between us and destroy him where he is most vulnerable."

I swallowed. Warfare was not for me. If it was, I would have been a Red.

"I'll send Hubric to help you when he is done arranging things here. Watch for him."

"And Rakturan?" I asked.

Her face was tight when she said, "The Dark Prince stays with me. I have need of him."

She turned and strode away, purpose in every movement and I watched her go with concern. Jalla was planning something and Rakturan was the key to whatever it was. That worried me. Was my theory correct that Rakturan could watch me through visions?

Ironic, isn't it? He watches you and you watch everyone else.

Chapter Two

Leng and I hadn't talked last night – we'd been too busy fighting and managing problems and then we'd collapsed into sleep. And now that we were alone in the attic, I felt oddly shy. I glanced up to see him lean against the window frame, a smile flickering on his face before he bit his lip.

We're here, too, but sure, ignore the dragons. Everyone does.

"You're alive," he said. His voice was magnetic. It drew me in and made me want to hear more.

"I should probably mention that I've been seeing you in visions," I said awkwardly.

He chuckled. "As long as you aren't dreaming about anyone else."

I felt my face heat, but I didn't need to tell him I'd been seeing other people in visions, too. That wasn't what he meant. His true meaning made a lump form in my throat. He wanted me to be his alone. Someone – other than Raolcan – wanted me to be his.

"I've been worried about you," I said. "You've been doing dangerous things."

He laughed. "More dangerous than leading an army of dragons? I knew you were different when you came to Dragon School."

He was smirking and the way he looked at me ... I had to look away. That much emotion made me feel overpowered.

"How was I different?" Better to distract him with conversation.

"Purples always choose their dragons. And bonds are formed that are close. But they take years. Ahlskibi barely tolerated me that first year even though he chose me. We weren't friends until I was through training. He certainly didn't like me touching him! But Raolcan let you in like a true friend right from the beginning." He licked his lips. "The thing about Purples is that they can read people so well – even when they aren't listening to their thoughts – that they know who a person is right away. They can warm up to someone over time, of course, and they have strong instincts about who they might come to like, but to attach to a human that quickly? You had to be pretty special. Pure of heart. Full of truth. Rare."

I looked up to meet his eyes and I could barely breathe. I felt like I was tingling all over with his gaze on me. He approved of me – maybe even admired me. I didn't think another human had ever felt that way. Especially not someone so incredibly amazing as Leng. He stunned me with his easy ability to do anything necessary. I was bowled over with his confidence and quiet authority – and he liked *me*!

Okay, that's nice. Now settle down before you give us all an emotional hangover.

Leng stepped forward and took my hand. I was suddenly glad that it was free to take. It was nice to only need one crutch again.

"I hope you still feel the same way about me," he said. "But I understand if you don't."

I looked away, suddenly nervous. How could I tell him that he made me feel better, bigger, fuller when I was with him?

Just tell him that and put us all out of our misery!

I was startled when Ahlskibi snorted, filling the attic with a puff of smoke.

"Leng, you know I'm ... I'm in love with you."

I glanced up, nervously, and was surprised when he took my face gently in one hand and kissed me.

"Good." He smiled. "It would be awkward if I was the only one."

I laughed, so nervous now that my body felt like it was awash with acid, making every part of me feel delighted and ill at the same time, like one person couldn't hold so much emotion.

He kissed me again.

"We might not have many of these moments left," he said, eyes sad.

I nodded. After all, we were about to try to set a trap for an army.

"As long as I'm alive, I want to have these moments. But Leng?"

"Yes?" his voice was husky.

"What if things change after?"

"How would they change?"

I shrugged. How did I put into words my fears? Raolcan was a prince. I was blood sisters to a crazy Baojang War Leader. I knew the True Dominar and the Chosen One by their first names. He was the brother of the Dominar. How could things not change?

He pulled me into a hug and I closed my eyes, reveling in the feel of being perfectly and totally safe.

"No matter how they change, Amel, it won't change how I care for you. You have my word on that."

I sniffed, trying to keep from crying and trying to remember this moment all at once.

There was a cough on the other side of the room and my eyelids flared bright red for a moment.

"Alright you old goon, we're just about done," Leng growled.

I laughed and a moment later Leng's chest shook from his own laughter. When he relaxed the hug, I stepped back.

"I guess we should get ready to go before these two burn down the Castel after all." I gave Raolcan a pointed look, but he was still snickering.

Chasing an army! Now that's a lot more fun than kissing is!

I didn't agree.

Chapter Three

I *think you should hold the Pipe,* Raolcan said as I finished packing his saddle. Leng and I had found provisions and water to restock our dragons and warm cloaks and clothing to wrap around ourselves now that Autumn was here. I was grateful for the thick fur cloak and wool scarf.

Holding the Pipe wasn't a good idea. I'd seen what that Pipe could do and now that we knew our enemies wanted the dragons, it was too dangerous for me to hold it. I couldn't protect it.

I don't trust anyone but you and I can hardly carry it in my mouth indefinitely.

Why not? Did it taste bad?

Ha ha. How about you carry a twig around in your mouth and after a few hours when you feel like screaming we'll talk again.

Admittedly, that couldn't be comfortable. How had he held it in there while he was flaming and fighting?

I'm a dragon of many talents. But seriously, I tucked it under my tongue.

Raolcan spat the Pipe onto the ground where it bounced slightly with a *ting.* I was about to scold him that he might damage it – but wasn't that what we wanted?

We'll keep it safe until we can dispose of it somehow. It would probably be best to give it back to the Elders.

That made a lot of sense.

"What's that thing?" Leng asked as I gingerly picked up the slobbery pipe, trying to wipe it with an old curtain from the corner of the attic.

"It's the Pipe of Wings. It can control dragons," I said casually.

Ahlskibi growled behind me.

"I'm not using it, Ahlskibi!" I protested, but he gave me a wicked look. Raolcan better explain this quickly or I'd be nothing more than a smoking pair of boots.

"What happened to your eye, old fella?" Leng asked Raolcan, changing the subject.

"He lost it in a battle against the Dusk Covenant," I said quietly.

"It makes me think of one of the Ibrenicus Prophecies. Have you read this one?" he asked.

"*When the people of the earth sound horn of battle,*
And the land trembles and is torn,
When the skies are rent in sorrow,
And the depths bring help no more,
Then the lame and the blind shall lead them,
And guide them from the storm."

I looked at Raolcan.

I'm not blind. I'm just missing an eye. Just like you aren't lame. Tell this fool to quote something else.

Well, he was feeling cranky!

"Raolcan says he's not blind," I said.

Leng laughed and gestured for me to come over to Raolcan's blind side before he snuck a kiss.

"We'd better take off," he whispered.

Don't think I didn't see that. I don't need an eye to see.

He didn't?

It's one of the advantages of reading minds. I can track anyone anywhere and if I really concentrate, I can even see where walls and objects are through their minds.

Handy. I wished I could make up for my bad leg so easily.

I didn't say it was easy. It's a crutch. And one that's hard to use if I'm distracted.

Was he ready to fly?

Always.

I smiled at Leng as Raolcan helped to nudge me up into the saddle. I didn't really need the extra help anymore, but it was still nice to have – and it felt less humiliating all the time.

You have a prince lifting you into a saddle – and that's humiliating?

I strapped in quickly, stowing my crutch and then Raolcan was ambling across the attic floor, climbing up the window ledge and leaping through, his wings spread to catch the air as we fell and then lifted, soaring upward into the pink morning sky.

I would never get sick of the feeling of flying. The freedom was worth the price.

Play the pipe now to call the dragons.

But didn't we decide it was unethical?

Not when I'm telling you to do it.

I pulled out the pipe, my nose wrinkling when I remembered his slobber dripping from it.

Get over yourself.

And then I put it to my lips and played my three-note call. Leng and Ahlskibi leveled off beside us while below us in the sky city colorful dragons swirled up into the air like flocks of birds over a dewy field.

They joined us slowly, lazy despite the brisk Fall air, a group here and a straggler there, and then we were flapping hard to gain height and hit an airstream heading south.

Would we even be able to catch Iskaris? He was probably riding one of those Silver dragons that guarded the Dominar. He probably had hundreds of Ifrits with him and they could move as quickly as any dragon. And they had a big head start.

But he also has an army to lead. Men on horses and marching on foot. It's too great an asset to leave behind. And the army has to travel by the road while we can fly directly over the mountains.

But would he stay with them or fly on ahead?

It's impossible to know for sure, but judging by his own insecurity, I would guess he will stay with them. He doesn't expect us to catch up now that he has gained a head start and he won't want to appear anywhere without a horde at his back. It would make him look weak. And people who steal power instead of earning it are always afraid that people will find out they are frauds.

But the Dominion wouldn't see him as a fraud. To them, the mask was the Dominar, not the man.

He can't trust that. He knows the truth – that he has no right to his authority. He is always afraid that everyone else knows it too.

What a terrible way to live your life.

A surprising number of people live that way. Dragons, too.

Why would a dragon live a lie?

Not all dragons have a rider like you, Amel.

We winged our way south and I pressed my cheek against Raolcan's neck, enjoying the feeling of belonging. If only every hour could be as beautiful as this one.

Chapter Four

You don't really make camp with dragons, you just find a likely hillside, preferably near water, and stop flying for the night. Our massive dragon army cleaned the mountainside bare of any animal or plant they could find. I hadn't realized that dragons would tear up grass like a horse.

Ugh. Don't compare us to those mindless creatures. Even humans eat salad sometimes.

We were heading due south through the Dragon Snout Mountains. Iskaris' army would have had to go southeast of Leedris City to skirt around them, taking the longer route by road to eventually swing south and head to the twin cities, Dominion City and Sky City. If we planned to ambush them, we would need to stage ourselves somewhere along that path before they arrived. Raolcan thought the spot where the road wound between a mountain range and thick forest would be the best place to pin them down.

It would be better in the mountains, but they will avoid mountains on foot – which is how we will get ahead of them. The river is also a possibility. There is a bridge across it, and if we destroyed the bridge they would be in trouble. Ifrits don't do well with water and the horses and men wouldn't be able to cross. But could we reach the river before the army did and have enough time to set a trap?

I was brewing tea on the fire as Leng gathered more wood for it. We'd pulled a pair of fallen trees from nearby to serve as benches, but we were the only humans and none of the dragons needed a fire to warm them. And if they changed their minds they could set one for themselves.

They're happy to be traveling with us. We dragons have taken a strong dislike to the Ifrits.

Did the dragon army realize that we were fighting to maintain their buffer against extinction?

They know it is a possibility. We have always known. I don't know how many of them realize how close this battle will be. We are not very humble, in general.

That was an understatement.

"I think the river is our best bet," Leng said as he dropped a saddlebag beside me.

He opened the top flap fishing out bread, butter, and cheese from the depths of it. I was beginning to miss hot meals. The last time I'd had one was the broth Dax fed me when I was recovering. I accepted the bread and cheese with a smile, though. It was still better than dried meat.

"Raolcan agrees with you, but I'm worried about that. If we destroy the bridge before they arrive, then they will know that we are there, and they won't walk into the trap. If we leave it intact, then we will have to destroy it while they are crossing it. People will die without warning. Those are the only ways to use the bridge as a trap and if we do either, then our own army won't be able to cross when it gets there."

"Warning them won't make it any easier for them to die," Leng said, but he chewed his lip like he was trying to find a way to tell me something. "Maybe you should let me lead this ambush, Amel. I don't think war is easy on you."

"Is it easy on you?" It had better not be! He had better not love death or killing.

"Of course not!" He sounded offended. "You'd have to be heartless to find it easy but ... it needs to be done or worse things will happen."

Everyone else understood that better than I did.

My mind flashed suddenly to a vision of Savette. She looked thin and worn, her face drawn and her dress dirty around the hem. Both of her palms were on a table and she leaned hard on them as if they were barely holding her up. Beneath them was a map.

"Days at best," an advisor was saying to her. "We've fought hard Chosen One and spent lives like water for you. When will you admit it is time to surrender? Starie Atrelan and her demons of dust are too strong for us. You keep saying that allies are coming, but none are here. Our water is contaminated, our food stores used up, our forces down to the bitter edge of the sword."

"Not yet," Savette said, her expression taut.

"Please, Chosen One, don't make us all die for you."

"Five more days, Casadis. Just five more."

His voice was quiet when he said, "We'll be lucky to last until dawn."

My eyes snapped back to Leng and I gasped.

"Was that one of your visions? Who did you see? Shonan?"

I shook my head. "Savette. Her army is spent."

"Defeated?" he was pale.

"Not yet."

"Then there is still hope. We need to stay the course. If Iskaris joins the battle with his forces that will be the end of Savette's army. It needs to be the bridge, Amel."

I nodded in agreement, finishing my meal in silence. Time was running out. We were facing down battle after battle to even have a hope of freedom and there was no guarantee that any of us would survive this.

I looked up at Leng. There was no guarantee that he would survive.

"Are you okay?" He shifted closer to me on the fallen log, concern all over his face.

I studied his every feature, trying to memorize them, trying to remember this moment.

"We'll make it in time, Amel. Don't be afraid."

He started to smile, but I leaned forward and kissed him, cutting off whatever he was going to say next. I was done with his gentle sweet kisses. I wanted to show him - maybe in this last chance that I had – how much I cared about him.

His arms wrapped around me and he kissed me back, all restraint gone in his matching intensity.

When eventually we broke for air he asked, "What was that for?"

"I don't want you to forget me."

He licked his lips. "I don't think that's even possible."

He leaned in for another kiss but the spell was broken by a gruff voice.

"Leave them alone for a few hours and this is what you get." Hubric strode in from the darkness and sat down beside the fire. "Oh, do carry on.

Anything you can do on your own you can do with me here – or did you marry when I wasn't around, too?"

I felt the blood rushing to my face as we broke apart, scooting to leave room between us on the fallen log.

Chapter Five

"It has to be the river," Leng said to Hubric as we drank the last of the pot of caf and prepared to fly again. "By my estimation, we can be there by nightfall and the forces on foot will be days away even if the Ifrits and dragons help them go more quickly. The bridge will bottleneck their forces."

He was drawing on the ground, showing the road, bridge, and river.

"It won't affect the dragons or Ifrits. The dragons can fly over the water and legend has it that the Ifrits can ghost under it. Destroying a bridge won't stop them." Hubric's objection echoed my own.

"But it will stop the army and the Magikas and the others will be forced to wait and defend them."

Hubric shook his head. "Or they might choose to carry on without the regular army and leave them there while the Magikas rebuild."

Leng had a firm set to his expression. "There isn't anywhere better to stage this. It's our best bet. We need to leave for there now, so we can assess the situation and plan the details of the trap."

Hubric weighed him carefully. "If you're so certain, then perhaps it's best."

What was he thinking behind those hooded eyes? Did he see something we didn't? I stared at the lines Leng had drawn, trying to visualize the plan as he saw it and trying not to think of the people who would die at our design.

"Trust me," Leng said firmly. Hubric nodded and I joined him.

"As you say, Purple." Hubric was already up, wrapping his caf pot in thick leather and stowing it in place for the journey.

When his back was turned I gave Leng a fleeting kiss and a smile. There was something so satisfying about that simple gesture. I couldn't seem to get enough of it.

"I trust your plan," I whispered.

"Fly safe, heart of my heart."

It was misty in the mountains and chilly and I wrapped my scarf snuggly around my neck before tightening the last straps on our baggage.

"Ready?" I asked Raolcan.

Always.

We leapt into the mist, the droplets of water chilling me as we rose up and above of them in a puff of vapor. The sun was bright and cool above the clouds and only the highest mountains peeked out of the fog.

Kyrowat and Ahlskibi popped up out of the thick blanket and then a few dozen more dragons and a few dozen more until it was hundreds of us winging our way to the river pass. I pulled out my maps to review the area we were flying to. Leng's plans made a lot of sense, but I couldn't help the anxious feeling that welled up in me at the idea of trying to trap an army, Ifrits and all.

I tucked away the map, pushing that feeling down, and reached for my book of prophecies. I hoped Talsan didn't mind that I was still using his. I thought that perhaps I'd always use his copy. It meant something to me after all this time. My fingers traced the passage Leng had quoted.

When the people of the earth sound horn of battle,
And the land trembles and is torn,
When the skies are rent in sorrow,
And the depths bring help no more,
Then the lame and the blind shall lead them,
And guide them from the storm.

I understood the references to battle and war. And the earth tearing apart and producing Ifrits was becoming as common as torn clothing. I shivered at the thought of that. But what did it mean about the depths bringing no more help? What help came from the deep? Troglodytes?

They had 'gifted' me with my visions – and whether that was a help or not was still to be seen. They'd also helped me gain the Pipe which was just sitting there ready to be unleashed on their people. Why leave it there? Why had they not removed it years earlier, knowing what it could do?

Perhaps they couldn't get to it without you.

But they were powerful and magical.

It hurts them to be above the ground. And I seem to remember it being a terrible battle to get your hands on that thing through the Kah'deem.

But they were the ones who gave it to Baojang!

A long time ago. Things have changed.

They seemed to be glad I had it.

I think I should point out – again – that being good and being on Amel's side are not always the same thing.

What was that supposed to mean?

Only that they could be a force of good but at the same time sometimes work at cross purposes to you. Like Rakturan.

I wasn't sure I agreed with that. If I was right in what I thought – and I hoped I was! – then all right-thinking people would agree with me.

We didn't stop for breaks of more than a minute or two for the rest of the day. The dragons seemed content enough. Flying was natural to them and they enjoyed air more than land, but I was getting sleepy when the mist burned away in the afternoon sun and we emerged from the mountains.

There was the river, winding out before us like a silver ribbon. It made me shiver with memories of Talsan and the Ifrit under the water. It hadn't been too far from here that I'd almost been killed. I was glad when no one suggested stopping at Backwater Manor. We flew on, tracing the winding river.

There it is. The bridge.

As usual, Raolcan's eyes were better than mine, but I scoured the golden landscape along the silver river, looking for a bridge. There were mounds along the river like small hummocks. They stretched all across the plain and into the nearby forest as if a farmer had stacked hay through the wild grasses and trees.

There! There was the bridge. It crossed the river at a narrow point where the water rushed and gurgled over dragon-sized boulders, steep cliffs on either side. Built with rock and carefully dressed stone, it was an amazing sight. For a country girl used to ferries, seeing a bridge was still a surprise. Someone had carefully planned each stone of this structure before putting it into place. Someone very clever.

A Magika.

But why did the countryside around it look so peculiar?

We're not the first to arrive here.

As if responding to his thought, Ahlskibi dove toward the ground like an arrow shooting out of the sky. Leng! Was he okay?

The bumps along the river unfolded into dozens of dragons.

Chapter Six

Dragons? Here? It was as if they had laid an ambush for us!

Leng isn't the only one to think the bridge makes a good place to ambush someone. His brother thinks the same way.

His brother? Raolcan leaned into a spiral and beneath us I could finally see Shonan standing between a Red and a Gold dragon as he spoke to his brother. What were they saying? I leaned to the side, trying to see as Raolcan slowly leaned into his own landing in front of them. Leng embraced his brother and they broke apart before Raolcan's feet hit the turf. Where was Rasipaer?

Back to Ashana. These dragons have taken turns carrying Shonan. None are bonded to him. It is a strange alliance and a slightly uncomfortable one.

Kyrowat was close on our heels and Hubric leapt off his dragon before Kyrowat had finished landing, earning him a grunt from the old dragon.

"A bit off course, aren't you Shonan?" he asked gruffly. "I'm pretty sure our Chosen One needs you on the fields around Dominion City."

"I'm needed here," Shonan said tightly. His voice sounded nervous despite its usual strength. I shifted uncomfortably in my saddle. In my experience, that voice of authority was rarely nervous and something in me – the part that stood up and took notice whenever Shonan was around – was screaming at me to fight with him to fix whatever that thing was.

"In the middle of an empty road?" Hubric prodded. Why was he baiting Shonan?

He has his reasons. He can feel there is more to it than the bald face of things – and you must think so, too. Remember the promise Shonan made to the Troglodytes? After all, you were the one who made it through him.

My eyes grew wide at the memory of gripping the handles of the Kah'deem and seeing the world through Shonan's eyes. The Troglodytes had demanded that he topple the imposter Dominar before they would ratify a treaty with him – and I'd agreed to it through his voice.

"In exchange for a new treaty with the dragons, I am required to challenge and destroy the current Dominar."

"The pretender," Leng said with tight lips. "Which is perfect timing. We plan to stop his army here at this bridge and defeat as many of them as we can with these dragons, our allies."

Shonan looked worried but still very controlled. "Haz'drazen was very strict in her renegotiations – and the Troglodyte Elders even more strict. They gave me a long list of things that will nullify the treaty and forcing any dragon to serve us – other than those sent to us by the lottery system – will mandate an immediate termination of the treaty. Did you force these dragons to follow you here?"

"They're here of their own will," Hubric said carefully.

But were they? After all, they might be in line with us and our goals now, but originally I had called them inexorably to myself without them having any will of their own.

Shonan nodded with a look of relief and we began to choose a hidden place with a good view of the road and bridge to set up our camp.

"I arrived here only yesterday," Shonan said as we moved to a nearby hillside. "We fought in the south with Savette until we realized that the Dominar had moved north to Leedris. He had business there with the Magikas – or so our captives told us. Why he would leave a battle over his capital city for that ..."

"They were manufacturing Ifrits in the north and channeling them through Leedris to send to the war," Leng explained as we laid out the camp.

I busied myself gathering rocks to ring the fire. My recently injured leg was stiff from all the riding, but a little bending was good for it. If I didn't move it, I would heal with less mobility. I knew how these things worked.

"A wise Dominar would not leave his city simply for that." Shonan sniffed.

"I think he was waiting for word from Ko'Torenth and the Rock Eaters about a possible alliance. They must have been planning to meet there – away from the conflict," Leng said. "They spoke of those other nations often. But always quietly and always with a sense of uncertainty."

"They want the dragons. They always have," Shonan said as he and Leng set up the tents. I couldn't help shaking my head. How long had it taken me to realize what Shonan saw immediately?

Hubric set down the wood beside me and set to making a fire as I put his caf grounds into a pot. If we were going to wait, we might as well drink something hot. This cold was going to be the death of me. It sank right into my bones and chilled me so I couldn't get warm again.

I hate winter. We should fly back to Baojang when it gets really cold.

That was definitely not an option!

Maybe we can go invade their territory. You know, take a turn at the whole invasion thing. And they can try defense and watching their beloved cities burned to the ground...

I hoped we wouldn't do something so foolish. If I were ever Dominar, I would do everything in my power to prevent war.

By now you should realize that being too cautious can lead to as a much trouble as being too aggressive. Wisdom is not simply following a set rule or principle – it's knowing how to apply the right rule or principle to the present situation.

Fortunately, I would never be the Dominar. Shonan would be the one weighing those things.

"But we will be here to protect the dragons and carry on our side of the bargain and they will help us to that goal," Shonan said, bringing a pot and waterskin to the fire. "As long as we don't break the terms. That's why I'm here. I must fulfill our side of the agreement."

I pulled out a few vegetables that Leng and I had scavenged from the Castel at Leedris and a small bag of barley. A soup would be nice on a day like this. The Pipe fell out of my bag and onto the grass. Quickly, I snatched it back up, replacing it in the bag, but when the noise around the campfire suddenly quieted, I looked up.

Shonan stared at me, his face ghost-white and his eyes wide.

"What is that?" There was danger in his voice.

Chapter Seven

"It's the Pipe of Wings," I said, tension building inside me as I held my bag close. What if he asked for it? I couldn't give it to him. I'd already given it to Roalcan. But could I say no to the true Dominar?

"I saw a picture of it in a book," Shonan said. His words were slow and deliberate, like he was trying to be very clear. "Under the drawing, it was stated that this was the Pipe of Wings, an ancient artifact of Baojang, gifted to them by the Troglodytes long ago but lost to their use."

"That's true," I said, my mouth feeling drier than it should. "I acquired it in Baojang."

His eyes met mine and his anxious expression was plain. His face was taut and small lines appeared around his eyes and between his eyebrows.

"And can it be used to force dragons to do you will, Amel? Is that how you have come here with a dragon army?"

"It's not like that," I began, but the look of horror filling his face cut me off.

"Can be used for the control of dragons?" His voice was higher than usual. "Answer me plainly."

"What are you afraid of?" I glanced around the fire.

Everyone was frozen in place. Leng's stick still poked the fire, but the tip of it was ablaze and he didn't even notice. Hubric tilted his head to the side like he could hear what we weren't saying.

"Amel, there was a list of things in our treaty that, if broken, nullified the treaty. One of them was use of any magic device to influence or control a dragon, including the whips Magikas – and Dragon Riders training new dragons - use." He cleared his throat. "Your pipe was on the list. It must not be used."

"I gave it to Raolcan. I can't give it to you," I said, feeling a bead of sweat on my forehead.

Shonan ran a hand over his face. "I can't believe it. After all that. After the promises I made. After everything that happened. It's all been for nothing."

"But it hasn't," I protested.

"If Amel just found out and if she stops using it, then we haven't broken the treaty," Leng said, throwing his burning stick into the fire like he was waking up from a trance. His stance was stiff and his eyes took on a new intensity as he quickly tried to solve the problem. "Raolcan keeps the Pipe. I'm sure that's fine since he is a dragon. Amel doesn't use it again. You kill Iskaris. And there we have it, our bargain is kept."

"I doubt they will see it that way," Shonan said. He looked sick. His face was practically green as he slumped to sit on the ground, head in his hands.

But it was the Troglodyte's who gave me the gift that gifted me the Pipe. They had been watching me all along – and occasionally commenting. They'd known when they were making the treaty with Shonan that I had the Pipe, so they must be fine with it.

"Are you certain that they meant using this Pipe?" I asked him. "Maybe it's a misunderstanding?"

He pulled himself to his feet, but he wouldn't look at me. "It's a disaster."

"What happens if we break our side of the treaty?" I asked. Leng and Hubric turned from me to look at Shonan. Everything was hanging on his words.

"Then we forfeit our right to take dragons for training and riding. The other portions of the treaty remain – we will defend the dragons and they us – but no more Dragon Riders. Without them, the strength of the Dominion is gone."

"And the dragons we work with now?" Hubric asked. "What about them?"

"They remain. But for how long? Our nation is doomed by this folly."

But they *knew*! They made the treaty with him *knowing* that I had the Pipe. They knew I had used it and would keep on using it!

They'd tricked him.

They'd tricked me.

I had always thought that the Troglodytes were good. After all, they rescued me. They opposed the Ifrits. They gave me a gift. But they'd purposely deceived Shonan. I felt like the bottom was dropping out of my world.

Just like with Rakturan, things are more complicated than that.

With Rakturan they weren't complicated. He just made them that way. He claimed to be loyal to Savette but he didn't love the Dominion. The Troglodytes pretended they were here to help us, but they manipulated us into betraying our nation.

"And you don't need to keep your side of the bargain to retake the Dominar's mask, do you?" Leng asked Shonan. "Since that was a part of it."

"I still need to do that." His voice was quiet. "Or the rest of the treaty is gone, too, and every dragon becomes our enemy."

And so, we were caught. We must fulfill what was left of the bargain but lose the reward of it.

They didn't negotiate for you, Amel. That's the difference. They negotiated on behalf of the dragons.

And did Raolcan think they did the right thing? Did he think it was fair that they trapped me into betraying my people?

I think they are looking out for their own. That doesn't make them bad. It makes them ... shrewd.

No one could even look at me. Hubric stared into the fire, his face so intense that he could have lit it with his expression. Leng stood halfway between Shonan and me, looking back and forth like he was torn.

I pulled myself to my feet, leaned into my crutch and limped away. I was so angry. I felt like a pawn who'd been played by giant hands into a position I hadn't asked for and didn't want. It wasn't me who wanted that Pipe. Wasn't me who thought it needed to be played. In fact, I'd given it to Raolcan! And they'd known all along that they were setting me up to ruin everything. Everything.

I wanted to bite through something and chew. I wanted to bite one of those Troglodytes with their creepy translucent skin and shake them until their glowing insides faded to dark.

Violent much?

I was too angry to answer. I didn't want to hear from Raolcan if he didn't take my side. He could just go congratulate the Troglodytes on their shrewdness while I sat here and thought about my predicament.

Maybe my rage was too strong. Or maybe I just deserved a lot better than this. Maybe, for once in my life, I should demand to be treated better.

Chapter Eight

"Shonan has calmed down," Leng said, joining me in the dark. My back was to the fire and I had hobbled out of hearing range. I didn't want to see or hear anyone right now. Not even Raolcan. "I explained that you couldn't possibly have known. We agreed on a plan of attack, and we'll set it up in the morning. Ahlskibi tells me that Raolcan is asking the dragons to help. We can't demand anything, but they can still choose to help us."

Well, good for them. Nice to know they had everything sorted out and that everyone was feeling calm and hopeful.

"He's not mad at you, Amel. When Hubric told us how you got the Pipe – well, it's obvious that you were maneuvered into this. You couldn't have stopped it. No one blames you."

That made it so much worse. I was humiliated by that – by being maneuvered and tricked and pushed into place like a fool. I hated myself for being a fool. They didn't *blame* me?

"You're going to need to say something, eventually. We need you for your part of the ambush. And I know you, Amel. You aren't so angry that you'll want this to fail."

They needed me to be a pawn, too. No. I was no one's pawn. I was no one's tool. I was done with being blown from place to place for purpose after purpose. I wasn't the one wearing a mask or even wearing the final uniform of a Dragon Rider.

"Listen, it's natural for the pressure to get to you at this point – to feel overwhelmed and like you don't have what it takes to keep going. We're all feeling it. It's been months of pushing and fighting and desperation."

I was just a girl with a crutch who was really angry that everyone seemed to be seeing the world differently than her – and in their version, she was just a piece to be slotted in the correct part of the puzzle. I gritted my teeth. Enough.

The Troglodytes thought they could manipulate me and use me a piece on their game board, did they? Well, they had better look out because I wouldn't be played.

DESTROY OUR ENEMIES, CALLER.

I flinched at their voices in my head.

But it seemed to me that I was the one up here risking everything – my life, my Dominion, my friends – while they were tucked safely underground making demands and ridiculous contracts. They wanted me to destroy their enemies while they undermined what I loved. Nope. If they wanted me to destroy their enemies, then they would keep this contract with Shonan intact. They would not break it because they maneuvered me to get the Pipe.

DESTROY OUR ENEMIES.

Only if you keep the contract.

RETURN THE PIPE.

I always meant to return it. They knew that. They just pushed me here because they thought it was a way to gain the upper hand. I would only agree if they agreed to my terms, too.

ALL WILL BE FORGIVEN, THE CONTRACT KEPT INTACT.

I froze. Did they mean that? They would honor the contract if I destroyed the Ifrits and returned the pipe?

They seem to be saying that.

Oh, Raolcan was willing to weigh in now that things were looking up?

I was giving you space. You seemed to need it.

Hmmph. I'd have to decide if I was going to forgive him.

Of course, you'll forgive me. You love me. Besides, it's not in your nature to hold a grudge. I'm a little surprised you lost your temper, but I suppose even the sweetest honey has a fly or two in it from time to time.

My eyes widened. I should make him eat feet for saying that! He was treating my reaction like it was trivial!

There's the spirit.

Agreed, I said silently to the Troglodytes. I hadn't forgiven them for this. But I would have to work with them.

AGREED.

I gritted my teeth to turn to Leng. He was still beside me, refusing to walk away despite everything.

"Don't hold this against me, Amel. Don't push me away. It's not me who put you in this position."

"Thank you for standing up for me," I said. My voice was tighter than I would have liked. I was still smarting under the humiliation of being forced and maneuvered like I had been. "Thank you for explaining that I never meant to cause this."

"I know it's true," he said. He sighed. "Don't crack under the pressure, Amel. Stay with me. We can do this together, but we need to stay focus. We can't let it break us."

"I have a way to fix it. The whole thing with the deal and the Trogs and everything."

"Let's go back to the fire, Amel." Was he afraid I was lying to myself, that I would crack if I tried to fix it? "We all need some rest. I'm exhausted. These last months ... Whatever the Dominion becomes, you'll be one of the brightest parts left in it, Amel. It will all have been worth it, knowing you're still shining here somewhere. And Shonan – we can be friends again even after he is Dominar once more. I'm getting used to the idea. I think I could keep it a secret between us, find ways to communicate or slip through the guards to visit him. I'm almost looking forward to it."

I laughed lightly, feeling the anger and frustration melting away.

"In fact, I hope you'll help me sneak around Dominion City," he smiled roguishly.

"I'm not much good at sneaking," I said, brandishing my crutch.

"Then I guess we'll be caught because I won't do it without you." He kissed the top of my head and wrapped an arm around me.

Of course, things were tough. Of course, there were forces and people trying to force me into the path they'd set. It would always be like that, but I would always have Leng.

And me.

Leng. He was faithful and on *my* side.

Oh, the burn of it! You have no faith.

You weren't on my side. Don't even try to lie about that.

I just ... see a bigger picture than you do.

Are you suggesting that I am not as smart as you? That I'm blind somehow?

Only that you are human. And that means we'll never be exactly the same. And that's okay.

That sounded a bit like an insult.

It's an apology.

Raolcan? Apologizing?

I know. I even surprised myself.

Chapter Nine

My sleep was troubled. I didn't know if I was dreaming or seeing visions. Savette flashed through my mind, kneeling in the mud, rain pouring over her. Was she crying or was that me? I dreamed of a room I'd never been in – a long marble room gleaming and white. Carved dragons ringed the bases of the pillars. Dragons were carved in snarling poses around the base of a dais and a tall white throne carved of marble sat astride the backs of a tangle of dragons. There were no steps up to the throne. One would have to climb up on the snouts or shoulders of the dragons to reach the towering seat.

I woke with a gasp. Something had felt strangely familiar about that place.

I felt that, too. But why would the throne room of the Dominion feel familiar to you?

Perhaps, one day, I would deliver messages there. Perhaps I would kneel before Shonan in his masked crown and bring messages of peace and prosperity from around the Dominion. I would like that.

We have a long way to go before we get there. We have a war to win first. It's easy to lose heart after so many battles, but I know you. You have a huge heart.

I drank my caf that morning with a feeling of peace. I was ready for the next stage. I would find a way to help win this war – one piece at a time – starting here with this ambush. We'd keep the enemy pinned here while Baojang traveled to support us. Then, we'd sweep south and join Savette in her fight and when it was all done, I would return the Pipe to the Troglodytes and all this would be over. We would be at peace again. I just needed to be strong and steady and not give in to worry.

I felt a hand slip into mine and Leng smiled down at me.

I smiled back. "Thank you for helping me find my way again."

"Of course," he said. "Are you ready?"

I nodded, taking one last deep breath. We all had our roles here. This morning, Shonan would stage on the hillside here with the dragons under his command. They would wait to quell any Ifrits or dragons who made the leap over the bridge after the army was forced to stop. Leng and a group of dragons, who Raolcan assured us had volunteered for the role, were set to spend the morning blocking the bridge with piled rocks and then to defend it. We'd debated destroying the bridge – still my own preference – but in the end Shonan argued that it would make it difficult to clear later when Baojang wanted to cross. We needed their army to reinforce Savette.

Hubric had already flown off on his own journey – he was to scout for the oncoming army and try to stay hidden. It was hard to plan an ambush without knowing when your enemy would arrive.

I wasn't excited about my role. Raolcan and I were going to fly rings around the bridge and hills, high up in the sky. From there, Raolcan could direct dragons and – if utterly necessary – I could use the Pipe to affect them.

"Remember, only use the Pipe as a last resort," Shonan said from beside the fire, as if he was reading my mind. "I don't really believe that you can change the Troglodytes minds, but any further infractions can only set them further against the treaty."

He ran a hand over his face.

"We'll succeed, brother." Leng let go of my hand to clap his brother on the shoulder.

Shonan nodded, but his face was screwed up in thought. "The main thing, for all of us, is to keep the Dominar and his army from reaching Dominion City. Whatever sacrifice that requires is worth making. Even if that brings displeasure from our allies. I woke with a deep feeling that this battle today or tomorrow – whenever they arrive – will change everything. It bears great significance for me."

"It's just that mask," Leng said. "The heaviness of it weighs on you even now. If we defeat Iskaris today, you will have to don it again."

"I'm not afraid. I won't shrink back," Shonan said, his eyes on the landscape beyond the bridge, but his voice was pitched low and almost intimate as he spoke to us. "I'm willing to bear the burden of it for my people and this time I won't do it alone, right brother?"

His eyes, when they finally met Leng's, were full of hope mixed with anxiety.

"It will be different," Leng assured him. They were two sides of a coin standing side by side with shoulders back and eyes looking unflinchingly into the distance. "We'll change tradition. I won't abandon you. The fate of a nation shouldn't be borne by one man alone with no support. It should never have been that way."

"There's a reason they place the throne so high above the people," Shonan said, his voice still laced with worry. "And it's not because a ruler looks good up there. It's to emphasize how separate he is. Separation from the rest of humanity is a terrible punishment."

His eyes looked haunted as he remembered his past. What would it take to choose to bear that burden? What sort of big heart would you have to have to accept it, knowing there was no way out, knowing it would be so lonely?

On an impulse I hobbled over and hugged him. "We won't make you do this alone."

He seemed stunned when I pulled back, his arm still open as if he were reaching to hug me back but couldn't quite bring himself to do it.

"See?" Leng said with a chuckle. "You'll even get surprise hugs sometimes."

I felt my face heating. I wasn't used to displaying my emotions so clearly, but I guess I was infected by the same sense of foreboding that he was. For some reason, this battle on the horizon felt different. Maybe we were all cracking just a little under the pressure.

Chapter Ten

We'd been circling for two hours and I was feeling antsy. I didn't like waiting.

At least you have something to watch.

Leng and his dragons were putting the final touches on the rubble-filled bridge. No human was going to cross that any time soon – definitely not on horseback and definitely not with dragons in his way. Ahlskibi straddled the center of it like a dragon from lore sitting on a pile of gold.

On the south side of the bridge, Shonan had finished arranging his own dragon troops and cleared the top of the highest nearby hill of brush and stones. I wasn't sure why.

He's preparing a stage for battle. If Iskaris slips by him today he will have failed the Troglodytes.

I returned to my Ibrenicus prophecies, reading over and over the same passage.

"*When the people of the earth sound horn of battle,*
And the land trembles and is torn,
When the skies are rent in sorrow,
And the depths bring help no more,
Then the lame and the blind shall lead them,
And guide them from the storm."

I found it unsettling. How could the lame and blind lead? What did it say about the destruction of a war if there were only lame and blind left to do that? It made me nervous. Over and over again these prophecies had been fulfilled. I'd seen it. I'd relied on it. I'd found guidance in the words and thoughts of them. I was as certain of their truth as I was of my own name. What did I do with one that made me feel so off-kilter?

I chewed my lip, watching the horizon. There was a small black blip too far out for me to see what it was. A bird? No. There was a trail behind it of smoke. Strange.

I tucked the book away in my pocket and leaned forward over Raolcan's neck, trying to strain to see the figure. There was something familiar about it ... was that Hubric already?

A burst of light surrounded the figure – flames? And then I noticed two other small dots. They moved too quickly for me to make out what they were doing. If they were flying in formation, then they were very bad at it.

As they grew closer, I began to make out details. Three dragons with riders. Two of them flamed at the third as he ducked and wove. His tail smoked as he flew, as if it were on fire.

Raolcan reared back suddenly, and then a fist of our own dragons – positioned on the north side of the bridge – launched. They rocketed toward the three dragons and my heart raced as I watched them quickly meet the others in the air.

Hubric on Kyrowat, both blackened and battered, dropped as the other dragons formed a shield to protect them, taking the full fury of the pair of silver dragons on themselves. We should have sent more scouts. We shouldn't have sent Hubric alone.

Kyrowat flew erratically to the hill where Shonan was stationed while the dragons Raolcan had sent attacked the Silvers. I shut my eyes when a big Black dragon bit down on the slender arching neck of the lead Silver, severing it so violently that I could almost hear the crunch.

I wouldn't look at what happened next. I swallowed, willing my belly to calm down. With trembling hands, I tightened the scarf that held my hair back from my eyes.

It's done now.

I glanced to where Hubric and Kyrowat had landed on the tallest hill to speak to Shonan.

Iskaris is with his army. The Ifrits and dragons are in the vanguard. Hubric estimates them an hour out. He should have just looked and returned, but he was tempted by curiosity and took too long watching them. When he was on his return route to us, their own scouts – those two Silvers – attacked him and Kyrowat. They are battered but fine.

Hopefully, Shonan was persuading him to rest.

Even as I thought that, Kyrowat leapt into the air, heading north by northwest back to the Dragon Snout mountains.

Shonan has sent him to bring word to Jalla of where the ambush is set and that it will spring today. We need her army to hurry to form the other side of the pincher. We won't be able to hold them otherwise.

But he was hurt!

Better hurt than dead. He sends a last message to you – stay alive.

I should be sending that message to him! Why had he been so curious that he had lingered near the enemy?

The Magikas were assembled. They were performing a magic unusual for them. Hubric was curious.

What sort of magic?

He thought they might be able to make their own bridge.

I looked down at the bridge we'd so carefully blocked and arranged for defense and my heart stuttered. We were in real trouble if that were true.

Chapter Eleven

There should be more things we could do to prepare. Surely there was something left undone that could be done ahead of time – some kind of preparation that would make all the difference.

You're just terrible at waiting.

But I was great at worrying and as the hours ticked by to noon, I felt worry burning as hot in my belly as the sun burned on my back.

That's life I'm afraid. Days, months, even years of anticipation all burned up in a few hot minutes of the final action. It leaves nothing but ashes and dust behind and maybe ... if you are very lucky ... success.

But what was success?

Continued love. Love that hasn't died. Isn't that why we fight? So that tomorrow the people we love will still be here for us to enjoy?

I glanced down to where Leng sat astraddle Ahlskibi. I'd be gutted if I lost him. I laid a hand on Raolcan's neck. And Raolcan, too.

Can I assume then, that all is forgiven?

I shouldn't have had that outburst. I just felt so cornered lately. This – everything – was such an enormous task and sometimes it felt like I had no decisions in it, like it was driving me instead of me driving it.

It is driving you. It's like we were in a river and when we chose to swim down the branch we did it narrowed and narrowed and now it's rushing around us, too fast to stop and too angry to fight. We can only let us take us over the falls and hope we all survive.

I swallowed, watching the horizon and thinking about what he said. I hoped we survived. On the road to the north, I thought I saw the first movement all day. It was strange that there hadn't been any casual travelers.

Heading toward a war? Anyone with half a grain of sense would be heading away from Dominion City or hunkered down in a place where they think they can survive.

True. Which meant that movement was certainly the army of Iskaris.

It is. They will arrive this afternoon.

And before them was a cloud of smoke with flashes of silver. It broke off from the main army as I watched, speeding toward us.

They know we are here now. They are trying to hit us with a hammer of force rather than wait for us to spring a trap. Dividing an army is usually a bad tactic, but in this case, it makes sense. The army on foot can't cross this chasm until we are dealt with and only the Ifrits and dragons can deal with us.

My belly clenched at his words. I hated battle. I hated the results. I hated Ifrits. Thank goodness there were no innocents here and nothing that could be set on fire.

Raolcan felt tense, too, his wide circles narrowing and his mind distant as he gave orders to the dragons around us. A group of Reds swooped up, swirling in the air above the bridge in time with us.

I felt like every inch of my skin was reporting to my brain, like my eyes were flitting from one thing to the next, like my breath was coming too quickly.

It is. Calm down.

I focused on long slow breaths as the Ifrits went from faraway smoke to clear shapes swarming toward us. What were they carrying?

Magikas. Uh oh. They have a plan, too.

I held on tight as Raolcan led the first charge with the Reds. I knew the plan. We would fly along the road, flaming along the right side of the army to keep them hemmed in on the road beside the forest.

We dove toward the line of Ifirits and I held on tight, trying to stay flat across Raolcan's neck.

This is the fun part! See us roar, Ifrits!

We swept beside the leader of the Ifrit horde. He towered, mountainous in size, swirling flames dancing in the caverns where his eyes and mouth should have been. His arms were full of Magikas. They looked almost as if they were hanging in swaths of black smoke, but their eyes were closed and their hands glowed with light. What exactly were they planning? What sort of nerve would it take to let one of those monsters carry you?

Raolcan flamed as we swept by the first Ifrit and then flaming again and again as we passed dozens more. His flight path was erratic, dodging and weaving to avoid any defense they might mount.

They ignored him and the Reds who followed us in the flaming charge. I heard cries from some of the Magikas, but the Ifrits were intent on their goal – the raging river and the bridge that crossed it. They didn't slow or stop. What would they do when they got there?

Raolcan pulled up before we reached the end of the line, somersaulting backward the way we came. I held on tight, eyes clenched against the dizzying roll and the spinning landscape. I tried not to take too big of breaths. All I could smell was burnt cloth and flesh with the overpowering smoky smell of Ifrits mixed in with everything else.

Their sheer numbers worried me. In every other Ifrit encounter, escape had been our main goal. There was no escape here. Here we must meet them head on and win.

We will!

But as they rushed toward the tumbling river set in the cradle of Autumn fields, I didn't share his good spirits. There were simply too many of them, and what possessed these Magikas to allow dust demons to carry them to the edge of the river? They had a plan and I didn't think that bridge building accounted for it.

I stole a glance over my shoulder as we hurtled toward the river, trying to count the Ifrits, but my mental count stuttered to a halt as the Silver dragons rose above their heads, picking up speed now that we were close to the river. I was certain that I saw the glint of a silver mask on one of the riders.

Chapter Twelve

We reached the river and wheeled to face the enemy. Somehow the current below us looked angrier, stronger, as if in reaction to our enemy.

The first Ifrit hit the bank of the river the moment we turned, tossing the Magikas he carried to the ground. He placed himself in front of the Magikas as the next Ifrit quickly imitated him, depositing his cargo and forming up along the bank. So. They would serve as a shield, ignoring the current bridge entirely.

Raolcan roared and then every dragon with us rose from the ground or poured in from the surrounding forest and hills. The roars joining his made the earth below us tremble. Ahlskibi scrambled up into the air from the bridge as the smaller rocks they'd piled on the bridge trembled and fell to the river below. Leng kept his seat with a calm expression. He held a short sword in one hand, ready to defend our bottleneck on the bridge.

I clamped my hands around my ears, bracing against the sound. When it was over, twenty Ifrits faced us, shoulder to shoulder along the riverbank. Behind them, more rows of Ifrits formed. I tried not to shudder at their sheer numbers.

The first one opened his cavern mouth and laughed. Or at least, I thought it was a laugh. The sound – like roaring flames and breaking branches – gave me chills.

I clenched my jaw, preparing for the response. I was not wrong to brace myself. We were hurtling forward before I had time to realize what was happening and then it was all I could do to hold on as Raolcan swooped in among the Ifrits, dodging arms and roaring mouths, blazing his own fire into one smoky monster after another.

The world was flame and smoke, spinning horizons, choking dust, and acid fear. It was my heart in my throat and my mouth gasping for air. It was twenty dragons pulling an Ifrit from the fray and shredding it to pieces in their powerful jaws.

Another Ifrit was drawn out the same way. I saw glimpses of him being shredded as Raolcan barrel rolled out of an engagement.

There was a knot of Magikas below – maybe twenty? – they linked hands in a circle, light filling the circle and bubbling up like a spurting fountain above their heads. Didn't they need to be near one of those power wells to do that?

Remember, we are not far from the Feet of the River, a place of great power.

I remembered that place. I swallowed, thinking about how much power it was rumored to have. Raolcan dove toward a group of Magikas but was batted aside by an Ifrit, sending us into a deadly spin. I gripped tightly to him, bracing for the impact of the ground. It didn't come. I opened my eyes to see he'd pulled us out of the tumble and was gaining height.

It was hard to keep up with the action – I didn't know how Raolcan stayed on top of everything, guiding an army as he fought and fending off attacks with only one eye to watch for them.

Beneath us, the battle swirled, lines of colorful dragons diving in arcs into a mass of dust demon clouds and flower-like patterns of Magikas holding hands and pulling up golden fountains of light. As I watched, the light from the seven flowers rose, linked and rushed toward the river. I was expecting the bridge to form so they could race across the water.

I didn't expect it to hit the existing bridge with the force of a thousand dragon fires. Ahlskibi leapt from the rubble just in time, Leng clinging to his back. A flurry of other dragons took flight like a startled murder of crows. Beneath where they had crouched, the bridge cracked, split and then broke into a thousand shards, spilling through the air and plummeting into the canyon, choking the river.

I gasped as the water rose for a few moments before boiling over the make-shift dam and thundering onward down the river.

The bridge was gone.

But why? Shouldn't they be building a bridge of their own?

A second spurt of light began in one of the flowers but was extinguished as a line of Red dragons burst through the Ifrits guards, flaming the flower of Magikas. Men and woman fell to the ground, their robes aflame and their screams silent in the clash and chaos of the battle.

It wasn't enough. The other six flowers were already working, purple light bubbling up around them. It met in the middle, swirling as it coalesced into a glowing rope of thousands of light strands. Wind whipped up around us, pulling toward the flowers and one of the Ifrits was whipped off his feet, swirling into the mass of woven light until he disappeared. All around them, on the ground, spiderwebs of darkness pulled from the ground into the circles of Magikas, leaving the ground behind it dull and lifeless as if something had been sucked out of it.

The rope of light spurted upward, swirling as it stretched across the river so suddenly that it might have been a rainbow springing to life. The end of it slammed into the ground, making everything nearby shudder and then coalesced from light into a thick bridge that looked like metal.

Sky steel, unless I am mistaken.

The Magikas stood utterly still, their hands still linked, their light still feeding the bridge.

And now we see their plan. With our bridge gone and theirs in its place, they control who crosses on it. Not only can their army cross, but our Baojang reinforcements will arrive to find their trap sprung and their way blocked. I suspect that once the Magikas leave, this temporary bridge will leave, too.

We hadn't trapped them. They'd trapped us.

I felt the blood draining from my face.

Across the river, enhanced by magic or some other trick, Shonan's voice rose, filling every ear.

"Come to me, Dominar. Come and claim a final victory, or lose your mask in defeat!"

Didn't he realize the situation we were in? This wasn't the time for a one on one battle. We were in the throes of defeat!

Not quite yet.

And if he was locked in battle, there would be no escape.

There is no escape for any of us. We win today, or we die trying.

Chapter Thirteen

Raolcan spun as the silver dragons streaked by. He dove, suddenly, with a furious flapping of wings and his neck shot forward, his mouth opening and biting down on the neck of the Silver. His victim thrashed against the hold, knocking his body into Raolcans and bringing his rider side by side with me.

My eyes widened as the man in ornate silver-trimmed armor narrowed his eyes. His helm was an open-mouthed dragon and an angry scar ran down his cheek. I'd never been so close to a dragoon when he was flying. The look on his face froze my blood. He reached for his sword and I scrambled to free my crutch from Raolcan's saddle.

It was tied too tightly. It wouldn't pull free. I worked at it, almost feeling the blade of my adversary plunging through me. Any moment now it would. Any moment...

The crutch pulled free and I gripped it in both hands, spinning to defend myself. My eyes widened when I saw an empty saddle where my enemy had been. What ...?

I looked from dragon to dragon around me. It wasn't Raolcan. He was still shaking the Silver dragon as its wing began to droop and the added weight made us sink toward the ground.

Sink.

Whoever had helped us must be above us now. I looked from the empty saddle and the torn leather straps, my gaze following an invisible line upward. I grimaced when I finally saw the rider, limp and broken in Ahlskibi's mouth. Leng was leaning forward in the saddle, his mouth a grim, determined line.

I signed a thank you and breathed a sigh of relief, strapping the crutch to my arm so I wouldn't lose it. I should keep it close. Next time, Leng might not be so close.

Raolcan dropped the Silver to the ground, climbing back into the descending clouds. A dark storm front was rolling our way. Between dark blue clouds, rays of gold pierced the sky, illuminating tiny spots along the hillside in halos of gold while the rest of the landscape grew dark.

One golden gilded the hilltop Shonan had prepared and sparkled along the wings of the Silver dragon who landed before it.

Paaaalk. Iskaris rides him. A proud dragon, sworn to service and trained to defend. He does not care who wears the mask, he is loyal to it regardless.

Maybe we could persuade him to defend the real Dominar.

The real Dominar is the one in the mask.

The real Dominar was Shonan.

What we know is true and what everyone else knows is true are different. We can't just demand that they see the truth we do. We need to find a way to show them. Would you change your mind just because someone shouted that Iskaris was Dominar?

Hardly.

Then let the true Dominar prove his point.

He was about to. Raolcan was already moving to his next target, but my eyes were glued to the showdown beyond us. Iskaris dismounted from his dragon and strode to the center of the hill, his single arm holding a sword at ready stance. Shonan had his own sword out – the only two one-armed men I knew, and they were ready to fight. I swallowed. Why would Iskaris fight when he didn't have to?

Even the worst of us can't silence the voice in our heads saying, 'Maybe you are nothing after all.' Even Iskaris needs to prove to himself that it isn't true – that he has the right to be the Dominar. He knows Shonan – knows he is no great swordsman – knows his weaknesses in a way that only a faithful guard could. He knows he can win. The temptation to silence him in such a public way is too much for him. Shonan knew it would be true.

But could Shonan win?

Raolcan wheeled to the side, avoiding an Ifrit hand that smacked the air around us. Behind us, dragons were grouping again, ready for a second assault on the Ifrits. We had numbers on our side, but were they enough? I swallowed as I realized how many dragons lay on the ground already.

The Silvers are no longer our problem. They are guarding Iskaris on the hill. The Magikas fight to hold their bridge in place. They can't hurt us with fire while they are occupied with that. Only the Ifrits need concern us now.

But that wasn't so easy. For every Ifrit our dragons shredded, we lost multiple dragons. I watched as a Gold was snatched from the air and hurtled into the rocks below, breaking his back over the granite. Carefully, I counted Ifrits and then dragons and then Ifrits again.

We didn't have the numbers.

We have the spirit!

Shonan would have to face Iskaris alone. We could spare no one to guard him.

He'll be fine.

And we didn't have the numbers.

Stop worrying so much.

We dove toward the Ifrits, but even in the middle of the smoke and flame, as Raolcan helped lure an Ifrit after him to let a group of Greens pounce on it, I was still trying to find some way we could turn the tide on them. There had to be something more that we could do than just fight.

The time for planning is over. Now it's time to put our heads down and rip and tear!

Raolcan was giddy with the excitement of it, reveling in every Ifrit he tore to shreds.

For each one I destroy, hundreds of humans and dragons are saved.

But I was watching the hillside where another battle was being fought in snake-like sword stances and the road beyond where the silhouettes of a human army marched across the land like a swarm of ants. Time was running out.

Chapter Fourteen

"The army will be here before we can finish off the Ifrits," Leng called to me. Ahlskibi had flown to level with Raolcan as Raolcan spiraled upward to get a better look at the battlefield. This many hours into the battle we were all soot-streaked and exhausted. Behind us, on the hillside, Shonan and Iskaris still fought, their stances and sudden lunges slowing as the weariness of a long battle overcame them.

Leng's gaze swept to them every few minutes, his body language tense. One-armed fighting wasn't the same as two-armed. One slip could be a disaster. Worse, Iskaris' experience and heavier musculature were beginning to show. A knot grew in my belly as the swordplay stretched out longer and longer.

Below us, dragons tore another Ifrit to pieces, but our numbers had lessened, and the shoals of colored dragons were thinner ribbons than they had been before. A dozen Ifrits still stood, protecting the Magikas, and now Iskaris' army was almost here.

Ten minutes.

Even Raolcan was sounding tense. Too many broken dragons littered the riverbanks, some of them swept down the river like fallen leaves.

"If they make it here first, they'll rush across the river and this whole ambush will have failed!" Leng said, his face screwed up in concentration as he considered the approaching army.

But what could we do? Any direct attack on the Magikas would be a suicide mission with the Ifrits still guarding them.

I swallowed.

Some things are worth dying for.

"We need to attack the Magikas as hard and fast as we can," I called back. "Ignore the Ifrits and go straight to them!"

Leng nodded grimly, rubbing a hand over his face like he could wipe away the task in front of him. I gripped my cane, took the Pipe out of the saddlebags and tied it around my neck. Whatever came next, we needed to be ready.

Unstrap the bags. There is nothing in them so precious as the extra seconds we can gain without them.

I hurried to comply and saw Leng doing the same.

"You still have my davari?" he asked as he worked.

I lifted a hand to show him, worry making my head feel light.

He smiled very briefly before calling out, "Don't lose it. The promise still stands!"

Before I could respond, Ahlskibi was plunging forward, Raolcan hot on his heels. I gripped his neck. We'd be okay, wouldn't we?

Of course! It takes a lot to bring this dragon down!

We fell toward the earth like meteors, wind whipping around us, other dragons rushing to fall in behind us. Raolcan dropped until I thought we would hit the ground. I was already bracing for impact when he suddenly swooped up, skimming the ground with his belly as he crashed through a knot of Magikas. They tumbled in all directions, their magical light that fed the bridge faded for a moment.

Already, the ones picking themselves up again were casting balls of flame at us as quickly as they could. Raolcan's neck arced around to grab one off the ground and shake him, tossing him into a woman who had both her hands lifted, flames surrounding them. Both of them fell to the ground, the flames sputtering out.

A quick glance showed me that two other knots had been disrupted, but one was already reforming, the Ifrit protectors around it having left the attacking dragons crumpled on the ground nearby.

Raolcan! On your right!

He spun just in time to avoid the Ifrit that sped toward us, jumping into the air, but his launch was interrupted as the Ifrit's hand grazed his wing tip, knocking us to the ground.

I cried out as my leg hit the ground – not hard and not for long, but enough to hurt! We tumbled, and I could tell Raolcan was maneuvering to avoid hurting me.

He scrambled up from the earth as soon as he could gain control of himself, clawing through dirt and over the fallen body of a dead White to try to get enough clearance to fly. A fireball splashed beside us, lighting the rocks and ground ablaze. I flinched from the flame, guarding my eyes with my forearm.

Raolcan leapt into the air as two more fireballs hit around us. I looked around, disoriented, but I was too dizzy to place where we were. Where was the river? The horizon wove in my vision and nausea filled me. I couldn't quite get my bearings ...

Humans and horses surged beneath us, channeling into a single stream.

The bridge!

They surged across the bridge of magic as Raolcan steadied himself and then swooped toward them like an arrow. He flamed across the bridge, sending humans and horses plunging to a watery death.

I held my breath, stiffened by terror as we turned to do it again.

My Raolcan.

My rock.

Fearless.

A second pass across the bridge and I was beginning to hope we could stem the tide of soldiers. Maybe we had a chance here! We could do it!

I clung to Raolcan's neck, channeling all the love and support I could into him.

We were going to make it!

A blow came from the side, knocking me loose from the saddle, I was flung hard against my straps. They creaked but held and then I was plummeting to the ground, dragged by Raolcan's heavier weight. Something had hit him from his blind side! I hadn't seen it coming to warn him.

Raolcan! Are you okay?

A cloud of reeking dust surrounded me. I couldn't breathe! I choked against it and then a second hit spun me in a new direction and with a *snap,* my strap broke and I was plummeting through the air, arms wind-milling as air whipped around my face.

I didn't know if I was screaming or not. Didn't know if the tightness gripping my heart was real or imagined, but the awful silence of my dragon's mind deafened me.

Something snatched me from the air at the same moment that I felt water spray on my face. I struggled against the grip, looking for Raolcan.

Where was he? Was he okay?

The dust was subsiding.

I thought that, perhaps, it was his purple form I saw sweeping down the roiling river and out of sight.

My heart burst.

Chapter Fifteen

"Don't fight me!"

I twisted to see Leng gripping my safety strap, hauling me up onto Ahlskibi's neck. We were flying low in the carved out riverway, along the water.

"Raolcan!" I gasped. "He went down the river!"

My crutch caught against Ahlskibi's saddle and Leng freed it, tucking it in beside me. Ahlskibi coughed, fell a little in the air, and then recovered, flapping up the bank of the river and then over the side. He was flying low to the earth.

"We have to go after him!" My gaze couldn't leave the river – not for a thank you, not to find comfort in Leng's eyes – I needed Raolcan to be okay. I didn't hear his voice in my mind no matter how hard I tried to listen. We needed to go after him. This battle meant nothing without my dragon whole and well.

"Ahlskibi is hurt," Leng said tightly at the same moment that I was jarred so hard that my teeth shut in a violent chatter and my neck jerked forward and then back.

I ripped my gaze from the river to the clods of flying dirt around us. Ahlskibi skidded along the ground, tearing a line through the grass on Shonan's side of the river. His great wings tangled around his neck and when he came to a stop he was limp and crumpled.

Leng leapt off his back racing to the head of his great dragon. I already knew there was nothing he could do. Dirt was packed around his head and forelegs from where he hit the ground.

Panicked, I scanned the world around me. It looked different from my place on the ground – tangled, chaotic, bloody. Dragons lay dead or dying in heaps, both near us and across the river. The army of Iskaris surged across the magical bridge, fanning out over the road and grassy hills to make space as more and more of them ran or rode or drove carts across the bridge. I watched as a knot of Magikas carefully crossed, holding their bubbling light in the center of their group the entire way across.

Up on the hill, Shonan and Iskaris still fought in a slow dance of death. Silver dragons ringed the hill, guarding the battle. All the other dragons – our dragons – were busy on the other bank, fighting the last of the shadowy Ifrits. Even if they won, we were too late. The ambush had failed.

Despair sunk into my heart as I carefully dismounted, leaning into my crutch. I hobbled up to where Leng stood by Ahlskibi's head. The Purple dragon's big eyes were closed but little steam bursts still came from his nostrils. Maybe he'd recover in a moment and we could go after Raolcan. He'd be okay. He'd wash up on the shore and we'd nurse him back to health and ...

My gaze met Leng's and I felt cold fill me, starting at my face and then spreading down to fill every part of me like freezing rain in winter filling a barrel and coating the sides with ice.

There were tears on Leng's face. Leng – who had faced torture and death. Leng – who had been hunted by the Dusk Covenant and tapped by Magikas to trap dragons. This Leng was crying.

I looked around at the dust and chaos, breathed in the pungent, eye-stinging smoke from patches of fire in the grass, heard the shouts of soldiers running just a dragon length from us as they ran to form up along the road and I realized that we were defeated. I couldn't catch a breath. I couldn't hold a thought. I didn't know what to do next.

There was only Shonan and his battle left to hope in. If he won ...

I gasped as a Silver dragon swooped down suddenly over us and yanked Leng off his feet. His eyes grew large and his mouth opened, but I didn't hear what he said before he was gone. Involuntarily, I reached toward him, feeling as if my heart had been wrenched from my chest. Not Leng, too!

I was yanked off of my own feet so suddenly that I lost my breath and then rough hands threw me over the back of a saddle. I grunted as the breath was knocked out of me. Wet leather and the smell of dragon filled my nose.

"Stay put," a rough voice said.

I lifted my head to see what was happening and received a cuff from a gloved hand in return.

"I said, stay put!"

I was shaking all over, my teeth chattering and my hands and feet trembling uncontrollably as we flew through the air. Not being able to see where we were going and lying belly-down over the back of a saddle without even being strapped in left me queasy and ill.

When the Silver landed, it knocked my breath out a second time, and then I felt the same rough hands winding rope around my wrists and ankles and then again around my middle, cinching it tightly to the saddle.

"There. You can watch your leader die before we move on. But don't try to escape. We don't have to leave you alive. It's only a courtesy to a fellow Rider."

I lifted my head carefully, expecting another blow, but the Dragon Rider who captured me was already dismounting. His gilded armor was dull in the shadow of the dark clouds above us, but his face had a noble cast to it and his dragon rider braids were familiar as he strode away from the Silver he'd left me tied to. The unfamiliar dragon rumbled under me. For the first time in a very long time, I felt fear at being on the back of a dragon.

All I could think about was how different this one was from my Raolcan.

I was trying not to think of Raolcan as dead. There had to be some other reason that I couldn't hear him in my mind. He would have survived the fall. He would be fine, floating in the river. Maybe he was hurt like Ahlskibi. Maybe he was just resting somewhere while he caught his breath. He'd been fighting for hours before he fell. He was probably tired. We were probably just too far apart to hear each other.

Excuses came faster than thought. But though my mind went through a thousand reasons, my heart welled up with sadness. It knew what I wouldn't admit – that only death would keep my dragon from saving me. Only death could keep us apart. And if he hadn't returned yet, he never would.

Chapter Sixteen

I didn't realize how close I was to the battle between Iskaris and Shonan until I heard Iskaris' voice.

"You weaken, boy."

Boy? Shonan had been a man for at least a decade. Did Iskaris really think that treating him like a child would mean anything?

My mind was racing. Shonan winning right now was our last and only hope. If he won, then he would pick up that mask and put it on and everyone would know Iskaris had deceived them and the Silver Dragon Riders and the men who followed Iskaris would have no choice but to switch their loyalties to Shonan. The Magikas would be another matter, but our dragons could deal with them. They were fighting the Ifrits and Magikas on the other side of the river, but we didn't need them there anymore. We needed them to help Shonan.

Part of me asked how they could help now when they couldn't help before, but the rest of my mind suppressed it. Shonan's battle was our only hope. The dragons were our only resource. I needed to match one with the other and it would work out.

But how? Raolcan was not here to direct them. I felt the dull pain where the Pipe dug into my chest between me and the Silver's saddle. Perhaps, if I wiggled around I could shift it out of my shirt and out to where I could grasp it in my lips and play it – not well, obviously, but playing it at all would do.

I twisted and wriggled, feeling like I was moving it by increments.

"You've got a live one there," a woman's voice said and then the rough voice of my captor responded.

"She's tied securely. She's going nowhere."

"Why capture her at all?"

"She's a Dragon Rider. Honor demands that the Dominar judge for himself what to do with her."

As if I wasn't already motivated enough. I knew exactly what Iskaris would do to me. I wriggled more, feeling the Pipe jab at my throat. Success! It was almost out of my shirt. I glanced up to see if anyone was watching me.

The guards were focused on the battle between Iskaris and Shonan. I watched as Iskaris made a tired lunge and Shonan barely evaded it. He was getting too slow. That lunge nearly had him. Sweat poured down the true Dominar's face, glittering in the light through the parted clouds. His dark face was grim but there was a sense to his expression, as if a part of him were tucked far away from all this – untouchable, unstainable.

Across the ring from me, Leng watched from the back of a saddle. He seemed unharmed, just as I was. He was tied, just as I was, to the back of a Silver dragon, but where Shonan seemed almost peaceful as he battled, Leng's face was torn with anxiety. This was his brother, fighting for his life. His dragon lay out in a field, vulnerable and hurt. And there was nothing I could do for him about either of those things.

I turned my attention back to the Pipe, my heart squeezing painfully in my chest. Where was the magic when you needed it? Where were the miracles?

The Pipe fell loose of my collar, still hanging on the leather string Hubric had made for it. It lay in a tiny ridge on the leather saddle and I leaned the weight of my head against my cheek on the saddle and carefully edged my face closer, trying to take the mouthpiece in my lips without knocking the Pipe loose from its perch. The seconds felt too long and the delicate maneuvering made my shaking worse.

After long seconds, I managed to grasp it, hoping beyond hope that it was still set to dragons.

I blew as hard as I could into the Pipe, note after note after note. Any help would be appreciated!

A rough hand yanked the pipe from my mouth and cut the leather strap.

"All that to blow a whistle? And who do you think is coming for you? Do you have a pack of dogs out there somewhere?" My captor laughed.

My eyes teared as I looked past him to see that he was right. No one could help us now. The air around me was filling with forest moths of every size and color. Their delicate wings were lit with gold around the edges as they flew in and out of the golden beam of light over the hill, but they brought no hope and no help.

The Pipe, it seemed, had been reset to butterflies.

Bitter despair filled me, as tears leaked from my eyes. Through my blurry vision, I saw Shonan look up into the sunbeam and smile at the moths above him. They swirled around him like the throngs that would hail him if they knew who he was, settling on his shoulders and the crown of his head. He looked so monarch-like in that moment that I wondered at the Silver Dragon Riders for not seeing it and bowing the knee to him.

They didn't.

Instead, Iskaris leapt like a snake, his sword stinging with such speed that it was as if he had been storing it up for that moment. He plunged his sword through Shonan's chest and as the true Dominar sank to his knees, Iskaris spun in an unfolding dance that ended when his sword swept across Shonan's throat.

I gasped.

Across the hill from me, I heard Leng's cry of despair as clearly as if he was beside me.

Everyone was silent for a heartbeat.

"Well, that's done, then," my captor said as if this shattering moment didn't matter at all.

Chapter Seventeen

"Witness this day, that the traitor is defeated!" Iskaris called, holding his sword over his head like he thought he was a hero. "Your Dominar's authority upheld."

I couldn't take my eyes off of Shonan. I hadn't ever actually believed this was possible. I hadn't thought it could happen.

Tears blinded me. Despite all my anxiety and worry, I had never really believed that we would fail – that Shonan wouldn't regain his rightful crown. That Leng and I wouldn't visit him in Dominion City and watch with pride from afar as he ruled again.

There was no happily ever after without Shonan.

Iskaris' words echoed in my head as I watched the rest of their army flooding over the bridge. With every heartbeat, they pounded that nail into my heart. Defeated. Defeated. Defeated.

Nearby the Silver Dragon Riders shifted uncomfortably, still loyal to Iskaris, but with grim expressions on their faces.

"Gather our wounded and our captives. We march now, to rid the Dominion of the Lightbringers and their schemes!" Iskaris' voice rang out firm.

No more dragons filled the skies. Any still living must have fled with the death of Shonan and disappearance of Raolcan. I had no Pipe to call them back.

Where was Ahlskibi? Had someone killed him as he lay wounded on the ground?

Where was Raolcan? I needed him so badly and I couldn't stop hoping ... couldn't believe ... no! I would not give up hope for my dragon!

Magikas swarmed across their bridge as the last of the army trickled onto the road beyond and joined the others winding their way along the twisting path. I bit my lip as I watched Ifrits go where the Magikas sent, speeding across the landscape – clouds of dusty intent.

Iskaris adjusted his mask, wiping blood off his sword in the grass. He pointed to Shonan. "Someone toss this traitor into the river."

My heart felt like it was tearing apart as they scooped Shonan up out of the grass, dragging him across the turf toward the river. The look on Leng's face broke me. If I was despairing, he was hopeless.

This couldn't be real.

Raolcan! Please, can you hear me? Please!

No thoughts came to me from Raolcan and I bit the inside of my cheek to try to keep from crying. He was not dead. I wouldn't believe that.

My mind felt thick. It was hard to think. The landscape was even shifting colors as the golden beams that pierced the clouds only moments ago disappeared now as more clouds moved in. From their dark depths, the first swirl of icy snow began to fall.

There was a cry and I looked up to see one of the Silver Dragon Riders pointing to the land across the river. The bridge the Magikas had made faded away. On the road from the north, a swell of black figures stormed across the ground, finally reaching the river – just moments too late. Their foreign dress marked them as the armies of Baojang and their stony expressions were as grim as when they raced through the warrens unafraid of sudden death.

They were led by a wave of creatures hovering in a uniform block – Sentries. If I still had the Pipe I could call them to come. They descended in an unsettling mass on a single Magika who had been forgotten or left for dead before the bridge was removed. He fell to the ground under the swarm and I looked quickly away. I knew how they killed their victims.

At the head of the army, three dragons flew: White, Gold, and Purple.

Jalla's hand extended out as she pointed toward our hill, her bearing regal and her cold expression unconcerned about the sudden setback. Behind her, Renn rode awkwardly as if he no longer was the rider of his own dragon.

Would they come for us? Of course not. There was an army here and only a few dragons and Sentries who could cross without a bridge. Beside her, I saw Hubric gesturing toward us as if encouraging her to fly to our rescue anyway, but Rakturan slashed a hand through the air in negation. He would never allow her to risk herself – or the army – for the two of us. His bright gaze met mine across the field and I knew for certain that there would be no rescue.

All my hopes and plans were destroyed with my army. At least Hubric had survived it. I felt one last surge of gratitude toward Shonan as the guards Iskaris had sent with his remains hurled him over the side of the bank into the boiling river.

Like a Purple bolt of lightning, Kyrowat leapt after him, surging upward a moment later, further down the river. In Hubric's arms, Shonan's corpse lay like a sleeping child. He'd be buried and his grave marked. At least he would be given that honor. Heaviness descended on my heart as if I was the one being buried, as if I was the one with a heavy stone laid over me to mark the end. It felt as if it really was me about to be buried.

Chapter Eighteen

The Silver Rider mounted up, his body blocking my view as he strapped himself in.

"I've got you until we make camp," he said gruffly. "No squirming. It makes Yarobet nervous. He doesn't like this whistle of yours."

"Who are you?" I asked. I was craning my neck, trying to catch a glimpse of Leng when the dragon he was tied to leapt into the air and I lost sight of it entirely.

"I'm Ralk Wheelspinner, Silver Dragon Rider and Guardian of the Dominar and the Dominion. Don't mistake my civility for mercy. You deserve the punishment that all traitors to the throne deserve." He said it so matter-of-factly as if it were obvious.

"What if I told you the man in that mask isn't the Dominar?" I asked as Yarobet's muscles beneath me bunched and then he launched into the air with a suddenness that knocked my breath out.

"I'd tell you that you're a fool. The mask is the Dominar. And I'd tell you to save your treason for the Magikas. They'll handle your imprisonment after tonight."

"He stole that mask from the true Dominar. He was a guard – just like you – a dragoon. Until he ripped the crown off his master's head and tried to kill him."

"Tried?"

"I stopped him."

He laughed. "That's a good story. A girl who can barely walk stops a dragoon and yet somehow he still steals a kingdom. Keep telling that story and maybe someone will take pity on you for your insanity and spare your life."

We climbed into the sky, the light snow swirling around us. Even my thick fur-lined cloak couldn't keep the wind from making my hands and feet numb. It felt, almost, as if someone had torn the sky and snow was falling out.

My heart lurched when we plunged through the black clouds to the bright sky above them. Kyrowat was waiting there for us, as if he expected us. All around, Silver after Silver popped through the clouds, but he stayed there, steady and solid, a cranky look in his eyes, a grizzled rider on his back and in the rider's arms the corpse of our hopes. They were stained with soot and sweat, but they still seemed untouchable. My eyes filled with tears as I caught Hubric's red-rimmed gaze.

Yarobet reared, flaming a warning but Kyrowat held his place as Hubric signed rapidly to me.

Remember the prophecies.

He nodded briskly and then Kyrowat dropped back into the clouds and out of sight, leaving me a prisoner while he went to bury our friend. I tried to keep tears of despair from overwhelming me. What good were the prophecies now? That's what Hubric spent his last word to me on? Tonight, when the Magikas had me, I would likely be tortured or killed and *that* was what he wanted to say? Not that he would save me, not that he would look for Raolcan, just to remember the prophecies?

We were at the end of the dream, at the broken edge of the bridge of hope. I'd been such a fool to think it could turn out any other way.

I'd been such a fool to believe in happy endings.

All of that was done. The only ending left was the one where they made me eat my hopes and dreams like a cannibal living on her own soul until the last bite took my life with it.

I didn't sleep or dream, but I did fall into something other than alertness as we flew slowly south. Ralk flew circles around the army, but from my position tied to the saddle, it was hard to make out any clear sight of where we were or what we were doing.

The hours faded and the crisp cold of a Fall night descended.

Eventually, we were circling over dozens of tiny red flowers that multiplied new flowers every few minutes. Fires, my weary mind told me. The army is below us, lighting fires. The dragons circle to protect their Dominar below.

Protect him from what? There was nothing left to fight him with.

Protect him from you, my mind said.

I laughed aloud.

"Ready for landing?" Ralk asked, as if it mattered whether I responded, but the landing was gentler as if Yarobet was trying not to hurt me, and I realized as Ralk's rough hands untied me that he was not intentionally harsh with me. He was just a man doing an unpleasant job, bringing a traitor to justice.

The internal part of me that watched the world from within must have broken in the fight because it was laughing now. Laughing at the men who served traitors thinking they were defending *against* traitors, laughing that Ralk was probably a good man with a good dragon and yet his good actions were destroying the last shred of good in the Dominion.

A deep voice startled him as he was finishing the job of pulling me down from Yarobet's back. He shifted in an almost protective stance over me.

"That's the girl you took prisoner? The Purple?"

"Yes, Dominar." He saluted.

He took my arms and turned me to show me to the Dominar. Iskaris stood in a dark shadow behind one of the pavilions. Firelight reflected on his mask, and on the helms of the five dragoons clustered around him – but faintly and from afar. We were on the far end of a dragon picket. Likely, that pavilion was his, guarded and tended by dragoons.

"She had a pipe with her."

Where had Iskaris heard of the Pipe? Did he realize what it did?

"Here, Dominar."

In the faint light from a nearby fire, something glimmered in the dark as it changed hands. The Pipe of Wings. In the hands, now, of one of our worst enemies.

"Interesting. Take her to the Magikas and give them this pipe as well." He handed back the object. "They are ready for her."

Fear stabbed through me as Ralk saluted and then marched me through the darkness. He stayed slow enough for me to hobble in the dark on a crutch, but kept a hand pinched uncomfortably on my shoulder.

"Don't risk your life in a fool's move," he murmured when I paused too long to catch my breath. "There's no one on this side of the river who can help you now."

As if triggered by his words, a vision flashed across my mind of Hubric and Rakturan carefully laying Shonan in a freshly dug hole. They climbed out, and Enkenay lay his mighty head down beside the hole and breathed into it. Shadows danced as the fire stream seemed to go on and on and on.

Ralk's grip tightened. "Come on."

I stumbled after him to the perimeter of a brightly colored orange silk tent. A pair of Magikas stood at the door, their ostentatious robes road worn and grimy. Around us were the sounds of tired soldiers pitching camp – eating, tired, tending wounded, tending horses, snoring.

"Special Delivery," Ralk said, pushing me forward and shoving the Pipe into the hand of one of the Magikas.

I gasped as they opened the door of the pavilion, so I could stumble in.

Inside the tent, a dark figure in a cloak stood, back turned to me.

Chapter Nineteen

The pavilion was too opulent for something thrown together in a hurry. From the silk tent to the patterned rugs laid over the dirt of the floor to the folding chairs and tables, I couldn't help but think that I hadn't seen pack horses or wagon trains to carry this much stuff. There were even a chest and a large mirror on one side of the tent. Was it possible that someone had met the army coming from the other direction?

Tall candelabras stood around the pavilion, lighting the tent brightly despite nightfall and Magikas stood quietly around the perimeter. Their sharp eyes watched me as I stumbled into the tent, but none of them spoke or moved to intercept me. Were they busy connecting to the veins of magic in the earth underneath me? Or were they waiting for the dark figure to turn?

I swallowed. Leng was not here. I would have thought that if they were going to interrogate me, they would interrogate him, too.

"I'm not going to interrogate you," the figure said, turning, finally, and lowering the hood of her cloak.

My mouth felt dry. Why was my good leg so weak? It felt as if it wouldn't hold my weight and my arm holding my crutch trembled.

I fought to remain in control as Starie Atrelan ran her hands through her long red hair to push it out of her face. Her black blindfold was not comforting to me. Darkness still escaped around the edges of it and seemed to pierce right through the cloth so that I could feel the oily touch of it on my skin.

I cleared my throat and glanced around to where the Magikas shifted uncomfortably, their faces white and eyes wide.

"I came to rein in a troublesome gelding, only to find an old friend was here." Starie smiled and I felt my own lips turning down in horror. Her smile was as wrong as a flower growing out of a corpse. "So, of course, I had to invite you to my tent."

My mind was racing. A troublesome gelding? Did she mean Iskaris? Had she traveled north to bring him back to Dominion City? But why would she leave her armies behind?

"They are in competent hands," she said.

Could she read my mind now?

Starie took a step forward, and the Magikas on either side flinched. She waved a hand, dismissively.

"I'll send for you when I need you. Stay close."

They scurried from the tent like mice from an opened box and I felt my jaw drop. Magikas – the most powerful people of the Dominion – *scurried* when Starie spoke?

"They fear me with good reason."

She really could read my mind.

"You should practice better mental discipline. Your thoughts are not hard to read." She gestured to one of the folding chairs. "Sit. Before you fall over. I don't want you dead before your time."

I sat carefully. Did she mean she didn't want to harm me, or that she didn't want to harm me *yet?*

"Yet. I have plans for you. Have you lost your voice? Or has fear made off with it?"

I cleared my throat as Starie sat regally in the folding chair opposite to me. Her smile had morphed into the grin of a cat playing with its food.

"I don't fear you," I said.

"Don't lie to me." But her words sounded like she was enjoying the lie. "I will know."

"Why are you here?" I tried. After all, if I could get her talking, perhaps I could find a weakness.

"There are no weaknesses to find. But I am happy to talk. It's why I called for you. Oh! And for one other thing."

She snapped her fingers and a Magika ducked his head into the tent. Starie held out a hand, palm up, and he rushed forward, placed the Pipe of Wings in her hand and then bowed low before striding out. He walked with dignity, but even I noticed his steps were too quick. He was afraid.

"An interesting trinket," Starie said, playing with the Pipe in her hands. She moved the lever from where it was set to butterflies. "And you called butterflies with it. Appropriate. You're a butterfly kind of girl."

I willed my mouth to stillness. I needed to keep my thoughts from thinking – Raolcan. I would think of Raolcan.

"Your dragon. Ah. Even the subconscious can betray you. Did you realize that?" Starie sounded so much older than she had before – she had grown up from the petty child whining for her own way.

Her head shot up from studying the Pipe to pin me with her hidden gaze. "Your friend Savette sees the light, doesn't she?"

We both knew that.

"And I see the darkness," Starie said. "Tell me, Amel, what is the night sky, but darkness? What is the universe, but deep, fathomless darkness? What is the ocean, the cavern, the heart and mind of man but endless darkness? When you stand in bright light it blinds you, but in the darkness, your eyes grow wider. You think that darkness has stunted me? What a joke! It has opened my eyes. I grow to fill the darkness, to fill the never-ending void. I am already greater than you think. Imagine what I shall become before the end."

I shivered.

"Yes," she said. "I see that you comprehend."

She twisted the Pipe in her hands, but she wouldn't be able to play it. At least I had that to comfort me. Jalla hadn't been able to do anything with it no matter what she tried.

Only *I* could play the Pipe.

Starie laughed, lifted the Pipe to her lips and played three notes so crystal perfect that it was like she had been playing all her life.

Gnats swarmed into the tent, biting and filling my eyes, nose, and mouth. She played again, and they were gone, leaving me coughing and gasping for air.

I felt like I couldn't breathe, like the world was going dark, and everything around me was being sapped of color. She couldn't ... wouldn't ...

"Don't underestimate me." Starie tucked the Pipe down the neck of her dress. "Anything you have, I can take."

My heartbeat filled my ears, pounding, pounding, pounding until my head was swimming and my vision was dotted with bright, lightning-bug lights.

She had the Pipe.

She could control dragons.

It was all over.

"For you ... it is all over." Her voice had a lull to it like a song for a child.

And then in the middle of my panic, a faint voice rang in my mind.

Amel?

Raolcan! He was alive.

Where are you?

I'm here! I'm here!

Dragon School: Starie Night

Chapter One

I*'m coming for you.*

Relief flooded through me. Was Raolcan hurt? How far had the river taken him before he surfaced?

Not far enough – not as far as the Feet of the River. I could have used the healing there.

You're hurt?

Not mortally.

If he was hurt, then he needed to rest. He needed to recover. He could come for me later.

Amel, nothing – not even death – will keep me from coming to your aid.

How were we even talking over such a long distance?

Our bond strengthens and grows. But now I must be quiet for a time.

Whatever he needed, he should have. I was just so happy he was alive. The tiny candle of hope I'd been carrying flared into a fire of hope.

"Don't think a conversation with your dragon changes anything," Starie said as she rose from her seat and turned to look at me over her shoulder.

I had almost forgotten where I was in my excitement over Raolcan, but now it all crashed back in on me. I was Starie Atrelan's prisoner. I was in her magnificent pavilion. She thought she could use me for her own purposes.

"I want to use you as bait in my trap for Savette," she said with a smile. "But for now, I have things to attend to, including bringing that masked man back to his senses. You'll be guarded by my Magikas tonight. Don't try to escape. I had them keep Leng Shardson. I remember the two of you being friendly. After all, you nursed him back to health all that time ago. I doubt you'd like to see the things I could do to him if you try to escape. I'll see you in the morning, Amel, we'll have much to discuss then."

She snapped her fingers and a pair of Magikas hurried through the doorway.

"You know your orders," she said to them. They bowed and seized me by the arms, pulling me up out of the chair. They had to drag my toes, carrying me in their haste. I couldn't possibly use my crutch when they held me this way and the tip of it bumped uselessly along the ground as we hurried out.

They pulled me through the darkness in silence as my mind raced. I was in the hands of the most dangerous person in the Dominion – Starie Atrelan. These Magikas served her like slaves – something I never would have expected from such powerful people! Worse, she had the Pipe of Wings – control over dragons everywhere. But there was good news – my dragon was alive, Leng was alive, and Jalla's army was untouched, even if it couldn't reach us yet.

What I needed now, more than ever, was to keep my head. There would be an opening somewhere for escape – or even better – to bring down Starie completely. But if I let my emotions take control of me, I would lose the opportunity. I needed to focus. I needed to be cold as the wind and hard as the rock to see the right moment to strike. This was not natural to me.

The tent they took me to was guarded by two Magikas. Their hands glowed and radiating out from them was a dome of faint purple light. The tent was surrounded by the dome and as we stepped into it, I felt a shiver go through me and a lasting chill stayed under my skin.

"She's your problem now," one of the Magikas dragging me said. "The Chosen One says to deliver this prisoner back to her pavilion at dawn."

The female Magika he handed me to shifted irritably. "Don't give her to me. Push her into the tent. You know how hard it is to concentrate like this."

He grunted and complied, but not before I saw the two guards frowning and shaking their heads at him. Whatever they were doing required concentration, did it? Hmmm. Every scrap of information I could gather would help.

I stumbled into the dark tent. The flap closed behind me so quickly that all I saw was a quick glimpse of some sort of pallet on the ground and nothing else. I tripped over something metallic with a *ding* and landed painfully on the ground, my crutch twisted under me.

"Amel? Is that you?" The whisper filled the tent.

I gasped in relief. "Leng! Are you hurt?"

"No," his own relief leaked into his voice and a moment later I felt strong hands helping me to sit up and unstrap my crutch. "Did they torture you?"

"No."

Strong arms pulled me to him and I leaned into Leng's chest.

"Amel, I'm so sorry – about Raolcan, about everything."

I leaned into him, letting the tears finally leak down my face as I pressed my cheek against his strong chest.

"How is Ahlskibi?"

"Alive. He's hurt, though. I can't hear his voice anymore. We're too far away."

I had forgotten that most Purples didn't have the range that Raolcan did.

"Leng, I'm so sorry about Shonan. I had hoped ... I had been counting on ... he was one of a kind."

Leng didn't say anything but I felt his chest shaking with silent sobs. I wrapped my arms around him, hugging him tightly as if I could hold him together with just my arms.

"I love you, Amel," he said, eventually. "If I didn't have you..."

His voice faltered, like he couldn't even say the next thought out loud. He let go of me for a moment to wrap our cloaks around us and some sort of threadbare blanket the Magikas must have left behind.

"I love you, too," I said.

"Can I hold you tonight?"

"Yes."

I don't know when I fell asleep, but his sweet breathing as I slowly drifted off was the only thing keeping me sane. Maybe I was doing the same thing for him.

Chapter Two

Morning came too quickly. We were given water and a thick porridge and a single candle to eat it by before the sun came up.

The Magika left us with a terse reminder. "Eat. The Chosen One wants you at dawn."

We did eat, but between bites, Leng tested the magic barrier surrounding the tent. He peeked his head out the side of the tent, running his hands across the barrier.

"It keeps us in," he whispered to me. "I can't force my way through. It's as tough as glass."

Neither of us dared to talk more about escape – not when every word could possibly be heard by our captors. I didn't dare tell him that Raolcan knew where we were or that there might be some way to topple Starie if I were careful. I did take out my book of prophecies and together we read again the prophecy that he'd quoted to me only a few days ago. It felt like a lifetime had passed since that day.

"*When the people of the earth sound horn of battle,*
And the land trembles and is torn,
When the skies are rent in sorrow,
And the depths bring help no more,
Then the lame and the blind shall lead them,
And guide them from the storm."

"There's something there," Leng said when we were finished. "It just keeps picking at me, like there's something I should be seeing there..."

"Well," I said, grimly, "the depths won't be bringing help anymore. The Troglodytes won't be coming to save me. Now, it's up to me to appease them."

"And didn't it look like the skies were tearing when Shonan died?" His voice faltered a little over the word 'died' like he could barely get it out. "When all that snow fell out of them, it was like they'd been ripped."

"Neither of us is blind," I said with a half smile. We were grasping at straws. We just wanted to have hope in something.

He held my hand as we finished our breakfast, like he couldn't bear to not be in physical contact with me. I couldn't bear it either. We were both drifting out beyond the point of no return. It was as if we had swum out into the ocean and been pulled by a current to a place where no one had ever been. We couldn't swim back and no one was coming for us. I just wanted those last hours to be full of him. I resented Starie for taking me from him. I resented our breakfast every time he let go of my hand to take a bite. I just wanted to hold on to him forever.

When we were done, he helped me strap on my crutch and gently brushed my hair from my face and helped me straighten it. His big fingers were surprisingly quick as they braided the stray hairs back. I bit my lip nervously at the sweetness of the gesture and then cupped his face in one of my hands to quickly steal a kiss.

He held my palm to his face and smiled boyishly.

"You don't have to rush. It's not like you're taking something I don't want to give."

Shyly, I stretched forward and kissed him slowly, lingering over the closeness, resting in the acceptance and welcome of his answering embrace. If these were our last hours or days, they would be sweet ones.

A cough broke us apart. "Time to leave."

I felt my cheeks heating as Leng moved to let me hobble to the side of the female Magika.

"I don't care what you do in here. But when we leave you obey, or you suffer the consequences," she said, as if she was giving us some sort of gift. Maybe she was. I didn't know how Magikas handled their prisoners other than the time we found them torturing Leng and Savette. Maybe not torturing us was a mercy from them.

My belly squirmed at the thought of that, but I schooled my expression to blankness and followed her out of the tent and through the camp.

The army camped here was larger than the one that had crossed the bridge. Clearly, Starie had brought them with her. Voices called across the camp as the first light of dawn lit up the snow-crusted field. Fires exploded in sparks as new wood was tossed in and pots or kettles were arranged over them. Sleepy soldiers stumbled out of tents or back into them in the general chaos of a huge group of people sleeping and eating out of doors.

"No distractions," my guard said, poking my back with a finger. I hobbled on.

"You're a Magika," I said, for lack of a better subject to talk about. "Have you been in the Dusk Covenant for long?"

She barked a laugh. "Oh, look at the lip on this girl! So, because I use magic you assume I belong to the Dusk Covenant? They should be flattered."

"Don't you? Don't you all serve the Dusk Covenant and their Chosen One now? Aren't you working with elements from Baojang and the Rock Eaters and Ko'Torenth to trade our dragons for power?"

Her eyebrows rose and she smirked.

"Sometimes, Dragon Rider, knowing only half the story is worse than knowing nothing. Your tongue is full of half-truths and half-understanding."

"Then enlighten me," I countered. I could see Starie's orange pavilion ahead, dusted in white snow. We would be there soon and before we arrived I was hoping for some shred of information to use against her.

"We – the Magikas of the Dominion – are the heart of this land. We are the power it was built on. It is we who craft dragonsteel. It is we who built the great cities of the sky and the wonders of this land - the bridges, statues, and healing arches. If we are telling you that something is wrong here, if we are saying that a treaty needs to be made with foreign lands, if we are the ones negotiating the price of it, shouldn't the rest of you listen?

"Our agenda here is the only thing left that can save the world. But no, you fool beast-riders and your misread prophecies think you know better, don't you? You just keep messing everything up, throwing up a half-obstacle here or thwarting a carefully laid subtlety there – like a dragon in a spun-glass shop crashing around and breaking everything. If this was left to you, the entire Dominion would be a burnt-out husk by now. You should be grateful for us."

We were at the entrance to Starie's pavilion now, but I wished we weren't. I wanted to hear more. The Magikas, it seemed, saw the world through a very different lens.

"Show respect in there. The Chosen One is our last hope."

She stalked away before I could answer or even ask her name.

Chapter Three

"Amel, excellent. You'll be traveling with me today," Starie Atrelan said as I entered her pavilion. She was seated before the large gilded mirror, brushing her long red hair while around her servants bustled packing up her blankets, folding chairs, and rugs.

I watched her arm where the tattoo ran up it. She'd received that in the mountains at the Dawn's Gate, but I was still puzzled about how. She caught my gaze in her mirror and grinned wider.

"I treasure your ignorance, Amel. It amuses me to no end."

I *amused* her?

"You wonder how I was marked when you are certain that only your false Chosen One could be marked, hmm?" She handed the brush to a servant beside her and tucked her hair back.

Something strange in the mirror caught my eye, but when I turned to look at it, there wasn't anything there, only a strange distortion that made the inside of the pavilion look different. Even Starie looked distorted for a moment, like a watery current was running through her.

A servant threw a black cloth over the mirror as Starie finished with it. I chewed the inside of my cheek watching as they carted it away. There had been something there. Definitely. Hadn't there? Or was my mind playing tricks on me?

Starie adjusted a leather cord around her neck, smirking at me. The Pipe of Wings hung from it, like an amulet of power. And of course, that was what it was. With it, she had nullified our dragon allies. With it, she could conquer the world.

"And I will," she whispered as she closed the distance between us. "And now, Amel, we go over the rules. It's handy that you brought a friend with you. Handy for me, that is. If you try to escape, I'll have one of his limbs removed with you watching. Try to take the Pipe from me, and I will do the same. Give me trouble? I will have the Magikas torture him in front of you when we stop for the night. Understand?"

I swallowed. I understood very well what Magikas could do to a man. And I was under no illusions that Starie had a heart.

"I understand."

"Good. Follow me."

She strode from the pavilion and I hobbled along behind her. The bright light of dawn was already spreading over the horizon and Starie's golden dragon was waiting.

"You'll ride behind me," she said. I felt my eyes growing wide. Why did Starie Atrelan want me to ride behind her? And would her dragon even allow that? After all, she already had taken from me what she wanted - the Pipe. "I want so much more than that. We have a lot of catching up to do."

A sick feeling welled up within me. What more could Starie want from me? And would I be able to give it without compromising the people I loved? The more I was around her, the more chance there was that I would do something that displeased her - and Leng would suffer the consequences.

Starie mounted promptly and then nodded her head briskly to a pair of Magikas who, grimacing, helped me up on the back of the saddle. The golden dragon snapped and snarled. Starie made an irritated clicking sound with her tongue until he settled himself. Golds had thick armor and the ridges cut uncomfortably into my thighs where the saddle didn't protect them.

All I could think about was the dragon I was supposed to be riding today. I hadn't heard from him again since that quick moment of assuring me he was still alive. Was he hurt? Was he with friends? Was there anything I could do to help him? The silence in reply to my thoughts was deafening.

The servants finished decamping and around us guards began to form up - mostly Dragon Riders, their faces steely and hard - with Magikas sitting behind them in the saddles two, three or four to each dragon. They wouldn't be able to fly all day like that.

"My actual army is not far," Starie said casually as I watched one of the groups of Magikas pushing Leng to their dragon. Our eyes met for a brief moment - just long enough to share a burst of courage and hope. "We'll rejoin them now that the task here is complete. We have something we need to bring south as quickly as possible."

She meant the Pipe, of course. With that she would win handily over Savette, but why was she being so mysterious about it? I glanced north, looking as far as my feeble human eyes could. I saw figures on the road, but no dragons and no Sentries. Likely, Jalla and her army were still building a bridge or finding another road to Dominion City. I couldn't rely on them for help. Anything I came up with, I'd need to be able to do myself.

At Starie's signal, the dragons around her leapt into the air and her servants and the Magikas unassigned to a dragon started down the road. Our own dragon took to the air, and Starie called back to me, "And now, Amel Leabrought, you will tell me everything you know or have learned about Savette Leedris."

Chapter Four

Around us, the snow had begun again, in little whirls and glittering puffs as if the world were trying to make up for the darkness of the times with diamond specks of sparkle.

I'd lost track of Leng in the flurry of dragons, but I noticed something about the enemy dragons around us. Their riders were dressed differently than the norm, their dragon rider braids tied up in topknots and their clothing bedecked with capes and jewelry instead of scarves. Interesting. It was as if their new allegiance had severed ties with the old and they felt the need to express that in what they wore and how they conducted themselves.

As if reading my mind, Starie answered my thoughts.

"It's a new age, Amel. The times and values you are devoted to are past. This is the future."

New fashions were the future?

"What do you know about Magikas and their power?" Her question had a testing note to its tone.

"They harness power from seams beneath the earth's surface." It felt strange to have my enemy – a fearsome wielder of dark power – engaged in such a simple conversation with me. Even now, black light emanated from her. It was hard to see it dead on, but it turned the edges of my vision blurry in a way that made my head ache. If I tried to look right at it, it wasn't there, and yet it was always present in the edges of my vision.

"In part, yes," she agreed as our dragon climbed higher through the swirling snow. The plains below were still dull, despite the dawn and the clinging wet cold seemed to penetrate through my clothing to my very bones. "But there is so much more than that. Magikas pull power from everything around them. And everything has some of the residue of the power that created it still within – people do, of course, but also grass and trees and even rocks."

"Rocks?"

"Where do you think Ifrits come from? They are creatures of life and dust. Sure, the life is needed to fill them, but so also is the dust. But that is not what we're discussing just now." She signaled to a nearby rider and our dragons all shifted to a slightly changed course. I kept my eyes on Starie. Perhaps, in the middle of this seemingly irrelevant conversation, she could tell me something about herself and if I was wise, perhaps I could use that to free us all. "Magikas pull on that leftover power - but it takes a toll on what they pull it from. There are deposits of it left in the earth from when the world began. Large, deep deposits and it is better if they pull their power from there. Not just better - but more effective. It's like the difference between harnessing the power of water from a raging river or harnessing it from gathering it drop by drop on a dewy field. You comprehend?"

I nodded, but she was facing forward and couldn't see. She seemed to take my agreement for granted.

"And now, those stores are mostly used up."

Wait. What? They were mostly used up? But that didn't make any sense. The Magikas I'd encountered were still using magic. They were throwing fireballs and building bridges and burning those resources up like there was an unlimited supply.

"People, it would seem, are terrible conservationists," Starie remarked indifferently. "I thought so from the moment I understood what I'm telling you now. They know their supply is limited. They know it can't go on forever and yet they use, use, use. Why? Because when it runs out that will be someone else's problem."

It was true that people were endlessly adaptable. If we ran out of linen for clothing, we would move to wool. If we could no longer grow rice, we would eat oats with as much enjoyment.

"There are ways to supplement it, of course. Ways to magnify the power that's left. But some of them don't want to lose the power that comes from tapping into the power of the earth. Have you ever asked yourself why so many Magikas are part of the Dusk Covenant? Haven't you noticed that none of them are with your precious Lightbringers? We don't care about your ridiculous claims to truth. We don't care about your romantic ideas about faithfulness to a lost ideal. We are concerned - and rightfully so - with our impending loss of power. We don't want to watch the Dominion die and her rivals eat what's left like ravens fighting over a half-eaten carcass in a field."

"You've allied with Ko'Torenth, Baojang and the Rock Eaters to destroy the Dominion," I said, unable to keep silent in the face of her lies. "Don't tell me you are trying to save our land!"

She laughed. "They should never have let you into Dragon School. They certainly shouldn't have released you out into the world with such a poor education. Grandis Elfar has been saying that all along, and she's right. It's only the woefully uneducated like you who can stand in our way now - and if you only knew ... but, of course, I am telling you.

"Listen, Amel. We aren't trying to destroy the Dominion. We're trying to save it - or at least save what we can. And yes, that means selling part of it to outsiders to keep what we can. And most of all, it means tapping into our strongest resource to buy friends where we can, so this whole country isn't overrun and our entire population isn't swallowed up by a stronger, more powerful nation. Yes, we've been making friends. Yes, we are giving them the dragons as a tribute gift - and as soon as possible! Yes, we will be giving them about two-thirds of Dominion held cities. What, exactly, did you expect would come as a result of the waste and irresponsibility of these last years?

"This is the last hope of our land. We must raise up defenders who can help us - Ifrits. We must destroy the dissenters. We must build a land strong enough to withstand the devastation to come. You think that you and your friends are going to save the Dominion? You're the reason this land is dying! It's only we - the last few people who really understand - the people at this world's dusk, who have made a covenant together to keep a remnant of this place alive - it is only we who can save the world now. And you're going to help us. It's time to begin."

Chapter Five

The clouds below us were clearing and the dragons dropped lower in the sky. As Starie talked, I was watching the landscape rolling under us. We were approaching the twin sky cities at the heart of the Dominion. I couldn't see them yet, but the fields below had changed from tall wild grasses to fenced pastures and tilled fields. Small specks of villages dotted the land below, but there was no smoke drifting up into the air. Were there still villagers in those little hamlets? Or had they fled the conflict?

When all of this was over, the Dominion would be in a precarious situation no matter who won the war. Our cities were devastated, our crops dying in the fields, unharvested. Winter approached, and with it would come hard, bare times unless we could end this quickly and take the time we needed to rebuild and store what crops we could salvage.

My belly twisted at the thought of taking care of all of these people. With Shonan gone, Leedris Castel fallen, and hundreds of our best dead or dying, who would lead us? Would Savette step up to take that role? Should I be worried that she was married to Rakturan? He would always hold his allegiance to Baojang above his allegiance to the Dominion.

"You should stop fretting about things that will never be your responsibility," Starie said airily. I hated that she could catch the edges of my thoughts.

She directed her dragons with her hand signals as she spoke in a way that reminded me of Grandis Elfar. Where was the Grandis? I would have expected her not to leave Starie's side. Was it possible that Starie had left her in charge of something? Something too important to leave unprotected? And if that was the case, what did that say about my enemies? Perhaps their trust was fractured. Perhaps I could use that to find a weakness ...

"If taking you out of Dragon School has made you that devious, then I take it back - it's a good thing you left."

I didn't care what Starie thought. I only cared about bringing down her reign of evil. Where was the frightened girl who had been forced to join the Magikas? The last time I'd talked to Starie, she had been a very different person.

"We've all had to grow up in the last months, Amel. Don't think you're the only one who has had to stretch into a new role. But now, we get to the point of this talk. Tell me about Savette Leedris."

"She's the Chosen One," I said, firmly. I knew it was true. I had seen the signs.

"No, no, that's me. Let's try this again. How did Savette acquire her power? It does not come from tapping the resources of the living earth like the power of the Magikas does."

"No, it doesn't. Savette's power comes from truth."

"That's an interesting perspective - though likely flawed. When did she first start to show her power?"

"She was taken by the Dusk Covenant," I said. "You know that. And she was brutally tortured."

"And that brought out her ability?"

"Yes."

“It wasn’t present before that?”

“No.”

She was silent a long time and I took the time to study the landscape, trying to gauge how many days it would take for the armies of Baojang to catch up with us.

"Power often comes from suffering," Starie said. "Yours or another's – it hardly seems to matter. I find it interesting. After all, we are the only two people I know who have a power different from that of the Magikas."

Then she didn't know about Rakturan. Or about Ephretti. Or about me. Because all of us had tasted Savette's truth-power and used it to help others.

"What sort of power do you have, Starie Atrelan?" I asked.

She turned around in the saddle so she could look at me face to face through her black blindfold. A smile curved across her face and I shuddered.

I was growing to loathe Starie's smiles. It was true that suffering and difficulty matured a person. I was deeper and stronger than I had been. So was Savette. The problem with Starie maturing, though, was that she had matured into something more deeply herself: she'd started as a self-centered, vindictive child. Now, she was all that but multiplied by a hundred and aged into a person who could wield power well to achieve her goals. Would I be able to find a weakness in her at all, or had she already shored up every opening? Was there any hope against an opponent who was clearly miles ahead of me in reaching her goals?

"I have the power of mirrors, Amel." I felt an icy stab go through me at her words. The memory of her mirror distorting flashed through my mind. What could you do that was magical with mirrors? "Where the Magikas need deep flows of life-force to draw on, I need only those droplets, because I can multiply them by mirroring their power back and forth and back and forth concentrating it to do as I will. I can tap the edges of their minds and amplify what is there. I can take the power of someone like Savette and mirror that, too. How do you think I achieved these marks?" She held up the arm that had been marked in the dragons' test. "It's easy enough to mirror another's power ... if you know the trick. And the dragons weren't watching for that. It never occurred to them to guard their tricks against counterfeit."

What did that mean for the coming battle? Could she mirror back at us everything we came up with? Maybe I should push her off here while I still could. I studied the straps holding her in place, weighing whether I could cut them or unfasten them quickly enough to pull them off in time. I wasn't tied in like she was and I was pretty sure that she could knock me loose before I could loosen her safety lines.

"How do you think that I hear your thoughts, Amel?" Her smile twisted, giving her an almost mischievous look that was at odds with her intensity. "I'm mirroring them back to you. It's the reason that I know I won't ... can't ... be beaten. Whatever you or your friends try to send my way, I can send back with twice the force. There's no way to beat someone who knows you better than you know yourself."

Chapter Six

We were headed toward a cluster of foothills when the dragons began to descend. Around the base of the hills, a massive camp was set up. Tents in rows, campfires, picket lines, and a long line of caged wagons filled the dips and valleys around the foothills and a massive set of three pavilions was set up on the hillside, so the leaders could overlook the camp. Jalla would approve - or she'd kill them all without a thought. I was almost starting to miss my 'blood sister.' I had a feeling that she wouldn't be hindered too much by mirror magic. Jalla had little to hide and revealing her secrets wouldn't stop her from ruthlessly destroying you.

Raolcan? I called out, hoping beyond hope that I would hear him.

There was no response. I took a long steadying breath. He was alive, wherever he was. I needed to manage my own business and wait. He would come as soon as he could and if he was anywhere near Jalla's camp, Hubric and Kyrowat would be helping him heal. They would take care of him. I just had to trust and focus on what *I* could do.

Starie was occupied with the landing, leaving me to study her camp. I didn't like what I saw. The guards circling the camp seemed attentive and the dragon section of the pickets was manned by Dragon Riders in proper leathers, though these ones were also dressed non-traditionally. I was most puzzled by the cages on wagons. They reminded me – in an uncomfortable way – of the wagons Savette, Hubric and I had been loaded into to be brought to Dominion City, except these ones had roofs, which made them difficult to peer into from above.

Arriving at this new camp made me feel like a drum was beating in my mind, slowly, one beat at a time, but it was speeding up with every step we took toward the final battle. Eventually, we would run out of time.

We landed in a clearing at the center of the camp. Whoever laid the encampment out had carefully thought through dragon landings. Starie's dragons circled in the sky waiting for their opportunity as dragons landed one by one, quickly hurrying off to the pickets. Dusk was descending, and I was already shivering and looking longingly at the fires as we landed in the field.

Starie's golden dragon snapped at the Dragon Rider who ran up to take his reins and Starie cursed at him, kicking him hard with her heel. There was no love lost there. Perhaps that was where her weakness lay, but she could have used the Pipe at any time if she really wanted to. Why didn't she use it to calm the Gold?

"I'm not going to waste my time getting to know a flying horse cart." She must have heard the edge of my thoughts. She turned to me as I slid off his back and adjusted my crutch. "You can cajole a person - or dragon - to do your will, or you can remind them who gives the orders. I'd rather train him to listen all the time and do as he's told. Then I can rely on him when there's nothing forcing him to obey."

Which was fine in theory, but in practice, the dragon hated her. And *that* was definitely a weakness.

"I'm done with you for tonight, Amel. Don't forget the agreement. You need to be on your best behavior." Her icy gaze swept the frosty camp. The snow was starting to swirl again, gathering in footprints in the mud and waiting long minutes before melting away as if it never was.

I watched the snow as a Magika hurried to my side and laid a powerful hand on my shoulder. Other Magikas rushed to greet Starie and on the hill. The door to the center pavilion opened as a familiar figure stepped out.

Grandis Elfar.

Perhaps the precious thing she was guarding for Starie was her army.

Starie climbed the hill, mostly ignoring the Magikas and nobles hurrying to fawn over her. I wanted to watch her greet Grandis Elfar - that greeting would be telling - but the Magika pushed me forward.

"Don't make me ask twice," he said, as if a push were a gentle request, but I knew better than to fight over that. I hobbled forward, responding to the pressure of his hand as he guided me through the camp, dodging hurrying servants and cursing soldiers, weaving between full tents and crackling fires. The soldiers were in good spirits, joking and calling to one another, but more than one sneer was directed at me.

It didn't take long to realize where the Magika was headed. Dread filled me as I watched the long train of caged wagons growing nearer. I scanned the area around my path, looking for any other option - any way to negotiate or cajole the Magika into keeping me out of those cages. - but there were no other options.

As if he were reading my mind, the Magika leaned in to make sure I could hear him as he said, "If you ask me, the cages are a waste of time. You're all traitors to the Dominion and you should die a traitor's death. As quickly as possible."

I studied the nearest cage as we drew level with it. A puff of smoke surprised me, and I stumbled slightly. As the Magika cursed, leaping back from the cage, the edge of a purple snout poked out and I caught a glimpse of the dragon inside.

"Rasipaer!" I said.

I thought he might almost be smiling in greeting, but the Magika pulled me away, forcing me back to the path.

"All you Dragon Riders are alike, fawning over the creatures as if they wouldn't take your arm off in a second if they were given half a chance!"

Someone hadn't had a good experience with dragons. From what I could tell, he'd probably earned whatever wrath he'd received. We reached the next caged wagon, and he angled us toward the door. A few figures were huddled at one end, but in the fading light, their faces were impossible to see.

The Magika called out and a guard hurried over from a few wagons down, keys jangling in his hand.

"Would you hurry it up? I want to drop this prisoner off so I can get some hot grub and warm up. Do you know how cold it is out here?"

“I have one, too,” a voice from behind me said. I tried to twist to look, but the Magika holding me slapped my face. “Eyes ahead!”

The guard with the jangling keys turned the lock and opened the door with a squeal of unused metal. “Here, move them in. Let’s get this over with.”

The Magika pushed me forward and I hobbled to the wagon, climbing awkwardly up the steps to the door. After a moment he grew impatient and shoved me in.

There was a growl from behind me. "Treat her with respect!"

Leng! I had just enough time to feel relief and then he was shoved in after me and the door was locked behind us. We were trapped.

Chapter Seven

I pulled myself to my feet, Leng reaching to help me as a voice from the other end of the cage interrupted us.

"I knew I'd see you again, Amel Leafbrought. And still alive. I was betting you would be."

I peered through the darkness. Ashana Willowspring stood at the other end of the cage, a pair of Dragon Riders on either side of her, purple scarves fluttering at their elbows and knees.

The murmur of our guard's voice drifted away in the night, joining the sounds of the camp - a constant dull noise, but with no clear words or sounds standing out from the rest. The worry knotting my belly mixed with the sounds to give me a dull headache. I limped forward, stiff and sore from a day of flying behind Starie.

I saluted. "For now."

Ashana looked us up and down. "Your dragons?"

Leng shook his head. "Ahlskibi lives - I think - but he was badly injured in our last battle and I don't know where he is. Captured, perhaps."

"Raolcan is alive," I said. "But I lost contact with him."

Ashana nodded briskly. "These are Eluci Daggerworn and Peln Vendris. We were taken by the Dusk Covenant two days ago."

"These cages seem well built," Leng said, joining the others. I followed him, worry filling me. I didn't like that they had us in these caged wagons. There was something about this that seemed strange. Why take prisoners this way? It was almost as if they had planned for it.

"I don't think they are for humans," Eluci said, braiding her hair absently as she spoke. "We've checked and rechecked them and they're built very solidly - overbuilt, really - no human would need something so strong to hold them. Why waste the resources and increase the weight for no reason?"

"What pulls them?" I asked. No single horse could pull something so heavy - not even a team of horses.

"They are using dragons to pull them." Ashana shivered. "Dragons are not made to be draft animals."

"We weren't made to be caged," Leng said.

"So, they built them for dragons then?" I asked, quietly.

Ashana nodded. "And they built them a long time ago - before this war started. I think they only have put us in here temporarily."

"If they want our dragons," Leng said, "They need to keep us alive. Every Dragon Rider they kill is one less dragon they can use."

Ashana nodded. "We concluded the same thing. But the Council and all other Dragon Riders are divided. Some are loyal to the Dominar. Others of us find ourselves drawn, instead, to our dragons."

Beside her, Peln shifted irritably.

Ashana laid a hand on his arm. "If I speak to these two it is because I trust them."

"She's not even a full Dragon Rider," he objected, pointing to me.

"Hubric Duneshifter says I am," I said quietly. "If you have so few Dragon Riders to call on, why worry about whether my title is formalized?"

"Because to formally be raised to the title you must pass tests and inspections that verify you have what it takes to join our ranks." Peln was frowning. "With Dragon School in complete disarray, it's impossible to determine these things. You could betray us thinking you were doing the right thing."

Ashana clicked her tongue. "Enough. Hubric said you were ready?"

I nodded.

"Then let it be so. She is raised a Full Dragon Rider of the Purple."

"You can't just-" Peln started, but Ashana threw up a hand.

"I can, and I did. Now, enough squabbling. We have limited time to hatch a plan before they decide to do something more than keep us in cages."

"They plan to use me as bait," I said calmly. "To trip up Savette Leedris."

"And you're fine with that plan?" Peln asked. "Savette Leedris and her rebellion are the last hope of saving our dragons. Do you know what they plan to do to them?"

"Yes."

He looked shocked. "And you're fine with that?"

"Of course not. I won't let her use me."

There was the sound of feet outside the cage and a call as two soldiers passed, calling drunkenly back and forth to each other. We all fell silent, huddling closer in the night.

"We'll wait until the guard changes to speak more on this," Ashana said.

"More waiting," Peln grumbled.

Ashana rubbed the bridge of her nose between her fingers. Her patience must be growing thin trapped with Peln all this time.

"We all have dragons we are worried about, Peln. Taking it out on each other doesn't help anything."

Peln had the good grace to look embarrassed before mumbling a 'sorry' and sitting down. Ashana sat down next to him and we all followed suit, forming a ring in the bottom of the cage. I missed the benches we'd had the last time. My bad leg always hurt when I sat on the ground. It was hard to get it into a comfortable position.

"First," Ashana said, "You'll catch me up on everything that has happened since last I saw you-"

“Actually,” Leng interrupted, “Now that we’re in the same place, I was hoping you’d grant my request.”

Chapter Eight

The dark of night was falling now, and the night was moonless. The only light in our cage was coming from the cookfires of the camp a little way off. I shivered, huddling into my cloak. What was Leng talking about? Ashana was hardly in a position to grant anything from the inside of a cage. And yet, she had an ironic twist to her lips as she looked back and forth between us and he was almost vibrating with the tension of whatever his request was.

"In the middle of a war?" She raised an eyebrow.

"Yes." I loved how firm and certain Leng's voice was. No matter how confused or unsteady I was, he was always a sure thing.

"With our enemies currently winning? With us caged like animals, and the fate of the world in our useless hands?" Her gaze bored into him.

"What other time would there be?"

He was smiling slightly and in the velvet darkness, he reached out and took my hand. I felt warmer - safer - despite where we were.

The caress of his calloused palm against mine – so real, so safe, so certain – comforted me.

My eyes strained in the darkness to see him, only seeing hints and flickers of his expression when the light caught it the right way. I shivered, conscious of the strange incongruence of the safety I felt with him and the evil all around us.

This was us. Two leaves rushing down the same waterfall side by side. Two doves huddling on the same branch in the storm. Two flickering candles holding off the dark of the night. Maybe someday there would be peace and sipping tea in safety together, but for now, a clinging grip of two hands, flickers of emotion in the corners of the mouth, hope in the eyes – this was enough. I could rest in this. I could treasure it forever.

Ashana laughed. "Well, if I am going to die tomorrow, I might as well help a pair of lovers marry tonight."

Beside her, Peln groaned, but my heart was beating a mile a minute. I had forgotten about Leng's request! He was asking her to marry us in the middle of a prison in an enemy camp!

My gaze drifted to the soldiers outside bent on destroying the land we loved, to the pavilions on the hilltop where Starie, Grandis Elfar, and their cohorts plotted the destruction of our dragons, to the darkness beyond the camp where somewhere our beloved dragons fought for their lives.

I would have liked Raolcan to be here. But I wouldn't miss this one chance. Besides, he probably would be complaining that it was too mushy for him. He would want us focused on defeating Starie and setting her army ablaze.

Coming...

Raolcan! I could barely sense him, but he was there - and he was coming! Excitement welled up for my dragon and for Leng. I felt like I could take down this entire enemy camp with the intensity and energy that filled me.

"Do you want to marry Leng Shardson, Amel Leafbrought?" Ashana asked, slicing through my reverie.

Of course, I did! The only thing I wanted more right now was victory.

"Yes," I said.

"Don't tell me. You're just going to say, 'you're married,' like you did when you raised her to Dragon Rider," Peln objected. "We have traditions and ceremonies for a reason First Rider!"

"We do," Ashana said, authority in her voice. "Ceremonies and traditions are vital to the future of the Dragon Riders and always have been so in our past. Through these traditions, we find meaning and our place in this world. We come to understand our shared values and agree to keep our promises as a group. But what are the fires of war and the famine of adversity but a kind of ceremony all their own, inducting us into a deeper kind of life?"

Maybe this wasn't a formal ceremony, but her words felt formal. And we were in the core of a war right now, we'd been swallowed down the throat of battle and found ourselves in the churning belly of conflict.

"A marriage between Dragon Riders," Ashana continued, "is different than most other marriages. Both Riders are dedicated to their own tasks, their loyalties to their dragons and to their Color, but at the same time, you are promising to have a greater loyalty to one another. It is complicated and not without strain. Dragon Riders rarely marry and are rarely given permission to marry. Do you understand that?"

"And maybe it would be a good reason not to do this now," Peln grumbled, but I didn't care that he objected. The whole world could object, and it wouldn't' change my mind.

Leng loosened his grip on my hand. Was he afraid? I felt a stab of uncertainty until I remembered he was the one who had pushed for this. He was the one who had interrupted Ashana to ask all over again. He was simply letting off the pressure, so I could decide for myself. I gripped his hand tighter to assure him that I was with him. I wanted this. No cost was too high for the chance to call him my own.

"Yes," I agreed, and this time I was proud that my voice wasn't shaking at all.

"Yes," Leng echoed.

"It is only because of the great loyalty and dedication that you have already shown that I am offering you this opportunity. I trust you will not falter in your other duties, that you understand that you are servants of the Dominion and that your own commitments will often have to come second to that. You are committing to seeking the good of the other above your own, to lifelong loyalty and to an intertwined life. Are these things what you want? Is this the truth as you see it?"

"They're true," Leng said, and his words were like granite. My breath was just a bit faster at the thought of him beside me through the days ahead. I felt warmth spreading through me at the knowledge that in these hard times, these toughest of tough days, he wanted to promise to keep loving me, to stay by my side, to keep loyalty to me close to his heart.

"Yes," I said aloud and this time my voice was quivering, not with uncertainty but with an intensity of emotion that I hadn't expected. I'd hoped for his love, but I'd been almost too afraid to hope that he'd offer me this - a future.

When I'd joined Dragon School I'd been looking for a purpose in life- and I'd found it. I hadn't expected the family that came with it and I'd certainly never expected this – a permanent place in someone's heart - a place guaranteed by promises and truth.

"Then we don't need a ceremony," Ashana said. "As the head of the Purple Dragon Riders, you have my permission. You are married."

I leaned into Leng, closing my eyes to savor the moment. I could smell his warm musk and feel his strength against me. If Raolcan was here, he'd be teasing us and laughing at us for getting married in a cage in an enemy camp, but nothing about our love had been normal or predictable. It made sense that our commitment to each other would take place in an unexpected way. I was just grateful for him - for his love, his strength, and the sudden hope that sprang up in me as I held his hand. Surely, in a world where Leng could exist, not everything was dark and hopeless!

"I have something more to say," Leng said, almost shyly. He turned so he could hold my arms, bringing his face down close to mine, almost intimately. "No matter what comes, Amel, I'm yours. I won't ever stop loving you, stop protecting you, stop helping you. No matter how our circumstances change, or how we change, I vow not to leave, not to give up, not to give half-heartedly. From here on, I am yours."

Heat flooded me and I was suddenly very aware of him so close to me.

"I promise the same thing, Leng. We've been through too much to ever walk away from each other. We've saved each other's lives over and over. No matter what happens next, I love you and I promise to be there for you."

The moment felt precious – like a perfect drop of dew on a sunny morning, like a feather floating in the air. I wanted to hold on to it forever.

"And now, you talk." Ashana's tone changed to something that had a growl behind it. Beside her, the other two Dragon Riders seemed to perk up. "Tell me everything that has happened since last I saw you."

"At least let them kiss first," Eluci said, speaking up for the first time. "It's not a proper wedding without a kiss."

And she was right.

Leng gathered me in his arms, feeling in the dark to find my waist with one arm and to cup my face with the other hand. His lips were hot and gentle, fierce but yielding. As if it were the seal on the promise we'd made, it seemed to brand our new place with each other onto my heart and into my flesh. I wanted it to go on and on, to lose myself in the moment and forget the war and the cold metal surrounding us as I fell into him. I felt my cheeks heating, as if the blaze within couldn't be kept inside. He was mine! Mine!

I should have stayed away. I finally get close enough to hear you and I get this! I did not *come back for squishiness! There's a war to win, Amel. Am I going to have to come down there and do this myself?*

Chapter Nine

We talked long into the night, sharing information before we drifted off to sleep. When the Dragon Riders were finally talked out, I slept curled up against Leng, sharing the warmth under both of our fur-lined cloaks. There was something so precious about laying my head on his chest and listening to him breathe as I fell asleep and something so fleeting about the way our shared warmth would flee with any movement under the cloaks. It, like the preciousness of the moment, was too fragile to last.

I woke to the squeal of the cage door as it opened and a Magika called from outside the cage. "We're here for the cripple. Send her out."

I untangled myself from my cloak and pulled myself up, adjusting my crutch and cloak. Outside, the Magika cursed and pulled one of his magic whips from inside his own cloak.

"No need for that," Leng said from beside me, sleep still thick in his voice. "She is only gathering her crutch."

He looked up at me, concern in his eyes. We were together in life now, our fates intertwined. He hurried to stand, pulling a scarf from where it was tied around his waist and wrapping it quickly around my hips and cinching it tight. I knew what that meant now. Dragon Riders didn't give out scarves without a deep meaning and this scarf – wrapped around as much of me as he could get it – had the deepest meaning of all the scarves I wore. I liked the feel of it there – like a snug reminder that we were tied together now.

“Don't worry,” I whispered.

“Be safe, heart of my heart.”

His fingers brushed mine in a goodbye before I hobbled out of the cage, sending him a last fleeting look as I left.

Would I see him again?

That question had weighed heavily on me before, but now it had a heavier feeling to it, as if our commitments to each other made the link between us both more powerful and also more significant. If one of us fell, it would drag the other down in a way that wasn't possible before. If one of us rose, it would pull the other up, too. It was a strange thing to feel, but just as precious as that fragile warmth and in a way, it kept me warm inside as the Magika pulled me roughly down the steps.

He was no longer patient enough to let me walk at my own pace, gripping my elbow to pull me through the skim of snow that coated the tents and ground and made everything seem brighter somehow.

"This whip isn't for show. Keep up or feel its bite."

I ignored him. I was already going as fast as I could. Whipping me would only slow me more. These Magikas were on edge - too on edge to realize the idiocy of their threats. I needed to focus on that. Where there was edgy behavior, there was weakness and where there was weakness, there would be opportunity. If I watched carefully, I might find out what that opportunity was.

We hadn't settled on a plan last night. Ashana's account had been simple enough. Having rescued the refugees in the warrens and brought them to the lands of Haz'drazen, the Dragon Queen had been kind enough to deliver her to the Dawn's Gate. After the chaos there had subsided, she'd hitched a ride to Sky City and helped the Lightbringers in their underground work there until Rasipaer had returned. After that, she'd been running messages for Savette along with the other Purples loyal to the true Chosen One. It was while they were running a message to Casaban that they had been caught by Starie's Magikas and Ifrits and pulled from the sky. None of that helped with a plan. And I needed a plan and needed it quickly.

"Have you been a Magika long?" I asked my guard, making conversation as we slipped through the wet grass and slick layer of snow.

"What's it to you?"

"I'm just making conversation."

"Save it. We all know your fate. There's no point getting to close to someone who has only one purpose."

"As a prisoner?" I asked, poking to see if I could get anything more out of him.

"As bait. Either you will be tortured for your friend to see or you'll be left alive long enough to draw her out of Sky City and bring her into the reach of the Chosen One. After that, all you'll be good for is raising an Ifrit."

I shivered, but not from the cold. I knew how they raised Ifrits. Somewhere around here, there was a dust demon made from the life of my old friend Tomas.

I wondered, idly, as if my mind were trying to distract itself, how the Ifrits did in the snow. They didn't like water. They hid under rivers and avoided them when they could. They liked to stay in touch with the dust from which they came. How did they cope on a landscape coated in frozen water?

We had a long walk to Starie's pavilion. My guard, strangely enough, seemed to be a favorite in the camp. At every campfire we passed, someone called out a greeting to him or bowed respectfully. He returned their calls with comments equally cheerful. How strange. To me, he was the boogeyman come alive. To them, he was a buddy.

Starie's soldiers worked industriously to break their camp despite the early hour, packing up tents and pots onto packhorses and carts. We'd be leaving soon, I could tell. I wondered if I should expect to ride with Starie again. It seemed that she wanted to keep me close.

The pavilion was open to the air, the door flung wide despite the cold and snow. Starie and Grandis Elfar stood close together, speaking in low, intense tones as the servants around Starie packed up the pavilion. They finished speaking as we entered the tent, the Magika bowing as he arrived.

"Your prisoner, Chosen One."

"Return to your duties."

He bowed and left, but the Grandis took his place beside me, looking me up and down and circling me as she did so.

"Not healed, then, are you?" she said, her eyes narrowing. "And yet you have survived. I never would have credited it."

"I thought you had faith in me," I replied. It still stung that the most fair-minded and kind of the Grandis had proved to be my enemy.

"I never said that."

“I thought you cared about the students of Dragon School.”

Her face grew hard. “I care about the Chosen One, Starie Atrelan. She is our only hope to keep this world from drying up like a rag left in the sun. And

I'll sacrifice anyone and anything that I have to if it means keeping her alive." She shot a look over her shoulder at Starie. "Remember that. And don't grow so soft that you fail us all."

She stormed off, leaving me with a creased brow and more questions than ever before.

Chapter Ten

Starie's expression was furious when I finally looked at her. The Grandis might be her ally, but there was no love lost there. Was that why the Magikas were so jumpy? Was it because their leadership was fracturing? Perhaps it was why she kept seeking me out. They said it was lonely at the top. It must be even lonelier when your friends were nervous of you and you couldn't be left alone with your conscience.

One of the servants brushed too closely to Starie and the false Chosen One spun, her mouth firming in rage. She tilted her head to one side and there was a burst of dark light around the servant woman's face. My gut twisted as dark ooze ran from the servant's eyes and she fell to the ground, lifeless.

I swallowed, a tremor running up and down my legs. I had almost grown used to Starie and her black mirror magic. Had I begun to think of her as tame instead of the evil killer she was?

That heartlessness! This was the woman the Dusk Covenant wanted to lead us. I bit my lip, letting the taste of blood remind me of what was real.

"You waste what's left of the world's magic just to settle an irritation?" I asked, not able to control the warble of emotion in my tone. A woman who would kill out of annoyance would kill for anything.

"I didn't waste it. Remember what I told you? I use mirrors to enhance magic."

I looked around. There were no mirrors nearby. They'd already been packed. There wasn't even a shiny object nearby.

"It's the eyes. You know how they say that the eyes reflect the soul? It's true. They reflect everything and that's all the mirror that I need."

Starie crossed to the last table that hadn't been packed yet, picking up a battered book from the tabletop. "Did you know that there's a book about me? But, of course, you did. You have your own book of Ibrenicus prophecies. It's scary how accurate it is. Scary for my enemies, that is. Have you read it, Amel?"

"I have." My hand drifted unconsciously to the pocket that held my own copy of the prophecies.

"Listen to this one," Starie said.

"Corrupted in the last days and trickling from the earth,
Dying in a bloom of power
The old passes and the new comes
Mirror of the old but amplified
Greater than the power which gave it birth.

Accurate, don't you think?"

It was accurate. The prophecies always were. But they didn't necessarily mean what she thought they did. Perhaps it meant that our nation and power structure was shifting, not the magic systems like her mirror magic.

"I found my power that way," Starie continued, striding out of the pavilion to where a line of dragons was being readied. Grandis Elfar was at their head, pointing and ordering servants and soldiers around like a High Castelan might. "Grandis Elfar brought me to the Healing Arches with a group of Magikas. It was the first time that they called up an Ifrit – ever – right there, from the pool of magic in the Healing Arches. It's funny what you said about how they brought out Savette's power through suffering because that's exactly how it happened for me, too."

Around us, there was a bustle as the first soldiers and caged wagons began their journey along the road. Everyone else was issuing orders or following them, gathering supplies or strapping them in place, extinguishing fires, drinking a last cup of tea, cinching straps and calling back and forth or up and down lines of men and women in squeaking leathers or clinking armor. Even the Magikas, usually slow and dignified in their movements, were hustling and hurried as they prepared to march.

Anxiety filled me as I watched them work. All these people were working against the future of the Dominion – whether they knew it or not.

A servant ran up with a breakfast tray for Starie and she accepted a bowl of porridge and gestured to me to take one.

"Eat now. There will be no more for a while."

"Thank you." I took the offered food and began to eat, but I wasn't distracted by the moving people or the hustle of the camp, my attention was fully on Starie. I had a feeling that what she was telling me was deeply important.

"The Magikas gathered around the arches while the Dragon Riders stayed nearby. We were transporting them, and also working as a security force, but I ... I was curious. I wanted to know how they were going to do it. I'd heard the whispers that they were raising an army for the Dusk Covenant. I knew why it mattered ... but I didn't know at what cost."

She stopped to take a bite and I ate, too.

But I wasn't thinking about the food. I even kept my face clear of emotion when I watched Rasipaer's caged wagon rumble past, pulled by a pair of furious dragons. Magikas in dark robes whipped them from either side to keep them going. Fury and bile rose in me equally. There would be a way to end this. I would make one if I had to.

Around Starie's throat, the Pipe of Wings flashed silver. I forced my gaze from it. I didn't dare show how badly I needed it back.

"I left my post and stood just behind the circle, watching. They were having trouble drawing up enough of the power from the well and someone suggested that if they could just start the flow of power then the rest might pour into it. It was in that moment that someone noticed me - Jasin Heedrunner, a Magika apprentice. He pointed across to where I was standing and before I knew it they had tied my hands and feet and drawn a knife. I thought I was dead. I thought they were furious that I'd been spying on them. I didn't realize until later that it was my blood that they needed for the life power. What they did ... I won't tell you. Not because I want to protect you. Not because I don't think it should be spoken of. Because I don't want it duplicated."

She turned from her breakfast to look into my eyes through that fear-inducing black veil and the spooky gaze made me freeze in place. I swallowed, my legs feeling like jelly under me. She wouldn't tell me about how she was tortured because she thought people might want to try it for themselves? What kind of person would think that?

Her mouth was a determined line. "I don't want anyone else to have what I have. Because it was the things they did to me - the terrible way that I suffered - that changed everything. I remember looking into Grandis Elfar's eyes during the worst of it. She'd come closer then to plead for me – I think. It was the reflection of myself - of what was being done to me - in the black depths of her eyes that triggered something in me. I reached into that blackness, dove as deep as I could, and the mirror magic bubbled up. It reversed all my wounds. It killed the ones who had tortured me. It touched me with that deep, reflected darkness – and in the rebound of their power, it brought to me the first of my pure soldiers. Creatures of blood and dust. Pure of intent. Born of darkness."

"Ifrits," I whispered.

"Yes." She smiled in that eerie way she had of only letting the edges of her mouth turn upward.

"Ifrits. And with them a darkness that has filled me and fueled me ever since. Do you know how to end suffering and bring the magic back into the world, Amel?"

"Yes."

She laughed. "Oh, I doubt that. You're doing everything in your power to stop it. You want the suffering and madness of this place to continue. I don't. I want it to end. And I know how to fix everything."

I couldn't help myself. I had to ask.

"How do you fix everything, Starie?"

"I end it."

Chapter Eleven

We traveled the rest of the morning in silence. Starie wanted me close to her, but she seemed to be done telling me her secrets. There was no love lost between her and the Grandis, though it was the Grandis who bound my hands when they loaded me onto the back of Starie's dragon.

"You wouldn't want her to push you off," she said by way of explanation. Starie had laughed at that as if it was the biggest joke in the world. After her revelations to me, she shouldn't be so certain. I could almost do that without a qualm. When Jalla had wanted me to kill her war leader, I had never really considered obeying. This was different. This person wanted to destroy the world.

We traveled until noon, the dragons flying loops and circles to stay with the army and the Magikas whipping the walking dragons mercilessly to force them to pull the caged carts. Most of the carts held a dragon or sometimes even two of them, packed in the cages so tightly that they were like extra blankets stuffed into a chest. There were only two cages that held people and I watched the one with my new husband in it often.

Eventually, we reached the plains between the twin sky cities, angling to a spot just north of the torn and muddy plains. As the scene slowly grew clearer and clearer, I felt my breath quickening and my belly knotting.

It was here, in these mud holes and chewed up earth, that the battle for our future was being fought. It was in the ragged remains of Sky City and the stark silhouette of Dominion City that the generals and castelans planned the moves of their armies and dragons. It wasn't until we were closer that I could make out the sprawling camps of soldiers. Between the two armies, fragmented walls in various states of dilapidation wove twisting lines. Defenders clustered at the haphazard walls, clouds of Ifrits or bursts of colorful dragons breaking up the otherwise monotonous mud-tones of the battlefield. How many days had they fought? How many weeks.

"Many. The end draws near," Starie said. "We have pushed them almost to the edge of Sky City. We have ground them into paste beneath the feet of our soldiers. Our Ifrits have torn down their defenses and shattered their dragons. The end draws near. But none of us wants to lay siege to a city. A siege could go on for years. Best to draw them out. And that, of course, is why you are here."

On the north end of the battlefield where the landscape began to rise toward the northern mountains and hills, someone had erected a massive platform. It was on that platform that we landed when the sun was at its zenith.

Rocks had been thrown into a pile larger than my village to create the base of the platform, a timber floor laid over the rocks and a pair of towers built on the northern side of it. The south side was free of obstacles – clearly built to look out over the battle. Strange that no one was fighting here. Both armies were far away in the field below.

"There's no military advantage to the platform," Starie said. "Unless I am here."

Grandis Elfar landed beside us. The Magikas she was transporting dismounted immediately, spreading out across the platform.

She was careful not to look at Starie as she spoke. "I'll meet with the Generals immediately. Your purpose remains the same?"

Starie's voice sounded firm. "Yes. I'll draw out the pretender. Only then, can we strike a final blow."

Elfar nodded, still looking into the distance rather than at her protégé. "And the Dominar?"

"Is less than a day behind us. He and his army will be here in time for the final victory."

"Good." Her dragon kicked off again and she was gone before I could wonder why she wouldn't look at me.

"She takes her duties seriously. She always has. It is hard for her when it is time to make necessary sacrifices," Starie said. She was scanning the battle below us. From here, picking out details was hard. All I could see was the ebb and flow of masses of black-clad soldiers. The occasional school of dragons or cloud of Ifrits was easy to pick out against the monotones but seeing a single soldier in that mass of bodies would be impossible. What was she looking for?

"There," she said eventually, pointing to a place in the field. Behind me, other dragons were landing and offloading their Magika cargoes, while below us on the ground – and a little way off from the platform, Starie's army was parking the cages and stowing their cargo wagons. I followed Starie's finger with my gaze. "See the bright light around her?"

Savette! I could see her there, across the battlefield. Starie was right that her people and their ragged wall were pushed up almost to the base of Sky City. Still, she fought, white light pouring from her hands as she disintegrated a cloud of Ifrits. It was amazing to see, even from so far away.

"Dismount," Starie said, cutting the rope binding my hands.

The dark light from her eyes was even more intense now, as if proximity to Savette's light made them brighter – or was that darker?

I rubbed my wrists awkwardly after so many hours of being tied up and then followed her down. We were standing at the edge of the platform and the drop beneath us made me think of Dragon School.

"I'm glad that I had time to tell you why everything must be this way. It will make what comes next easier."

I looked from Starie to the drop and back again. There was no one else here. If I timed a push just right I could knock her off the platform. I could end this now.

I lunged before I thought, pushing off with my crutch and rushing toward her with all the speed I could muster. Fear and courage pulsed through my veins so that all I could hear was the roar of them as I flew through the air.

I froze, neither foot touching the ground. No!

Around me, darkness pushed. I couldn't see, couldn't breathe, could even hear. And the edges of my vision, there was nothing but the mind-bending darkness of Starie's mirror magic and the pull of it as it tried to refract me into nothingness.

Chapter Twelve

I woke up to a hard surface under me and a pounding headache. My face hurt. I reached up and felt blood.

Someone was standing over me. Between her boots, I could see the battle raging on the fields below. Savette stood at the front of her troops, flaring with light again and again. Even from here I could tell her head was held high.

I flashed into her eyes for a moment and felt her movements – lightning quick as she spun. A massive Ifrit bubbled up from the dust in front of her. He snatched up one of her wide-eyed soldiers, cracking the man in half in his monstrous grip and then tossing him aside like a fallen leaf. Savette's arm shot out and with it came her light. The Ifrit flared with light for a moment and then dissipated in a burst of dust and ashes. Around Savette, her soldiers doubled over in coughing and hacking, but when their eyes met hers there was nothing in them but utter devotion. These men and women would fight and die for her.

There was a battle cry from nearby and a line of soldiers rushed toward her position. I recognized the man at the front. General Honorspur was exactly as he had been the day I met him – when Starie killed another general before his eyes. Now, he fought for the false Chosen One, rushing toward Savette, his men a vanguard before him.

The soldiers around Savette seemed to gain courage rather than melt away. They swelled forward, calling out her name.

"Savette Leedris! The Chosen One!"

The first clash of steel on steel was joined by Savette's flare of light.

I snapped back into my own mind, panting from the intensity of the battle below. Now only tiny figures on the massive field below, the armies crashed together like waves across the sand. I had the strangest feeling that someone was looking through my eyes. That had better not be Rakturan!

The boots in front of my face shifted and a voice growled.

"You can stay down there or get up. It won't matter. Either way, this fight is done for you."

I looked up at Grandis Elfar. How long had I been unconscious? It must have taken her at least a little time to meet with the generals. Had it been hours? Days?

"We could put up a dome around her," one of the Magikas offered.

"Unnecessary," the Grandis said. "You have your own work and I can deal with this stray."

It was strange to see her here, standing over me. She'd been doing her best to avoid Starie and me. Perhaps her conscience troubled her. Had she received what she hoped from helping Starie to power – from maneuvering things to put her in power? She didn't seem to have the prestige or honor I would have expected from someone in her place.

Guards stood a few steps away, but they weren't needed. The Grandis held one of the dragon whips in her hand. It was unfurled, ready to lash out at a moment's notice. That was more than enough to keep me in check.

"It's done for you too, from what I've seen," I said, my voice rougher than I had expected. I raised a hand to my cheek and felt blood. Fighting dizziness, I sat up. My arm hurt where the crutch was digging into the skin. It had torn a divot through my forearm when I fell, but the blood there was already dry, a scab forming over it.

Grandis Elfar didn't respond. Interesting. When I was angry – when something cut too deep – that was when I didn't speak. She was angry, too. I needed to spread division here. That was my only hope against an enemy with such an advantage.

"Is that General Honorspur in the field? How strange. I would have thought that a man of his position would be somewhere safe, not slogging through mud with his troops."

"The General is honored to fight with them," the Grandis said, but I heard the note of tension in her voice.

"Is he? Or did Starie use her eye-magic on him? Did she look him in the eyes and tell him what to do so that he thought it was his own idea?" I pulled myself painfully to my feet. "Has she been doing that to you? Maybe it wasn't really your idea to bring her to Dominion City and announce her as the Chosen One."

"Of course it was," the Grandis said, but her eyes were on the field, watching General Honorspur and she was answering me as if I were her equal, as if I had the right to question her. No person at her level of importance would do that unless they wanted to talk – unless they hoped that I had the insight they needed to make sense of something they'd suspected for a long time.

"Was it your idea to bring an innocent girl – someone in your charge – to a violent magical ritual?" Her head shook almost imperceptibly. She probably didn't realize she'd even moved. I pushed harder. "Was it your idea to let them-"

"The prophecies have been fulfilled in her," the Grandis' voice was quiet. Was she afraid that if she spoke louder she would shatter the lie?

I matched her quiet tone. "Which ones?"

She began to quote the prophecies, but out of order. I frowned as I listened. Was there a thread running through them?

"*Corrupted in the last days and trickling from the earth,*
Dying in a bloom of power
The old passes and the new comes
Mirror of the old but amplified
Greater than the power which gave it birth."
"*In dust and deception, I am made,*
Bound by water and blood.
Who may retrain the dust storm or calm the call of water?
Who may feed the maw of the earth?
Is it not you, dark one?
Is it not your dusk descending upon us?
"*Twice dead, she rises.*
Her rising a sign of salvation.
Favor from the heavens.
Relief from the fires of hell."

The Grandis paused for a moment. "She died that day. I'm sure of it. Died in body and in soul. Twice dead." Her face went pale as she spoke the next words. "*Twice blind but still seeing, The only bulwark against the dark*"

"And what makes you think that she didn't trick you into thinking those words applied to her?" I asked. "What makes you gamble your future on them."

The whipcrack startled me. The tip of it hit me across the face, splitting the skin in a burning line. I shuddered, a cry escaping my lips. I almost missed her next words as my brain fought to maintain consciousness. My hand was holding my torn face, the other one gripping the crutch in a jelly-like wobble. Inside, my emotions warred against a sudden thought 'oathbreaker.'

The lash did more than sting my face – it sent a stab of magic through my brain triggering every stray thread of guilt or shame that was lodged there. I felt, deeply, the guilt of being rescued when he fell. I felt the heavy burden of the deaths of innocents in Vanika, the deaths of soldiers in the warrens – my fault and every other breached covenant and willful deception of my short life. I shuddered under the weight of it.

Grandis Elfar waited until I recovered enough to look her in the eye. Her words were a hiss.

"I believe."

Chapter Thirteen

Raolcan! I called mentally, bracing myself against the continued effects of the whiplash. I couldn't allow myself to admit the guilt it forced into my mind. It would have no control over me.

I held my injured face, pushing back tears. Carefully, I unwound the scarf Ashana had given me when I became a Color, holding it against my right cheek. There was a split on the bridge of my nose, too, but most of the damage was to the cheek. It stung, but not as bad as the pain inside.

I'm here.

I gasped in relief, all thought of physical or mental pain evaporating at the feel of his mind. He was here! He was finally here! So many days of longing and hoping, of worrying and wondering and he was here!

I choked back my sob, scanning the sky for him. Grandis Elfar was already marching away, and the guards she had left drew in tighter around me. Magikas or not, they didn't stand a chance against Raolcan!

He wasn't over the battlefield. I studied it carefully, noticing the surge as Savette's smaller force rushed forward and General Honorspur's line opened up, letting them in like a flood.

He wasn't over the towers at the back of the platform. Starie was on one of them, the Pipe held to her lips. My breath caught as I heard the sound of it playing out a tune I'd never heard before. If Raolcan was in the sky, was he being controlled by her?

Not in the sky. Not affected by the Pipe.

Then why was he so quiet? It wasn't like my dragon to be quiet when there were people to mock and enemies to fight.

I looked to the north and my breath caught in my throat.

The Dominar had arrived. His army marched forward and without stopping for rest they hurried down the road toward the field of battle. In minutes, they would be there – reinforcing the already greater forces arrayed against the Lightbringers. There was no way Savette could stand against that! We needed to do something right now!

And then I saw him.

He was surrounded by Magikas, whips in hand.

They'd tied a chain around his neck – many chains, enough for each of them to hold one. And chains were wrapped around his eyes. No!

His head hung as he walked, his snout almost bumping along the ground. That was not my dragon – tied like that, humiliated like that. It must be a different purple. It was hard to see at these distances.

It's me.

What had they done to him? How badly was he injured?

Not badly enough that I can't walk.

Or fly?

My wings are not damaged.

But somehow, he'd fallen into their hands. Somehow, they'd wrapped him in chains and pulled him across the ground like one of the horses he despised.

I thought for sure that if he washed up further down the shore that Hubric would find him.

I didn't wash up along the shore. I was plucked out of the water by a stray Ifrit. He brought me to Iskaris. Apparently, he has a list of people and dragons that he'd rather see tortured than killed.

Had he tortured Raolcan?

Beyond putting me in chains?

I held my breath.

No.

Then why was he so quiet? Why was he walking so strangely? Was he embarrassed that he'd been captured? Was he ashamed that he wouldn't be flying to my rescue today?

I didn't care about any of that! I was just glad he was alive!

It takes a lot of concentration for me to walk right now – although I'm getting used to it. It makes me less talkative.

Why?

There was no answer.

"He's back." Starie sounded smug as she joined me at the edge of the platform. It took me a full breath to realize that she meant the Dominar, not Raolcan.

She was still grasping the Pipe. She played a second set of notes and I clenched my jaw as dragons soared out of Savette's gathered army and above them in Sky City, to swirl above the battle for a moment before diving down toward their own allies.

I flinched when they struck. I spun toward Starie, fists clenched.

She waved a finger at me. "Oh no, Amel. Remember? I can knock you out with a single glance."

The dark light behind her blindfold flared for a moment and my heart stuttered in response.

"I don't think your friend has noticed that you're here. Let's draw her attention, hmmm?" She smiled in her odd way and then her voice was amplified over the field of battle. "Savette Leedris."

Below the battle seemed to almost stutter to a halt as soldiers looked her way. I couldn't tell if Savette was looking, but her light strikes stopped for a moment.

"Let's make this personal!" Starie continued. "I have your friend. You have one hour to surrender, or I'll cut her throat right in front of you."

Sweat soaked me so suddenly that I shivered. I felt lightheaded, and not just from the blood soaking the scarf I held to my face, or that first head wound. I was trapped here. Leng was trapped. Raolcan was trapped. There was no way out this time.

And I still didn't know what Raolcan wasn't telling me.

Starie was going to beat us by seeking out own fears and using them against us. It was her reflection magic all over again, but you could hold a mirror up to another mirror, couldn't you?

"What will you do when all of this is over?" I asked, breathlessly. Surely there was some way that I could reflect her back at herself.

"Rule." Starie seemed unconcerned. Her gaze was on Savette. The light bursts hadn't started up again yet, but now the Dominar's forces had almost finished joining the Dusk Covenant army in the fields below.

"But what will you rule? The purpose of the Chosen One will be over. Magic will be mostly spent. The population of the Dominion decimated in this war. Your allies fearful of your dark gaze. You'll never be certain if their thoughts are their own or only a reflection of yours. They aren't your friends. They're barely even your allies."

The muscle of her jaw clenched and then unclenched.

"Shut up."

I'd struck a nerve. But I'd have to keep on striking at it if I was going to defeat Starie Atrelan. If only I had Raolcan's help. He was great at knowing exactly what to say to people. If only he'd just tell me what he wasn't saying!

I'm blind. I lost the other eye, too.

Chapter Fourteen

I felt like I was falling. The bottom had dropped out of my world and I was falling through whatever was underneath the earth I stood on. Falling, falling, falling ...

My knee hit the stone and I wavered, barely catching myself with the crutch. This couldn't be true.

It. Must. Not. Be. True.

I knew it was a mistake to tell you.

This is what he'd been hiding! Was this also how he had been captured?

It's hard to fight blind.

I felt as if I were deflating. I was losing myself second by second, melting away like a candle thrown in a fire.

On the field below, Savette surged forward, toward the platform, toward me.

"Yes!" Starie's sound of victory was barely audible.

I watched, helplessly, as she pushed forward, spreading her troops dangerously thin.

I felt ill. I would be the cause of her defeat. I'd already been the cause of Raolcan's and of Shonan's. I couldn't bear one more. Memories of Vanika burning in the night flashed across my mind. So many dead because of me. So many defeated. I couldn't bear even one more.

I'm a little insulted that you think I'm defeated.

I tried not to answer. Anything I said would hurt him. But I couldn't help but think that he was lying to bolster my spirits.

Remember when I told you how I could compensate for one missing eye? I can read the minds of the people around me – I can even see what they are seeing if I concentrate.

That's why he had to concentrate to walk.

Exactly.

And to fly …?

I don't know yet, but I expect it would be the same. You should have more confidence in me, Amel.

He'd never see another sunset. Never see a drop of dew on a flower, the spider-work of frost across a rock, the delicate flakes of a first snow.

Not with my own eyes – but I'm already getting better at this. In time … who knows? It's a little addictive to flick from mind to mind watching everything from a thousand pairs of eyes instead of just one.

My eyesight was blurry as hot tears splashed down my face. I sobbed raggedly, trying to control myself and failing. I thought the lowest point of my life would be the burning of Vanika. The wounds from that on my psyche still hadn't fully closed. But this … this was somehow more painful. It was worse than the slash of the Grandis' whip.

What I see now is different – like if the world were colored by emotions. Like if you could taste and smell the things you see – even from far away. I can see you up there. You need to stop looking so indigo.

Indigo?

You look like you might throw yourself off that platform.

I swallowed. Would it really hurt anyone if I did? It might actually save this war.

It would kill me. Do you think my life is worth nothing just because I can't use my eyes? Don't insult me! Is your life worth nothing because of your leg? You've done things that no one with two working legs could do. It's not over yet, Amel. Not even close.

I swallowed. Beside me, Starie whooped and threw a whip to a Magika nearby. He closed in tighter to guard me.

"I'm going down to face her," Starie said, the darkness flaring from behind her blindfold. "One on one. Dark versus light. It's time to finish this once and for all."

"You should take a cluster of Magikas with you," Grandis Elfar said, walking up from behind us.

"You know it's better for me to go alone," Starie said, coolly.

A vein bulged in Grandis Elfar's forehead. She didn't like Starie telling her what she knew. Had I planted enough seeds of doubt? Would she stand against her protégé?

"It's better not to risk our Chosen One," Grandis Elfar said, licking her lips. She refused to meet Starie's blindfolded gaze. "Stay with the hostage and I will go down and convince Savette Leedris to come to you. Alone."

"Look me in the eye and say that again."

It was working!

"Without you, this alliance will fracture," Grandis Elfar said, still not meeting Starie's gaze. "The Generals follow you. The people have faith in you. Only you can fulfill the prophecies and lead us to a new era. If you go down there and die for no reason, all of that is lost. Look," she pointed toward the Dominar's army. "Even the Dominar is moving to higher ground."

I followed her pointing finger. A formation of Silver Dragons flew toward a single room-sized platform dangling from the edge of Dominion City. Instead of walls, the sides of the round room were made entirely of arches. They must have been huge. As I watched, the figure of the Dominar on his dragon grew smaller and smaller until it reached the hanging room and entered through the arches on the side.

"I'm not the kind of coward who directs battles from a safe Observatory," Starie said, coldly.

The Grandis face darkened as Starie spun suddenly and crossed the distance between them, grabbing Grandis Elfar by the scarf and pulling her in so they were almost nose to nose. They were close enough for me to hear her, though her voice was barely above a whisper.

"And what about when all of this is over, Grandis? What about then?"

Starie was waiting for the Grandis to meet her eye. I could tell she was, but the seeds of doubt were too deep. The seconds stretched, and when the Grandis refused to meet her gaze, Starie pushed her away.

"Look after the prisoner," she ordered. "If the hour passes without their surrender – or if I fall – kill her. At least you're good at doing that."

She stormed away, fury filling her face.

Chapter Fifteen

The look on the Grandis' face as Starie walked away made me shudder. I had one hour with this woman. One hour to escape or I would die. Or worse – Savette would surrender.

Allies are almost here.

I looked to the north, but my dull human eyes couldn't see anything coming from that direction. Above us, though, the Silver dragons still circled below the Observatory. From here, I could just make out the silhouette of the Dominar in the arches. I didn't know how he was signaling the army below, but they were moving differently since he arrived. If I had the Pipe those few dragons wouldn't be enough to stop me.

Focus. One thing at a time.

"Grandis Elfar?" I needed her attention if I was going to do anything now.

The Grandis turned to look at me, the battle laid out behind her. I saw a pair of silver dragons drop from their place surrounding the Observatory and dive toward our end of the battlefield.

"Don't speak to me. I know what you've done. You've sown division among us. The Chosen One wouldn't be running headlong into battle with minimal guards if it hadn't been for you. Look!" She dragged me up and forward, grabbing the scarf around my neck and shoving me to the edge of the platform so that I was leaning precariously over the edge, held only by her grip. "Look and tell me what you see!"

The Silver Dragons plummeted toward us at full speed. Were they coming for Grandis Elfar? For me?

"Tell me!" she demanded.

I choked against the scarf wrapped around my neck, gagging and gasping. She pulled me back from the edge – only enough to catch my breath in quick pants. As soon as I could form words I began to talk. I started at the western end of the battlefield.

"The Lightbringers are fading in strength. Some of them have retreated to Sky City, those who remain on the ground are only the most devoted ... or the dead."

"Go on."

"Savette has plunged too far into enemy lines. Her soldiers are almost cut off from their own lines, fighting a battle on all sides. Starie is moving toward her, but there is a lot of ground to cover. She's barely left the platform. The battle is still hot across the entire field. It hasn't stopped just because those two have a vendetta to deal with."

"Continue."

"There are two Silver dragons. They've reached the base of the platform and-"

They were taking the prisoners! That was Ashana they'd loaded up on one of them and there! There was Leng, his hands bound, his eyes searching frantically for me. Where were they taking him?

"See? They're taking your friends to the Dominar. You think you've split us up with your words, but it is you who are divided. I can count the minutes of your life on my fingers."

Surely it hadn't been that long yet! Was she planning to kill me prematurely?

Something glimmered in the distance to the north-east as the Silver dragons launched into the air. Leng couldn't sign with his hands ties, but his gaze never left me. When I finally tore my gaze from him. I felt like I was tearing myself in half.

"I'm not done yet," I said.

"You will be when I slide my knife across your throat."

"I mean I'm not done describing the battlefield."

She laughed harshly. "Don't let me stop you."

"From the north, the armies of Baojang are entering the fray. I can see the Sentries at the front of their ranks. They descend."

"What?!"

I was yanked back to the platform, coughing and clutching my throat as Grandis Elfar stepped to the edge, stretching to look north-east.

"They're led by Jalla, the Winged Prince," I said through my raw throat. "She is so feared in Baojang, that their war leaders united under her in a single day. She comes not to join you, but to finish you."

I thought I might see her in the distance, a flash of gold across the sky. The Silver dragon bearing Leng was growing smaller and smaller. There was suddenly a lot of activity around the Observatory.

"Baojang stands with the Lightbringers," I continued, this time, louder. "Baojang has read the prophecies. Savette Leedris is the one they call the Hasa'leen, the bringer of light."

The Magikas around us shifted uncomfortably, but Grandis Elfar was still looking to the north-east, her hands clenched in fists. I remembered those hands teaching me to oil and care for tack. What could have turned her so far against the truth?

"I was so certain ..." she whispered. "How could they choose your side?"

"It's like the prophecies said:

In secret, their doom is sealed.

In secret, it is wrought.

Evil brings its own demise.

The dusk may still be fought.

How could you have turned on your own people, Grandis? How could you have chosen to serve the Dusk Covenant?"

"I believed ..."

Keep pushing! I've almost found a way out...

There were three dots heading toward us, dodging Ifrits and dragons as they came. I could almost pick them out by color. Gold. Purple. White.

"*And the people will be free of terror and the nations of uproar,*

when the Chosen One brings truth to the heart of the Dominion,

when the dominion of darkness comes to an end." I quoted.

Grandis Elfar wasn't looking at me. She was watching those dots like her life depended on it.

"You're misquoting the prophecies," she said.

"Or maybe it's you who has been misquoting them all this time."

They weren't dots anymore. They were dragons – and they were heading right for us. I could almost see Jalla's flint-hard face when I quoted one last final prophecy.

"*Advised by folly and deception,*
Reflection but not the truth,
Dark falls twixt the cities,
And all her children scatter.
Woe to her mother.
Woe to the one who gave her birth."

I paused a moment before I asked. "That's you, isn't Grandis Elfar? After all, you're her advisor. You're the one who birthed that child of darkness."

Her slap rang across my face, so hard that it seemed to loosen my bones. I felt the whip wound open up again as hot fluid dripped down my cheek.

Chapter Sixteen

I didn't have time to be shocked, didn't have time to wonder if any part of me was going to survive unscathed after all of this was done. I reeled back and then the Grandis was whipping me, fury in her eyes.

Crack!

I threw my arm up over my face to protect it and felt the sharp agony of the whip's snake-like strike on my arm. My Dragon Rider leathers squeaked as the leather pulled at them but they protected me from the worst of it.

I stole a glance at the Grandis from behind my arm. She'd turned her back to the battle below us and the Magikas guard was turning inward, too, focused on our private battle instead of the armies clashing below. Frustration and uncertainty painted the Grandis' face as she channeled her emotions into her strikes.

Crack!

The whip shot out again, slashing across my ribcage.

Crack!

The leathers protected my skin from splitting, but each whipcrack was like a blow and this one knocked me backward. I barely managed to keep my balance on the crutch.

Crack!

This time the whipcrack hit my leg. Growls of appreciation escaped the nearest Magika. Grandis Elfar wasn't the only one who needed a release for her pent-up emotions. If I could keep them off balance and focused on me, maybe I could distract them for long enough that they'd forget why they were really here.

The Grandis wasn't speaking, but her face was red and her lips trembled as if she wanted to say something but the words wouldn't form.

Crack!

This time, the whip wrapped around my crutch, pulling it out from under me. I crashed to the ground, barely breaking my own fall. My bad leg twisted under me awkwardly. Was it broken? I couldn't feel if it was.

With the surge of urgency pulsing through me, I couldn't feel much of anything.

I scrambled up, pressed the button on my crutch and with a flicking motion, I let the retractable end shoot out.

This time, when the tip of the whip snaked toward me, I caught it on the crutch and jerked it toward me.

The Grandis stumbled forward, her teeth gritted and a snarl on her face and she pulled back. I twisted to one side, carefully balancing on my crutch, and then pushing all my weight onto my good leg so I could pull the crutch to the side with a quick snap.

The Grandis cried out, startled as she tripped, falling to one knee, and finally freed her whip.

"I don't have to wait a full hour, girl." She pulled a wicked-looking curved knife as long as my forearm from a sheath at her belt and started forward again.

I moved into a defensive position, bracing myself against my crutch. The Grandis nodded to the Magika beside her and he nodded back. What-?

I tried to take a step back, but I was frozen in place. The smile on the Magika's face was all I needed to see to know who was responsible. I didn't need him to raise his glowing hand or wink at me – though he did.

The Grandis bounced the flat back of the knife across her other palm as she walked toward me.

In the distance, I could hear shouting. It seemed to be growing closer, but I couldn't move to look at it, and my captors were preoccupied.

"I suppose I could wait the full hour before I finish you off," Grandis Elfar said, speculatively. "You don't need to be *whole* to work as bait, do you? After all, you aren't whole now."

If she thought that old insult had any power over me anymore, she could think again. I was so much more than the body I'd been given. I was so much more than the limitations others might try to put on me. I wasn't going to die a cowering cripple. I would never be that again. When she slit my throat with that knife, I would die a Purple Dragon Rider, human to the Prince of Dragons, married to Leng Shardson, Lightbringer.

In my wildest dreams, I couldn't have asked for more than that.

Yes! Yes! Finally, you get it!

When it's done, get to Haz'drazen as quickly as you can and see if she can save you. And take care of Leng.

The Grandis raised the knife. Her eyes were so close that I could see my own face reflected in the pupils, I was proud that I looked so calm. I was ... wait ... was that ...?

Fire flashed past me, incinerating the Magika holding my bonds. I dove to the ground as screams and a howling wind of sudden flames filled the air around me.

I rolled to the side to see the Grandis running, the curved knife in her hand. She dodged a burning Magika leaving him to stumble off the edge of the platform with an agonized scream. But she wasn't fast enough.

A golden blur flashed past me. Jalla and Renn rode Ahummal like angels of death. Ahummal's tail smacked my shoulder and I flinched at the accidental hit, but my eyes grew wider as Jalla carefully drew her big sword.

She leaned out precisely from Ahummal – like a master clothier preparing to cut cloth – and then, in a single, decisive movement, she lopped the Grandis' head off her running body.

Chapter Seventeen

I pulled myself to my feet, looking around me at the chaos. There wasn't a guard or Magika still standing on the platform. I stood, alone, in a tiny clear spot between clouds of smoke. Behind me, the wooden towers roared in flames while Ahummal carefully flamed any part of them not already consumed. No one ran to put out the fires. No one worked to assemble a counter-attack. Ahummal circled the platform and set down beside me.

"We're even now," Jalla said, flicking her blade to one side to shake the last drops of blood off it. "Twice blood sisters, but equal in debt. This alliance is going to be good for us!" She grinned, and my eyes widened. Only Jalla would find this amusing. Only Jalla wouldn't even flinch after single-handedly devastating a pair of towers and a half a dozen Magikas! "Good job distracting them. The Snake Prince is going to be envious of my tally. He's never taken down so many magic-users at one time."

Was my mouth hanging open? Yes. I shut it quickly.

"Well, I don't have time to sit and girl talk right now. We have a war to win and Renn is feeling ill." He looked ill. His face was green and his hands gripped Ahummal's reins like they were the only thing keeping him tethered to reality. If I had ever wished revenge on Renn for his betrayal and moral weakness ... well, he certainly looked like a man who was suffering. What would a lifetime of being married to Jalla be like?

Ahummal launched into the air and she was gone before I could thank her for saving my life or even ask her to carry me off the smoking platform. I gritted my teeth against the pain and hobbled to the stairs. If I waited too long, I'd run out of time. The tower end of the platform was already engulfed, black smoke swirling up through the leaping flames and embracing the sky.

I hurried down the steps and then stopped. Between me and any allies was an army of soldiers, generals, Magikas and Ifrits bent on my destruction. Now that I was on the ground, I'd lost perspective. Even the caged wagons were too far away to hobble to easily.

I watched as a squad of soldiers ran by, surrounding a Magika. His hands were alight with magical energy, and his intense gaze focused far away. In their wake, an Ifirit followed. I shrank back into the platform's supporting stones. I didn't want to catch his eye.

When they were past, I shuffled out from my hiding place, blinking at the obstacle before me. I couldn't stay here – not with a fire raging behind me. No one was even bothering to fight it. They all had bigger worries. I also couldn't just stroll across a battlefield. I stood frozen, fear and worry clouding my mind.

A shadow fell over me.

I looked up, shielding my face with a hand, but all I saw was a dragon's belly as he swooped over my head. He landed a few feet away.

Raolcan!

Amel!

Chains wreathed his neck, rattling as he settled onto the ground. His eyes, blind now, were also swathed with metal chains, as if they could lock up his vision with their metal weight.

I hurried to him, throwing my arms around his huge neck and nestling my cheek against his.

Sorry it took so long. It was hard to convince the guards to unlock the chains.

He managed *that*?

I'm not proud of it. We aren't supposed to use our mental voices to manipulate humans.

I didn't care about that. I only cared that he was alive and with me again. I tugged at the chains around his eyes.

Leave them. We have other things to deal with right now. Can you ride without a saddle?

If he was careful with me. And I could hold the chains, unless he thought that would hurt.

Don't baby me. I'm not a weakling. Look at me! With these chains on me, I look twice as tough as ever! Those Reds and their gnarled scales don't have anything on this chain look!

He still had his sense of humor.

I smiled, kissed his cheek and then hobbled to his side to mount. He helped me, pushing me up onto his back with the help of his snout.

I find that in life there are a lot of times where you can choose to either cry or laugh. I'd rather laugh.

In the middle of a battle?

Especially then!

With our lives in the balance?

What better time?

I laughed, too.

Okay, let's show these dust demons what a blind dragon and lame rider can do!

Blind and lame ... that reminded me of something.

It should. It's from the prophecies:

When the people of the earth sound horn of battle,
And the land trembles and is torn,
When the skies are rent in sorrow,
And the depths bring help no more,
Then the lame and the blind shall lead them,
And guide them from the storm.

We rose up into the air and I tried to orient myself to see what was happening in the chaos of the battle. Jalla was flying back to her ranks. A White dragon – Enkenay! – closed in on Savette. Hubric ... where was Hubric? ... There! He was at the cages, a fleet of Sentries at his back. They were fighting the guards as a unit. That was something I'd never expected to see!

When my eyes settled on Starie – not far now from Savette – I almost froze. She looked like she was looking right at me despite the distance and the blindfold. She lifted the Pipe in the air and waved it at me before blowing it fiercely.

Uh oh.

Chapter Eighteen

Raolcan froze beneath me for a moment and we fell like a stone.

No, no, no, no!

His wings spread out suddenly, like a human who threw out his arms when he tripped to keep from falling face-first on the ground. and our descent eased. I scanned the sky, my heart rising into my throat as all around us, dragons dropped from the sky like meteors.

Hubric and Kyrowat had been close to the earth when they dropped, and the older dragon looked unharmed. Hubric scrambled off him, his movements frantic as he rushed to his dragon's head.

I can't hear their thoughts.

Everyone or just the dragons?

Just the dragons.

I could hear my own heartbeat pulsing in my head and my breath came quickly. Were they dead? I'd played that Pipe many times and never actually hurt the dragons ...

It was different. I don't think they are dead. I think they are trapped ... it's like they are behind stone doors I can't access.

Stone doors?

Mentally.

We needed to join Hubric. We could decide what to do then.

Agreed.

Hubric took up a position at Kyrowat's head, his short sword drawn and a fierce look on his face, though none of the guards around the cages was coming for him. They seemed as shocked as he was by the dragons' fall. A pair of legs stuck out from under Kyrowat's belly and an arm from under his neck. He must have crushed a pair of guards when he fell. How many other people had been crushed across the battlefield? I glanced behind me. Chaos ruled across the plains.

Keep your eyes ahead!

I snapped to obey the order.

It's easier to see if I only have your mind to read. Easier than reading hundreds of minds at once. It means I can still talk to you and think about other things.

What else was he thinking about?

The kind of magic that can take the call of the Pipe and amplify it almost as if the dragons affected were mirrors facing each other, reflecting that one note over and over and over.

We were getting close to Kyrowat now and I gasped at his open eyes. Tears leaked from them, but he was unresponsive otherwise. Weren't the eyes the mirror to the soul? Could Starie have somehow used her mirror magic to multiply the effects of the Pipe and to have them reverberate back and forth from one dragon to another and to another?

It's a crazy thought, but not a bad explanation. After all, what do I have that none of these other dragons have?

Let me guess, ravishing good looks and a rapier wit.

True. But I was referring to blindness. She can't use my eyes against me.

I had a flashback to Grandis Elfar refusing to meet Starie's gaze. There was something to this theory. It had to do with the eyes. We needed to get that Pipe back from her before every dragon on this field of battle died. They were defenseless like this.

Raolcan landed close to Kyrowat. Hubric spun toward us, sword raised. His shoulders sunk with relief and his eyes closed for a moment when he saw us.

"Amel! Skies and stars, I thought you were dead! And that old lizard of yours, too!"

Sure. Pick on me when you know I can't talk back because your dragon is unconscious.

"Is Kyrowat okay?"

"I don't know what's wrong with him," he said, pointing to Kyrowat. "He just fell – they all did."

His eyes narrowed when he looked at Raolcan.

"Starie," I gasped, sliding off of Raolcan's back to limp to the cages. The guards were down, the Sentries and their riders ringing the cages. "I think her mirror magic uses the reflection of their eyes."

Hubric squatted down, staring Kyrowat in the eye. He waved a hand, but his dragon was unresponsive. He hung his head for a moment and then startled, tugging suddenly at the arm sticking out from under Kyrowat.

"Here. Ask Raolcan to give Kyro a push. I'm never gonna get this guy out otherwise."

I frowned, watching him speechlessly. Had the old man mentally snapped with his dragon down and incapacitated?

Raolcan hissed a steamy laugh before leaning forward to help.

You forgot something, Amel, but Hubric didn't. How do you open a cage?

"Ah! Here it is!" Hubric said, pulling the fallen guard out from under Kyrowat and tugging a leather strap from around his neck. "The key!"

I grabbed it from his hand and hurried to the first cage. Eluci was pressed against the door.

"Hurry!" she said, as I fumbled for the right key on the ring. "They took the others – Leng, Ashana, Peln."

Around me, the buzz of the Sentries was making my hair stand on end, but they were the only ones standing between us and our enemies.

I'm still here ...

And my mighty dragon, of course. I found the key and slipped it into the lock, quickly opening the door. Eluci stumbled out of it and down to the ground and I shoved the keys in her face.

"Take the keys! I need to go stop this madness!"

"The war?" she looked aghast, as if I'd gone crazy in the hours since she'd seen me.

"No, what it's doing to the dragons. Free the prisoners!"

I hobbled back to where Hubric was kneeling beside his dragon, holding Kyrowat's snout in his hands. "Whatever magic this is – he can't stay like this forever. It will kill him."

I gripped his shoulder until he turned to me. "I'm going to find a way to stop it."

He nodded.

"If I don't make it back ..." I paused. "Leng is in the Observatory." I pointed to the place where it hung beneath Dominion City. "He's a prisoner there. So is Ashana."

Hubric nodded, gripping my hand on his shoulder. "Go fix this, apprentice."

I laughed. How long ago had it been since the day he adopted me as his apprentice and gave me this crutch.

It had only been a few months ago.

It felt like a lifetime.

"And don't die!" he called as I mounted Raolcan carefully and we rose, again, into the sky.

Chapter Nineteen

Look! Do you see Starie?

I scanned the field of battle as we rose into the air. The battle raged on two fronts, the Dusk Covenant versus the Lightbringers at the very edge of the base of Sky City, and our Baojang allies versus the Dusk Covenant below Dominion City. Despite the sudden chaos born of dragons falling from the sky, the armies were already regrouping. A red flag unfurled from the Observatory – a sign of what, exactly? I didn't know. It wasn't hard to find Starie. I looked for the most chaotic spot of the battle. There! A nimbus of black light circled her.

The falling dragons had slowed her in her quest to meet Savette on the field of battle. Both of them were diverting from their paths, trying to move around fallen or dead dragons. I swallowed at the sight of an entire squad of soldiers climbing up on the rib cage of a White, slashing and hacking at those who passed below, as if the dragon were only higher ground and not a living thing.

There was something strange about the soldiers that Starie encountered on her way to fight Savette. They seemed confused ... disoriented.

She's doing the same thing to them that she did to the dragons. She doesn't have the Pipe to reach them all at once, but she uses the reflection in their eyes to amplify her power and to entangle them.

I swallowed. Who could resist a magic like that?

Savette can. Her eyes are so full of light that no darkness can enter there, and no reflection can be stolen from her.

What would happen when they met face to face? Would the world end then?

I doubt it. The world has seen evil and good meet before.

Before they met, I needed to get to her. We needed that Pipe. If the dragons were left like this, many more would die. I would not stand by and watch my friends die for no reason – and that included my dragon friends.

In that case, I need you to trust me.

I always trust you, Raolcan. I'm so sorry that I wasn't there when you were hurt. I'm sorry that you were taken captive when it should have been my tender care to help you, not the rough chains of enemies! I'm sorry that you've lost your eyes to save me.

I'm the worst thing for you, but you keep on loving me.

Amel, my dear girl, my spider. You need to remember something.

He was flying faster than I ever remembered flying so that it took almost all my concentration to hold on. The battlefield blurred beneath us.

What did I need to remember at a moment like this?

You need to remember that you *are why I'm here. We're in this together. Neither of us can succeed alone.*

Succeed at what?

Victory. Now, enough of flashing that big heart around. I need you to trust me.

I do trust you!

Take off that lovely scarf that Leng gave you – the one around your waist.

How did he know it was lovely?

Allow me some assumptions. Tie it around your eyes.

Around my eyes? Then how would he fly?

After you tie it on, I'll have to focus so I can navigate. You'll hold one of these chains and drop down beside Starie and I'll tell you what to do. You have to get that Pipe before she realizes that you're above her. Are you able to do that?

I swallowed. a sour taste filling my mouth. Sweat broke out across my body. I wasn't really the most athletic person...

You can do it. We're almost there. Catch this chain!

He whipped his head in a complicated fashion and two of the dangling chains his captors had used to lead him whipped up beside me. I grabbed one of them in shaking hands and tucked it under my thigh to hold it in place while I got ready.

The blur of the armies below slowly came into focus as Raolcan slowed, curving in a spiral. My hand shook as I realized what I was going to do.

Scarf on!

I unraveled the scarf and quickly tied it around my eyes.

Hold on to the chain.

I wiped my hands on my leathers and then gripped it with both hands.

Could I do this?

I wasn't sure.

You have to. It's our only chance.

I could hear the chain rattling in my shaking hands, the din of the battle growing louder. Starie was shouting something over the rush of voices.

"Face me, Lightbringer! Face me and show the world that darkness overcomes light! Or are you trying to extend your life by seconds? I will catch you! You cannot run from my power!"

Jump!

I couldn't ... I couldn't ... I did!

The air whipped around me and I braced my grip for the impact. Even gripping as hard as I could my whole body jarred when I reached the end of the chain. Could my joints pop loose? It felt like some of them had. I swallowed back a cry, listening for directions.

Left! Reach to your left and grab!

I felt almost as if I had just missed someone.

She can read the edges of your thoughts. Don't think, do!

I pawed the air with wild abandon. There was a shriek as I grabbed something to my left – hair! I tugged as hard as I could.

Yes! Now let go and feel for the strap around her neck!

I raked my hand across a face, ignoring the cursing and found the strap, gripping it as hard as I could. I felt the leather cord jerk up, and for a moment my arms screamed in pain as I was being pulled upward with one arm and pulling Starie upward with the other. The sockets of my shoulders felt like they were ripping in two.

Then, all at once, the leather cord snapped, and I was swinging back and forth through the air on the end of the chain. I jammed the leather cord into my Dragon Rider leathers before feeling to see if the Pipe was there.

We had it!

I tugged my blindfold off and reached for the chain with my other hand. As I adjusted my grip, light surrounded me and with a clap like a thunderbolt, we were spinning through the air, tumbling end over end, my only link to Raolcan – to life – my grip on that snapping, whipsawing chain.

Dragon School: Ascendant Light

Chapter One

Hold on! Raolcan called to me as we tumbled through the air. I didn't dare close my eyes. What if Raolcan needed to see through them?

Thwack!

I cried out as one of the loose chains hit my hands. Though I flinched away, I didn't dare let go. The tiny bones in my hands ached from the hit.

Just one more se-

He hit the ground first – sliding through the mud – and I landed next to him with a rib-cracking hit.

They aren't cracked. They just hurt a lot.

I gasped. Breathing was so hard! Why did everything hurt so much? I coughed, doubling over. My breath wheezing and painful. How did he know my ribs weren't cracked? They felt cracked.

We couldn't stay on the ground. I had the Pipe now. I had to blow it and rescue the dragons from the mirror magic enslaving them. I pushed against the thick mud, only seeming to sink in deeper.

If they were cracked, you wouldn't be moving like that. You're sore, but you're fine.

It coated my hands and the front of my leathers – an inch thick of soft clay. I tried to wipe it off to clean my hands, but it only seemed to smear it.

On your feet!

He seemed tight – like he was close to snapping. I struggled in the mud to stand. We'd skidded to the side of a downed dragon. His rider, a Red was standing at his head, swinging his sword wildly at anyone who came near, friend or foe.

"You won't touch him! Not one of you!"

Arrows flew around him, some of them flying past and landing around us in the thick mud.

I fought the mud to try to stand. My good leg was too deeply dug into the clay – almost knee deep now – and my crutch was worse. Its narrow point jabbed deep into the mud. It couldn't hold my weight.

Blow the Pipe!

What if it made things worse? I tried again to wipe my hand on my pants, but in the end, it was a clay-smeared hand that reached into my leathers and pulled out the Pipe. I checked the lever. This was it, wasn't it? I didn't want to blow the wrong note. What if I made it worse?

Just do it! There's no time to second guess!

I closed my eyes, raised the Pipe to my lips and blew my three-note tune, clear as a bell. Dax would be proud.

Look.

I opened my eyes to see the Red shaking himself, his rider still screaming threats from in front of him. Clay and mud sprayed the field around us in every direction as the great Red shook like a dog on a rainy day.

I almost breathed a sigh of relief when a cry to my right caught my attention. The Dusk Covenant army was swarming toward us, throwing logs or planks in the mud in front of them to gain a better position. I looked quickly to the other side to see the Lightbringer's side doing the same thing. I felt like I was swept up in a vortex of passion and fury.

So, that was why they had been fighting for so long in this field! Even moving a few feet took extra effort! But now I was stuck between them. Really stuck. I couldn't pull my foot out of the mud and my crutch had only a hand's width of length not swallowed by clay.

I was trying not to panic. Remember not to panic!

Yells and arrows shot around me as I tugged my foot, my breath coming faster and faster. I half-sobbed, frustration and fear warring for control of my thoughts and then Raolcan's neck shot around lightning quick. His head went past me and the heat and smell of his flame filled the air. A moment later, he drew his head back to level with me. Did he know how spooky he looked with chains across his eyes?

I look tough! No one wants to mess with me.

Like he didn't look tough before. He was a dragon. He always looked tough.

Don't judge me by my bad breath.

What?

He opened his mouth wide and then twisted so he could take me gently in his jaws and pull me from the mud. I grimaced, worried about his sharp teeth. What if he broke me in half? What if he accidentally flamed me?

I was more worried that you'd swoon from my breath.

It *was* terrible. What had he been eating?

Horses. Cats. Fluffy bunnies.

Tease! I clutched my crutch, pulling it with me as he lifted me up from the clay with a loud sucking sound and then arched his neck around to place me on his back, clay, mud and all. We were in the air before I could even settle, swirling upward into the sky.

Around us, dazed dragons pulled themselves back out of the mud and into the air. I hurried to tuck the Pipe back into my leathers. I couldn't afford to lose it again. Especially not now.

Oh no.

What now?

A second blast hit us, rocking us back and forth, but this time Raolcan kept his place in the sky. We spun to look at the source of the blast. Fear filled me.

Savette and Starie stood in an empty circle of mud. Anyone and anything that had been around them before had either fled or been pushed back from their blasts of power. Starie's dark light pulsed out from her blindfold and Savette's white light shone brighter than ever. They were knee deep in mud. It coated their clothing and stuck to their feet. At the edges where they met, sparks and sprays of light crackled and popped.

My vision shifted, suddenly, to Savette's perspective.

"I come to claim your soul," Starie said, her smug smile taking on a new life as she flared to life with the darkness of deception and mirror magic.

"Today, your lies end. Today truth will win," Savette challenged. Her light flared out to match Starie's light.

"You can't beat me," Starie challenged. "I have something you don't have."

"What's that?"

"I have nothing to love. Which means I have nothing to lose."

I snapped back to my own mind again, but my eyes lingered on the two challengers, standing across from each other, grim determination in every line of their bodies.

Only one of them could survive this final conflict.

Chapter Two

It won't be a fair battle.

Why? Because good would always win?

Has that been your experience, Amel? Has good always won?

Well, no. Of course not.

Then think about it. Why won't the battle be fair?

Because Starie was a cheater. No matter what the battle was, she would find a way to cheat.

Exactly. Look around you.

All around us, the Ifrits seemed to be waking up. They'd been fighting all along, but their sudden increase in speed and deadliness caught me off guard. Had they even been trying before?

They come for her. She is their Chosen One. Their dust lives in the power of the dark light in her. Like all creatures born of deception, they follow no rules.

They were all moving in the same direction, flinging men, horses, and dragons out of their paths as they scrambled toward their goal – the clash between the Chosen Ones. What would happen to Savette when they arrived?

We have another problem.

No other problems mattered right now. The fate of the world rested on this!

Look at the Observatory. Is that our problem?

I swiveled to look to the distant hanging room. Two wooden "X's" were being lowered from the arches. Was that a third I saw them preparing in the opening of another arch? I thought I could see figures chained to them. What was with Iskaris and those horrific things?

He's mad. Completely mad. But this time it is Leng strapped to one of those.

Anxiety rose up and choked me. A sound escaped my lips like the cross between a sob and a curse. What about Savette? My gaze swung to her little circle of light as the shadows around her closed in, and then back to the wooden "X's" being lowered and then back to Savette. She still had a fighting chance. Leng didn't.

The fate of the world rests on Savette's shoulders.

The fate of *my* world rested on Leng's.

Some people say you need to remember that there's a difference between personal and important. Savette's battle is more important. Leng's is more personal.

So, I should help Savette and leave my husband to his fate? Is that what he was saying?

I'm saying that you have to make a decision. Personal or important?

Personal *was* important. You could find a hundred thousand people to care about important. In fact, there were thousands of them on the battlefield today. But no one else would take care of the personal. No one but me.

If you go for Leng, everything we worked for to help Savette might be for nothing.

If I didn't help him, then the world we saved wouldn't be worth saving. It would be full of people like me who coldly calculated victory over devotion. That would never be me. I'd watch the world burn first.

I never expected anything less from you.

We were already turning in the air. My dragon was with me!

And as always, you prove again why my loyalties lie with you, Amel Leafbrought.

An Ifrit towered in front of us, suddenly stretching and narrowing to a tall, thin pillar to block our path. Raolcan dodged his first blow, but he had to be careful. I had no saddle and nothing to hold on to but his chain collar. Worse, I was slick with clay.

My dragon dodged again, turning a little too far in his dodge and sending me sprawling across his back. I tried to right myself, but a third dodge left me dangling off his back. The chain bit into my fingers while the wind howled around my loose legs. I kicked to try to get momentum to pull myself back up, but it wasn't enough.

Sorry! I didn't see the turn clearly enough.

It was amazing we were both still alive, but my muscles were aching already, burning as if someone had thrown hot coals over my biceps and shoulders.

We swung to the side and I could feel the burst of air from the Ifrit's swipe whip my hair out of its braid. I turned to look at the dust demon – Raolcan needed my eyes! – only to have the Ifirit burst into dust and rain from the sky in a chalky cloud. I blinked rapidly to clear my eyes.

From out of the puff of glittering dust, Kyrowat and Enkenay flew. Rakturan – still glowing with the light he'd used against the Ifrit – gave me a Baojang salute as he passed.

Hubric! Could he help me before my arms gave out?

Kyrowat swooped in close and as he ducked under Raolcan, my dragon called to me.

Drop! Now!

I let go of the chain and fell onto Kyrowat, my tailbone aching from the blow of hitting his bony spine. Hubric reached out and stabilized me as I landed on his dragon's neck.

"Easy now. Skies and stars you're a mess!"

"It's nice to see you, too."

"We'll set down in friendly territory, so you can get back on your dragon."

Kyrowat swooped low over the heads of soldiers fighting in the field. I tried not to see the details, but try as I might, they still burned into my eyes – things I couldn't forget, wouldn't forget, for the rest of my life. War was not a pretty thing, though armor and swords and dragons decked out in armor might be. It was a place of horror and misery. A place a person might beg the stars and skies that he could only leave. The seconds would feel like hours as he cried for relief - until his life was snatched away by muddy hands. I shivered and clung to Kyrowat.

I glanced back over my shoulder to see Rakturan rushing toward his beloved wife, his dragon glowing as brightly as he was.

We were following Raolcan across the Dusk Covenant army, taking arrows on Kyrowat's belly and dodging clumps of Ifirits. As if they had been called by a Pipe, they were closing in toward Starie, ignoring anyone else unless they were in the path to her.

I glanced behind us every few seconds. The Ifrits had clustered in so tightly around Starie and Savette that it was almost impossible to make them out through the clouds of dust demons.

What should I do about the dragons? Should I be directing them with the Pipe right now or leaving them alone?

We can't direct them right now. We're going for Leng. Save the Pipe for when it's useful.

Rakturan was harder to see as we flew further away, but this time when I glanced back I saw light shooting from him and blasting a path through the dust demons toward Savette.

The Observatory was right over the field of battle, but I hadn't realized how far Baojang had already pushed. The battle line between them and the Dusk Covenant was right beneath the Observatory, close to the base of Dominion City.

Some of the War Leaders were already trying to secure the ropes and cables that hauled boxes and baskets up to the sky city. If Jalla didn't rein them in, they would try to sack the city before she could stop them.

Worry about your own business. Jalla can mind hers just fine.

She was on the frontlines – of course! – waving that huge sword of hers around and shouting her troops onward from the back of Renn's Gold dragon. Ahummal looked almost as disconcerted as his real rider as she spurred him on into the carnage of the front line. Raolcan couldn't possibly hold a grudge toward him now.

Just because Jalla makes him do good things doesn't make him a good dragon.

But didn't it? Were we what we did or were we something detached from our deeds? I didn't see how you could separate the two.

Can we be philosophical later? Distracting yourself from this situation isn't going to make it go away!

I hadn't looked up this whole time. I didn't want to see Leng on that "X." If I did, it would make it real.

Not looking won't make it not real. Ignoring the truth never saves anyone.

I looked up ... and my heart broke.

Chapter Three

It was worse than if it was me.

It was worse.

My heart was stuttering so badly I thought it might stop and my hands shook violently as Hubric pushed me off of Kyrowat's back. He was saying something, but I couldn't hear it over the din of battle and the roaring of immobilizing terror in my ears. I couldn't lose Leng before I ever really had him. I couldn't.

Hubric shoved me forward. He'd set us down behind the frontlines of Baojang and our allies poured around us like a river around a rock as they rushed to the fray. Trust the people of Baojang to hurry to battle!

I stumbled in the direction he'd pushed me, seeing the rushing soldiers, drawn blades, furious expressions, and brightly colored clothing but not really taking it in. I hobbled forward anyway, the occasional hand shoving me out of the way. I felt like I couldn't think. The world around me was a teary blur.

Shake out of it!

The crowd parted and then a path cleared to my purple dragon. Puffs of smoke and a little trail of fire kept a narrow path clear for me. He really shouldn't flame around his allies.

They shouldn't wave pointy blades near my human. Fair is fair. I didn't kill any of them. Now, stop panicking and mount up. Let's go save your husband!

I scrambled forward, letting him boost me onto his back and we leapt up again into the air. Below me, a series of screams and gurgles reminded me that the Sentries were fighting, too.

I don't even wish that kind of death on the Dusk Covenant.

Didn't he?

A burst of light so bright and at the same time the opposite of that – black as night – pulsed across the battlefield with a powerful burst. It was stronger than the swipe of an Ifrit. I flew off my feet, sight gone, sound gone.

My entire world was white light.

My vision returned suddenly. My arms ached from holding the chain as I dangled from Raolcan's back. Enkenay and Kyrowat burst through a cloud of dust. Hubric nodded to me as Rakturan dove beneath Raolcan.

Wait. Hadn't this just happened?

But not like this. It had been different.

Drop! Now!

I landed on Enkenay's ghostly neck, Rakturan stabilizing me. My jaw dropped, and I spun to face his blind-folded gaze.

"Wha-"

"No time," his accent sounded thicker since his time back in Baojang. We spiraled upward, higher and higher. I caught a glimpse of Raolcan following us. "I must return to Savette as quickly as possible. She needs my added strength.

"Wha-?"

"When their power collides – truth versus deception – it reacts. It explodes." We were still climbing, passing now out of the reach of even the Ifrits. "But the false one has these mirrors - they reflect back the past. Her mirror magic shot us – the whole battlefield – back into the past. I could see it all happening. It will happen again. It's going to make this last battle ... complicated."

"You should be fighting her!" I protested. If she could send us backward, even a minute backward, we'd have to fight the same battle over and over!

"I will stand against her. And I will stand with my bride. But first I must entrust this to you."

"Entrust what?"

"The night you were taken captive after the trap failed, Baojang waited on the other side of the river, but Enkenay and I flew across to spy on them. I saw the false Chosen One talking to the Dominar. I crept close and I heard everything. She said she needed to rein him in, that he was out of control.

She said that he'd destroy everything. And then she took something from him."

"What?"

"You know how I can see through your eyes sometimes?"

"I knew that was you!" My guess was right!

"And you can see through Savette's?"

"Yes."

"Starie Atrelan can see through the eyes of the Dominar – more than that. She can control his actions. She said as much when she took it. And watching them now – it's true. It's true. He's like a puppet in a street show, not a man at all. It's that mirror magic of hers. Everything shiny is fair game – even crowns."

"What did she take?"

"She took his free will. He's her puppet now. But a puppet with a crown. The mask and not the man. He'll never be the man again, only the mask forever."

I looked at the clouds around us, heavy and dark. This news was heavier. I shivered.

"Why bring me here to tell me this?"

"In a moment we'll dive back into battle. I'll help my bride to fight. She needs me by her side if she's going to stand a chance at victory. But someone – you – needs to destroy the false Dominar. With Starie in his mind, there is no stopping what he could do."

"Why me?"

His bandaged gaze seemed to pierce me. "I trust you. I've seen what you hide from the world."

Raolcan appeared from the clouds, leveling off beside us and drawing in very close. Rakturan leaned far out to the side and snagged one of his flapping chains. He pulled my dragon closer and began to help me across to his back. I obeyed his wordless directions almost mechanically, too afraid of the implications of what he was saying to be afraid of the crazy thing I was doing – changing dragons in mid-air.

"What do I hide from the world?" I asked as I settled on Raolcan and Rakturan handed me the chain.

"Indomitable strength."

I grabbed his arm as he tried to remove it, meeting what I hoped was his gaze through the wrapped bandages.

"Thank you, Prince Rakturan. For everything." I released him and looked down to adjust my grip on the chain.

He was gone before I could look up again, diving headlong through the clouds to the battle below.

That's our cue to go, too.

Chapter Four

We broke the cloud cover, spiraling down instead of piercing through the dark clouds as Rakturan had. He was already near the clearing where Savette and Starie battled. Light and dark bolts of light streaked between them, countered or dodged or transformed into something else before they could hit their opponent.

The clothing of the two women swirled and flapped in the rising wind as it howled from the east, the muddy edges of cloaks and dresses flinging water and dirt into the air like tarnished ocean spray.

The wind caused the Ifrits to shimmer and waver and the sky cities to almost seem as if they were swaying.

I think they are *swaying.*

I braced myself against Raolcan's back. We needed a proper saddle. We also needed to get to the Observatory, now for both Leng's sake and the fight against Iskaris. Raolcan was already flying in that direction, keeping us high to avoid the fray below.

Everything was easier to see from here and despite the urgency, it was hard to tear my eyes away from the Chosen One battling the false Chosen One in that empty circle of ground. The mud didn't stop them – hardly seemed to affect them. In some places it had hardened from their battle, in others, it was still thick and soft. No one, man or beast, could enter that circle and live – though that didn't stop the horde of Ifrits from trying.

With the suddenness of the howling wind, Rakturan and Enkenay dove into the circle, landing just behind Savette. Rakturan's sword was out, slicing and slashing at the Ifrits who stepped into the circle. He was like a weathervane turning in the wind. When Savette moved left, Rakturan and Enkenay moved to stay at her back. When she dodged right, they dodged with her. When she stepped forward, they did, too. I could watch them all day. Their battle was a dance of magic, power, and determination.

Rakturan's light joined Savette's feeding it as she fought. They were growing slowly distant as we flew to the Observatory, but I kept one eye on Leng and one eye on her.

I was worried about him. He seemed to be struggling against his bonds, but so high up, if he freed himself, what hope would he have? The fall was too far. If he could just hold on!

He can't just give in. That's what you love about him.

He shouldn't die, either!

With the added power of Rakturan, Savette pushed forward. Starie stumbled, catching herself at the last minute on the corpse of a dragon and pulling herself back to her feet. Yes! She was tiring! Together, they were too strong for her.

I could feel the cheer building inside me. We could still win this war! We could!

Like a silver arrow shooting from a bow, the Dominar launched from the Observatory on dragon-back. The circling dragons who were guarding the Observatory swirled into a line, flapping hard to catch up to their leader and surround him in an honor guard. Sunlight glinted from his crown and mask, as he searched the battlefield. What was he looking for?

He comes to aid Starie.

His pointing finger proved Raolcan right. But now they were flying right toward us and we would have to make a decision. Would we follow them and fight Iskaris like I had promised Rakturan, or would I rush to the aid of my husband? I'd already made that decision. Already decided that the personal outweighed the important.

Hurry, Raolcan, hurry!

Amel, we have a problem.

The Dominar and his Silvers were headed straight for us.

There wasn't time to dodge them. There wasn't time for delay. We needed to get to Leng! How much time would he have before the cords holding him failed? Or worse, until he wiggled free of them. Why couldn't he sit still?

Hang on tight! This might get crazy!

The Silver dragons swooped past us so quickly and forcefully that I was rocked in my seat as wings beat against me and flames singed my hair. I held on to the chain, white-knuckled, my only thought for Leng.

Please let us get to him in time, please!

Why would Iskaris string him up there as bait if he wasn't going to stay around to guard the prisoners?

He knows what he is doing. He's distracting you and anyone else who might care about dragon riders.

A trap?

Remember – he's controlled by Starie. Aren't traps like this her way of dealing with opponents?

They were. And yet, I couldn't ignore it.

Silvers still shot past, flaming and snapping at us as they passed, but they had a goal and we weren't it. They refused to be distracted. When the last one jostled us and Raolcan could finally get wing space, I almost breathed a sigh of relief, but we still had a long way to go. Where was Hubric? I could use his help?

We were getting closer. Any moment now. Any moment ...

The Observatory was so close that I could see Leng's face when the Magikas stepped out, filling the windows. Hands lit up like torches, they opened fire on us, throwing one ball of fire after another. The first one splashed across Raolcan's face, but he dodged the next and the next.

Raolcan? Are you okay?

He didn't stop flying, didn't stop pushing right into the teeth of the fireballs. Why didn't he slow?

One of the Magikas was leaning over the edge of the arch. He pulled a wicked looking knife from his pocket and began to saw at the rope one of the "X's" hung from. He kept glancing up, looking at us as if he was trying to finish before we could get there.

Hold on tight! These fireballs keep pressing me backward. If I duck under them...

He leaned to the side, leaving me breathless as I fought to keep my seat. With no saddle, my bad leg was useless for holding on and I slipped to the side, dangling again by the chain. There was a horrific scream and I gasped, looking wide-eyed at the "X" plunging to the earth. Had that been Peln? I didn't have time to scream before a second plunged after it. That was Ashana!

Raolcan was flapping as hard as he could, but I was a dead weight hanging from a chain around his neck, swinging and swaying so hard that I thought my arms would give way. A fireball splashed across his chest, the fringes of it singing my hands.

No, no, no!

The last "X" plummeted past and I screamed as my gaze locked with Leng's. The grip of my hands slipped down the chain and I was tumbling with nothing beneath me but air and mud.

Chapter Five

Boom!

Light seared across my vision. For a second, I thought I saw Starie through Savette's eyes. She was cursing, her hands flung outward with dark light crackling from her fingertips. My pupils burned so deeply that they felt like they'd been branded. This time – even without Starie's curses – I knew what had happened.

Please, be before they fell! Please be before they fell! But I couldn't count on luck or the favor of the skies and stars to let this time-mirror land in my favor. What if when it happened everything went worse?

But how could it be worse than this?

My vision cleared suddenly.

We're back. This time hold on harder!

This time I had a better plan. The Silvers dove out of the arches, shooting toward us but I fumbled in my jacket and whipped out the Pipe, raising it to my lips and blowing. This time I had them!

Nothing. They didn't slow. They hit us with the edges of their wings and flamed at us just like last time. What-?

Starie is in their minds, just like she's in Iskaris'. You can't take control where she already has.

My brilliant plan was gone.

My eyes were glued to the wooden "X" they had tied Leng to. It swayed in the wind. What did it feel like to be him, dangling out over a muddy battlefield so far in the air that you could see birds flying beneath you?

I bit my lip. My breath was coming too fast. This couldn't happen. We had to stop it.

I ducked low as Raolcan darted forward, under the Silvers. I blew the Pipe again, knowing it would do no good to gain their help, but still hoping, hoping that somehow I could stop this.

The gusts of wind shook me as our speed increased and then from below, three figures began to grow. They were climbing through the sky like birds, but these birds were purple.

They heard the Pipe!

I recognized them! Hubric rode Kyrowat, but with him were Rasipaer – his proud neck jutting out – and Ahlskibi – whole and well!

His wound was not mortal. He just needed deep rest to heal. But they were caged. Rasipaer in the cage you saw until Eluci set him free. And Ahlskibi was a prisoner of the troops with the Dominar.

My breath caught in my throat as they joined us. We had a chance! If we could just get there before the Magikas had the brilliant idea of cutting the ropes...

We were all flying at full speed, hurrying toward the hanging crosses. What if they cut the ropes while we were still cutting the prisoners loose?

I couldn't watch Leng fall again!

He was heart of my heart, life of my life.

Concentrate. Focus. See the hooks at the top of the crosses?

The cables the crosses hung from were fitted with hooks. Where did Iskaris keep finding these torture devices? Did he have them commissioned?

No. They are common in sky cities. Usually, they don't hang vertically like this. Usually, cables are affixed to the loops at each end of the beams and they hang horizontally. They are used to carry heavy loads up from the ground to the sky city above. They tie ropes around those hooks to secure the cargo. If you slip one of my chains over the end of the hook, I can still catch the weight if they cut the rope.

But could he? The beams were heavy and Leng would be attached to them, making them even heavier. Could he carry that much weight from a chain around his neck?

I should start doubting you every time you have a plan. I bet you won't like it any more than I do. What am I, a cat?

A cat?

An animal who doesn't know how to work?

That was a harsh judgment of cats!

We were almost at the beams.

Show me a cat that works for his dinner and I'll take it back.

"Leng!"

His wrists were bloody where the straps dug into them and his face was white and drawn.

"Amel." He sounded like he was in pain.

Quickly, I hooked the chain onto the hook and glanced over to where Hubric was reaching across to hook Ahlskibi's chain into the hook on Ashana's beam. Would he be fast enough to help Peln, too? What would he do there? Kyrowat had no chains weighing him down – and nothing with which to catch a falling cross.

"I'm here, Leng. Let me cut you loose."

I pulled a belt knife from my pocket, sawing at the strap around his wrist. The seconds dragged out, too long, too long.

Behind me, I heard the same piercing scream I'd heard before as Peln's "X" broke free of the cable.

Determined not to let that happen to Leng, I sawed harder. The strap broke.

Feet next so he didn't fall. I sawed at the cord around the first one. The seconds dragging out too long. There!

The other foot now.

Hurry!

I fumbled with the knife and it fell, glinting in the air on the way down. Leng would have a pocket knife. I looked up at his pale face to ask the question.

"Do-"

He dropped out of sight so quickly that I barely had time to gasp before Raolcan plunged down, too, dragged to the earth by the weight of the heavy cross.

Chapter Six

I craned to the side, searching for Leng and the heavy cross ... there! He was almost on top of an Ifrit! If we didn't level off...

Hold on!

I dug my fingers under the chain around Raolcan's neck, holding on for dear life as he whipsawed back and forth, his wings flapping with powerful strokes. He was trying to level us off, but the cross was heavy. He had to let it pull us to the ground!

And land on an Ifrit's head? I can see through the eyes of the fighters below. They struggle to fight as he tears them to pieces. He's supposed to be joining the others around the Dominar, but he is distracted by the screaming people and the fire and mud. He wants to destroy, rend, and grind to dust. He will not stop until-

Shake out of it, Raolcan! Get out of his head!

Wow... Yeah. Good call.

Beneath us, chaos reigned as soldiers ran or charged through puffs of smoke and deep mud holes. The boards and logs they'd thrown across the mud did little to give them solid ground. I could see the Ifrit roaring and leaping, still right beneath us, see the cross dangling at the end of the chain.

These were all farm fields except for the army encampment. None of that stands now. Not even the garrison.

I hadn't noticed that – I should have. I'd been in that garrison – but I had other things on my mind. Where was Leng? Why couldn't I see him?

He's freed his other hand.

We were sinking as Raolcan's strength faded.

Lower.

Lower.

The cross fell into the dust of the Ifrit and it looked up, eyes ablaze and mouth opening wide. Like a snake, it seemed to open wider than the Ifrit was until the flaming void swallowed the cross whole with a spine-shuddering *snap*.

Someone was screaming. They were screaming so loud.

We fell, but to the side, avoiding the Ifrit, and soaring in an unexpected arc out of the danger below and to a little rise at the base of the city.

I wished that person would stop screaming. I wished I could breath easier. I wished I didn't feel so light headed. The world was going black...

Seriously, stop screaming.

Hands shook me.

There was ground under me and Raolcan's hot scales against my back. Hands shook me.

"Amel? Amel, are you okay? Talk to me! Tell me you're okay!"

I opened my eyes. Dark, steady eyes met mine. They were beautiful. More beautiful than a thousand sunsets. More precious than a thousand diamonds. More-

We get the picture.

Leng! He was alive! How was he alive?

"Leng!" I gasped, reaching for him. My voice shook and the side of my face was twitching uncontrollably.

He had already cut his own bonds and climbed up the chain. Didn't you know that? You were the one looking down there. I literally *saw it through your eyes.*

All I'd seen was that mouth.

You need to work on observational skills. Thank the skies and stars that you have me! You'd be lost on your own.

"You had me worried there, heart of my heart." His hug crushed me. His arms were so thick and strong. He was alive. Breathing. Living. His face scruffier than it should be and his scent musky.

Being taken prisoner and kept in a cage isn't great for personal hygiene.

"You're alive," I breathed, burying my face into his neck and drinking in the bliss of his warm skin.

"So is Ashana. Ahlskibi saved her in time."

I dragged my face reluctantly from his neck to see Ashana and Hubric walking toward us. Ahlskibi and Kyrowat followed.

Leng kissed my forehead affectionately. "I need to check on my friend. Don't fly off anywhere."

He ran to Ahlskibi as I adjusted my crutch.

"Peln?" I asked, looking around me. We were on a heap of rubble so close to the base of the city that it was out of the battle – for now. It looked as if there had been a building here before. Maybe one of the storage buildings where goods were shipped up and down from the city. It was hard to tell with the whole thing a heap of rubble.

Ashana shook her head, rubbing her wounded wrists. Hubric handed her a roll of white fabric and handed me a waterskin.

"Go easy on it. It's all I have," he said. It was all I could do not to gulp it down. How long had it been since I'd eaten or drunk anything? I was all turned around. I didn't know how long I'd passed out this time or last time. I had no idea what time it was or what day it was.

"Something strange has been happening," Ashana said.

"Time," I said, passing the waterskin back to Hubric. "When Savette and Starie clash, sometimes it triggers those big pulses and somehow Starie's mirror magic is sending us a few minutes backward in time."

Ashana paled. "So I really did ..."

"Die?" I asked.

She nodded.

"I think so. I also know we can't rely on those. What if next time it works against us rather than in our favor?"

She shivered. "Nothing we achieve is certain."

My mouth firmed into a grim line. We had a job to do and a nation to save. We didn't have time to get upset about having to fight the same battle twice. We would do what it took to win, no matter what that was. The sun was setting in the distance, making the shadows around us grow long.

"We need a plan," Ashana said. "Can you blow that whistle again to get the dragons' attention?"

Hubric and I exchanged a guilty look.

"I shouldn't be blowing it at all," I said. "The dragon Elders said they would forfeit our treaty with them if we forced the dragons to act with this Pipe, or if we didn't replace the Dominar."

Ashana looked around at the battle in the distance and her firm expression grew firmer. "If we don't gather the dragons, they'll die one by one out there. Blow the Pipe. If we live through this, we can worry about the consequences later."

"And the Dominar?"

Ashana sighed. "I'm good with dragons, not with succession. Why don't you leave the dragons to me and I'll leave the coup attempt to you?"

"It's not a coup attempt," I said.

She rolled her eyes. "Isn't it? In war, we all do things we aren't proud of, girl. Now, blow that whistle."

There was no point in arguing with her.

I lifted the Pipe and blew the three notes.

Chapter Seven

That's not good.

What now? Every time I turned around, things got more complicated!

Really not good!

I searched the battlefield nearby but saw nothing. I looked to the sky where dragons were rising up and headed toward us. Still, nothing. How far away was he looking?

We need to get higher in the air to see for sure.

I hobbled around to where he could help me mount and let him push me up his back. We needed a new saddle. Soon.

When all this is over you can have whatever saddle you want.

Behind me, Ashana, Hubric, and Leng were already rushing to mount up, too. The nice thing about purples was that you never had to tell them anything. They always already knew.

We leapt into the sky and rose under the city. It felt strange to fly so close to a sky city without a single Black dragon rushing to challenge you. They were all occupied with the battle below.

Something about the battle looked strange. I watched, looking for the pattern.

Yes. It's there. See it?

The last Ifrit straggled in to join Iskaris, forming up in his phalanx of Ifrits like a cloud of dust moving back in time to return to the point of origin. The prophecy sprang to my mind unbidden:

In dust and deception, I am made,

Bound by water and blood.

Who may retrain the dust storm or calm the call of water?

Who may feed the maw of the earth?

Is it not you, dark one?

Is it not your dusk descending upon us?

Raolcan finished the quote:

"Is it not your armies drawn up against us,

Your dark the counter to our light,

Your rebirth the horror of our deaths?"

That part had always mystified me.

Look closer.

I squinted my eyes, looking but seeing nothing.

Closer.

I scanned the muddy field at the bodies laying across the battlefield. Our nation would be mourning for the rest of our lives for the fallen here. As I watched, one of the figures seemed to crumble like dust – and then I startled as a burst of dust puffed up from him, growing, growing, growing to the size of an Ifrit.

That's what I'm worried about. They are raising our dead into Ifrits.

No!

Nothing is too horrible for the Dusk Covenant. They only want one thing.

Power.

To hold back their own fated demise. The tighter you grasp at what is yours, the faster you lose it. The only way to keep love, to nurture life, is to give it up for the loved one. But that's not the way of the Dusk Covenant. Oh no, they'll strangle themselves with their desperate grip.

A second Ifrit rose from the battlefield.

A third.

But this wasn't over and that wasn't the only prophecy. Another came to mind.

"But one shall rise,

To stand in the place of the other,

to bear the debt of nations,

to give up the breath of life to dispel the dust of death.

To give up her future for the future of the nations,

Her love for the loves of their hearts.

Her last strength their boon,
Her last gasp, their hope.
Her last flight, their salvation."

I didn't want to believe that was about me. I wasn't ready to die today.

We each only have one life to spend. If my time is up, I'm glad I spent part of it with you and I'm glad I spent it this way.

I was glad to have known Raolcan, too. But that didn't make me ready to die.

He sounded grim as he said, *Would you give up everything to save your people?*

I think I've proved that I would.

Then let's take a last flight.

Just below us, dragons began to gather, arriving in ones or twos, some with riders, some without. I watched a Gold swivel suddenly and rip the throat out of a Black. Wait ... I lifted the Pipe.

Stop. Not all of them are allies, even if all are dragons. Let dragons deal with dragons.

If he was sure ...

I am.

I swallowed down fear as a group of ten Reds arrived, worn and ragged. Their riders were bloodstained and muddy, weapons held in their hands. Those ones had better be on our side.

Stop worrying about the dragons. Ashana will deal with them. She's better at that than you are anyway.

I turned back to where the Ifrits rose out of the mud and dirt. Only Savette could stop that. None of the rest of us could do anything to fight Starie – not with her level of power. Someone had to do something soon, though. An army raised from the dead could only grow.

Baojang was already feeling the blow of the new Ifrits as they plunged into their ranks. Sentries tumbled through the air, their riders spread-eagled as they fell from the saddles. One of the War Leaders raised a staff and then the army charged toward the coming dust demons. Their courage would never cease to amaze me, but there wouldn't be enough of them, couldn't be enough of them.

Strange, that Jalla hadn't been forced to come here and join me. She was still at the head of her army, fighting like Death's handmaiden. Ahummal was a dragon, and I had blown the Pipe – shouldn't she be forced to join us, too

I told him he was exempt.

He could do that?

After he began to fly this direction.

Jalla must have loved that – someone else determining what she could and couldn't do.

Her spirit is only matched by yours.

But they were being beaten back. One corner of the Baojang wedge folded and then dust demons were tearing into their ranks so far behind the front line that nothing and no one would be able to stop them. The line was in disarray. I looked frantically to the clusters of dragons preparing to counterattack. They weren't ready yet. I looked back at Baojang, shuddering as men and animals were trampled by stampeding Ifrits.

There was a cry from behind us – from the sky city – and we spun in the air to look. I couldn't see where it was coming from until I looked up.

Chapter Eight

Ropes fell from the sky – a hundred, no – a thousand ropes of every thickness from arm-thick cables to ropes no wider than my finger. Raolcan dodged to the side to avoid a massive cable, and then he kicked forward, speeding away from the city.

Wha-?

Trust me.

Once we'd cleared the lip of the sky city, he slowed enough for me to look back.

I saw them. First, a pair of Magikas fell from the open windows, their fireballs flying in every direction splashed uselessly against the ground or faded out in the sky.

And then the people who pushed them out appeared.

Citizens of Dominion City descended on the ropes. People in armor, people in everyday street clothes, people with swords and knives and hammers, with axes and makes-shift polearms, people on hanging crates being freighted down by pulley systems, people in harnesses descending on their own, people in uniform and out, in every color and clothing imaginable.

My jaw dropped. And my eyes teared up. We'd thought this was only our battle. We'd begun to think we were the ones about to save the citizens of Dominion City. And now here they were coming to save us. These were fathers and mothers, bakers and grocers and cobblers, city guards and criminals, all descending together to stem the tide of war.

We couldn't let them sacrifice in vain. We couldn't let them die easily. In fact, we couldn't afford to lose them at all. We needed to end this war – now!

– before we lost the life of our nation, the courageous people who had built it day after day with the sweat of their brows and with tears and effort.

Ahlskibi climbed up through the jungle of ropes, squirming to join us where we hovered.

"Amel!" Leng called. "Ashana is taking over the fight below, but she's asking you to wait before you go charging off. She's sending the Reds to help you!"

How did she know I was about to go charging off?

You don't become First Rider of the Purple by being an idiot.

Apparently not.

Leng and Ahlskibi closed in the rest of the way. Long enough for me to recognize the tension in Leng's face. He was ready for battle.

"If what Rakturan says is true, then we have to take out Iskaris, the false Dominar," I said to him. "That's our only priority. If we don't do that, then Savette can't possibly win."

He nodded briskly. The Reds were drawing near, their progress slowed by the need to avoid hurting citizens descending from the city.

"Don't worry about anything else," Leng said. "Ashana and Hubric will have it covered."

"Just Ashana!"

I startled at the words as Hubric and Kyrowat joined us.

"You didn't think I'd stay back here and let you get all the legends sung about you without me, hmmm?" he asked, but there was a tension in the way he sat in Kyrowat's saddle. We all knew what we were doing. We were going to die for the Dominion.

And if we were going to die, then it didn't feel right not to call on every resource. It didn't feel right to let the citizens of Dominion City come to our aid without asking for every advantage we could have.

Fighting back fear and reluctance I reached out, trying, hoping. Would the Troglodytes hear me?

Help! I called.

CALLER. YOU CALL US AGAIN.

Please! I asked. Please, will you help us?

DESTROY THE PRETENDER. RETURN THE PIPE.

Yes, that's what I was trying to do! I just needed all the help I could get.

OUR CHAMPION FIGHTS.

I looked toward where Rakturan was fighting, his sword flashing with bursts of light from the blade as he slashed and hacked at Ifrits to defend his bride's back.

OUR CALLER MUST DO AS PROMISED.

So, they wouldn't help? They could, but they wouldn't?

DO AS PROMISED.

Great. Just great. Below us, Ifrits pounded into Baojang. The citizen reinforcements ran to help, but even I could see they would be of little use to the battle. Inspiring as their desperate charge was, it was only that – desperate.

Ashana and her dragons scrambled to pull together enough dragons to help them.

I gritted my teeth as the Reds finally joined us. I signed "follow me" but a blast sent us spinning backward. Everything was suddenly white.

Not this again. I thought I could hear a curse from nearby.

Maybe it will work to your advantage again.

Or maybe it wouldn't. I felt nervous, licking my lips as my eyes slowly blinked back to reality. Raolcan righted his spin and we were flying between ropes, dodging descending citizens. They cheered us as we passed.

"The Dragons of the Dominion!"

"Dragons!"

"Dominion City and the Sky People!"

This time I wouldn't beg a Troglodyte for help. This time we'd just go. I started waving to Leng and Hubric before they could even join me. Raolcan was slicing through the sky. If all we had was time, then we couldn't afford to waste it.

Onward!

We plunged forward over the fields of battle, Ahlskibi and Kyrowat hot on our heels. The Reds would just have to catch up. We had a goal. We had a mission. We were going to show Iskaris what it was like to be brought down.

Take that, Troglodytes! You withhold your help at our darkest hour? All for some maneuvering you don't even have to do? Well, you can negotiate with Ifrits then, after we're all dead.

Those are dark thoughts –

WE COME.

Wait. What?

Chapter Nine

The snow began while I was still struggling to process what was happening. The first flake fell like a butterfly curious about the chaos below. It drifted back and forth – so gently, so randomly, that it almost seemed to have a mind of its own.

It drifted down past us as we streaked across the sky toward Iskaris. It tumbled over the heads of the citizenry of Dominion City, ignoring their terrified but grim expressions and brandished weapons, as it drifted past to where the line of Baojang was growing thinner, where Jalla battled from dragon-back to try to get to her stranded troops, past where Ifrits screamed and hissed, smoke and dust billowing around them, to settle – forlorn – in the mud. A moment later, it was trampled.

But it was only a scout before a greater army. Its brothers fell, an enraged army, on the people below. It dumped from the heavens in a heavy blanket as flake after flake fell relentlessly over the broad swath of mud in the middle of the field and even dared to drift up to the magical battle where Savette and Starie still fought. Both women - though dressed lightly and dripping in sweat – ignored the flakes.

I would have ignored them, too. But the field the snowflakes were landing on – that broad stretch of mud in the center of the battlefield – opened up at that moment, as if it thought it were a sky full of snow, too.

A split began at the center of the field, widening slowly. As we swooped over it, a thunderous crack sounded across the valley. My heart stuttered at the sound of it ripping through the air. Raolcan slowed for a moment, almost hovering over the crack. Kyrowat and Ahlskibi pulled up on either side. The dragons looked at each other and then we were speeding over the fields again, the ground blurring under us, the snow blinding us, a lace curtain of white filling our vision more and more the faster we went. My face and hands were wet. Melting snow clung to my hair and leathers. I shivered.

A gust of wind blew the snow veil away and through the descending darkness, I saw Iskaris maneuvering his Ifrits to the platform the Grandis and Starie had held me captive on. The towers were gone, and the platform blackened.

Before my eyes, a line of Ifrits tore them up and threw them away, revealing a circular base of stones interlocked together. At the edges, crumbling bases of what used to be arches told me one thing: this was once an ancient healing arch. It was once a place of great power.

Iskaris climbed up the crumbling remains of stairs, standing at the edge of the ancient platform, his single arm outstretched. The Ifrits lined up before him like ranks of soldiers. At a second signal, they stood at what must be attention for an Ifrit. They seemed to almost hold the same shape for a moment.

I had the surreal feeling that what I was seeing couldn't be real. Or maybe I wasn't real. Because this hope and love in my heart and this army of evil couldn't both survive in the same world. I hoped that Ibrenicus had been right about this, as he had been about so many other things. I hoped that our sacrifice would be enough to stop them.

Iskaris pointed forward and the Ifrits swirled toward the battle at his command.

Despite the descending darkness as the sun faded to red on the horizon, the light of Savette, Rakturan, and Starie's magic lit the field.

In that light, I saw the Silver dragons and riders swarm around Iskaris.

They saw us coming, and while we might be a ragged, scattered team, we were still a threat to them. I felt a surge of pride at the thought. We wouldn't die as cowards. We could make even Dominion Dragoons sweat with our ferocity.

Ferocity! Raolcan echoed.

The Reds had finally caught up, surging past us, their greater wingspan overtaking the Purples. Their leader waved to me and I waved back as they passed. Here we go.

Run, silver fishes. This is our reef!

Did that intimidate anyone?

It should! They've never felt the wrath of the Raolcan!

I laughed. I shouldn't be laughing. I should be hyperventilating or sweating through my clothes or something. Instead, I was laughing like a fool, head thrown back and face lifted into the breeze.

I shut my eyes as Raolcan maneuvered in and out of the silver dragons.

Keep them shut. I don't even need them. I have these shiners beat! I can smell their fear, see their miscalculations in the color fluctuations of their minds.

Oh yeah. I forgot that he needed my eyes. I opened them quickly. We plunged through heavy flakes of snow as Raolcan headed off a Silver dragon, grabbing the other dragon's tail with his teeth and shaking him. He flung the dragon away and pounced after another one like a cat chasing chickens.

The intelligence differential is about the same.

What?

I am so much smarter than they are.

Very humble.

Very true.

I lost track of the others fighting. Between the dark and the snow, I was disoriented but Raolcan was having the time of his life, chasing and charging after every Silver he could see. It should have been hard to disrupt dragons and riders trained for fighting, but the snow that blinded both me and our opponents was no hindrance to my dragon.

See? I told you being blind wasn't all bad. I can still see their minds. They can't see anything at all.

As long as he still knew where the ground was.

Seriously? You doubt me again? When will you learn that I'm limitless?

Wait! Not him.

Not who?

That Silver and his rider. That's Ralk Wheelspinner. He wasn't unkind to me when he was my captor. I don't want to see him die.

You realize he's the enemy, right?

I realize he can be a captive. He doesn't have to die.

Fine. He's the last of them anyway.

Really? We were so close! We were so close!

And then I gasped. Not because I was hurt. Not because I was crazy, but because that burst of light stole my vision again.

No! Not now! Not when things were going our way!

I chewed my lip as I waited for my vision to clear. I could only hope that things hadn't become worse for us.

We were flying over the battlefield studying the widening crack, but this time there was no snow. Well, that could be worse, right? All it meant was that we were going to have to fight the Silvers again and this time without being soaking wet from melting snow.

And without the surprise of snow cloaking our attack or the veil of it to disguise my pounces ...

I swallowed. I was too tired to do the same things over and over, fighting a battle only to have to fight it again a moment later. Being rejected by creatures from beneath the earth only to have them give me cryptic answers after all. If I saw a chance – any chance – to end this constant cycle I was going to grab it. I didn't care what it was. I didn't care what the consequence was. I was going to end it.

WE'RE HERE.

There was a boom and a loud squeal like metal bending and then the earth in the center of the field pulled farther back and the ghostly forms of Troglodytes slowly climbed out of the void below.

Chapter Ten

It was hard to concentrate on diving toward the Silver dragons when I knew that Troglodytes were squeezing through the crack in the earth and entering the battlefield. How did they get here so quickly? How was that even possible.

Remember the last time that you talked to them? When you promised to return he Pipe and defeat Iskaris?

How could I forget?

I think it's likely that they planned to help you then. Maybe they were already on their way.

Then why did they make me think that they'd abandoned us? Why did they make me work so hard for their favor when they were planning to give it anyway?

They admire you. They might even like you.

It was hard to think of them as liking anyone. They felt so – other – so different from who we were as humans and dragons.

Do you think so? Interesting. I never thought like that. To me, they have always just been – like the moon and sun, like the tides and rocks below.

The Reds passed us again, streaking toward the Silver dragons, their leader waving politely. Déjà vu didn't even begin to explain the strange feeling of living a patch of my life a second time. I stole a glance at Leng over on Ahlskibi.

No distractions!

And then I turned quickly to look back at the Troglodytes, their knobbly toes left raking marks across the mud and the last rays of the setting sun glinted oddly off their slightly glowing skin.

We have our own business to deal with. Leave them to theirs.

I glanced to the other side to see Savette leap into the air, light spinning around her and flashing in every direction as she landed. Three Ifrits were knocked off their feet, but Starie held up a hand almost nonchalantly and the power deflected in a thousand other directions. Nothing could stick to Starie Atrelan.

Rakturan turned his back on the Ifrit he'd just slain to link hands with his wife.

I flashed into her mind for a moment.

Starie was distracted, her gaze drifting constantly to Iskaris, though new Ifrits continued to pop up in the muddy swath of ground between us.

"I return, bride and morning light," Rakturan said. "Take my heart, my strength, and my light. All is yours to use as you will."

His look of devotion was almost shocking. I'd never seen anything like it from the man. But I'd never been in Savette's mind when he was looking at her before. There was love there, mixed with bittersweet loyalty and strength.

"My heart warms to see you one last time, Dark Prince," she said, a sweet depth in her voice. "I would have done anything short of failing in my purpose if it meant seeing your face again."

Already her glow was stronger. When he leaned in to steal a kiss, I snapped back to my own mind, but my gaze lingered on them. What would happen next?

When they both raised the other hand, white light shot out from both of them, meeting in the middle to slice toward Starie.

I need your eyes up front!

We were almost at the platform. Moonlight glinted on Iskaris' masked crown as he shifted his hands to urge his Ifrits forward – if they were his.

If Rakturan was right, Starie was controlling them through him. That might explain her distraction. How did Savette and Rakturan avoid her controlling them with her mirror magic?

No time for thinking!

We dodged as a Silver plunged toward us, diving out of the way and then spinning so Raolcan could take his flame on his underbelly. I held the chains as tightly as I could, jerking and straining against his maneuvers.

But if I had to guess, I'd say that the light probably protects them.

My dragon! A warrior and a scholar!

And a great charmer with the ladies – but you wouldn't know about that.

One day, I'd meet one of these fictional lady dragons.

Hold on!

We were dodging again. From the corner of my eye, I saw a Red dragged to the ground by a pair of Silvers. One of them plucked the rider from his dragon's back, snapping him in half in a single bite. A shudder of terror ran through me and my gasp sounded more like a pained cry.

We circled to the side as Raolcan chased after a Silver. His rider was distracted with trying to catch Ahlskibi off guard. All around us, Reds fell from the sky. We were losing. Without the surprise attack through the snow, they had seen us coming and they were too used to training and fighting alongside each other. We were no match for them.

Got him!

Raolcan grabbed the Silver's tail, yanking him backward at the same time that Ahlskibi whirled and crunched the Silver's head in his jaws. Ahlskibi wrenched his head back and forth like a dog fighting for a stick, and then released the dragon, letting him fall from the sky. I watched in grim horror as his rider screamed throughout the fall to his death. That could be me. It could be all of us.

It was already most of us.

I'd lost track of Hubric in the fighting and I didn't see him now. Leng on Ahlskibi was with us, but as the Silvers re-entered formation, a chill formed in me.

The Reds were gone – obliterated. We'd only escaped because we were at the tail end of the fighting.

I craned my neck back to look for help. Across the field of battle, Ashana finally had the other dragons formed up, heading into battle, but she was going to the aid of the warriors in the field, not to our aid. There would be no help for us.

Leng was signing something. It wasn't a sign I knew. He always forgot that I hadn't been at Dragon School for very long.

When the odds are stacked against you, throw something at that stack! If nothing else, it will be fun to watch it topple.

We were diving so suddenly that a scream wrenched from my throat. My hair was streaming behind me, my eyes watering. Raolcan's neck was stretched as far forward as it would go. A Silver dragon barely managed to dodge our flight. We were a meteor descending from the heavens. I wouldn't be surprised if there were flames around us as we shot down from the sky toward the ancient stone of the ruined healing arches.

Someone was yelling from behind us.

I think Leng's mad that we went first. He and Ahlskibi are a pair of gloryhogs!

And then we struck the stones with a mighty *crack*. Crumbling rock flew in every direction. The smell of char was heavy in the air. We skidded out of control until we came to a stop – finally – just behind the terrifying figure of Iskaris – the false Dominar – the crown-stealer.

If I had been afraid before, it was nothing compared to this.

Chapter Eleven

Ahlskibi's aim wasn't as accurate as Raolcan's. He careened across the platform. Skidding and spinning, flaming randomly at anything that moved. I ducked low, protecting my face with my arms in case he hit me. What was he thinking?

It's a dragon fear response. He doesn't like what Leng is telling him. Not one bit.

What was my husband telling him?

I looked up to see Leng leap off of Ahlskibi's back, sword in hand. He sprang into a fighting stance and gave a shout. Iskaris spun, his masked crown gleaming in the light of the rising moon. The intricate dragons in the carved crown seemed to gleam with a light of their own. He drew a blade with his lone hand, but his head tilted to the side in curiosity.

"My brother's blood calls out for you," Leng called. "Come. Face me. I will join your death to his."

"Brother?" Iskaris was not loud, but his voice seemed to ring across the platform. Was that natural to him, or an effect of the masked crown?

"Shonan, Dominar of these lands."

Iskaris' laugh was mocking. "He was your brother? I killed him before your eyes!"

"I haven't forgotten."

"Boy, I've killed a thousand men and I'll kill a thousand more. I can add you to the tally if you're so set on it."

"You stole a crown that isn't yours, stole a nation that didn't belong to you, stole the lives of innocents. It's time you paid for that."

Iskaris slashed his sword through the air dramatically. "I've never taken anything that didn't already belong to me. This whole land and every soul within it ... they're mine."

What was Leng thinking? If Shonan couldn't defeat Iskaris one on one, why did Leng think he could? I felt ill watching him mock a man like Iskaris - ill with worry. I didn't want to watch my love slain on these stones any more than I'd wanted to watch Shonan die. Couldn't there be another way? After all, we had two dragons just sitting here while they threw comments back and forth? Why didn't they try to knock this imposter off his feet?

Raolcan moved subtlely and Ahlskibi – now riderless – joined him. Flames burst from their mouths, hot and quick, narrowly missing Leng as they concentrated their power to destroy one single target.

The Dominar laughed as their flames washed over him, never touching his skin, though it singed the guards around him.

"I suppose you don't know much about the dragon crown, do you? I didn't at first, either. But it makes a lot of sense. If a man is going to lead a kingdom of dragons, he'll need to be immune to their flames. Whoever crafted this crown was ingenious. As long as I'm wearing it, the flame does nothing to me. Your dragons are useless."

A half dozen Silver dragons descended suddenly, surrounding our dragons with their bulk. Not only was their flame useless, they were also blocked from physically interfering with the fight.

And now Leng was trapped into a fight with Iskaris. There was no way out.

They circled each other, blades up. I couldn't see Iskaris' face, but I didn't need to, to know he was smiling. Just as he dragged Shonan out of the circle to die, just as he stole his life and Dominion, just as he fought him to his last breath and then brutally murdered him – so he would do that to Leng – to the one who was more precious to me than the skies and the stars.

I reached toward Raolcan, but all I felt in him was matching horror. There was no way out of this.

My breath came in short gasps, my heart pounded so hard that my head hurt. There was no way out. Unless ... but those flashes backward in time didn't come when you needed them most.

They didn't come when Iskaris' blade darted out and nicked Leng's hand before the battle had even begun.

They didn't come when Iskaris laughed wickedly.

"You'll die like your brother and I will have everything. Do you know what it was like to serve as a dragoon all those years? I watched the crown go to that boy. He had nothing to recommend himself to anyone. He had no reason to be given it, but the law doesn't care about fair. It didn't care about how hard I worked. It didn't care that I was better than him, smarter than him, faster than him. It didn't care that he gave such weak orders, that he ignored good advice. When we fled on the ground, carrying his litter, all I could think of was what a fool I'd been to hope in a man. All men let you down. Every human story is a sad story."

I wanted to scream that it wasn't true. But how could I say that? Every human story eventually ended in death. Oh, you could put it off for a while – maybe for a long time. You could do meaningful things and love people and make life worth living, but in the end, we all had to turn and face the long shadow. In the end, we all had to look back and see the errors, the failings, the weakness. In the end, there was no way across that terrible chasm except to leap – and we had to leap alone. He was right. Every human story was a sad story.

And as I looked out over the battlefield I saw that playing out in a thousand individual dramas as dragons fell from the sky and smashed on the ground below, as soldiers died in blood and fear, as those citizens who ran bravely into danger when anyone else would have fled, dashed against the Ifrit army like surf on the shore, as Baojang – noble, proud Baojang – was whittled to a sliver, as even our Troglodyte allies began to stumble, to fall into the mud like candles sinking in a swamp. I looked over to Savette and Rakturan, the last hopes of two nations. Starie raised a hand and they both stumbled, dropping to one knee. Even there, it would not be enough.

"And this sad story needs an audience," Iskaris said, easily parrying Leng's charging rush and swatting him aside. "You're not good for much beyond destroying plans, cripple." He was talking to me! "Let's see how badly you destroy this man's plans just by watching. Come down off that dragon."

Why would I do that? He had to know there was no reason that I would!

The Silver dragons pulled in tighter so that Ahlskibi and Raolcan had to back up. There were more of them, too. The surviving Silvers from our battle slowly rejoined the ranks. Three of them dragged a purple dragon to join us at the edge of the platform. Kyrowat! Hubric clung to his back, but both were muddy and injured, surrounded by Silver dragons.

"Come down, or watch these loyal Silvers melt your dragons into oblivion with their flame. And if they so much as twitch – my dragoons will flame you to smoking bones and ash."

I scrambled off of Raolcan's back, adjusted my crutch and hobbled forward. He knew how to make me obey. I'd do anything for my dragon.

Leng, face screwed up in concentration, attempted to leap under Iskaris' reach, but the older man stepped out of range at the last second, smacking Leng's back with the flat of his sword.

"A little closer."

I hobbled closer.

"Good. Stay there. It will keep us both focused and give an audience for what is coming."

"And what is that?" I asked.

"When I finish chopping this man into mince, you can tell the world what you saw. You can tell them how I destroyed all challengers and how you – somehow a catalyst for the Lightbringers – are now bending the knee to me and to the Chosen One."

I tried to shoot a determined look at Leng, but he was concentrated on Iskaris. Why couldn't one of those blasts come? This would be the right time! This would be the perfect time for it!

Nothing happened except that Iskaris and Leng sped up, their blows and counter-blows beginning to blur with movement.

"Stay back!" Iskaris called to his dragoons as they shifted impatiently around the perimeter. "This battle is between me and the boy. The regular rules apply. If my crown is taken from me, it is taken fairly. But, it won't be. There is no threat here."

I bit my lip, leaned on the crutch and hoped against hope that Leng would stay quick, that he wouldn't let Iskaris get the better of him, that he still had a chance.

Every story might be a sad story, Amel, but that's not the whole story. Why do you think that Ibrenicus wrote down the prophecies? Why do you think that the Lightbringers cling to them? Why do you think that the power of truth in Savette's magic is still enough to fling back Ifrits and push Starie's mirror magic away?

Why?

Because this life is only the beginning. And that chasm you must leap is only the beginning. I believe with all my heart that once it's been leapt you will be surprised to realize that it wasn't as deep as you thought it was and that it never had the power to swallow you up.

He was just saying that because I thought we were going to die and he was trying to cheer me up.

I'm certain that it's true. And Amel?

Yes?

You won't really have to jump that chasm entirely alone. If you die, I won't be far behind. And when you enter the life beyond this life, I'll be right there to fly into that sky of skies with you. There's nothing so dark that hope can't burn. There's nothing so tempestuous that it can blow out the flame of truth. There's nothing so empty that it can't be filled with love. Don't give up yet. We have so much more to do.

I wanted to believe him. I could feel that there was somehow more that he wanted to tell me but couldn't. I wanted to believe that, too. But the dark of the night and the cold of the air and the terrible cries of men, women, and dragons dying were finally the last things to crack me.

Chapter Twelve

I was still standing to the side of the fight between Iskaris and Leng, leaning heavily on my brass crutch, ignoring the way the straps bit into my arm. After the way it had been flung here and there while I was dropped and caught, hobbling and lifted, riding and sitting, it was a wonder that the straps hadn't broken yet.

It was whole. But I was not. I always had something to hold on to. I always had some purpose, some goal, some hope. But here, watching everything washing away I felt like I'd been broken into pieces.

You haven't been.

Like I'd lost some part of myself – my sanity maybe. I was barely holding on to clear thoughts.

You are still sane.

I was helpless. There was nothing I could do but stand still and watch my dreams shatter.

You are never without help – as long as I live.

I squinted my eyes and furrowed my brow and hoped for a burst of power to turn back time and change everything, but still, nothing came.

See? You're still hoping.

I watched Leng dodge a blow from Iskaris, but the edge of the larger man's blade bit into the side of Leng's calf as he dodged. Blood flecked the burnt wood beneath his feet. He spun into the next form of the dance of swords, but Iskaris was faster. He moved like lightning, barely seeming to be hindered by his missing arm. His blade flashed and stung, more aggressive than artful. With his power and muscle behind the sword work, he didn't need to be artful.

He glanced at me from time to time as if watching to see if I was still there. Why did he care so much?

He sounds like Iskaris, but he thinks like Starie. She controls him, though a shadow of him still remains. And she has always wanted to make you pay for something you didn't do. She's always seen you as a potential threat. She wants to watch as you lose Leng.

And she would. There would be nothing I could do to stop it.

The Silvers surrounded Raolcan, Ahlskibi, and Kyrowat. Whether they were once good or bad men, they served that mask. They'd always served it. Maybe people from the outside looking in wouldn't understand that. Maybe they'd find our ways and culture confusing, but you had to serve something. You had to be loyal to something. This Dragon crown was what our people were loyal to. This dragon mask hid the man because it was the mask itself that was important.

These Dragon Riders would keep my dragons from moving to help. Ifrits divided us from the rest of our allies. There was no way to cross their deadly clouded forms to bring aid.

That left only Leng and me free to move, and he was tiring quickly as he fought off Iskaris. His attacks had faded, leaving only defensive parries and dodges as he was pressed backward in a circle. It was just like when Shonan fought Iskaris.

Just like when he died at the hands of this man. Two brothers – companions in life, joined in death.

I shivered in the cold and black of the night. I could see my own breath escaping through my parting lips, like my soul escaping to the world beyond. Leng's breath gusted out, pale and white in the bright moonlight. We were nothing but breath, spent in a few short months. We were the last gasp of the Dominion trying to stay alive, but she was slain. Slain and in her final death throes.

Stop and remember.

Remember what?

It's always darkest before the dawn.

Dawn was a long way off.

Remember the prophecies, Amel. 'When the skies are rent in sorrow,
And the depths bring help no more,

Then the lame and the blind shall lead them,

And guide them from the storm.'

It's our time to guide the peoples.

But how? We were both trapped. There was nothing either of us could do. Any move by us would kill us both.

Iskaris beat on Leng's sword, driving him backward. He fought to keep the blade back but sweat dripped down his face and his movements were growing slower.

'But one shall rise,

To stand in the place of the other,

to bear the debt of nations,

to give up the breath of life to dispel the dust of death'

I think you're that one, Amel. I think now is that time. It will take self-sacrifice, but that's why we're here. We're here for our people. We're here to stand for them and take down this evil.

What was I supposed to do? I couldn't even hobble fast enough to jump between Leng and Iskaris. They'd just dodge out of the way.

I don't know how this is going to work out. I just know that you need to be ready. Remember some of the first words of the book of prophecy, Amel, "When your salvation is near, you may lay hold of it. Do not wait. Do not doubt. Seize life while you still have breath and peace before it has dissolved like snow." If there's an opportunity, whatever it is, you have to take it.

I swallowed. Maybe I'd already missed the opportunity. Maybe it had come and gone while I was busy doing something else.

And then it happened.

Chapter Thirteen

Iskaris jabbed at Leng and Leng spun to the side in a sudden burst of speed, reversing the direction they were turning in. Now, as Iskaris forced him back, he was backing up toward me. He parried and dodged and danced, a wisp in the wind, a reed dancing on the shore. Leng's movements were more graceful than I'd ever expected. I hadn't realized how incredibly skilled he was with a sword.

As he passed me, being driven backward, our eyes met for a moment – like a touch, like a caress, like a last goodbye.

He stumbled, distracted by our shared moment and I gasped as he barely managed to parry a jab from Iskaris. He was on one knee – so close I could almost touch him. Iskaris advanced, his gaze never wavering from Leng as he unleashed a series of strikes toward my kneeling husband.

Iskaris didn't seem to even realize I was there as he passed within inches of me – as he stopped so close I could touch him.

My heart leapt into my throat. An opportunity ... or a trap? I didn't – couldn't – hesitate. A sudden memory came to me of tending to Shonan when he lost his arm. Unbidden, his face swam into my mind. Another memory was hot on its heels – Iskaris dragging the limp form of the Dominar out of the circle right before we fled the warrens.

I gasped.

I reached out, and it seemed as if the moments stretched to minutes as I chose my spot and grabbed, grasping the sides of his mask, and ripping it away. It stuck for a moment and I had to throw my weight backward against it.

There was the sound of something snapping – a leather cord, perhaps? And then all I heard was the gasping as I fell to the ground, hugging the Dragon Crown to my chest. The spikes along the top bit into my chin and jaw, but I didn't care. Now that I had it, it would take more than pain to take it away again.

"I ... Iskaris?" I recognized that voice. Ralk Wheelspinner – the Silver who had held me captive – broke away from where he stood, guarding our Purple dragons. His mouth was open, shock flooding his pale face.

Hadn't they heard him mocking us? Hadn't they realized who he was?

Even if they did – they couldn't admit it. Not and remain true to their vows. But now ... now they can say what they would have wanted to say.

"It can't be," one of them muttered. "He died when they fled. Died guarding the ... Dominar."

Iskaris spun from their shocked gazes, finally finding his opening in that moment of distraction. He kicked Leng back and my husband went sprawling across the platform. His sword tumbled away.

"No!" I cried, pulling myself to my feet.

Iskaris stormed forward, sword held out. Two paces and he'd be close enough to ram it through Leng. There was no one close enough to stop him. No one but Ralk, but why would Ralk do anything to his Dominar?

The seconds dragged like weeks.

I glanced up, taking in our situation with a single glance.

Savette and Rakturan were on their knees, a triumphant Starie poised above them. Our armies were overrun with Ifrits. The last glowing Troglodyte fell as I looked up, the mud coating his fallen body as he rolled across the field. Leng lay helpless on the platform.

We were beaten.

It was all over.

All because of this betrayer who had stolen the mask from the true Dominar and ... put ... it ... on.

I didn't second guess it.

Didn't dare.

I just put the mask on my head.

"Stop him," I ordered, raising my hand to point to Iskaris. Somehow, my voice seemed larger, deeper, fuller – the voice of the Dominar.

Chapter Fourteen

It was a heartbeat before the dragoons understood what had happened. They looked at me, stunned, shocked. Even Iskaris spun to look.

Another heartbeat before Ralk saluted.

One more and the other dragoons joined him.

Raolcan barrelled forward, darting past them all to launch himself at Iskaris. He grabbed the betrayer in his mouth, barreling over the edge of the platform and into the darkness.

I gasped – but the sound was muffled by the heavy mask and crown. They were so heavy that already my head hurt. No time. No time to think about that.

We had barely moved an inch before Raolcan was back, blood coating his snout. Whatever he had done had been quick.

Leng was the first to move, scrambling to his feet and whistling for Ahlskibi. I hobbled to Raolcan, meaning to mount, but finding it impossible.

Ummm ... should I pick you up? I'm afraid my mouth is a bit of a mess ...

"Dominar! If you please!" Ralk Wheelspinner was at my side, a dragon saddle in his arms. I stepped back as he hurried to saddle Raolcan.

It's his saddle. The one you were tied to.

When he was finished he dropped to one knee and a chill settled deep in my body as the other dragoons dropped with him, fists pressed over hearts, heads bowed.

"We live to serve, Dominar."

I was their Dominar.

Forever.

I reached up and felt the heavy crown. There would be no way out of this now. I was as much a prisoner to it as I had been in those cages. As much a prisoner as I had been when I was tied to Ralk's saddle.

I turned to look for Leng. He sat on top of Ahlskibi staring at me, a look of apprehension on his face. Had I ever seen him so stunned? So worried?

Tears filled my eyes as I realized how great the barrier was between us now.

Light burst over us suddenly, and with a sigh of relief, I let it take me. We would go back in time. I would choose something different. Something other than this.

It was all going to be okay. Thank the Skies and Stars for Savette and her magic!

I opened my eyes as the bright light faded.

The moon glinted over the helms of the dragoons still bending on one knee.

No.

No.

No.

Yes.

Chapter Fifteen

I stared at the dragoons kneeling before me.

Do something.

I cleared my throat.

"I accept your loyalty. We fight now with Savette Leedris and our Baojang allies. Go through the field and tell our generals and our troops their new orders: we band together against the Ifrit horde."

"Dominar?" Ralk Wheelspinner's voice was full of respect. "If we go, we will leave you unprotected. You are our charge now, and we are your bodyguards."

There's no getting out of that. They live their lives to serve the Dominar – whoever that is.

I was protected enough with Hubric and Raolcan and ... Leng. I could barely meet his eyes through the mask and what I saw made me flinch.

"Then you'll have to hurry, won't you?" I replied. My voice still felt louder, deeper, more resonate. It didn't feel like it was me talking at all.

The dragoons bowed lower and then hurried to mount their dragons – all except for Ralk Wheelspinner.

"One of us must stay with you, Dominar," he said. "Always."

To do what? Keep someone else from snatching the crown off my head?

Among other things. But yes – they were off their guard. They should never have allowed that to happen. I suspect that like so many others, they underestimated you, judging you by that brass crutch rather than by your iron will.

I turned my back on Ralk and mounted Raolcan. The saddle was comfortable and a bit of a relief after riding bareback for the whole battle – and that was irritating. What right did Ralk have to make my life easier? What right did the dragoons have to guard me?

The right of blood. They've given theirs to defend the Dominar.

The false Dominar! Iskaris. While he was killing the true Dominar!

It's more complicated than that. I know you don't like complicated - but it is.

I frowned and strapped in. Next stop, dealing with the Ifrits. I turned to look at them when I felt something strange, like a thought trying to enter my mind from outside. It was as if I was being drawn to feed anger into the Ifrits rather than redirect them. As if I wanted to make them attack instead of retreat.

I wanted, suddenly, the opposite of everything I'd thought I did. I wanted to take power and rule this land as Dominar without those fool Lightbringers. I'd throw the Troglodytes out, too, while I was at it! I'd–

Raolcan snapped to attention, his head rising so suddenly that I thought we would take off into the air, but instead I saw what looked like a faint arch of light spring up from the battlefield, from the place where the Troglodytes had fallen, and arch over the battlefield to touch his head. He snarled and shook.

All thought vibrated from my mind as I struggled to hold on, and then he was done. I felt like myself again. Immediately, I raised my hands, knowing somehow that it would stop the Ifrits in their tracks.

They froze.

All across the battlefield, they froze into pillars of air and fire, immobile but still present. What had happened to me that for a moment I had been on their side?

Starie. She took hold of you through the mask and crown, just like she did to Iskaris.

I shuddered.

Did you know I was born on a mountain?

What? Wait. The first prophecy I had ever heard spoke of a mountain. I had thought it was about Savette, but hadn't Ralcan said that these prophecies could be about more than one person?

Born high on the mountain,
Blazing bright under the sun's demise,
Twice blind but still seeing,

The only bulwark against the dark
Watch as the arches proclaim
Dominion of Light.

Convenient.

Sometimes magic is convenient.

And strange. Where had that magic come from?

Dragon magic. I did mention I was a prince, right? Sometimes, we can tap just a little of the power of the Troglodytes – if they're willing, that is.

But it seemed just a little too easy that he drew upon that now.

Easy? I've been saving up that favor all my life. I didn't use it until today, and I'll never get it back. Easy, maybe. But not without cost.

My dragon would never stop surprising me.

And I wanted the prophecy to be about him. I wanted everything from here on in to be ruled by Light. I wanted peace. I wanted my people to be safe. I wanted the killing to be over and a happy ending for everyone – or at least everyone who could have one.

I glanced over at Leng, but he was strangely silent, his back straight, and his face staring out into the field beyond. Hubric and Kyrowat snuck up beside him and my old mentor leaned in to speak to him. They both glanced at me before putting their heads back together.

That was how it was going to be from now on, wasn't it? Everyone else – and me.

This crown, this mask, was my cage.

I looked out over the battlefield, watching as the Silver dragons set down among clusters of men in the fields. Slowly, one group after another stopped fighting.

A hush washed over the land.

You did that.

And it was worth it, wasn't it?

I watched a young soldier climb up on a mud hill and raise a banner. As the wind took it I could almost make out the moonlit crest.

It's the flag of the Lightbringers.

A knot of white dragons swirled out of Dominion City, soaring down to the field below.

They were waiting to bring healing. Waiting for the end. Someone always has to mop up at the end.

They should have been there for the actual fighting. What good were they when everyone was fighting and dying?

What can I say? That's Whites for you.

He seemed remarkably unaffected by our sudden entrapment. Wasn't he as torn as I was?

Remember, we were willing to die for our nation. Are we not willing to live for them, too? One day after another, giving ourselves to make them thrive?

I felt tears prick my eyes. I tried with all my might not to look at Leng. I had been willing to die. I wasn't sure I was willing to live like this.

I might like seeing you receive the respect you deserve.

Locked in a sky city, surrounded by Silvers?

Who says you have to be that kind of Dominar? Who gets to say who you will become?

I didn't know. There were probably rules.

When have I *ever found a rule I couldn't break?*

I almost laughed at that.

And then something below us twitched.

The Ifrits were waking up again.

Chapter Sixteen

It started small. A movement here, a twitch there, but the moment that the first Ifrit shook himself back to life and rushed forward, my heart leapt into my throat. They weren't finished. Ending Iskaris' reign had not been enough to stop them.

What could we do now?

I flashed into Savette's mind so suddenly that I reeled from the shift. She was looking out over the fields, too. I watched through her eyes as the first Ifrit woke enough to launch himself at the soldiers still laying down their arms. Her gaze shot back to Starie, standing above her, a look of triumph in her eyes.

"See?" Starie said. "Your pet has destroyed my pet, but it is of no concern to us. I have many, many pets."

"She's not my pet," Savette said through gritted teeth. "But you wouldn't know that, because you don't know what the word 'friend' means."

"It means nothing," Starie said, her smile gone. "And now I'll take your last pet."

She turned to Rakturan, a calculating look in her eyes, but Rakturan wasn't looking at her. He was looking at Savette, his eyes full of love and confidence.

"I knew who you were from the moment I saw you after the fall of Vanika," he said to her. "Hasa'leen. The bringer of light. I knew that day what your fate would be."

"And you married me anyway?" Her voice was full of wonder.

"Face me!" Starie demanded from the sidelines, but whatever magic she was using to fight them wasn't enough to break their focus.

"I love you, Savette Leedris. I love you as a woman and I love you as the Chosen One, the one who will save both our peoples. I'm not here to stop you. I'm here to help you."

"You've always been here to help me." Her voice was adoring.

"And I've always known what I would help you to do."

Her vision was blurry with tears, but I didn't think she was sad. She was grateful and so full of love that it was flowing from her tears.

He began to quote the prophecy that I thought was meant for me, but it was so obvious from his lips that it had always been about Savette. How could it not be?

"*But one shall rise,*

To stand in the place of the other,

to bear the debt of nations,

to give up the breath of life to dispel the dust of death."

"And that one is me," Savette said.

"Face me!" Starie screamed, breaking the tension of the moment, but Savette didn't face her. Instead, she stood and Rakturan stood with her.

The light they had been holding in their other hands faded out and they joined both hands stepping toward each other. I could tell he was about to kiss her before he did. I could almost feel her racing heart and the hope surging in her veins as she stood on tiptoe and leaned into his embrace.

Light surged bright and full and I fell from her mind.

I couldn't tear my gaze away from the light where they had been standing only a moment before. It was so bright it burned my eyes. It was so bright that time seemed to stop – not just for me, but for everyone.

And then, the two of them were rising up in the air, though nothing but magic seemed to propel them upward. As they kissed, power came up and through them and burst outward – so bright that it blinded me, but I refused to shut my eyes.

Somehow, I could almost make out the pair of them locked in their embrace. And around them, Starie and her Ifrits burst into dust. Dust rained down everywhere and blew in the howling winds whipping up around them.

When the light finally faded, the sun was coming up.

I blinked rapidly, my eyes tender and sore from the light.

There were no more Ifrits, though there was dust in the air everywhere and sweeping across the muddy fields. It had begun to snow while we were all frozen in place and everyone – humans and dragons alike – had an inch of snow on their heads.

And out in the center of the battlefield where once there had been a garrison, between the two sky cities, a massive white statue rose into the air, twice the height of any dragon.

I barely choked back a sob as the details of the statue registered. It was as if Savette and Rakturan had frozen in their last embrace, floating forever on the top of a swirling pillar of white stone.

At the base of the statue, a white, glowing dragon shifted his weight slightly and the snow that had piled up on him fell free.

Enkenay stood guard over his humans.

Chapter Seventeen

And then I did cry. I cried for my friend and her husband and for the hundreds of others who would wake up this morning with loved ones lost forever. And I cried for myself and the future I would never see.

After what felt like a very long time, I pulled myself together enough to look around me.

Silver dragons ringed the broken healing arches, their dragoons facing outward on guard for me. And inside the ancient circle stood a solitary man, his own sword drawn, his back to me.

The gold and pink of the morning lit the edges of his figure, but all the rest was dark - as unknown as his thoughts. A long shadow clung to him, spilling across the platform.

Leng.

He hasn't left you.

Neither had Raolcan. My great dragon lay with his head nestled on his forepaws. He yawned dramatically as he spoke with his mind.

Well, you are strapped to my back. I'd have to kill you to get you off and as much as I'd like to find a nice horse to eat, it's not worth killing you for my appetite.

Eventually, he'd stop joking about the horses.

Stop being a fool and get down off my back and go talk to your husband.

The best thing a girl can do, is listen to her dragon.

I unbuckled my straps and slid down off his back and hobbled forward.

All across the ruined valley, people were picking themselves up and helping those around them. Fires – tiny specks of light with plumes of smoke above them – were being lit and tents set up. As people everywhere did, the citizens of the Dominion were gathering themselves, counting their losses, quelling the tides of war.

They're your people now. Yours to direct and protect.

I shivered violently. I was not ready.

Fortunately, there were no eyes on me yet. I could see movement from the fields – movement in this direction – but everyone else was too far away to see how crushed I was by the burden of this crown. All the Silver dragoons had their backs to me. Their eyes were on potential threats, not on my weakness. Not on my hobbling, ridiculous self. Who would ever mistake me for a Dominar?

Everyone. Everyone will see you as nothing but the Dominar from this moment on.

I could throw the crown away – give it away. I could give it to Leng.

It can't be given. Not really. Such a thing is no gift.

Can't be stolen – you saw that with Iskaris. He made a terrible Dominar, not just because he was an evil man, but because he always knew he was a fraud. Why wasn't he here leading his armies in the war? Why did he go north chasing after a whisper? He knew he had no right to lead.

It can't be thrown away.

And the way our ancestors set it up, it can't even be chosen or pursued.

It can only be accepted. Can you accept it?

I swallowed.

And do you realize yet what the consequences will be if you do not?

More war. More death. More evil.

Yes.

I had no choice.

There's always a choice, but sometimes there's only one good choice.

Then I would just have to find a way to make that choice.

Leng still hadn't looked back at me. He must hear me coming. My crutch tapped metallically on the ancient stones.

I chewed my lip, trying to think of what to say. A thousand fragments came to mind from 'It's not my fault' to 'I'm sorry' to 'Do you hate me?' They were all terrible beginnings.

So, I straightened my spine, and took the last step to stand side by side with him. I didn't look at his face as I began to speak. I looked instead at the people pouring out of the twin sky cities on ropes and lifts or dragon-back, bringing – no doubt – medical supplies and blankets and food. I looked to them – my people, my life now – to find the courage for my next words.

"When you thought it would be Shonan, you said you were used to the idea. You said it might even be fun to see him in secret, to sneak into his rooms, to be his eyes in the world beyond his palace."

He didn't reply.

"I didn't have a choice, Leng. I could take up the helm, or let you and everyone else die."

Still nothing.

"Don't you think I'm as devastated by this as you are? Don't you know that I still want that little farm and those dragons and a life with you?"

The silence was so deafening that I almost glanced over to be sure it was him at all.

"Is it impossible for you to accept me like this?"

On an impulse, I dragged the crown from my head, letting it fall to the side in my free hand. I spun to look at him, my loose hair obscuring my vision as badly as my tears. My lower lip trembled uncontrollably. I sucked in a deep breath, trying to still it.

A warm hand reached up, and brushed my hair aside, tucking it behind my ear. Leng's face was suddenly so close that I could feel his warm breath on my cheeks.

"Is that what you think, heart of my heart? You think it is impossible for me to love you as the Dominar?"

"Isn't it?"

"Never. I'll die before I stop loving you. They'll rip me to pieces and watch my heart stop beating and still I'll want my life to be yours."

"Then why do you stand with your back to me?"

A tear slipped from his eye, though the rest of his face was hard as stone. "The Dominar gives up all right to her life before. The Dominar has no family. Trust me! I of all people know that! The Dominar has no friends." His voice was rock hard. "The Dominar has no husband."

I dropped the Dragon Crown, ignoring the clang as it hit the stones and grabbed his hand with mine. I was shaking from the intensity of the moment. My hand was cold as ice.

"This Dominar does."

I stood up on tiptoes and kissed him gently, afraid he would push me away. His kiss was bittersweet, as if he were afraid it would end at any moment.

"I plan to change a lot of things," I said, drawing back so I could watch his eyes. "I plan to fix a lot of things. I hope that you'll help me. I hope that you'll stick by my side and help me know what to fix and how to fix it. And I hope you'll do it as my husband. I made promises to you and a spiky hat doesn't change any of them."

I tried to smile, but my lips were trembling so much that it was hard. What if he couldn't take the burden of what I was thrusting on him? After all, I had wanted to give it away. What if he did, too?

He looked up, finally and he smiled – a little mischievously. "It might still be fun to sneak a bit and meet in secret ..."

I laughed and after a moment he joined me, and as we laughed together the tension melted away. His fingers entwined around mine and he leaned in so close that his cheek brushed mine and then his lips dragged gently across my cheek to find my lips and seal the promise.

Chapter Eighteen

The dragon throne was as intimidatingly large in person as it had been when I'd seen it in my mind. I had not been able to climb it – not with my bad leg – and Raolcan had been forced to help me up. Perhaps it could be replaced with something practical.

Don't you dare. For once there's a room that fits me and a chair that keeps you too high above the ground to get into trouble. I'm not losing that!

He was sitting at the base of the throne as the last officials left the room. Seven days after the great battle and I still wasn't used to being in charge. I still had trouble trusting the generals and administrators and dignitaries who had been happy enough to serve Iskaris just as they had Shonan.

And with good reason. Traitor once, traitor ever.

I'd been replacing them as much as possible with Lightbringers as suggested by Hubric, but too many of the Lightbringers had fallen in the war and there was no way to fully replace all the people who made me suspicious.

We'll just do the best we can.

And we were definitely doing that.

In the wake of the battle, we'd spent the first day establishing my authority and returning rule of law to the twin sky cities. It had taken longer to sort out the wounded, bury the dead, restore transportation and communication between the cities. And all of that had taken meetings. Meetings about food stores and fresh water, meetings about dwindling coffers and weakened fortifications, meetings about sending loyal Castelans back to their own cities to quell rebellions and return order. It would be years before we could restore the Dominion to what she had been.

Restore? We'll make her twice the land she ever was. Better than the days of Haz! With your crown and my mind ...

Raolcan was still wearing those chains wrapped around his eyes. I thought they must be uncomfortable, but he wouldn't budge on removing them.

I earned them. I'm wearing them. They make me look terrifying. Did you see how the generals looked at me?

Like a dog who hadn't been housebroken.

Like a dragon so tough he wears chains.

Either way, my next meeting would be with Ashana. She was going to have to sort out Dragon School. In a perfect world, I would like to do that myself.

You can only live one life at a time. And it will never be the same again, anyway. We have a new deal now with the Elders.

A deal that meant only dragons who wanted to be at the school would arrive. And they would be involved in choosing their own riders.

I could still remember how surprised I was when more Troglodytes crawled from the crack in the earth when the battle had finished on that strange pink and white morning. The first one had approached me on the ruins, his movements so slowly that eventually, we met him halfway, and there, in the swirling snow as his brothers retrieved their dead, I returned the Pipe of Wings.

IT IS DONE, CALLER.

That's all they said. And then they were gone, back down into the earth.

But if they feel like it, they could come back.

I hoped not. I hoped all would be peace between us now.

It will be. If you make my mother happy, that is.

I still felt queasy thinking about that part. Sometime soon I'd have to go back to the Dawn's Gate and give an account to Haz'drazen and seal the deal between Dominar and Queen of Dragons. But not today.

Today, I had an old friend to see before my next meeting.

I'll help you down.

I let him lift me down off the ridiculous throne, glad that the dragoons pretended not to notice the indignity of it. Their eyes stayed ever forward, still as statues. I'd put Ralk up as second in command of them – at least I knew he had some morality – but all of them worried me.

We'll deal with that in time.

I hobbled out of the throne room to the balcony beyond. My old friend Hubric was waiting for me there, looking out over the battlefield. The last troops of Baojang were still in sight as they marched away. Raolcan hadn't been sorry to see them begin packing.

I really do hate those Sentries. And I never even got to eat one. It seemed ungrateful after they fought with us.

But I was surprised to realize that I was sorry that they were leaving. I looked to the white statue at the center of the valley. Even from here, it stood out. It seemed to almost glow, as the eyes of the two people immortalized by it had glowed.

It had been just after the meeting with the Troglodytes that I insisted we go and look at that statue. I'd laid my hands on the base, wanting to feel where Savette had been. I knew she was gone. I knew she'd left for us.

Now, seven days after her sacrifice, it was even more clear what she'd done. Reports were coming in from around the Dominion. When she and Rakturan gave their lives in that last act of magic, it hadn't been just these Ifrits that exploded into dust – it had been all Ifrits in the Dominion – maybe even in the whole world.

The scourge was ended.

I ordered a plaque to be put up at the base of the statue. Everyone should know the words of the prophecy she had so perfectly fulfilled. I still shivered when I thought of it.

"Healing comes from the one who pays a steep price.
In this, victory will begin to grow like the first sprout of a mighty oak
And our hopes, bright as the dawn will rise over the horizon of our hearts.
And the people will be free of terror and the nations of uproar,
when the Chosen One brings truth to the heart of the Dominion,
when the dominion of darkness comes to an end."

I had been standing there under the statue when Jalla flew down on Ahummal. There wasn't even any point in pretending he was Renn's dragon anymore. He was hers as much as Baojang was – everything that girl wanted became hers eventually.

She leapt off the Gold with curt instructions to Renn. "Stay put."

Like with everything else that wasn't currently interesting to her, Jalla ignored the cold. The wind whipped through her dark curls and billowed her fur cloak out behind her, but she didn't try to draw the warmth of the cloak in, and she didn't huddle against the frigid blast. She was as straight-backed and confident looking as if artists were about to paint her portrait for the generations to follow. Maybe they were. I'd been told that tiny watercolors and ink drawings of that moment where we met under Savette's immortalized statue were already being sold on the streets of Dominion City. We both looked grander and more beautiful than we really were in the drawings, and the artists hadn't included the thick mud climbing up our boots.

We met under the statue, the wind blowing our hair into our eyes and the gaze of the armies on us. I knew how powerful the image was. Two rulers. Two nations. Meeting under the sign of sacrifice and truth. If peace could be found anywhere, couldn't it be here?

"I was far-sighted when I made you my blood-sister," she said with a laugh.

"I thought I earned that."

She shrugged. "It's all the same."

I followed her gaze as it drifted upward to the statue towering over us.

"We will always revere the Dark Prince and the choice he made to save us all," she said.

"He's bound to our Chosen One forever."

She smiled. "Exactly. As you and I are bonded. You won't forget that, will you?"

I swallowed. I knew that with Jalla every word counted. "You saw how I burned Vanika. You saw how I retrieved the Pipe of Wings."

"My victories," Jalla said, baring her teeth.

"My sacrifice."

"What of it?" Her bright eyes were hard as rocks.

"If my nation is threatened, what won't I do to keep it safe?"

Her eyebrows rose. "I've always been a personable prince. I like people. I bring them together. I create alliances. Is this not so?"

I felt my own eyebrows rising. Was she kidding?

"And so, Jalla, the Winged Prince of Baojang, will triumph again."

"And how do you expect that I'll do that for you this time?" My tone was drier than I'd meant it to be and the black gaze she shot in my direction told me it bit at her.

"By making an oath with me this day that we are blood-sisters and blood-nations. Today, we drenched this mud in the blood of our people, fighting side by side. Today, we drove off the Ifrit horde – our Dark Prince and your Chosen One. Today, we become family and we swear an oath of peace that will last as long as we both draw breath."

I blinked. Jalla wanted peace? Jalla wanted an ally? Was this the same Jalla who watched indifferently as men fell to their deaths? Was this the same Jalla who had been measuring my nation for her cities and armies?

The same Jalla who is a brilliant strategist and politician? That Jalla? The same Jalla who is honorable in her own way? I rather think so, yes.

"Well?" Jalla asked, her fists moving to her hips.

"Are you still marrying Renn?" I asked.

She looked taken aback but she grinned. "I think so."

"Good. Then yes, you have my oath."

"And you have mine." She grinned so wide that she looked more like a wolf than a human. "And I will send you Renn as my ambassador after we are wed. I can see you like him."

I felt the blood draining from my face under the masked crown. My eyes must be as wide as saucers.

"I jest." Jalla's laugh bit through my panic, but then her expression hardened. "But if you try to take advantage of us, don't think I won't do it."

"Understood," I said with a wry tone. There was Jalla for you. Promises and gifts – and a little threat to remind you who was boss.

"I always liked you, Amel. I'll visit from time to time, so we can play cards."

She took my hand in the ancient gesture of treaty-making and then she was striding back to Ahummal, chastising Renn for not being ready quick enough, and waving merrily as she leapt into the air.

I would never get used to Jalla. She was like a hurricane in human form.

A shame. She certainly seems to like you.

If you called that 'like.'

No, really, she likes you.

At least I didn't have to lead Baojang. I would never understand those people.

Now, seven days later, I was saying goodbye to another friend – a real friend.

"Hubric," I said as I joined him on the balcony.

He bowed, almost by instinct.

"You don't need to do that." My voice still sounded too loud in the mask.

"I do need to do it, Dominar. Some things have changed."

I touched my purple scarf – the one Hubric had given me so long ago. I knew it was precious the day he gave it to me – but not that it would be this precious. There was so little that I could keep of my old life.

"I said you were ready the day I gave you that," Hubric said. "I just didn't know how much you were ready for. If I could have handpicked a Dominar ... well."

I felt my cheeks heating behind the mask. "I have to ask you for something."

"I'm your man." He looked proud to say it.

"The Lightbringers – without them, without their help and their safehouses and their supplies – we would never have succeeded. Before you go off and do your own thing – I need you to deliver a series of messages for me." I pulled the cylinders out of my pocket, each perfect and white. There was a time when all I wanted to do was carry these. Now, I never would again. Reluctantly, I passed them to him. "And I hope that while you deliver these, you'll take the time to check on your network – help those who survived. You have all my authority and resources."

He smiled. "I'd hoped you'd think that way."

"These messages are the top priority. They will help restore order in our sky cities and give them hope. You understand?"

"That I'll have to put off personal plans until after I deliver these? Yes, I understand."

"Did you have personal plans?" I asked gently.

"I want to honor Haskell. And I have a promise to keep."

I smiled. I wanted to take off the mask, but I couldn't – not here in public.

"If anyone can be depended on to keep their promises – you can."

"You were my favorite apprentice, Amel Leafbrought," he said with red-rimmed eyes. "The best I ever trained. Purple to the core. Truth, loyalty, faithfulness. Stubborn and with a mind of your own. Difficult-"

"Hey!"

"I'm glad it's you sitting on that throne. Tell that old dog that he's got a good life by the fire now. Tell him not to bother bellyaching about it – we all knew he always wanted the life of ease."

Tell Hubric he's a rotten-toothed foot eater.

Hubric laughed as if he could hear Raolcan himself.

"Tell Raolcan that Kyrowat says there are worse things to eat than feet."

Tell him that he would know, not me.

I coughed, barely covering a laugh. "I think you two might want to talk in person. You have so many sweet things to say to each other."

Hubric smiled, but now he was tearful. "Keep making me proud, apprentice."

"Stay alive, Hubric," I said, throwing his old advice back at him. I wouldn't see him much after this. We both knew that. But I hoped I'd still see him sometimes. I'd grown to depend on Hubric. "And come see me from time to time. There's a message in there for you, too. Read it when you have a moment."

He smiled and then coughed again, as if he couldn't trust his own voice. Instead, he waved briskly and then hopped over the edge of the balcony like a much younger man might. I'd been a Dragon Rider long enough that I didn't worry. I just glanced casually over the side of the balcony, just in time to see him land lightly on his old mount and dart away.

You're never too old as long as you can fly.

My dragon joined me on the balcony and we looked out over the sky city and to the plains and the mountains beyond. Dominion City was strange to me – more foreign than Baojang had been – and my new role as the ultimate ruler not just of this city but of the whole nation, was even stranger.

What's in Hubric's message?

I was making him a part of my spy network. Never again would our enemies conspire against us without us knowing about it.

Hubric? A spy? The man is soaked in truth.

Then who better to spot a lie?

I watched the bustle below for a moment. All across the Dominion, the same sights would be seen as people fought and struggled to rebuild what we had lost. I wondered if back on their farm somewhere my family was doing the same thing. I wondered if they ever thought of me. They would never guess where I was now. I could hardly believe it myself. I wasn't made for this.

Don't worry – I was. I'll be here for every meeting and order, every edict and decision. I'll help you.

Then you'll get out of shape because you won't be flying.

Oh, I didn't mean here exactly. That would be boring. No, as soon as order is restored in this city, I think you should make a tour of the Dominion. Visit the land. See to the rebuilding. Visit Haz'drazen as promised. And maybe break in that dashing new Captain of the Dragoons you acquired.

As if on cue, my Captain of the Dragoons came striding out onto the balcony, the noon light glinting on his brand new armor and off a helm almost as shiny as my own masked crown.

I thought only Silver Dragon Riders were charged with the protection of the Dominar.

He insisted.

And that worked? It never seems to work for me.

I pulled the mask off my face. I wasn't supposed to. Not here in public. But I could never keep it on when Leng was around.

I can't keep my lunch down when Ahlskibi is around. He struts like the smallest rooster in a barnyard. Purples just don't look imposing next to Silvers. I tried to tell him, but he's too puffed up to listen.

Leng grinned sheepishly in his shiny new armor and held out a silver crutch, inlaid with gold dragons.

"I know you said nothing ornate," he said, offering it in exchange for my old battered crutch. "But I thought that maybe it would do for now while they repair the old one. I was certain that you wouldn't want it replaced, only repaired. Was I right?"

"Hubric gave it to me," I said with a smile. "How did you know I'd want to keep it?"

"Because you have the good sense not to throw away something useful or exchange something beloved for something more ornate." He looked around stealthily before taking the last step toward me. Raolcan slid across the doorway to the throne room, blocking the view to the balcony completely. "And because I know that a woman as faithful," here he kissed my forehead, "as smart," and my cheek, "and as magnificent," a quick kiss to the lips, "as you would want it that way."

"You won't leave me, Leng?"

He looked down at his shiny armor and back to me. "Would I have let them fit me for this silly get up if I was planning to leave?"

He pulled me close, kissing me gently, as his fingers found his davari on my finger. When we broke apart he deftly slid a second ring on the same finger – a simple circlet of pure gold.

"What is that?"

"The davari marked a promise made. This davara marks a promise kept. I-"

I never heard what he said next. I launched myself forward, nearly knocking him off his feet with my kiss. He could talk later.

All this kissing makes me ill. I swear I'm thinner. Gaunt even.

I didn't even care if Raolcan mocked us.

I'm losing my touch. But it's worth it, spider. It's worth it.

He sang something, giving us our mental privacy, a dragon lullaby, I thought. But in the song, he'd incorporated the prophecy that we both knew for sure and certain was about him.

He loses half the sun to save the world.

His crown he lays aside to choose one star, from a sky of stars.

One part, one place, one role: to be a mountain and an anchor in the storm.

Hope for the hopebringer, light for the lightbringer, wings for the lame.

He was hope and light just like the prophecies had promised ... and I couldn't have asked for a better dragon.

And to think – I could have chosen Starie Atrelan.

Enough.

Or what was that guy's name? Daedru Tevish?

We're a bit busy here ...

Sure, brush your dragon off. Don't even stop to think how lucky you are that I chose you.

I was lucky.

Especially now that I have a recommendation ...

Anything. Just give me a moment of privacy.

I'd like to pick the first location we travel to.

Sure, sure.

I'm going to remind you that you agreed to that. Are you still kissing? That can't be healthy. You're probably spreading germs.

Go eat feet.

No gratitude. That's humans for you. No gratitude at all.

THE END

Behind the Scenes:

USA Today bestselling author, Sarah K. L. Wilson loves spinning a yarn and if it paints a magical new world, twists something old into something reborn, or makes your heart pound with excitement ... all the better! Sarah hails from the rocky Canadian Shield in Northern Ontario -

learning patience and tenacity from the long months of icy cold - where she lives with her husband and two small boys. You might find her building fires in her woodstove and wishing she had a dragon handy to light them for her.

Sarah would like to thank **Harold Trammel, Eugenia Kollia,** and **Sarah Brown** for their incredible work in beta reading and proofreading this book. Without their big hearts and passion for stories, this book would not be the same.

DRAGON CHAMELEON

Amel and Raolcan might have found a happy ending, but the Dominion still has problems to be solved. What will they do about the dwindling magic, the nations that banded together against the Dominion and the tenuous bond with Haz'drazen?

Find out in DRAGON CHAMELEON: ROGUE'S QUEST, the next season of Dragon School.

DRAGON CHAMELEON: ROGUE'S QUEST

It's great to be a spy. Trust me. Who wouldn't want to leave everything, get pushed around by a haughty dragon, and do it all without fame or glory?

It takes a special kind of magic to hide in plain sight.

I've been hiding all my life but now I'm doing it for my country.

My partner in crime? A chameleon dragon who takes things *way* too seriously.

They keep telling me that the world hangs in the balance, but I try not to take things like explosions, spies, and illicit magic too seriously.

After all, I get to ride a dragon! That is ... when she lets me.

DRAGON CHAMELEON: ROGUE is episode one of a brand new series set in the world of DRAGON SCHOOL. It's the perfect beginning for readers new to this fantasy world but still contains hidden gems for long-time fans.

GET IT NOW.[1]

1. https://www.amazon.com/Dragon-Chameleon-Sarah-K-Wilson-ebook/dp/B07HQXJDGN